# AN OCEAN GAZES THROUGH HUMAN GLASS

## EMILY NGUYEN

RIVER GROVE
BOOKS

Published by River Grove Books
Austin, TX
www.rivergrovebooks.com





Distributed by River Grove Books

Design and composition by Greenleaf Book Group and Kim Lance
Cover design by Greenleaf Book Group and Kim Lance

Publisher's Cataloging-in-Publication data is available.

Print ISBN: 978-1-63299-657-2

eBook ISBN: 978-1-63299-658-9

First Edition

*Thank you to Joel Bahr and Chris Tran*

# ONE

"I WILL DEVOUR THE MOON."

This was one of the many inane things he'd said as a child. He dreamed of an ocean where cardboard ships and paper sails parted black waters, where a child's naïve navigation cut through the bobbing fields of meteors afloat in icy waters. He sailed past rotting fish, sideways upon the water's brim, desolated by the long-fallen fire. Collapsing stars dusted the horizons, their iron cores skipped across the water's mirror finish as if thrown by gods. Oh, how close the stars were to the touch when he stood upon the ocean.

Stellar anomalies were the easy catch. His curious touch would leave handprints in the stardust upon these once-beating iron hearts resting in their oceanic graves. He wanted the moon, always out of reach, ever tempting in a sky quickly drained of constellations. His cardboard craft sailed to the very edges of the ocean, where the water tumbled into oblivion over sharpened cliffs. Children have no notion of mortality, so with blissful ease, he took the fatal dive. He would fall through bottomless astral skies, back into the black of the ocean.

He could never sail far enough to touch the moon. There was no place where he could stand on his waterlogged ship and reach it like he reached extinguished stars, but astral skies offered him better opportunity. He would aim from above by tumbling over the edge of the world to catch the moon with outstretched arms. The moon was wiser, or at least competent enough to outwit the plans of a precocious child playing in a dream. If he fell like rain, then all it had to do was stay above the clouds.

His youthful vigor waned as the years went by, until reality finally imparted the idea that not all things pined for would be had. Settle for a lunar reflection over the ocean instead.

How could he ever eat the moon? No physical jaw could complete such a feat. But ah, why couldn't it be an abstract jaw? Children need a role model, Venner thought. Time was endless. Time did not struggle. No portion of existence could dam the onslaught. Children aspired. To become an endless ocean entranced his heart because that is the sort of strangeness children love. If he was the ocean, if there was enough of him, he could reach up into the evening skies and pluck the moon from its hole in existence. The moon would be his, forever gone because of him.

Five years went by, then ten, then more, and finally he stopped trying. Seafaring adventures were replaced with discontentment. He had dreamed as children do of knights and dragons. Now, he was supposed to dream about a decent retirement fund in twenty, or thirty, or more years.

*But if I could devour the moon*, turned the perpetual phrase of mind. The world moved on. He was here to finalize the business of his taxes. Settle the matter and be on to the next worry.

"I am the infinite ocean," whispered the former child sailor, reading his name off the header of his W2 form. But "Eram Venner" worked better for conventional conversation.

# TWO

VENNER'S SIGH COULD BARELY BE HEARD OVER THE RAPID clicks of the keyboard. Soft beams of light streamed in through partially closed blinds of his accountant's tiny corner office. The yellowed plastic shades on the windows reflected the bright orange and faded reds of the setting sun. These colors crawled across the paperwork arranged over the desk. Venner bit his lower lip to stifle another sigh, running a hand through his slicked hair. He slid his chair back a few inches to give himself more legroom, though it offered little relief given his excessive height and the scant space between his chair and the wall behind him. He hated the way he towered over everyone, even with his hunched shoulders and perpetually poor posture. There was nowhere he could hide. He dusted his knees and straightened his tie before leaning back in his seat, waiting and watching the accountant's hands work letter to symbol and back.

The desk was immaculate save for the paperwork. The documents themselves were neatly sorted and confidently bore multicolored tags and stickers. Annual taxation was a routine chore, but it was one he had never bothered to properly attempt on his own. Venner was a structures analyst by trade; safety was his purview and numbers his tools. If he could design metal to fly, he could very well fill boxes with deductions and withholdings.

Maybe it was the potential consequences of poor reporting that made him uncomfortable. Or perhaps it was sitting down and weighing his life in receipts that reminded him things were going terribly. Gawking eyes and chattering voices preyed on his inadequacies from within the cubical walls of his corporate workspace, denying him comfort even when he was miles away. He shifted in his seat, straightening his suit jacket, and felt where his phone rested in the inner pocket. He lifted it an inch out of the lining. It would be rude of him to produce his own distraction or to check the time so blatantly. He allowed the phone to resettle in its pocket.

There had to be a wall clock somewhere in this office. Fake dracaenas filled the space between aged bookshelves. Accounting handbooks leaned across geometric figurines on crooked shelves. Some bric-a-brac, like the grazing elk or the perched eagle devouring carrion, were easily identifiable. Others defied immediate understanding. The more mysterious items drew Venner in, muting the fluttering of fingers on keys.

An inelegant wrought silver paperweight in the shape of a cube captured his attention. Its metallic wiring climbed in an inexplicable pattern across the faces that coiled over its corners. Finer details were lost at this distance. How impatient was curiosity. It made his seat so small, the office so vast, and the figurines so beckoning in their motions.

Distraction made easy prey of consequence. At least until he would inevitably realize such flippant attention was in and of itself a consequence doled out by wasted time. A realization shortly followed by the misery of wasted effort and missed deadlines and a review tomorrow to be prepared for tonight. A review to prove that he was not a failed employee. By figure and sum, he had calculated so long ago how to get by in this life, flitting from one wonderful distraction to the next.

Now, years of ever-worsening habits had finally come tumbling down on him. Poor reporting on half-finished analyses received email summaries of chastising metric reviews. The inability to handle his own obsessions had set fire to all his prior achievements. The company advised him that he would need to take his work, his very livelihood, more seriously, and that continued poor performance would result in severance. From one distraction to another, his world had been nothing more than a simple toy meant to keep him busy. His world would devolve into a far more uncomfortable reality if his performance did not improve, and improve quickly.

The clattering of the keyboard suddenly stopped. Sunlight caught the accountant's odd smile, the curious turn of the head, the waggle of his finger in childish admonishment. His eyes were exhausted, his collar unbuttoned behind a crooked tie. He picked up a pen from his desk and held it like a cigarette while chewing the end of it for a moment before asking, "Have you heard any of what I've been saying for the past half-hour, Mr. Venner?" Venner started and sat immediately to attention. He grew flustered under the accountant's gaze of gentle suspicion. He shifted his hands to the armrests and began tapping his fingers.

Venner shrugged. "Enough, I suppose. I don't need to pay this year." He cleared his throat softly, gesturing with a nod of his head to the figurines around them. "A collector? They are interesting."

"Yes, they can be," said the accountant as he surveyed his domain. "I like to keep a few around in my workplace—for emergencies, you know. I'm a craftsman in my spare time." The accountant took a nearby figurine in hand. It was a lanky, dog-headed creature with an almost human musculature, hunched over on all fours, or sixes it seemed. A mess of hands and limbs bent the wrong way fit roughly in his grasp. "I like to give things life. Most of them fit quite well in their boxes, though some do occasionally get lost. I loathe cleaning up their messes, but good client retention demands that I do." The accountant flashed a wide grin, obviously amused by himself.

"You must be very talented," said Venner, leaning forward. "Such detail for something so extinct." *The wolfhound was loyal in life and given no choice in death. It was the eternal beast of the hunt, stuttering paw prints whimpering upon the ocean's gloam.* He was tempted to say these strange things aloud, but he bit his tongue and swallowed them down. The accountant gave a stifled chuckle, but such apparent mirth did not reflect on the face. "I'm sorry," added Venner quickly. "I meant the craft. I barely see artisan craft nowadays."

The accountant brought his hands together, tilted his head for a moment, then nodded. "Ah, that's no problem. Making's a dying art these days." Rudely interrupting, the accountant's phone started ringing.

The accountant looked to see who was calling, but did not immediately answer. He chewed on the end of a pen before glancing to Venner. "I need to take this call, very personal. Like one of those health checkups. My sincerest apologies," mumbled the accountant with little actual sincerity. Venner's curiosity was replaced with a mild frustration as the accountant set the dog-headed thing away. "But our business is more or less finished," continued the accountant. "No worry at all."

The accountant was soon engulfed in the midst of another conversation and beckoned Venner to leave when ready. A short handshake before the accountant paced into the hallway outside with a box of cigarettes in hand, leaving Venner alone in the office.

Venner collected his reports and found himself waiting in the chair. His gaze had again fallen onto that metal wrought box, lingering over details only clarified by closer examination. A moment of inspection, that would be enough to satisfy him.

This paperweight was a puzzle box, Venner realized, observing how it was displayed on its black stand and then how it sat in his palm. Though small enough to fit comfortably, it was heavier than he had expected. It had the heft of a good brick. The thin bronze plates were composed of moving faces, many of which were scratched from where they would shift against each other. Shift the plates in the right way and the box would open.

There were symbols etched across the surfaces, clues to aid in solving. The markers and hatched lines wavered in the light and did not seem to follow the transposition of space exactly, as if these half words just floated over the bronze. He ran his fingernail over the lines. Just good ink and poor lighting. At the creak of the door, Venner startled, fully expecting to be caught.

There was no one. The central heating had turned on, shifting the air and swaying doors on loose hinges. The blinds tapped and waved. It was not good to linger as he rolled the cube in his hands. Plates shuddered with quiet clicks of the mechanism fueling his fixation. He heeded his fear.

As he walked through the office door, an associate bade him good day. She had been setting the automatic climate control. Venner nodded as he passed her, keeping a tight grasp on his files and on the puzzle box in his pocket.

# THREE

NIGHT HAD FALLEN MORE QUICKLY THAN USUAL OVER THE city. Outside the office, there was no sign of the setting sun he had seen through the accountant's blinds. No stars either. Daylight had been replaced by the giants of the electrical grid, offering no chance for stellar dwarves. Venner acclimated to the open air, damp from recent rain. The rumble of the city, of distant traffic and sirens, replaced the hums of the climate system inside the office. The city loomed, making Venner feel quite unwelcome standing outside the accounting office. He was alone, even being without the inhuman company he expected scrounging around at night. Such rats had been slaughtered by the diligent piper. The city council was quite good with cleanliness it seemed.

A cool breeze stirred through Venner's hair and ruffled his clothes. It scattered through the bushes and trees, swirling around the high stonework of civilization. His breath condensed, reflecting the golden glow of the overhead light posts before it dissipated into the dark. He tugged on the collar of his coat.

Soon, he would be home. A long night of consequential preparation awaited him, building a defense to keep his career on track. His apartment was near downtown—close enough to visit social venues and entertainment when traffic was not too heavy, though he rarely did. He thought on occasion of moving closer to work; he disliked feeling so detached from his spreadsheets.

He remembered parking right in front of the office, but pressing a button on his key fob brought only a sharp, distant horn. The blinking taillights of his car seemed impossibly far away. It must have been his addled mind that distorted the distance—a momentary delusion brought on by the concern of nearly being fired. The parking lot can't be that big.

He hurried toward the sound of the horn. The open parking lot stretched endlessly before him. Murky clouds rushed overhead, which he took as evidence of time ticking just as fast. He walked until his footsteps seemed terribly loud, then stopped. All sound stopped with him. The wind had died down and so too had the traffic. He reached for his phone to check the time.

Instead of his phone, he found the puzzle box, which seemed to have gotten much pointier since last he had held it. Venner pulled the box from his pocket and the moonlight illuminated every crack and crevice. A thought pointed him back to the office, and then he remembered the accountant and his call. He had no way to verify whether the accountant was still inside. There was nothing weird about a man walking through the reception area, passing rows of cubicles and offices to a decidedly empty one just to deposit something he had stolen, nothing weird about being caught by the object's owner returning from a smoke break. Venner winced.

He found the doors of the office already locked, and the office lights dimmed. Nothing weird about a man knocking on the entrance. They would want to know why, and he did not want to explain. He replayed that spurious moment over and over in his head. He could leave the puzzle box behind then, by the entrance. It was a horrible idea, but at least he would be rid of the box. Someone would notice it there the next morning. After its solving, of course.

Distraction was his malady, and he should not have been so indulgent. But to suffer through such withdrawal just made him count moving plate after plate, unraveling the puzzle and fidgeting to the tune of his own denial. Fixation slayed all stuttering worries and provided momentary reprieve of any thought for his occupational instability.

His attention was consumed. Only occasionally did he look up to avoid various obstacles in his pacing. He furrowed his brow, clenched his teeth. Hermetic fixation left no room for failure. Nothing bothered him in his distractions. He traced the scuffs of prior solutions. Through the permutations of matching metal patterns and trailing mental notes about the number of clicks, the box opened with the tumble of gears of a revolving mechanism.

Venner was a collector himself, though not of statuettes. He had always been drawn to puzzle boxes like these, and it was never out of whimsy that he had acquired them. It was a compulsion, a true necessity, an open pit in his chest that needed to be filled. Throughout his entire time in the accountant's office, he'd never thought to just *not* steal that object of fascination.

The conventional never satisfied him. Those gimcrack toys were not difficult enough, or perhaps not unique enough, to do the trick. Back alley trinkets and treasures, however, spurred his mood, even if at the end he always found them empty. It was the action that sated as an actual meal, another furtive belief like the thoughts of immortal wolves and impossible water.

Tonight's puzzle box was empty as well. He traced the chamber inside with his thumb, finding scratch marks against one wall. He felt good. Good enough to . . . he stopped his thought and waited, squeezing the opened box. No, he did not feel good. Reevaluation bore dissatisfaction. He felt he had been presented a meal two times too small. He should have been sharper with the unraveling of the puzzle. Frustrated, he sniffed against the cold air and ran his thumb over the teeth of his lower jaw from point to ridges to point.

At last, his distraction was spent and the anxiety of work began to build on him once again. He put the box back in his pocket and glanced to the doors. His pacing had led him a good bit away, and it was easier to continue onwards to his car instead. All evidence of his thieving indecency thus would be lost. The moon was whisked away, behind the clouds. He wanted to focus his eyes on something. He kicked a pebble, sending it clattering into the darkness.

His work considered him an occupational hazard. However, hyper-fixation made good quality work, a job well done, and a nod of thanks. The same hyper-fixation sharpened absurd interactions and let spill those immortal wolves, tumbling stars, and feasting brine into open conversation because there was nothing else that could possibly be said. If only he could have controlled himself like he had in front of the accountant.

This week had been the culmination of his unmaking. Too many throes and not enough good work this quarter to compensate. He could never explain himself, and that made it all the worse. There were none who would defend him, but that was expected. Rare were the genial first impressions. "I am the infinite ocean," a phrase completely internalized to the point of habit, now slipped through his lips as an absentminded remark. And all relationships devolved from there. He knew he was the topic of gossip and conjecture, a bidding game in the break room. Lucky them that had bet on this week.

There was nothing better than a job well done. An immutable success, a consolatory metric that allowed him to ignore whatever else was wrong with his life. Everything in life. Venner groaned and forced anxious shoulders apart. *His everything*, the fragment of conversation flashed in his mind. That was his last conversation with Caide, the only person that seemed to ignore his madness without problem. Most likely out of pity, Venner acknowledged, but Caide's company was appreciated, however fragile.

He had told Caide that work was his everything. Work stifled the odd proclamation or the occasional insane gesture. Diligence devoured the day. It felt good, the satisfaction of having problems settled and solved. The puzzles, the conundrums, the next quarter's design improvement exalted him. He enjoyed the ever-chasing climb that kept his eyes away from himself.

Only his failures in workmanship proved him that much more the madman. While work provided adequate distraction from his internal absurdity, its potency had grown lethargic over the months.

Venner had even called work and distractions "childhood joy." He could not suppress his own disgust at this. There was such a belief in the system because children need structure, grades, checkpoints, scheduled triumph. Just another hyper-fixation, but it had worked. He did not think about oceans leaking inside typeface or dragons driven off the cartographer's map because someone forgot to close the lines. Water flowed off the edge into oblivion. It was drivel, but all of that was spoken when he was left too idle. Venner bit his tongue again.

Had he not achieved each desirable goalpost that was cemented within society as required? He must have been measured as some sort of success. The checklist had been filled proper with elevated projections: higher education, a promising career, then next to come some well-laid retirement fund, a house bought somewhere in the meantime. However, compatriots and romance were out of the question. Yet partial success had to guarantee partial happiness, somewhere.

It had to be too much for Caide. Not just a sentence or two lost in split second privacy, but a whole conversation in front of other coworkers. Undivided time towards facing the fact that Caide should be with better people, not oceans. It had hurt, hearing it from Caide that work could not save him.

What else did he have? Venner rubbed his hands over his face. They had not talked again since. If all these moments were plunged into nothingness, drowned beneath the waves of a dreaming ocean, he would be saved.

He exhaled loudly, his breath invisible now. Ah, where were the lights? He checked all around him but found nothing. What were once rows and rows of searing streetlights had disappeared into a seemingly infinite sea of night. His world had shrunk in his inattention, or perhaps it had grown all the more vast, engorged on his anxiety. He hated his free eyes and empty hands. The mind would find exercise in the exact thoughts that corroded his workplace standing. *Oceans do not eat.*

A blackout, it must have been. Even the lights of nearby buildings had been snuffed. Venner was left truly alone in an impenetrable darkness. His hand gripped his car keys tightly, clicking for the light as often as he could. The red taillights were in constant alert to their location, yet he felt nowhere closer. The mind cradled every loitering second, chasing hyperbole straight into the ravenous dark. His eyes would adjust in time, surely.

His footsteps, sliding against the gravel, irked him more and more with every step. The lights blinked again. Damn him if he actually thought the lights were getting smaller. He shook his head, forcing a few more ungainly steps. He should have known where his car was. He would simply walk there and then go home.

The red lights blinded him, igniting this time right before his face. He staggered back, his keys making a few clinks as they clattered to the ground. "Oh please," he whispered, catching his breath from the scare. He wanted relief—what an embarrassing feeling to want relief from a darkened parking lot. He knelt to the asphalt, set his tax documents aside, and pulled out his phone. Any kind of relief, please.

He scanned the ground with the light from his phone, eyes darting from shadow to shadow. His keys couldn't have fallen far. They were fortunately designed in a shape not conducive to rolling into despair. As for himself, however . . . . Was his phone running out of battery? The area illuminated felt oddly constrained, as if the darkness was moving in on him. He sighed, and tried to stop his dreadful thoughts, but his thoughts persisted nevertheless.

*On a Thursday night, a man raving in an anxiety attack was found outside Gilman & Co. Accounting Offices,* an imaginary headline from a particularly slow news hour flashed across his mind. Evidently, he was quite scared of the dark. Venner huffed. The silver glint of his keys at the edges of the light interrupted his self-chastising, and he snatched them without hesitation. Ah, this was fine. Of course it was. The phone battery was certainly draining now as he wiped the damp off the screen corner, revealing the red glare. He shut off his phone and the light with it. He was close enough to his car.

He collected his documents and proceeded to put his arms forward, trying to feel where his car was. He felt the cold metal bite into his skin and he traced from the damp roof down the smooth glass, eventually finding the tiny bumps and curves of the handle. The dew of leftover rain dripped off his hand. He wrapped his fingers under the handle and opened the door. The scrape of metal and heavy clicks of the locks sounded in the distance behind him. He half-turned, scanning the rest of the parking lot. He shut the door and opened it again, its mechanisms not sounding nearly as strange as that something else in the distance.

What a cruel trick that caught him off guard and nearly convinced him he was being mugged. People came and went in multitudes of cars. He wondered if he should include for his performance review his work on composite filaments and why the scraping of metal on asphalt sounded right above him.

Something cold brushed the back of his neck. Something sharp traced across his throat.

His first regret was letting go of the handle. His second was stumbling away from the car. His third and most damning of actions was running deeper into the darkened parking lot. He ran in no distinct direction, whether to office or street or car, he just wanted to find someone. His footsteps echoed alone in the night. Call the police. Pray that there is no gun.

Something caught his foot at the wrong rhythm and he fell, face first, onto asphalt. Something squeezed his head and pressed his face into the rough surface. His body tensed immediately. He clawed uselessly against the ground, unable to pull away.

Pain rang through his head as the sound of metal scraping revved louder and louder. Blood seeped from his cuts and scrapes. He couldn't breathe. His lungs burned. *Please, no.* A heavier weight pressed down upon his upper back from this monstrous machine. His ribs bowed, threatening to crack. Metal sliced through his clothes and into flesh. Hot muscle met the outside chill in utter agony. Pathetic flailing failed to disturb his perpetrator. He heard nothing but his own pounding heart, nothing but his own muffled cries, the nigh-silent begging to his torturer.

*Please. Please don't kill me.*

# FOUR

THE ACCOUNTANT'S FLASHLIGHT ILLUMINATED A MOTION-less body on the ground. Now, now. This case was no different than all the others. Calm down. Steady hands made for better work. The accountant unclipped a Gilman & Co. badge from his own person and hid it away in his pocket. He feared a repeat of coming into work with blood over his portrait. He had made it in time for this client. He sidestepped the growing pool of blood and flicked a steel lighter to ignite the end of a thin cigarette that shook on his lips. He inhaled deeply. He just needed to put the creature back in his wonderful box and pluck all these offending thoughts away.

No one had to know what had happened. His client was alive, even if barely. The dumb machine would be dealt with after. A moment's preoccupation in a phone call let slip this dirge, loose from its box. An assault by one of his crafted creatures would not look good on his record, never mind discussions of possible manslaughter.

Those that owned the city cared deeply for keeping the peace. They ran the city like clockwork. They watched with cleaners and handled business with couriers and enforcers. Punishment was swift against detractors. Not that they could have known this soon. He just needed to hurry up and fix the client, hope that he was outside anyone's attention.

# FIVE

SOOTHING COLD PIERCED THROUGH THE HEAT AND FIRE OF frantic panic. The sharpened distress of incoming terror bled away into an aching body and exhausted mind. Venner saw light through closed eyes, but his thoughts struggled against their own gravity. Lethargy shackled his reactions. Time made unknowable headways. He breathed, loud and heaving, because brainstem reflexes demanded air. Lungs filled with hurt. He wiped his tears away with his sleeve. Sight stunned him immediately.

He stared at the glaring red stoplight. Evening rains pattered down the windshield, streaming this way and that, obscuring the world before him. The hum of the engine was drowned by the water. His gaze dropped to the dashboard, to the steering wheel, and to his own unmangled body sitting in his car, waiting at an intersection. The dashboard lights lingered in afterimages, conjuring mild nausea. He covered his eyes with his hands.

What had just happened? His memory remained mute upon interrogation. He gripped his head harder, and the pain brought forth a few disconnected flashes. Something was wrong. Fear snarled like echoes of a distant thunder; the heat of trembling horror coursed through his veins. Then nothing. No words or names to be had. All was missing but one momentous feeling. The momentous inexplicable lived in the dark, not between the seams of his sweating touch over blind, searching eyes, but behind his hand, rapping metal across his knuckles, through his knuckles, and the final mulch that was him.

With a gasp, he dropped his hand and stared into the street. The white crossing light steadily blinked on and off. In the quiet of his car, in sullen disbelief, he rested over the steering wheel, burying his head in his arms. He counted the drops of rain, arbitrarily choosing which ones to include in the tally. All he wanted was a reprieve of any further aggravation and dishonest half-truths. Yet his frustrations fed in utter bliss in utter insolence against him. The rains intensified and he eventually gave up. Arithmetic would not save him.

Speeding cars splashed through the flooded streets. Someone honked behind him before cutting by, causing indistinct shouting from someone on the crosswalk. How long had he been waiting beneath the glow of neon signs and dim streetlights, trying to swallow his own helplessness? He looked up once more, fully expecting the scenery to change, for his car to disappear underneath him and leave him stranded back in that parking lot.

It did not. The world and its inhabitants felt perfectly still. He was shivering. With quick flicks, he turned on the heater and his headlights. The sharp brightness skimmed off the ripples and waves of the urban river. He debated turning on the radio, but his hand slid off the knob. There was nothing wrong with quiet. Something had attacked him. It lived in the dark, and it waited for him. His breathing caught in his dry throat.

He clutched at his heart. It felt as if, as if . . .

His mind stalled. No thought formed, nothing concrete to describe what he had felt. He inspected himself again, more closely this time. He expected tattered clothes and bloodied arms, but found no trace of harm or conflict. His tie was crisp, his suit as sharp as when he had left the workplace, his hands clean and dry. Physically, right now, he felt fine.

Venner's distress fell apart like a half-remembered dream. Memories slipped from their places. Nothing lived in the dark. Nothing waited for him. Effort failed the true course of events and rewrote the night over and over with false renditions. Terror murmured beneath the surface of his temperament. All that mental effort to speak of nothing. Then he remembered he had something to do.

Ah yes, his work. He watched another cycle of the pedestrian signal count down and the unfortunate wet bicyclist riding across the crosswalk.

"Go home," he muttered behind the rhythmic roll of the wipers, and he shifted the car into motion. Water blurred the lines of the outside world. All light, hazy, and lost at sea.

Thankfully, the drive home was uneventful, initially. Venner sighed as he drove along the slick road, a perfect expanse of wet blackness flanked by closed down shops and lonely apartments nestled in between. It had been nothing but a bad fall, he told himself. There was no solace in those words.

This was an unsolvable puzzle. Pieces were missing; memory misbehaved. Frustration coiled up every ligament of his body. He squeezed the steering wheel.

Once he was home, he could work his problems away. Work was a potent distraction for any illness, any state of mind. Work had to be. In the meantime, at every intersection, every turn, he found himself glancing in the rearview mirror. Sometimes he would see the brights of a car in waiting or nothing. No, he was not thankful for the nothingness. He dreaded the nothing. Work in mind, toys in hand just to avoid looking at nothing but himself.

The roads were thinning and winding. He counted cars to ease the encroaching loneliness. Perhaps it was just the bias of his anxiety that begat this solitude. The cars that followed him had turned away long ago, and many more went the opposite direction. It was preposterous to have such expectations of streetwise companionship. He pointed the rearview mirror away. The hazard would not matter much in the dead of night. Alone. He stepped on the gas and the engine revved. He didn't want to spend any more time outside than necessary. Finally, his attention turned to the road.

A dark shape appeared suddenly some twenty feet in front of his car. In a split second the distance between them closed, and he just had time to register a startled woman on a bike lit up in his headlights. In a panic he slammed the brakes. The car lost traction on the slick, swerved, and jumped the sidewalk. There was a screeching sound and the warping and shearing of metal mixed with the shattering of glass on concrete as the car smashed into a streetlight. The light pole landed on the roof of the passenger side, collapsing the cabin with its weight. The cacophony of the crash gave way to the quiet beating of the rain. Venner had been saved from certain death by his seatbelt.

He was a panting, haggard mess, staring in shock at the light pole through his shattered windshield. His thoughts tumbled with broken limbs, struck dumb. The wreck creaked and shuddered around him. Rain washed down the cracked concrete pole, collecting in pools on the dash and seats and floorboards. The dying splutters of his engine heaved the car forward once more, jerking him into reality, then lay cold. His heart rushed and burned.

Venner had not yet released his grip on the wheel—his knuckles were white and his fingers pulsed. He unclenched slowly. There was a dull pain in his hands where he started to rub. "Damn it," he whispered. All he wanted was to go home.

Wait, he had almost hit something—a woman on a bike! Was she buried now in steel? His eyes grew wide. He had to check, had to get help if she was hurt. He wrestled with his seatbelt and shouldered the door open, disturbing the shards of glass underfoot.

First aid mantras from a class long ago raced through is mind. *Check for breathing with the victim. Keep them warm. Stem any bleeding, if possible.* He climbed from the wreckage and turned to the front of the car, now embedded within the base of the light pole. The adjoining intersection signals turned red, blinking in warning. This lurid tint lurked over wet surfaces, swallowing all other color.

The crash was shallow enough to see that there was nothing pinned between the car and pole but that the damage severe enough to require a tow vehicle and probably a new engine. Faint relief that it was just him. A bit less luck and that would have been the end of it. He swallowed hard and watched leaking fuel trace the jagged wreck. He was alone in the midst of a slumbering commercial district where life remained undisturbed.

The clatter of a trashcan alerted him to a nearby alleyway. The waste bin rolled out into the light, gently settling against the wreckage. Where was she, the rider? With a second wind, that shameful anxiety swallowed his relief. Splashing his way into the alley, he was soon met by the bitter stench of rubbish. He saw nothing initially but ripped trash bags and water clattering on aluminum lids, but then he found a bike on its side in the corner of the alley, half hidden by ruined cardboard boxes. Its frame was bent and broken, its front wheel still slowly spinning.

"Does anyone need help?" he called. Had his voice always sounded so fragile? "Is anyone here?" The headlight from his ruined car sent his shadow high up the walls, tall enough to disappear into the night sky. Thunder rumbled in the distance and there was no one that answered him. A final scan of the alleyway satisfied him, and he returned to his car, intending to fish his phone from the wreckage and call emergency services.

He wanted to turn away from the sight of his mistakes. With trembling hands, he excavated the puzzle box from his pocket and replayed its solving. He looked momentarily up at the streaks of burned rubber. He could have killed someone.

With the red blinking lights of the intersection reflecting off its surface, the puzzle box denied him peace. There was no solution to living without consequence. He stepped back into the streets and brushed wet hair out of his eyes. He prodded the shorn metal carefully before reaching between to grab his phone from the passenger footwell. Serrated edges circled him uncomfortably close. The phone's slick glass face taunted his outstretched grasp up to his seething growl before finally growing bored and accommodating.

The sound of metal scraping through rushing water cut through his self-loathing with absolute ease. Across from the wreckage, it stood at least twice as tall as him—a deformed thing, hunched upon four arms and two crooked legs stitched out of red bone and metal plate and clad with glossy tendrils and rotting, dark flesh. The head of a dog seemed melted onto its human body. Life squirmed from within. Oil bled where skin tore, mixing with the rain. Wherever empty space allowed were carved eyes, slitted and yellow. All stared at him. The dog-headed thing rose, and Venner automatically backed away, almost stumbling in his haste.

"You have something of mine, Mr. Venner," said a man from a distance, voice familiar. It was the accountant standing behind his favored dog head. He leaned against the side of another idling car in the middle of the intersection, an umbrella in one hand and a cigarette in the other. A vicious glow flared across his face as he took another drag. The smoke wrapped upwards, seeping through the accountant's bared teeth. "I thought it was my fault you almost died, as if I've been negligent locking up my creations. You've really upset me." The accountant waved his cigarette in the air. "I regret playing hero to your wailing victim and all the time I spent on you. Forgive me as I extract a little vengeance." He spoke with the same finality as he would when closing financial statements.

"I can just give it back," said Venner, offering the puzzle box in hand, wincing at every movement of the dog head. "I'm sorry."

"Do you know what I found in that parking lot?" the accountant asked. "I found a barely breathing pile of viscera. You, I mean, and the broken body of one of my creatures. A creature dragged along asphalt, half-chewed and swallowed, missing limbs and faces. Missing answers to questions I don't know where to start asking. I couldn't salvage it unfortunately. Not many things are that capable of dismantling my darlings.

"What do you want if not this?" asked Venner.

"Peace at night," the accountant said, adjusting his umbrella. "I don't know what you did, but I know I would sleep better if you were dead. That's the sort of solace you can give back."

"I don't want to die."

"No one does. I've already seen you mangled. It wasn't impressive. I'll come to collect what's left of you after a warm dinner—maybe. I've had enough of tonight, if you would so kindly." The puzzle box dropped onto the ground and slowly filled with rain. There would be no further negotiation with the accountant. Venner ran.

# SIX

**THE ACCOUNTANT FOLDED HIS UMBRELLA, WATCHED HIS CLI-**
ent dash off, and then settled into his idling car. The dog head stayed
motionless. The accountant tapped his hand on the steering wheel to the
beat of his wipers until he felt it was enough. With a wave of the hand,
the hunt began with pants and heavy paws. He massaged his neck and
closed his eyes. It hurt, this aching body. In the throes of an afterhours
panic attack over an almost-dead client, he was but a heartbeat away
from skipping town.

Terrible, the crash, but lucky enough for him that Mr. Venner was
delayed to shorten this agonizing ordeal. He had planned for a midnight
visit at Venner's residence, but it was dangerous to overextend his presence in such a way. They were named Harken, those that owned the city,
those that provided for people like him all those absurd mystic remedies,
all those resources to practice sorcerous arts. Specialized healthcare of
the thaumaturge, a service growing rarer by the day, was what drew him
and many others to this metropolis. Magic wasn't a dying art; it was a
dying breed. Its degradation could barely be managed, leaving him with
a tightening pain throughout his body that was only worsening.

There was no ruckus allowed within the city hospice, no patience
for the ungrateful living. Harken's enforcers killed and collected the
refuse. The accountant knew that if he kept his head down, their
enforcers would never knock at his own door. It was nerve-wracking to
keep this tacit peace when the definition of peace was always changing
without warning.

Daylight incidents had occurred in this city without punishment before. Wendigo hunting a year back had led to a whole parade of dead animals flooding a midtown park. It had hardly been subtle, the explanation—a rash of wild dogs or exceptionally cruel teenagers—seemed to take well enough. Poor taste, but mundane. Yet people disappeared for having done much less, though maybe it was just their inability to blend into modern society. Too much of the inexplicable left unexplained led to too much background anxiety. If he staged Venner's death as part of the car accident, the city might not care, and he could continue on like nothing had happened.

He should heed the warning for careful driving in this weather. Car wrecks, straightforward as they were, could not doublespeak like Harken. Just go slower, stay westward where the streets were drier. The city stood silent outside his window, waiting. He could justify this violence. It was self-defense. His broken creation was proof.

The accountant rested his wrist over the shifter and took another drag. The decision to drive home, instead, gave way to parallel parking ahead of the crashed car. He turned off the headlights and waited. Normally he would trust the word of his creatures that the deed was done. Tonight, he wanted to be nearby just to make sure himself. He lowered the driver side window to let out the smoke and tapped the ashes into a tray he had taped to his cup holders.

The accountant saw from his rearview mirror someone else who lacked that nicotine patience. A woman in a cracked bicycle helmet and a dirty company jacket from a courier service emerged from that dark alleyway. Blood soaked one of her sleeves. She started to salvage what looked like a hard case from the shorn engine. She could only partially rescue the case and settled for prying apart the covers. She glanced around. When the accountant met her eyes, she flipped him off. She grabbed an unknown totem from the case, hid it under her jacket, and took off running.

The courier must have seen the entire exchange. She would report him to Harken, their enforcers without mercy. Troublemakers were worth more as cadavers. His body tightened under the thought of unavoidable punishment. It would be impossible to justify his creature hunting someone in the open streets. What were the chances that Venner would have clipped a courier tonight?

It—it was the courier's fault, or Venner's. If they had not crashed, things would not have devolved into this violence. Out in plain view, what was he thinking? It would have been well contained with one missing man the next morning. Hardly a lucky blessing, this crash had damned him. He lifted his fist but stopped short of hitting his horn. He squeezed and pulled on the steering wheel as if he were trying to wrest it from the dash. Maybe she wouldn't report him? He clung to this possibility with white knuckles and bared teeth. It could be no matter at all. People have gotten away with worse.

The accountant stepped back out into the rain and went to investigate the hard case. The dented steel was near indistinguishable from the wreckage. Whatever else was inside had been crushed beyond recognition, and he didn't have the strength to investigate further. Yet it had to glimmer. He had to notice. It was a black polished business card kept within the case lining. Harken. Oh gods.

There was no doubt now. His demise was guaranteed. He had not set out to obstruct Harken's business. Traffic accidents happen, and given how the courier patiently waited, and would have most likely continued to wait until Venner had calmly left with the proper authorities—police, medical, or otherwise—there was no problem. It was far from normal, however, planning to kill a man with a reanimated corpse. He could recall the creature, but intent to murder cannot be forgotten. He had shown himself willing to flout city laws.

The evening as a whole ended up tallying poorly for the accountant, and he dropped the card back into one of the crevices of the bent case. He could still leave the city. The enforcers were not omniscient, but he would have to deal with the courier witness to give himself more time.

He pulled a silver coin from his pocket and pointed it in the direction she had run. He should never have bothered. He should have let that man die. He should kill himself. Whatever she carried for Harken, the accountant hoped it could fence for enough to tide his escape to a haven far, far away.

"Fetch."

# SEVEN

**THE DOG HEAD FOLLOWED CLOSELY BEHIND, LUMBERING** slowly, but easily keeping pace with its long legs. Every block Venner ran, every intersection he crossed, appeared as one long façade. The dog head's presence nipped at his feet. Terrible looming buildings and ominous red lights flooded each and every way. Everywhere else was a sheet of darkness. Unfamiliar places, unfamiliar signs. It was a nightmare through and through.

Venner had no destination. There was no one who could help. He dared not stop, but he knew all the same that it was inevitable. It would catch him and it would kill him. His muscles burned and screamed for break.

What could he do? Bash its head in? He clutched his phone tightly in his hand. He tried to call the police, but nothing connected on the other side. The dull drone of busy lines crushed the spirit. Stop the record, advance the needle, or find someone that can—all options mocked his plight.

Where was he? If this was still the commercial district, a police station would be on the turn of capital square. The intersections provided no answers. Rarely could one read in a nightmare. Letters jumbled, crowding the green light–reflecting nameplates that swung in the wind.

His mental navigation was interrupted by the city turning underfoot. The needle lifted and the ambience turned into disquiet. Nothing physically changed around him—brick as brick and mortar as mortar—but a set of attentions had been shifted. The lights above him turned green.

He had paused in the middle of an intersection. He saw the headlights. Death in different ways, how spoiled for choice he was.

The air filled with screeching brakes. He ducked his head under his arms. The car missed him by inches. The wind blew over him. The smell of exhaust whiffed past. There was no safety or rest in the wake of the vehicle. One death passed hands into another.

He flinched as the dog head collided into him, and once again, he was pinned to the ground with many arms. Many eyes were filled with hunger as it began the excruciating ordeal that was too quickly becoming familiar.

Thunder and rain. The snarls of the pet most loyal. The rumble of a nearby engine. Somewhere nearby, red taillights blurred. They must have seen him. They must have seen it. *Get out of the car!* Desperate in his strangling, he thrashed and freed one arm. He threw his phone toward the taillights, and it clattered uselessly against the back windshield. That was the limit of his freedom. His chest either rattled from a heart in fever or the dog head in bliss. Pain stayed exhaustion. There would be no shock into unconsciousness. He would be awake in the maw of this creature, staring into the abyss of eyes. This was his consequence.

Strike went the lightning and belated roared the thunder. Then, silence. That strike shimmered before him, a solid hallucination. Having grown so accustomed to the night, the lightning was blinding. A long, luminescent spear impaled the maligned muzzle, contorting the dog head against its own body before cracking the ground around them upon exiting into the street. The dog head slumped quietly. Its arms went limp. A weapon of solid lightning and good aim, an impossible weapon.

Black oil stained the weapon's shaft where it met the monster. Venner reached out, unable to get up, and brushed oil from the weapon's surface. The spear pushed back. Its light warped on contact like an old television screen disturbed by a magnet. It was real enough to save him, real enough to reflect off the wet streets and his own exposed skin. The dog head decayed into ash in a gentle cascade. Black skin collapsed into its emptying cavities. Its crimson bones were left behind, bowed on the asphalt in reverence to the olden hunters victorious amongst savage beasts.

Footsteps were nearing and he had no more effort left to see whose they were. His view of the skies, now unobstructed by the dog head, were that of the moon perched upon the clouds, out of reach as always. The splendor seemed so formidable, so far in excess of childish dreams.

This view was replaced by the underside of an orange umbrella and the girl who held it. The rain tapped against the plastic. She seemed so bored of the violence surrounding them. A nonchalance born firmly from believing that nothing was wrong and that the world was mundane as ever. She could convince him that none of this was real.

She leaned down and whispered, "You are a very lucky man." She passed him by without another word and stopped beside the spear embedded within the creature.

Was he lucky? He certainly didn't feel lucky. Beside him, crimson ribs were cracked open, revealing the machine heart inside the once-living dog head. The heart bounced and struggled. A sickness grew in his stomach at the sounds of this fragile organ pumping itself apart.

At some point in their lives, people start claiming proficiency in distinguishing the fantastical from the real—to garner satisfaction in enjoying the magic and then explaining the trick. If the trick was not obvious, then the secondary satisfaction of at least knowing what was trickery would do. The person could not be had. No one wanted to play the fool and actually be known for believing in cryptids or the like. Belief was juvenile, lasting a few years under the evergreen tree. It was a failure to take things seriously enough, a failure of the checklist to give anything like madness any sort of satisfaction. Maybe it was just he who writhed at the feet of this hang up.

The world sought to damn him in his witness. Formed from liquid light, an ornate spear dripped into being from an open hole in the air. It crystallized and moonlight glistened inside its facets. It hung suspended over the mechanical heart. Madness took him by all his mental capacity and then swallowed him. He was not in the mood to argue the impossibility of these things. A lifetime's capacity for disbelief had been exhausted before a single night's end.

This spear plunged into the heart with no resistance, and its body disappeared into nothingness. The evidence of dog heads and spears made of solid lightning was swept away by the coming of another torrent. The orange umbrella came back into view.

# EIGHT

THE DRIVE WAS SILENT AND HAD JUST TIPPED OVER INTO BEING long. Venner had been collected by the girl with the orange umbrella and her driver. He did not know where they were going. A hospital, maybe. There was no argument. She had saved him, and at the moment, he wanted nothing more than to be away. End the night. Perhaps it was the shock, but conversation struck him as distasteful.

He sat in the rear seat, ruining the fabric with his wet clothes. The scant towel they had given him smelled of car wax and had already soaked through. He hung it uselessly over his head. The rough and tumble driving did not help his condition. Numb arms braced against the underside of the roof with little relief. His clothes were filthy and tattered; his body was equally shambled. His many wounds were still raw, and every dip and bump in the streets rubbed them against the rough seats. He tried to swallow his groans but did not always succeed.

Adrenaline ebbed, leaving behind exhaustion. His shaking hands fumbled with his seatbelt, eventually releasing the catch. He wanted very much to lie down. Another dip threw him against the door. Another groan. The lightning spear and the death of the dog head replayed in his mind. The accountant somewhere in the dark, waiting. There was a certain safety, Venner acknowledged, in riding in the back of a speeding car instead of running for his life. He squeezed his hand, trying what people did to wake up on command.

Regret for the theft of a single puzzle box, now lost somewhere in the city, consumed him. His worst fear should be no more than the missed bill or the tribulation of stolen identity. Conflicts found and solved within the confines of societal mechanisms. Why did the absurdity of this event have to intercede?

He preferred denial. He just needed to go home, check up on emails, get some dinner, finish up household chores, commit the rest of the time attending to the current pop culture show of the month, and sleep it off. And again, and again. Then maybe Caide would call out of the blue as he always did, asking to hang out that weekend. That would have been nice.

Delirious faculties like an impossible ocean and monstrous hunters needed to be starved out of his mind space through his work, his paradise.

Glancing to the rearview mirror, he found the driver glaring back. He ducked his gaze to the rental tag taped to the front windshield. The girl occupied herself with sights out the window, bouncing the umbrella from hand to hand as it leaned between her knees. She was smartly dressed in a white collar and blue ribbon tie. Her greatcoat sat folded on her lap.

The driver was much gruffer in her old leather bomber and turned to raise the heat in the car, filling the cabin with the stench of cigarettes. She passed a quick glance over to the girl, who said nothing, still preferring the outside views. The driver turned off the fan and cracked open the driver-side window, ignoring the water that seeped in. Without looking at him, the girl handed Venner something rectangular. His phone.

Venner murmured his thanks. The front wipers thumped back and forth. Rain obscured the streets and signs. Another bump sent Venner's head to the ceiling. His phone jumped out of his hands. The idea that he was not where he should be had hardly crystallized before he pushed it away. After all that had unfolded, he was not dead. His trembling heart might not survive a bout of self-induced paranoia.

He rubbed the back of his head and collected his phone off the floor. A reprieve from sinister driving let him lie down. The screen of his phone was cracked, and the casing was dented and scratched. He could still call the police and have them fix whatever was wrong. No more monsters. No more lightning trickery. No more terror. Venner remembered that image of the moon overhead. To hold that moon in his hands could very much convince him nothing was wrong with the world.

There were glimpses of conversation. "Weill," the girl said, "I was under the impression that such blatant disregard for the sanctity of this city was punishable by death. Or what did they call it? Repossession? And here we have a man and no one chasing."

He did not want to hear this. He focused on his phone instead. The dark screen erupted into distorted shapes as it was turned on. Bright colors melded into missed messages to read. The girl's words implied there were more dog heads at the end of every turn, sniffing at the intersections.

"Don't talk about this stuff in front of him," said the driver. She pulled down the brim of her cap while Venner scrolled through the late work emails. There was work to be done. Work. To. Be. Done.

"He is my concern now," said the girl. "My small, defiant indulgence against Harken. The city's lack of cooperation has generated less than stellar terms for the both of our organizations, but they cannot accost me. Their fault. Let them chase me in their frothing irritation if they have such a problem with my interference." She sounded bored.

He wanted them to ignore him, to stop talking about him. He shot an email in reply to nondestructive evaluation inquiries. He answered that minor composite indications should be well-screened by required testing, that there was no need for repair unless found grown afterwards, and that the streets were lined under the asphalt with the flayed skins of missing persons. He swallowed hard as he carefully edited his reply before sending, then ran a hand through his hair and dropped his phone onto his chest.

"May I ask," started Venner. "Can you take me home?" This was just a nightmare he was waiting to pass. If this was reality, and if he was going to die, he would prefer to die in ignorance. They did not answer him. "Then may I ask that I not have to listen to this talk of men and monsters?" The storm heaved upon its haunches and thunder rose from its throat.

"Who are you?" the girl asked. His lips twitched. He brought up his hands to stuff his mouth. He would not say anything about an ocean. He did much better when he presented himself unprompted. It was awkward now, but he could always make it worse. He was thankful of being in the backseat, where he did not have to face her. Where was the dreaming? Where was the mindlessness that assured him these were all lies, that the parking lot did not happen, that there was nothing out there watching and biding its time, that he could refuse the words that so crowded his mouth and tasted of brine?

# NINE

**Dreams were fickle. They served at once to calm Ven-**
ner and to taunt him. They were a phantom place he never quite knew
what to make of. *Stage set, everlasting night.* Underneath a grey expanse
of clouds waited an endless ocean existing across all horizons. It was
always here that he found himself an outcast lost at sea. He stood upon
a lonely beachhead, the only land to be had and just enough to barely
stand above the waves. A child version of him would pine for a boat or
gimcrack raft to sail to the ocean's edge where he would topple over the
ends of the water. That child's faint whims dredged up a small smile.

Salt-filled wind slipped over the ocean's surface, spraying water and
stirring lapping waves across his cramped rock. Some dreams had him
stranded on a sheer cliff edge or an empty shoreline stretching miles.
He preferred the shoreline, of course, given those options. The sand was
always cold and waterlogged, but he enjoyed that, no matter how far
back he walked, the breaking waves would always reach him.

The ocean functioned as expected. It never failed him; it was just
invasive. He relished the quiet and sheer control he had here. All good
memories stemmed from the ocean. Not the relief of barely passing in
society, but good, genuine success in the manner of good, honest work.
Satisfaction was supped from these waves. Exploration, adventure,
assurance—he felt he had everything he ever wanted as a child here. If
anything bothered him, then here was where they drowned and were
cleansed from the thought space. As an easily identified metric for progress, cleaning was nothing too complicated. It felt natural. Except . . .

Beyond the clouds was once the home of stars and moons. Now, all the stars had been diligently expunged. As a child, he'd been much more successful in that senseless dream of cleaning up. Maybe because children have no sense of scale or for the limits of their own bodies, but a younger Venner managed to erase many celestial bodies down to one. He'd carried out this campaign with pride.

He missed the energy of those younger years. There were so many corners of the ocean to explore, and he truly loved the vastness of it all—and the myriad ways to drown everything. Yet more than anything, he yearned for an empty ocean and that solitary moon to be devoured. The moon vexed him and cursed him with the knowledge of eating and jaws and failure. He did not love outgrowing his dream. The paradise, ruined.

A crick between his shoulders ached; he disliked remembering how close he had been to clearing that night sky. Hidden behind the cloud cover was one last moon and no more stars. He surveyed the silent ocean. Light from above swept the tops of rippling waves in white. The moon's reflection upon the water's surface mocked him. It was a surreptitious mark on his cleanliness he was always frustrated to witness. Even infinite water could not reach the heavens.

A weight pressing on his legs caught his attention. Hand-shaped things, body sold separately, scurried underfoot and overflowed his little rock island. These scuttling things were battered by the waves. Some were washed into the depths while others began climbing him. Things with many fingers or legs moved too quickly to count. There were pincers, too, sized too large for the bodies that carried them.

He scowled at the legfull things as he picked one up by the thorax or palm. Its shape shifted from angle to angle as it wriggled in his grasp. He underestimated its neck as it reached around, its mandibles drawing blood. Needlelike teeth pierced the skin between his fingers. It hurt, but was more annoying than painful. Venner ripped the thing off and with a snap of the arm, threw it into the ocean.

Rising waves climbed above him and swept the rest away, throwing him underwater. The legfull things paddled with thrashing fingers to stay afloat, but a current pulled them deeper. Venner watched the desperate things sink and seize as water entered their pores. A few came afloat on the surface, but he hoped they wouldn't linger. He loved them drowned and dead. Cleanliness next to godliness.

He tugged at the wet clothes around his shoulders and chest, alleviating some of the discomfort where they clung and stretched. He floated, suspended in this ocean, and was once again left alone. He smiled and gently held himself. The wound from that legfull thing began to irritate. He inspected his hand, finding mucus-like excretions mixed with blood. Bright neon traveled down his veins. He huffed, disturbing the water. He picked at the wound, pulling out threads of shimmering neon. The ends were picked up by the current and spiraled into the widening emptiness.

The neon strands were pulled arm length after arm length, tightening his skin from his hand to his shoulder, until a sudden jerk of impatience broke the line. Neon sparked at the snap, crisping his wound. He rubbed his hand and tasted the salt of the water.

Dropped from a careless sky, oily metallics rained down into the ocean. Red bones splashed into brine. He reached out to catch them and caught instead the skull of a dog head with too many orbits for too many eyes. Air bubbles leaked from these empty sockets. A preoccupation seemed to pant down his brain stem. If he had the chance, he would have liked to open this skull—to turn plates of bone in reverse of its creation and make what lied in its very center his. He was sure this dog skull was not empty.

☾

**DREAMS WERE AS THEY WERE. AS THE YEARS PASSED, HIS** strange visitations to an ocean had become rote, familiar even. Venner had been displaced from car into a spartan bedroom in a rented apartment—the driver's apartment, he remembered that. It was enough for someone to stay perhaps temporarily, but there wasn't much evidence of living except for the musk of tobacco and an off-tinge to the walls. The girl had told him aid would be arriving. He must have fallen unconscious after that. The clock on his phone told him an hour had passed. He did not remember falling asleep or even the end of that conversation, but he remembered the dream. His head ached.

Watching the streets below from the window of an unfamiliar bedroom, he counted the rare passing car in this tranquil midnight. Trees swayed in the wind. Branches dipped with rain. Lights in adjacent apartments slowly flickered out one by one. The night was hardly over. They had left his phone on the nightstand alongside a superstore bag full of discount T-shirts and rough-cut jeans. They'd been newly purchased, judging from the receipt dated within that uncounted hour, and were a bit of a loose fit, but he was grateful.

He kneeled on the floor, resting his back against the windowsill with his head sunk into his arms. Not too uncommon, but it was a small marvel for the waking world to hold the same solemnity as dreams. Despite uncertainty and fear, he'd found a moment of peace. Solving equations at work did not comfort as well as a devouring ocean picking teeth.

Yet a dream's assuredness never lasted long. If it was not a wave that toppled him over into wakefulness, it was the sinking into pitch-black depths. The ocean swallowed him, he supposed, when it had enough of him. These dreams never afforded him much sleep, yet he would wake feeling oddly satisfied with having cleaned the last bit of things in a place that did not exist. He heard muffled voices from the other room, his two supposed caretakers up and about still.

This counted as kidnapping. He had been taken away from his car, mugged. A pipe wrench begat pain and blood, and he was left to unknowns, locked away. *Mugged* was not the right word. He traced the veins of his imaginary neon wound. The rev of metal scraping was unforgettable. He had been in a car crash.

Reality demanded consequence, and he was currently guilty of possible manslaughter. No, there was no one there. He really had checked in that alleyway. He would be under exorbitant increases in insurance premiums if he did not land in jail. He flexed his phone between his hands. He would need to call the authorities—the police, a lawyer, an accountant. There was a sharp crack. The phone screen was further ruined.

Why would he need an accountant? That, that was not right. While he could never guarantee that every memory would come with rigid surety—for he forgot and misremembered as the living are wont to do—the memories of these past hours felt precariously thin. They stuttered and frayed like the images on an old VHS tape. He could rewind and rewatch till these paltry images were scrubbed away. Perhaps then he would see what lay underneath.

A heavy feeling of déjà vu quieted his thoughts. His perception kept flowing out to sea. He had drowned in that dream, yet here he was. He stood up despite his body crying out in soreness. He checked under his shirt. Whatever was done to pluck offending memories and heal his broken body had been carried out by skilled hands, but the scars were still very evident and very sensitive to the touch, almost as if this was more for visual comfort instead. Had he been healed by the same hands that stole a dog skull filled to the brim with brine out of his own grasp? Compulsion spurred him to drown all manner of dog heads. He corrected himself. There was no skull to be had in reality. The properties of a dream could not intercede in the waking world. He rubbed the teeth of his lower jaw with his thumb.

He had almost been killed twice by a raking beast commanded by a nameless accountant, near murders that had only been delayed.

The voices became heated on the other side of the bedroom wall, one voice especially so. The driver, he supposed. The voice was indistinct but violent. An argument perhaps. Confrontation would be unavoidable and he was far from home.

It was not too late to repair the fragile bulwark of his normality. It would be a substantial puzzle, but he could still fix this. He straightened his back slowly and rolled his shoulders, aching and hurting all the way, and rubbed his hand where the legfull thing from his dream had bit him. The checklist was not infallible, but it was there for a reason. As long as each day passed and those daily boxes of work and distraction were completed, he would find happiness. Just get home and he will figure it out from there. And the matter of murder? He knew he would not find his answer here. Going to the police was still a good option.

Venner leaned against the bedroom door. It was silent now save for the sound of another door closing. Slowly, he opened the bedroom door. He peered into the living room. The apartment was sparsely lit from the open blinds. Fairly quaint from what he could see, but more importantly, he could see nothing that could have had a voice. He didn't dare make a noise. He sidled out of the bedroom and carefully closed the door behind him. A hallway leading out of the apartment was in front of him. Beyond that was the front door.

The hallway was a terrible mess. The floor, which might have been hardwood, was layered with loose papers piled in manila folders and books stacked high against the walls. There would be noise on his path to liberation. He started slowly, planning every footfall through this paper wilderness. He was curious, however, about the yellowed pages in those marked manila folders as well as those that had collected in the crevices of waylaid books and open cardboard boxes. It was a makeshift library in this cramped hallway. He glanced behind him.

The moonlight was beautiful tonight. Soft and blue, it crept down from the windows and rolled across the room, collecting in half empty glasses of water. The girl's orange umbrella leaned against the couch. Water pooled around its wooden leg.

His attention shifted to the nearest paper stack, one nearly at eye level. He picked through the articles and reports. This was a library of odd things and even odder subject matter. Strange geometry was scribbled between notes on conventional geometry, delirious equations spilling down the margins.

Entranced, he flipped through the rest of this strange collection. Different sigils and different numbers to their names, then an endless stream of mundane reports and research findings. He read over documents with titles like "Testing and Prediction Modeling of Xifer-Idm Thaumaturgical Flicker Transience" or "Slip-Scape Analysis of Bolton Triggers in Gamma Chimeric Species (X-163)."

These research papers were well thumbed-through, judging by the added notes and circled figures. They were also surprisingly topical, many with dates that were only a couple of years old. It was a fine and respectable collection. People could be concerned with worse things. Like puzzle boxes piled just as high up the walls, monuments to his obsession. While this pocket archive was not as easily fit within the hand, it functioned to his service well enough. He replaced these plucked files atop their stack and then adjusted the base pages to be more secured against an errant knock.

Nestled amongst the papers were cluttered weights. Miniature statues, busts, and rocks were used to keep their charges guarded from drafts. Hidden amongst a stack of papers just besides him, missed in his initial search, a small blackstone idol of a resting bear stared up at him with bright jeweled eyes.

He picked up the strange idol, careful to not disturb its paper den. Polished, roughly sculpted obsidian, it shimmered with black and purple hues. His fingers brushed across its many facets, each one meticulously carved into tiny scenes of forests and creatures. Evergreens in blinding thickness, mountain ridges under distant winged things, and a winding brook. Shards of rusting metal pierced through the bear's skin. Brine would wick up the metal and cling to its patchy carved fur. It stared at him, this bear. Its fidelity to reality—or at least to a reality—captured his interest. It was easy to imagine this bear walking down the ocean shoreline toward him.

He lingered on the bear, idly scratching the other facets. He finally peeled away, satisfied by his decision, and rolled the idol in his hands. The scenery changed. The forest grew; the skies filled. A smile started at the corners of his mouth. He tapped at the edges. So reliable was distraction, so-called desire, and so full was this puzzle box.

"Good evening," said the girl, who had been watching his trespasses. She was shorter than he initially thought her, barely coming up to his chest. Her features were delicate, as if carved, and there was an unnatural stillness to the way she stood, as if she too were only a statue. She stood at the edge of the hallway, warden to her literary keep. A sense of austerity was hardly fettered by physical limitations with her straight back, sharp shoulders, and a quiet sidelong gaze that seemed to appraise him poorly. She brushed her long, dark hair with her hand and straightened her bangs, careful to keep one grey eye covered, before clasping her hands behind her back.

# TEN

**VENNER KEPT DILIGENT INSPECTION ON HIS CHOSEN PUZZLE** but acknowledged the girl. "Good evening," he said. She remained serene despite his dismissiveness. While watching him fidget, she straightened her blue ribbon tie, measuring with her fingers to help center it and set its proper length, and then patted down the rest of her attire. Venner traced over the obsidian stitching with an intrigued exactness. He turned and pressed, and the cracks of the idol began to split open.

She took him by the wrist and kept him from prodding further. The idol settled down in their grasp. "Congratulations. That took you no time at all," she said, gently prying the idol out of his hands. She reset the box with the same air of lightning mysticism and set it back where Venner had found it.

Venner snapped from his reverie, spluttering for words. He pulled away, holding up his hands, and bumped into a stack of papers. The pages cascaded down with a sharp flutter and settled around him. Venner cleared his throat, rubbing the bridge of his nose to cover the rising heat in his cheeks.

"Would you kindly stay for the night?" she asked. Her piercing gaze offered no alternative option. He glanced over to the momentary distraction again. He meant to escape, yet here he was because he could not leave well enough alone. *Leave. Run.* This was his chance. Yet he wanted an answer to this demanding feeling, to all the missing thoughts that ran amok in his head.

"Why am I here?" he asked.

The girl's silver earrings reflected the moonlight. *Someone stopped the music long ago, but the universe keeps pretending, humming along in celestial silence, practicing for a partner that will never come.* He cleared his throat again, feeling further embarrassment though his thoughts had gone unspoken. He despised the absurdity. He despised the way they looked at him. He despised himself for never failing to oblige these insane thoughts. He leaned against the wall in the open void of papers created by his misstep.

Blue ribbons were entwined in the girl's fingers. "We found you unconscious on the street," she said. "Mugged, I think. We called the police. They will take care of it." She was searching his expression, noting every jitter and tic. "Go back to sleep. Spend the night. Your trial will be taken care of by morning."

He said, softly, "Please don't lie to me."

She had nothing for him. No surprise, or pity, or anger. Just an impassiveness as she answered, "Are you sure?"

Venner thought carefully about the wanting feeling that dwelled within him. To be satiated would remove all handholds for denial. His nightmarish experience would be firmly corroborated. Here he had someone who understood, someone who may even offer solutions. The aid against a murderer, against another world's frightful unveiling, had to come from her. He was becoming quite convinced that nothing outside this room would be able to fill this hole. But death, or to be so close to death as to see the pits in bones and to smell the musk of poisoned ashes, invited a sobriety that cowed his head and sewed shut his mouth. He was caught in a child's fiction where simply mentioning the name of his danger would invite it back in.

"I'm sorry for staining the backseat. And the streets. And all the effort," he said. Then he laughed nervously. If this feeling was strong enough to commit thievery, then obviously it was enough to steal the direction of his life. She waved her hand to dismiss his concerns.

"I am always unlucky. All that effort to keep you sleeping, to make sure that as easily as you were stolen from your normal life you could be fit back in. Evidently, it has not taken in the slightest. I would have preferred to at least keep the mugging. It is calmer on the mind. There was a previous attempt on you to do the same mental adjustment. I should have taken that as warning that it was not for lack of effort the adjustment failed. Who are—" she started.

"Please, no," interrupted Venner. He slowly vetted further words as he wrung his hands. "I know what you asked. I think you asked before. Did I answer you?" It was insane to hate a benign, introductory question. Three words was what it took to undo him. The proper answer was his name, but he always felt compelled to answer wrong.

"No, you did not," she said.

*Thank you*, he mouthed. While she did not understand his reticence, she appeared to respect it. She took him by the hand and urged him. "Come," she said. "Please continue to be cooperative. I am enjoying this peace." She added softly, "Until Weill returns."

He followed her to the open kitchen. She seemed to have a distaste for artificial light, refusing the convenience of light switches and instead following where the moonlight, which streamed in through open windows, led her. On the counter stood a glass jar full of writhing white beetles. Their polished carapaces glimmered in the light as they turned their heads to see him. They had such tiny beady eyes. They were so fragile, but had looked so much more menacing in dreams.

"Eram Venner," he said, offering a handshake.

She touched her left earring and then traced her face where it was hidden by her hair. She said, "Claire Erishtal Iramir," and reciprocated, shaking twice, firm and practiced.

The sudden entranced behavior of the beetles warranted a moment of her investigation. "So you recognize them," Iramir said, noticing Venner rubbing the web of his hand. She uncapped the jar and gently plucked one from its brethren. Their collective trance was broken, and she nudged the escaping rest back into the jar to be resealed. "Even though you were asleep when it bit you." Iramir set the beetle onto the counter, letting its legs touch down and grip before dropping its weight. She stroked its hard carapace. It stood on its very tips to meet her.

"Look, I have never," Venner said. "I almost died. I mean, until tonight, I never have thought anything like monsters—it was not just a dog—anything so supernatural, so impossible, to be so real."

"Even in movies?" she said. Venner shrank, realizing his status as a normal person was being questioned. His terrified mind wrought violent consequences. Any of his responses could become his fatal lightning rod for her piercing weaponry.

"I can keep a secret," he pleaded. "I really have nothing to do with this. I don't know what happened. I don't know what's going on. I was just getting my taxes done." Fear struck him silent. What if, in the back-seat of that car, he'd said aloud how he thought himself water in fever to cleanse the skies? Words born from his delirious compulsion. Words someone else might attribute meaning to where they should not. If she knew, how could he explain himself? "I just, I just want to go home, please. I will do anything to be released from this dread."

The beetle, now free, tapped along the concrete top, exploring the opened bills and stranded protein bars. It tried to bite into the food, unable to comprehend the clear wrapping.

"These little machines eat memories," said Iramir. The beetle's antennae waved aloft as it raised its jaw, eager to try again. "Little memory machines with their bellies full of dreams," she said with a slight smile. "Not mine, from a cute advertisement actually. Your recent hours would hardly be missed. The real ones are extinct and hardly as handy. Mere machines now."

The machine rolled and tumbled in lonely playfulness as Iramir let it climb up and about her hand. It was so lively for a machine. "They were made by those who miss the coleoptera," she continued. "Their venom is replicated by a manufactured tonic. Everyone is nostalgic these days. A syringe would do just as well, but to be guised in rose colors comforts people, people who would wish upon an ocean for dead glory."

He was convinced then he had in fact said those words aloud in the car. "I'm sorry. I say things I can't control. Inane, maddening things." He gripped the edges of the table. "This is a bad dream."

"Do not start. We are long past that," she said. His hopes collapsed. He looked away in shame. "You are worth a quality creation and a flouting of the city rules. You are no creature of happenstance. Are you having fun?"

Venner tensed. No, of course he was not. He would have to be an idiot to think it all a joke. He had been hunted like vermin. Denial would not save him. Whatever shelter was found within the hoaxes of blurry photographs and shaking cameras could not cover the unmistakable veracity of his pain. "Shouldn't you be hiding who you are?"

"If you asked that a century ago, perhaps. It's far from necessary now. Who is going to believe you? The modern age is quite resistant to these sorts of revelations. You will get a newspaper mention, a few forum posts. All you will accomplish is revealing yourself to other people, people who might care a little bit more than I do. Weill is one of them, and I warn you, she is unconvinced that you were simply caught up in misfortune. There has to be reason. There has to be something devious."

"I don't want to be here. I don't want to be subjected to this questioning," said Venner. "What do I need to say for you to let me go?"

"Wild attacks do not happen. This is not the dark ages. Abject violence is rare and nothing bothers anyone anymore. There is simply nothing left to be wild, nothing that young and rash. Who did this to you? What would they want with you?"

"I suppose you asking me is a mercy," acknowledged Venner. Iramir leaned onto her elbows. "I don't know. I keep seeing the dog head and nothing more. I think it was his favorite." He paused. "You're waiting for something. You would have had me done away with already."

"Did I not tell you I would have it all taken care of—that I would have you right back home?" said Iramir. Venner nodded as he scratched at his palms. Was it cold sweat running down the back of his neck or one of those spears leisurely making its point? He didn't want to turn around.

"Or perhaps I should indulge my misgivings," Iramir continued. "Would some enlightenment cure you? The city would not send such a creature against you. Too much of a mess to clean up. A case like this can be swept away before the hour, settled and stamped, leaving the city as restful as ever. However, nothing has been cleaned up. Something is odd about your case and about you." Venner shrunk at the accusation.

"Unfortunate that I have not hidden my own intervention." Iramir waved. "The city is interested in you, taking the time to chew on your remains, and now they wait for my investigative results. What are the chances, may I ask, that whoever hounds you will come again? No harm in saving some effort."

Venner squirmed at the thought of another visit from a dog head. He silently watched Iramir pick up the beetle who had started climbing down the table leg. She offered it to Venner. "Would you like another try?" she asked. "You are right; we are waiting. There is a murderer to be found."

Venner offered a finger for the beetle to climb onto. It twitched at his touch, crawling away and balling up. Legfull things drowned in his ocean of faraway dreams; he wondered if he could drown the rest of these too. It would not be out of malice, as he glanced over to the jar of now-still things. Beady eyes hid behind carapace shields. He would simply like them better in that wetter, more familiar backdrop.

His dream ocean was always accompanied by a feeling of lost remembrance. So too was the dog head and the legfull things. There was another word to be had for the girl, one that he had not figured yet. There was the itch on the tip of the tongue, curling for that first syllable or the pinpricks in the back of his mind. The feeling demanded a name. Desire turned his stomach and squeezed his heart.

Alphabet and voice tumbled in the space of silence and leaked through the sieve of his mind. He closed his eyes and the ocean stirred behind them. The ocean swallowed concepts. Words and names were lost to the abyssal undertow. The idea of an apartment drowned, leaving him wading in brine. Slivers of hardened moonlight fell like snow and took in water. An icy spotlight, irreverent in the starless night, shone over the ocean's surface, over him. Its source, as Venner looked up, was his dear celestial heartache.

"Moon. You are the waning crescent moon," said Venner as he gasped for breath, pulling himself from the imagined water. The words now freed from nonexistence came tumbling out. "You are cursed and scorned, the last of your line. No more moons are born. Your legacy dies with you, and your world will be no more." The beetle in her hand shuddered and threw up salt water with a bubbling cry.

Her calm died when he spoke those words. Unease and resentment were the pallbearers. Venner covered his mouth, an effort far too late. It was cold in this apartment as he sunk into despair.

"What a sordid description," she said. A sharp viciousness came from her. She laid the beetle to rest over an opened envelope.

He was flanked by moonlight. Terror burned inside him. His searing organs skipped beats like they would if he had thoughtlessly driven over someone. Then came the sharp pangs of dread at the sound of approaching sirens. He had violated some rule he had unknowingly followed all his life. "I—I'm sorry."

"Stay," she said, a stern tongue accompanied by an even gaze. He had barely taken a step.

"I am so sorry," he breathed. Her grey eye was just like the moon floating in reflection upon the water's surface. Enough! He bit the skin of his hand. No more oceans. No more words. This was it. Whatever chance he had for normalcy had been dashed upon the rocks.

Iramir clasped her hands behind her back and looked down at the shivering Venner. "What are you?"

Venner refused an immediate answer. In his hesitation, he noticed a knocking slightly out-of-step with the fervid beating of his heart. The hallway door resounded with an impatient violence. This easy observation substituted the syllables of his unwilling answer.

"There is someone at the door," he said, but Iramir did not heed. The knocking came again. Louder, it threatened to tear the door from its hinges. "They are insistent."

"Are they?" she said.

"I'm not lying." Venner scowled. She waited, evidently pondering some thought as if she could not hear the noise.

She relented. "Stay in the corner, in the light." She slipped past him towards the entry hallway. Something thin and sharp in her hand reflected moonlight off its surface. A knife? Venner swallowed hard and did as he was told, stepping quietly towards the back of the room. Against the windows, he sidled up to the coffee table. His shadow obscured the room, and out of the need to cultivate better security, he pulled aside the curtains for a wider path of light. Iramir was in the passageway of crinkled pages. A sudden rattle of the doorknob caught him off guard.

Iramir tapped on her knuckles before grabbing the blackstone bear from its den. She rolled it carefully in the light back towards Venner. The heavy stone rumbled and creaked the wood. "Keep this in the light as well," she said.

Picking up the idol, Venner obliged. The rattling of the door slowly subsided, the knob turned, and the door opened in utter silence. Fear gripped him. He told his legs to move, but they flatly refused.

There was no more outside hallway to speak of. There was no more light from beyond. The door had opened to a solid black expanse. The interior lights flickered as their fuses lit, then burned one by one. Papers rustled softly in an intangible breeze before every stack tumbled down in gentle clatter.

Then a crunch as paper bent and crinkled. A footprint appeared from the edge of darkness, followed by a trail of footprints that led straight to them but appeared only on the pages. Heavy footfalls of a formless, invisible thing. An unfigure.

Iramir crossed her arms and glared at the unfigure. The knife, if that was what she clutched, was hidden out of view. "Leave." The footsteps paused.

And paused.

Dark, viscid blood dripped onto the pages in discordant patter. A spear of lightning that Venner had not seen thrown had impaled the unfigure somewhere. The only evidence was the blood and a weapon that had been suspended in midair before falling with the dull thud of a body landing.

The door multiplied in its frame. Wood and brick cracked apart to accommodate this sudden extradimensional space. The doors then slid across the walls, twisting and turning the apartment into nothing but entryways that circled them. The moonlight from the window was swallowed into these doorways. Venner staggered away from the malevolent architecture and slammed the blackstone idol onto the table, the only place where light lingered. Orphan moonlight danced in the glasses of water.

Iramir remained serene. The spear used to mark the invisible body had disappeared. She slipped her phone partially out from her pocket, turning on the flash at the same time. The bright light melted into physical quicksilver as she painted the air with it. Light was drawn like ink until the flash was completely consumed. Her nimble, shining spears stood at attention from where they were born. Venner did not like how far away he was from her, how alone he felt in this dimness.

The kitchen table cracked in half, and something tore the couch across the shortened room, charging towards them. An LED light spear embedded itself into the floorboards. Footsteps kept charging. Another spear struck closer to him. He could hear the pants of the unfigure. Then another spear far too close for comfort made contact with the distinct noise of flesh erupting. More blood leaked down the shaft of her weapon. Venner shook, his legs almost giving out. Footsteps retreated.

Her spears reformed at the ready, swaying in air before crystallizing. Iramir sighed and clicked her teeth, pulling at her ribbon tie as she glanced across her weapons. These LED spears were slow enough to visually track and perhaps more difficult to aim. More noises of pattering feet and vicious intentions paced the room, overlaying upon themselves and making the source difficult to pinpoint. An invisible touch brushed his shoulder. Venner clenched his teeth, picking up and throwing the half glass of water before him reflexively.

Glass shattered against the air. Water sprayed amongst the shattering, reflecting light like little stars. The droplets froze in place, a map of moonlight. LED spears tracked the unfigure with true precision. Weaponry flailed in the air from a writhing body coming quickly closer.

A spear dug into the wall above him with a harsh crack. Wet splinters clattered around him. His outstretched hand brushed against more wetness before snapping back. The splinters were not wood or drywall, but red bone. He scurried away from the invisible unfigure, bumping the coffee table and knocking the blackstone idol into darkness.

The blackstone idol rolled, traveling as if it could steer itself. It unfurled, pulling in mass from where there was none, and grew larger. "Cover your ears," she said. Venner raised his hands to his head but the sharp howl from an animal's throat pierced through. The sound echoed in his gut and rattled amongst the thunder. The planks were stripped from the floor and drywall from everywhere else with the swipe of a great claw. The scars trailed across the apartment as things of fur and bone and glass shattered and crumpled.

Venner cowered to avoid the destruction, staying in the faint glow of her weaponry the best he could. Iramir took to straightening her tie while she commanded spears to pin the larger bits of flying debris to the ground. A gigantic bear, born from the blackstone idol, materialized through the dust. It appeared wrapped in protruding steel and revealed too many teeth as it set to tearing apart each errant door. LEDs shielded him from thrown entryways fragments, but LED luster began to distort from continued use. Iramir walked over and clutched him tightly by the shoulder as if to provide reassurance.

The bear's attention snapped towards them. Its fur bristled as ursine muscle prepared to pounce. Hard light spears cracked under the weight of it barreling into them. Its claws ripped through the apartment walls and opened a hole to the outside. A starless night spied through. Rubble tumbled down the side of the building, demolishing the sidewalk and crushing an unfortunate car. The alarms joined the cacophony.

"Forgive the guardian spirit. It is not very smart, and Weill is not here to tame it. We will have to wait it out," whispered Iramir. Her limited weaponry were used to keep the aggravated bear away instead of hunting the intruder.

The unfigure stood up from its battering. Its invisibility singed at the edges, revealing its vivisected body. Skin hung like a mangled cloak. Doubled organs, clouded tubes, and jagged machinery whirred within its shambling form. Black holes for eyes leaked oil down a broken skull of metal and bone. It was far too reminiscent of a dog head.

The bear roared and leapt toward it. Another collapse of dusty structural instability followed. The bear pummeled the corpse, shaking the floor. Oil and flesh puddled together, and congealed beneath the bear, creating a slick upon the floorboards. Venner watched this oil stir with strands of gold and neon. He watched strands form almost words.

Black arms formed from the oil and tore like bullets through the bear. They scrambled and squeezed through the mountain of growling, ursine flesh, the unfigure's distended torso. The bear showed no signs of pain and dug its paws deep into the unfigure. Its bear jaws twitched anxiously for its meal. The unfigure grabbed desperately at the bear's face, teeth, eyes. The jaws closed over the skull. With a rolling crack, the bear devoured the unfigure.

A damp wind blew in through the hole in the wall, bringing cool relief to Venner's sweaty body. The infinite black that had settled into the room lifted. Outside, the moon and storm clouds returned to where they had always been. The hallway too was amongst its rightful place, properly singular. The silence was deafening in the absence of violence. He returned focus on the bear, but in its place was the small blackstone idol, full in its feast and sleeping. While the danger seemed to pass, this sense of urgency had no respite.

Iramir held a phone to her ear and gazed out from the hole at the streets below. Gathered around the crushed car, collateral damage from the brawl, were people dressed in pajamas and graveyard shift uniforms. "Weill, do you have anything to chase?" She tugged on the ends of her tie. "I do not care about Harken. Return now."

Venner stared at the oily puddle drying in the open air. Rainbow refractions off its surface made written speech. *The entropic dissolution of liquids cannot make words*, he chastised himself in yet another moment of madness. It was chaotic nonsense. However, he could not shake the association that there was an alphabet of a foreign language; there was meaning; there was intention too elemental to be misunderstood.

Out of the mute voice of an unfigure spoke, *I want to live.*

Iramir touched him on the arm. "Go to the roof and stay until I come to collect you. Just turn the corner and go straight up. You will not be far from me." Then she whispered something as equally foreign as the oil's alphabet into his ear. Venner heard her and understood. He left wordlessly, agreeing to her every suggestion. No argument, no outcry. He wanted to get away for a chance to breathe and hide from the sheer enormity of everything. The door of the apartment shut after him.

# ELEVEN

Iramir paced the ruined apartment unit, flipping the tarnished steel in her hands. All of this residential damage would make for a challenging apology. She would begin with a platter of sincere condolences for Weill, then offer her a plan for reparations—a task for later when she returned to the Library. As of late, she had been making a poor example of her station as figurehead above wonton chaos. She had to get the situation under control. Grimleer demanded inexhaustible competence from her. Why else would she be allowed to exist? She was vanguard of the Library. Through her light let the world be saved.

Rain invaded through the hole in the wall, soaking the walls and floorboards. Sirens wailed in the distance. Neighboring buildings obscured most sightlines, the city in claustrophobic contention looking in. The moon hung low in the sky. The sirens faded. Harken would not dare confront her directly. They were only good for waiting. Venner had made it to the rooftop, so reported her light. Some solitude from this destruction might ease his mind.

Iramir rubbed over her abdomen, controlling her breathing until the pain subsided. She would not frown, would not furl her brow. She would keep her back straight and her chin up. False confidence was better than none. The Library would question, and they would have their lies. She should have been better prepared against causing a scene, though her foray into the city should have long ended by now. It was an unseen turn, managing trade contracts between the Library and Harken to becoming embroiled in dark age savagery.

She patted down her clothes, making sure everything was spotless. No dust, but red blood. She pulled against the stain. It was not hers. Eram's then. She checked where he had cowered. Blood splashed the floor and rubble, unfortunately dried and ruined with oil. It was her responsibility to investigate the strangeness that was him. There would be other opportunities. She collected some of the shattered glass to dispose of later. A small pile of shards glittered on their bed of paper towels on the coffee table.

Shadows from the rain played in the remaining glass of water left behind. It was just water, she learned, as she inspected the glass closely. It beaded. It swayed to the weight of gravity. However, within the darkness kept behind closed doors, in the glass that Eram threw, this water was moonlight. Moonlight as pure as the present evening. A leak left in the transformation of the room? An exploit then, in the poor attention of her attackers. The pain was becoming quite bothersome.

Iramir navigated around the debris to the bathroom for some discount pain medication and a shower curtain. Weill kept nails and a hammer in a toolbox under the sink. Back in the living room, Iramir measured the shower curtain against the hole. Satisfied, she began nailing it to the wall. Hammer impacts loosened red bone scraps from the drywall. It was an expensive assault. Certainly out of the bounds of a mere sorcerer and crude textbook machinery. There had to be a sponsor, someone or something much more troublesome to deal with than a thug. Such material generosity in the current climate was hardly amiable. Eram was evidently very valuable.

The pain did not subside. Rechecking the box of medication she had left on the table, she found only empty blister packaging. She had already exceeded the recommended dose. Alternative medicine then, which advised her to release the spell of a spear that followed Eram. Perpetually poised, it had been wrapped around his neck, ready to silence him if necessary. Her pain abated a little as she held herself. She hurried out the door. Do not lose him in those unwatched minutes.

The Waning Crescent. That was what he had said. An omen for the end, if one believed in omens. She scowled at having to slow down, simply because her body would not cooperate. She stopped moving completely.

She had to wait out the pain. She used the wall for support and fixed her attention on just getting to the stairwell. Eram was proving himself apt. It was not an omen if her function and future integrity were already well documented and outlined.

She was not a full moon like any of her predecessors if Eram was referencing full-blooded lineage. Even her powers paled in comparison. Her crescent had been made from the scraps of those full moons fallen and shattered years ago. She was simply a stopgap to avoid facing the end of a lunar legacy, a reprieve of inevitability, however temporary. Her body could not last long. Mortality was a mere time limit as she aimed towards strengthening the Library and its positions.

She had a duty to fulfill: do not stray from the Library.

Eram had proven himself remarkably apt, actually. Not just by pulling fortune from thin air, but by being able to break down a guardian spirit's home and undo the magic that had created it. To reverse engineer those items was quite difficult, even with the blueprints. He'd done it in less than a minute. A beetle had been undone between the words of a single outburst.

Not that this was an entirely unique set of skills. Rarer creatures roamed the world with their peculiar senses, though not with the efficacy he had shown. A few of those enigmatic things had emerged from the depths of the Library. A distant probability, but misfortune knew her by name, and that was what she feared. Her matters liked to worsen.

If Eram was born from those depths, how then could she explain his existence out here, free from the Library? Not that she should entertain this thought for too long, but she wanted a contingency.

She could simply ask him, but it was also low-chance resolution. She did believe in his ignorance. For him to exalt her own origins and not understand the significance convinced her. The reputation of her Library often preceded her and never kindly. However he was excised, he had found the chance to establish himself outside, and needed stay there. It would be troublesome to keep him out of these instances, especially due to their irregular circumstances, but it was not like he actively sought such danger. It should be easy enough to set him back home, safe and sound.

# TWELVE

THE CITY HAD NO QUALMS ABOUT MAKING THE WORK OF A hound difficult.

Weill huffed. It was her job to sniff out where their strange man had come from and to find his pursuer. She started at the site of the jagged wreck of a car, examining the asphalt scars and the ravaged body of some nameless person. It lay slumped and disemboweled against the store front of a post office. Meat was smeared over glass and sidewalk. Struggling all the way, it'd been dragged from down the street by some large creature. Rain leisurely washed the blood away.

Claws marks crossed concrete. The sharp smell of ichor was in the air. Broken, inhuman fangs littered the ground along with glossy red shards of bone. She pocketed a few of them, saving a small shard to grind her teeth on. A quick lick revealed the taste of charcoal and slight notes of quicksilver. She gently chewed on the shard, letting the taste of magic linger on her tongue and fill her nostrils.

It tasted rotten and smelled of the sweat of too many people in too singular a body. Weill pulled a sour face because these people always tasted sour. Whoever owned these violent, red bone whelps was a body snatcher. They would soul hop from one to another for that glimmer of immortality. It was hardly immortality. Each generation down the line ruined more and more of the original person. Bodies decayed faster. Minds emptied out. Magic faded. Most people only cared about the last one. They jumped on and on until consequence hit them like a freight train.

Once the decay started, there was no stopping it. It could only be managed. Some pulled it fast with a bullet. Some chanced the slow burn, but that was like ignoring the public service announcements she'd heard since childhood. Maybe there was a cure somewhere, hidden like legends in the mist, but things always got worse. Magic exacted vengeance. Whatever that was left over from slow people got cleaned up in trash bags and incinerated. That was not a fun summer job.

Weill shrugged. It wasn't as if she knew what she would have done in their shoes. The perfect cure-all was a fun dream, magic without consequences, like winning the lottery and spending like mad. She bent down over the corpse and took hold of the head. Turning it in her hands, she found the bone of the temple and saw the crack that had split it. With her lighter, she sparked a flame and ignited the bone. Whatever residual magic that remained sizzled away, leaving only the imprint of a courier's brand.

So it was theft, then. The courier probably carried something good. Good things were always viciously owned. The body snatcher had seen a chance to improve their situation. They danced in front of the dragon, hoping that whatever scant treasures they could steal would save them. She stood up and stepped out into the street. Her boots squelched on meat. She wondered about the killing she could make running a power washing scheme.

Every drop of rain that landed upon Weill sizzled and evaporated as befitting a body of fire. She pulled a cigarette out of a teal carton. Holding it in her mouth, she cupped the end of the cigarette and blew. The end of the cigarette stayed cold. The shard of bone in her mouth hurt as she clenched her teeth. She spat it out.

Claire had told her not to worry, but how could Weill ignore all the signs? She had failed her thaumaturgy fitness evaluations five of the past six months. She had burn scars on her body from her own magic backflow, but she was made from fire. Magic decayed for everyone. No amount of exercise or healthy eating would help.

She slowed her breathing, imagining the roaring fire in her bosom. Her breath stirred into sparks, releasing a trail of burnt paper and nicotine. Image training was like learning to count numbers on your fingers. Some days were bad. This was a small victory, as she had saved another use of her lighter. She pulled up the zipper of her jacket to her neck. These midnight hours.

Cigarette burning pleasantly, she surveyed the crash underneath the flashing red lights of the intersection signals. She stalked around, tracing splatters, struggles, and trails. Creations of flesh and metal from the hands of a necromancer, most likely. It was expensive to be a necromancer nowadays. Sending a creation to chase a guy down the street simply wasn't a good investment. There was a steel hard case pinned between the car and pole. Courier package found, unless their mysterious man enjoyed flouting steel in his day job.

Weill pulled apart the wrecked engine with slight effort, bending the fender away. The hard case was freed. Latches swung and clicked against the metal as she checked inside, finding shattered chunks of crystal. A dull cobalt sheen reflected through the grey cloth used to wrap them. She draped the cloth carefully over a relatively clean patch of ground after sweeping scrap and meat away with her leg. With the items laid out, she pieced and aligned runes and ritual marks to the best of her knowledge. A whole obelisk once tallied up, but it was useless now. Judging by the foam inserts in the case, there was once a trio of them, but two had been taken.

She spun a piece of scrap metal between her fingers. The courier should've just been hit by the car. It would've been quicker. She stretched her shoulder. Bodies of fire shouldn't get sore, but she was getting more tired every day. What if one day her inner fire just snuffed out? She would keel over. That was it. Nothing to stop it, like the slowest, stupidest aneurysm ever.

Weill sniffed the air. Certainly, there was their mystery man, who'd been found far from this crash and then seemingly abandoned by this necromancer. A necromancer who strangely wanted to clean up witnesses when they would not even wipe down the crime scene. All in plain view of the city. A pet was too easily linked to its master. Maybe they expected to be able to leave the city immediately. The courier must've carried something amazing. Maybe the necromancer really hated their mystery man. To hell with the city, right? She certainly did not trust the mystery man.

She pinched the end of her cigarette, stowing the rest away for later. She had promised Claire that she would quit by the end of the year. The same promise made every year before. She replaced the obelisk shards into their housing, fluffing the cloth to prevent them from rubbing together in transit. The same necromantic scent lingered in these velvet notches. The remaining crystal obelisk could be used to sniff the others and their necromancer. She had tracked with less over greater distances. She checked the lining of the case and pulled out a black business card. It was marked with a single golden *H*.

Harken.

A voice cut through across the wreckage. "We blame the courier. The company responsible will be penalized." Weill spotted him standing opposite her, far across the wreck, dressed in a grey trench coat with a yellow lily pinned to his lapel. He held his black umbrella tightly, covering most of his face, and kept his limbs close and out of the rain.

"Piss off or I'll kill you," threatened Weill.

"Library business? We understand, but this is our property, our domain, and our jurisdiction. You're the trespasser here. Our work is frequent and necessary. You are not." The cleaner held a bronze plated box. Weill could see that it was opened and empty. "We've come to collect. Have tact. We would be poor servants to disrupt our masters' delicate relations. It's barely been a handful of hours. The ink still drips on their contracts."

"Call me servant again," she said, shoving her hands into her pockets. The puddles of water at her feet bubbled. "This is Library property. Evidence."

The cleaner tilted his head for a moment, "And the man? He too is evidence?" The cleaner smiled. "We suppose you will simply clean him up, remove the infractions, and drop him off home." He shook his head. "We didn't think the Library took charity cases anymore. He's been kept under your master's care for some time now. Is there a problem?"

Weill kicked the case closed. The melted lock steamed in the rain. "What do you want?" She scowled. Something moved down the street, and they both looked that way. It lumbered towards them, cyclopean-eyed with a dozen arms creaking in the air. Its flailing hands desperate for something to grab and crush. For the second time that day, Weill breathed fire, licking at the sparks.

"It looks like our thief's own little witness eater is a bit late," said the cleaner. He kept his gaze on the approaching creature. "We know who the thief is, and you will too. We're impatient and your master is slothful. Hunt with haste, hound. Lay your fires of divine punishment upon our thief, and we won't retaliate against your master's transgressions this time. Our masters agreed to the sanctity of this city, so do not involve the Library in our matters. A live man was not part of the planned shipping manifest."

"Should've let him die then," said Weill. She nodded at the grotesque thing. "Not my problem, right?"

The cleaner pulled a small folded letter from his sleeve and read. With a practiced motion at the wrists, he closed his umbrella. The streets rolled into sloping hills. Buildings collapsed like a closing pop-up book. Weill tapped the case with her boot and kicked it up into her arms. With a leap, she mounted the car wreck, holding onto the lamppost for stability. He held an open journal over his head in a poor attempt to keep dry.

He brought up a finger to his lips to silence her. Gravity settled sideways and Weill was left hanging with one hand gripping the wet metal and the other unwilling to let go of her evidence. The cleaner remained firmly planted on the street, as did the city and rain. The asphalt river, however, obeyed gravity's new direction and tripped the creature with the rushing undertow. Many hands slipped against a city maligned.

Concrete buckled and buildings dove into their foundations, shaking the earth. Weill heard the roughness of brick against mortar as the creature was crushed and ground between a corner barbershop and confectioners. Wasted sorcery dripped past them, swallowed by the storm drains.

"We're sure you have what you need," he said. "The Library will go through collections if you make more problems here. We do not forgive."

Weill felt her phone vibrating. The cleaner tapped the tip of his umbrella on the ground and twirled it upright to open it. The city reverted and Weill landed roughly on the ground. The car wreck had disappeared, the streetlight had been repaired, and the mail storefront was spotless. The cleaner had taken his leave. There was nothing more to be investigated. She was disappointed in losing the chance to use her magic. For Harken to tell her to hurry up made her gnash her teeth. Something was up, rotting like fish in the sun. Her phone started ringing, and she answered.

# THIRTEEN



VENNER WAS STRANDED ON THE ROOFTOP. HE LEANED AGAINST the exit that led down the quiet stairwell and held the door open with his foot. The rain still came down in a raging torrent, mocking his hatred of being wet. Water flowed down the cracked concrete steps. He took a deep breath and brushed a hand through his hair. No amount of fidgeting or hopeless wishes could quell this anxiety.

He struggled to understand why he was going along with this absurdity. He needed to find his murderer, an idea stolen from the silver screen, from daytime dramas of a stuffy sick day—from fantasy. Out there lingered dog heads and unfigure things that he could never have imagined, but he knew well how their claws felt scraping the inside of his heart, how they picked out a tortuous tune on every link of his spine. He had never been so far away from his life, from the safety of his career and his puzzles.

Things needed to be kept apart. They needed to be nicely delineated with colored tags and their own little boxes. Worlds apart! An entire other line of existence did not need to be meddled with. A divide that spanned further than his damned ocean needed to cleave the difference and deliver some relief to his mind. He could never be matched with these supernatural beings. He was mortal and powerless.

No amount of braying denial would change anything. He had been stolen from a death and carelessly thrust into existence's most heinous secret. Normality had died like a shot dog. Comfort had been dashed to the storm. Iramir assured him of a finite journey, that there was an end to this insanity. He could go back to sleep under her care and wake up to morning coffee and a commute.

Or he could stay up. He could find his murderer.

He would encounter more strange things like words in oil, more mysteries to be solved. He kept turning that phrase in his head, inspecting the kerning and the points of serifs. He had no puzzle box in hand to damn him, but he felt that same compulsion regardless. He needed to march himself into destructive consequence. He knew nothing and that was precisely why. The abstract puzzle was intoxicating to the mind, and he needed to have his prize.

There was someone at the landing of this flight of stairs. An opened, black umbrella covered their face even though they were sheltered from the rain within the stairwell. They wore a yellow lily pinned to their lapel. There were thirty other sets of tenants, perhaps, in this apartment building. Each landing had a painted floor number. There were no corners to spy down during Venner's trek to the stairwell, and so the number of units was easily estimated per floor. It was not impossible to think someone, especially with an umbrella, might want to take a quick trip to the rooftop—someone who appreciated viewing the storm.

"We would like it if you closed the door," said the man with the black umbrella and the yellow lily. His words sounded crimped and crinkled, as if he were made of paper. Venner stepped into the stairwell, gently letting the door rest on its latches. The rainstorm became muffled by the thick metal and the stairway river abated. Venner had not heard anyone make their way up. The acoustics of concrete brick towers offered no places to hide. "Thank you," this paper man said.

Venner knew his would-be murderer walked the streets, fully intent to finish the job. This could be another attempt on his life. Venner made his way down the stairs, taking care with each step to avoid slipping on water. His footsteps carried down to the ground floor. He stopped before the paper man. Under the dim, cyan light of aging fluorescents, they stood together. Venner tapped and drew his nails across the railing to the undulations of an imagined ocean. His compulsion mingled with his dreaming obsession. Through the stifled cries of the storm, he could pretend this ocean was everywhere around them.

This man was not his murderer. Paper disliked dogs and messy unfigures.

"What do you want?" Venner asked with measured cadence. Like with Iramir, he wanted to choose his words with precision, rewinding and editing out the idiocy. People were not made of paper.

He wanted to carve out the bits of his brain where these thoughts crept out so naturally. Their veracity utterly unknowable, but because the thought was had, the property of pure truth was always coupled. This was the reasoning of a child, but this mindful child stole his direction with wasteful toys and ocean dreams. He hated the face others made when he spoke his psychobabble. The turn of their mouths, the crossing of their arms, the false platitudes of understanding. He could not understand it himself. He would eventually be brought out of his rambling monologues, back to himself, but only after whoever he was speaking to was quite certain that he was mad.

Simply existing had never seemed as difficult as it did tonight. His skin didn't fit right. His skull felt incorrectly molded. The wrong shape of him had been stuffed and baked with too many other things.

Without emerging from the confines of his umbrella, the paper man pulled a black business card from the lining of his grey trench coat and held it out. Venner only stared at it where it hovered, shaking a little in the paper man's fragile hand. How long would the paper man wait while Venner considered the malformations of his own self? The paper man's face remained hidden despite the umbrella's shifting.

"We want you to call at your earliest convenience," the paper man said. Venner couldn't shake the image. Even though there was flesh on the man's hands, ink stains under his fingernails, and a body clothed and able, he was made of paper. Venner was certain of it.

"I—I can't." Venner held the railing tightly, as if the effort of words spilling out of him would throw him down the stairwell. "Please leave."

The paper man twirled the business card between his fingers for a moment. He shifted his weight. A hand went up to rub where his face would have been—perhaps his chin or brow. Then the paper man lifted his umbrella just enough to reveal a finger raised to his ink-stained lips.

"I find you a very curious thing," he said. "What are you so dying to say that it would cause you to perish on the spot?" Venner shook his head, legs buckling underneath him. The paper man kept his finger to his mouth and crouched before Venner. "I've cleaned up your blood. I've cleaned up all your forgotten things. The blood that filled my gutters was not of iron." Venner wondered if this macabre description was meant to strike up some sort of intimate connection.

"My forgotten things?" asked Venner before pulling away in realization. "Oh." Missing items to report: his car, his wallet, and his keys. He was not in the mood to ask for them back. Such items of consequence he wanted far away from him. "Then did you see what happened to me?"

The paper man crinkled. "No, I was there after the fact."

Venner imagined the forlorn scene of a paper man huddled underneath an umbrella, taking watch over city cleanup. A cruel wind blew rain into the canopy from underneath the umbrella's rim. A mouth with a finger placed to its lips distorted as paper took on water. The urban river flowed, salted with his blood. As water, Venner could reach out and take hold of the ankles, pulling the paper man under. Instead, Venner pinched the phantom wound on his hand. The ocean lived in dreams. The machinations of an outside world never bothered it. Yet now it spilled into this storm and all the children seas begot. Ever present. Suffocating.

The paper man smoothed some of the creases around his hand, adjusting his fingers so they wouldn't catch on the umbrella's handle. An ocean of dreams should not make the walls and stairs drip away into blank shapes. Venner clutched the frame of himself, scared by his own sensation. His cut hole in existence, shaped to his very exactness, dropped away from him, and names fell in silhouette, and silhouette fell into nothing. A castle upon the dotted shoreline defended against the waves. Here the brick and mortar called mortal man came tumbling down.

Venner clapped his hands together suddenly, trying to keep his perception grounded. He gasped for air from his silent drowning and felt his consciousness being pulled away, back out into the city and its paper men. Venner swallowed his bile and said, "May I tell you something that is simply wrong?"

The paper man tapped at his lips. "No one has ever asked my permission to speak. Yes, you may."

"You were folded wrong, against your binder's intentions. There is a hole in your seals where fatigue frays your beloved spic and span. A set of foreign eyes were slipped between your covers through that hole. How negligent was your creator. Sorcery folds your gilt edges upon itself and unfolds when you breathe. Every breath a little more loosens. Corners unravel. So is the fate of all finger puppets, paper man."

"Am I?" interrupted the paper man. His voice was a soft sort of surprise.

"You are not human," said Venner, who now suddenly found himself at the end of his words. One paper puzzle was a tad bit unraveled and Venner's mind a tad bit more restful. Unlike extinct beetles, there was no nostalgia that lined the pages of the paper man. The paper man lifted his finger from his mouth for an instant to speak but said nothing. Instead, he steadied himself just before uttering, once again keeping his finger where it was supposed to be.

"A bit of the wrong order now," the paper man gently chastised. There was no condemnation, just silent acceptance. This relief felt alien to Venner. "You are astute. What are you going to do about me then?"

The paper man was like the black pool of oil and neon script. *I want to live.* What a senseless phrase. So amorphous, so difficult to digest. The concept was immaterial and dripped from the pores of this living paper. What was he going to do about this phrase? Venner did not immediately have an answer. Paper men, unfigure things, were facets of a world that beheld its own living. All of it should be out of his concern, especially their frightful problems.

"I don't know," said Venner, "but I'm scared of this world too."

It was a long moment before the paper man decided to react. He slipped a pen from his pocket with a flick of the barrel, balanced the shaft of his umbrella against his shoulder, and carefully uncapped the pen within a single hand. His finger may as well have been glued to his lips with the way he clenched his jaw. His face remained hidden. He perched the business card on his knee and dipped the nib in his mouth. The umbrella swayed and began rolling with his movements.

Venner reached out to steady it, looking away. He didn't want to see any more frightening things and also respected the paper man for all the effort taken to hide his identity. It simply seemed rude to take advantage of this moment. The paper man wrote across his kneecap; the cardstock creased and pen nib slipped and smudged. Written on one side in decent legibility was a number too long for a phone. The paper man paused, having found Venner staring at the card. Venner let go of the umbrella as the paper man offered the card one more time. Drawn on the corner of the card were seven eyes.

"Good luck," said the paper man, capping his pen. Venner took the card from the paper man and flipped it over, revealing an *H* in maze-like gold. The number printed beneath it had been crossed out. The paper man began to move away from him.

"Wait," Venner said, snatching the ends of the trench coat. His grip crushed the paper. *Watch paper tear and bloat in salt water.* Like puzzle boxes, there was a blueprint, some obscure purpose, to the body of magic that could be solved and therefore undone. Solve why paper was and free that valuable headspace from the grips of madness. The paper man covered his own face with a hand, displaying patience even though he seemed to know better than to dawdle. Venner was shaking.

The paper man sighed softly. "I am not a puppet," he said, with his fingers free of his mouth. "I am free to do what I please." These words were whispered as if they could not be held to scrutiny. At last, Venner forced himself to let go. He understood that paper had enough clout to be left alone to its own devices. Venner spied the shadows of the stairs below them restructuring, settling into physical constructs.

"Please don't let me keep you," said Venner. Shifting concrete and liminal space must have allowed the paper man to be anywhere. No footsteps to be heard.

The paper man gestured down the stairwell. "Which floor?"

Venner stuttered, "Just the third." Two pairs of footsteps echoed—sounds that Venner found genuinely comforting. He walked somewhat behind the paper man, not wanting to accidentally glimpse the face he had so carefully kept concealed. His fingers ran around the edges of the card. "What is this for? You asked me to call, but you covered the actual number."

"To go home," answered the paper man. "A prospect you are quite eager for, I imagine." The paper man tapped at his lips again, letting go longer and longer each time. "What are you?"

Venner's throat collapsed in anticipation. He coughed and wiped sweating palms on his shirt. "Thank you, I guess, for letting me amuse you." He tried to slip by, racing the rest of the way to the third floor. The umbrella was laid across the railing, preventing his passage. The paper man would have none of it.

*I am a structural analyst on the cusp of getting fired. I just entered my mid-thirties. I collect puzzle boxes like an addiction. I dream about making a meal of a moon.* He hated this question, having failed many interviews because of it. "*I am the infinite ocean.*" Who else would say such psychobabble? No, the correct answer was always found by avoiding the first thought that came to mind, to read the situation and deliver an answer fully formulated to draw a smile from a prospective manager.

Venner bit his knuckles in defeat. The ease to which these poisoned words leaked between mental bulkheads was an insult to the decades of his life spent pretending to be sane. He was always beside himself, taping names to shapes that had lost them. It was exhausting. How wonderful would it be if he simply stopped and let everything tumble into madness, stripped of all context?

The paper man lifted the umbrella and settled it over his head, supposedly satisfied. Venner had missed a chance to see his face. "The infinite ocean," the paper man repeated. "We'll remember this." The concrete rippled to let the paper man through, and Venner stepped away in surprise. He gripped the railing until his fingers burned. Just one dream where he did not have to see that damned ocean.

# FOURTEEN

**VENNER HUDDLED UNDERNEATH THE MARKER FOR THE THIRD** floor, shivering in the cold. *I am the infinite ocean*, five poisoned words stuffed inside a man. If he held these words to be true, then why did he deny the concept so thoroughly? It was absurd, that was why. He could see himself, and he was not water. Sight was the most immediate, irrefutable proof of his personhood. But unlike those remarks forgotten by the hour, five poisoned words haunted him. Because it was true. Because it couldn't be true. The stairwell door opened, and Iramir appeared. Hopefully she wouldn't look at him.

She looked right at him, picking him apart with her unchanging nonchalance. In this night, in this storm, his world was broken apart not by monsters but by the betrayal of his own mind. He held on to the black card tightly, smudging the ink further.

Iramir slipped by him, sliding her hand across his arm. Venner looked to the lights, expecting to be interrogated again. Their buzz was constant, and light conformed to mundane expectations. She had found the pair of damp footprints, his and the paper man. She inspected the brickwork where the paper man had stepped through. The walls were properly sound.

She waited in the stairwell with him, listening to the distant echoes of rain and watching him flip the card in his hands. "I have advice for you," she said, "though by no means must you take it. That card belongs to the city, to Harken if you want a name, and the city does not like aberrations."

"Am I an aberration?" asked Venner.

"Is there something wrong with that?" asked Iramir. "This is a novel night for me as well." Stern and always discerning, that was her affect. Despite their differences in physicality, she certainly knew how to stand taller than him. The black card felt heavier. Her authority demanded that he answer. Should he tell her about the paper man? Should he wait for her to ask? He noticed the vulnerability of what was written upon this stock and given to him to keep. It was a vulnerability that Venner refused to betray. The paper man had managed to fold himself intimate.

"Should I avoid Harken, or is that a mere warning to keep in mind if I decide to call? You have your apprehensions after all," observed Venner. Grimacing, Iramir turned away from him. She settled herself and smoothed down her tie.

"We will see," she said. How common were the thoughts of endless water basins and paper humans within Iramir's world? Were they common enough that a paper man would hold a patience that Venner rarely knew?

"Do you know what I am?" asked Venner. He wanted any confident answer, and he was so convinced that Iramir could lay the tides to rest. For the slightest moment, concern crossed her face. Her fingers brushed against her lips as she caught herself.

"What would you like to be?" asked Iramir. It was as if she knew how best to punish his desire, how best to dredge out the ever-painful notion that he was abnormal. His pain must have been plain to see. She took him by the hand and splayed her fingers with his, deliberately taking the time to center her touch. Her hand was colder than he expected. "I have heard all manner of strange things before. So judgement is no concern. If someone asks you like this, why not take the chance? What would you like to be?"

Venner stared down at their interwoven hands. He felt her waver and then let go. Iramir wrung her hand and mouthed, *sorry*, another vulnerability given to him to hide. As briefly as he'd known her affectations, even this seemed an anomaly for her. It was such a pointed question, as if she had heard his oceanic confession.

Venner raised a finger and said, "One week ago. I would like to be who I was just a week ago. I don't need to have all my mistakes erased, but I want to be, ah, conventional. Is that the right word? I want to be able to rewind to the point that I can stop that final nail of my career. If it's at all possible for me to not need endless distractions, that would be even better. Without them, I end up thinking too much about myself, about what's wrong with me. I end up saying things that disgust other people. Work fills in that void. It provides the structure for detailed problem solving. Then I find a few more days have passed without any harm." Venner nodded. "Repeat this a few times more." He expected her to uncomfortably stare back at him the way his coworkers did. Even when he tried to mirror their mild, banal discussions, some stray phrase or detail would slip through and betray his otherness. He very much wanted to reword his reply.

"It is good to be diligent," said Iramir without any derision. "Purpose offers us the promise of salvation. However far down that path, there will be a point where enough work has been done to offer some sort of happiness. I hope you find that happiness, and I understand this night has been a stubborn obstacle to that. I have no intent to keep you. Your murderer will be slain, Harken will be pacified, and you will have your life back."

It was an answer spoken with good confidence, and Venner decided to push further. "Can you answer me this, Iramir: Am I human? It is an odd question, I know." Even if the question begged the only possible answer, it would be a comfort to hear it.

Instead of answering, Iramir held open the door to the third floor and said, "Now it is time to leave. You may stay in the apartment, but out of the wet living room. Unfortunately, I could do little about the hole."

The missing answer only unnerved Venner. Was he not perfectly presentable as a human? His form was his proof, and for Iramir to fail to corroborate only further unsettled him. Iramir seemed in no mood to argue, and he did not want to try.

The anxious mind ran away from the quandaries of his existence back to the paper man, only partially solved after all. The paper man was gone, tucked into the confines of the city that had made him. Venner sought solace by imagining how to pick apart the workings of crafted origami and how to prove to that man he was not an ocean.

Venner and Iramir walked down the hall together, following a trail of wet ashes leading from the elevator into the apartment. The apartment door had been ripped off the hinges and lay half-embedded into the wall. He did not remember this being caused by the unfigure.

"Excuse the door," she said. "Weill apparently forgot she had a key. Too quick to act, this guardian." The wet trail stamped across the paper-strewn corridor of the personal library. Iramir looked a bit deflated.

"Sorry," Venner said, having indeed remembered the mess he had made here. His gaze briefly flittered over the same titles he had read before, trying to glean anything else from them. The blood of the unfigure had dried a hazy purple on the papers. Ashes had been tracked into the bedroom where Venner had slept.

"I am intruding in Weill's home, and now because of me, it is ruined," replied Iramir. Across Weill's devastated apartment, a shower curtain had been nailed over the hole in the wall as a crude stop against the storm. The nails were within reach of Iramir's height.

"It is dangerous nailing that high on a chair instead of using an actual ladder," she admitted, noticing what Venner found amusing. The nails were quite crooked and poorly spaced.

"Is it?" Venner had to smile at something so mundane. What a rare occurrence now.

"I also ran out of nails," said Iramir, still stone faced. "The . . ." she half-shrugged, "bear kept eating them."

There was an open steel case on the floor. The lock and lining were melted and the contents missing. On the coffee table sat a chunk of cobalt crystal and red bone crudely cobbled together with masking tape. There were bits of shattered glass collected on a paper towel also on the table. He felt a sudden pang of guilt. He should have helped clean up. It was he that had dislodged the bear, after all.

Iramir took her greatcoat off the upturned couch and draped it over her shoulders. Venner rubbed his arms for warmth. There was noise in the bedroom, a thumping of something heavy against the wall. Venner flinched.

"That is Weill, having lost her security deposit. Do not mind, she is just searching for what she needs," Iramir said before heading to the kitchen and pulling open the heavy door of the refrigerator. "Do you want a drink? There is beer if it would suit you better tonight." Venner was still at the upturned couch, picking up more pieces of broken glass that had been missed. The interior light of the fridge bathed Iramir in an orange glow. She held up her choices in her hands. "Weill seems to hate all of them, however. Be that as it may."

"No, thank you." Holding the paper towel of shards, he headed toward the trash can in the kitchen. Iramir now held up a box of refrigerated cigarettes. Venner blinked twice before realizing Iramir expected an answer. He shook his head and disposed of the shards. Iramir sat next to the kitchen countertop with the white beetles. She had a small bottle of bright-red fruit punch with a straw. Venner bit his lip to avoid smiling again. Iramir noticed regardless, becoming bashful, and tugged on the ends of her tie. A white beetle that had been let out lapped the punch that dripped from the straw onto the counter.

"I—I want to understand you. This is, of course, because of what you are. There is no need to mistake it," said Iramir. Venner hung on that stutter. A sudden hope flared that it would lead to more friendly exchanges, and then the implications behind her words bit. It seemed she did know what he was—not human, at least not completely. By being more insistent, he could wring his proper definition from her, but he wasn't about to dwell on the anxiety he'd left behind in the stairwell. These minor moments of light interaction were a welcome reprieve.

"Can we avoid talking about me?" asked Venner. "There is nothing to understand. I will just wait in the quiet. Well, maybe I can find a way to help bolster the shower curtain a bit better." Yet a gravity directed his attention away from the hole in the wall and toward the dried puddle of oil that had expressed its desire to live. Venner tapped his fingers on the counter. He didn't want to be left alone with nothing to occupy his attention. He forced himself to attend to Iramir. She was on her phone, obviously willing to accommodate him, and if she was disappointed, it didn't show.

Venner asked, "What would you like to be? Think about your wildest dreams, Iramir. What do you want?"

"The stars," said Iramir, putting down her phone. "I would like to see the stars. I travel on business much of the time, city to city always. And while the brightest constellations occasionally beat light pollution,

I have been told the evenings far from civilization are something else." She shook her phone in conciliatory efforts. "You can travel the world in images, but you know, the real thing is better."

Venner had eaten all the stars that had once lit his ocean dream. He bit his lip. He often cherished the fact that the conversations of his extra-curricular experiences were self-defeating. By the wondrous property of taboo topics, he would never have an exchange last longer than a hand-ful of replies at most. This was good in that it spared him from further embarrassment, but he secretly still longed for connection. With Iramir, it could be possible. Absurdity had risen, been acknowledged, and here Iramir still stayed. As long as absurdity stayed submerged within uncon-scious thought, he could continue this conversation fine.

"Ah, there is no need to travel so far," he said. "It can get quite moun-tainous near here, and there is an observatory not far from the heart of the city. From there you can see down the city skyline. And after sunset, you see the towers lit and shining. Stars of our making. If you want to come." Venner shrugged. "Though, this is probably not the answer you want, and some would call the skyline callous."

"That would be quite nice if I had the time."

"Yes, I surmised that your sort of business does not handle off-hours well. You are still young though. I used to travel a lot for work as well, back when I used to do fit checks on satellites. It was always stressful. Every waking moment was a fixation on time and to be as efficient as possible. The schedule was daunting. I guess I would have liked to say I walked across the world and saw all their different skies, but I was always too busy to look up. But being busy was good, I think."

"Why did you stop?"

"I transferred to my current job, one that afforded me the chance to grow more insular over the years. I just poured more and more of myself into work. Looking outside began to inspire so many unwanted thoughts."

"Do you think you made the right decision, valuing work like that?" The question caught Venner off guard. He didn't know how to put his feelings into words. Iramir only waited for him, and he could not stand the silence.

"Work has to be," rushed Venner. "In children, my madness is imaginative. In my years, it is a concern. Work sets me the same as everyone. I am functioning. In the protection of my chosen distraction, I contribute to society. I can converse with others without attracting any sort of terrible attention. I am human, not a condition.

"Just stop thinking about it, they say, but I can't. It always devolves into that single predilection, of nothingness upon the water. Too much time with myself, too much time comparing myself to everyone else. Interaction is uncanny, as if I should not be there or doing this. This constant dread can't be normal.

"Behind the numbers and electric code of my computer screen are visual representations of almost-wolves and lost heads." Venner sliced across his neck with a finger. "To avoid sides of streets because there are pining spirits beneath my feet. To panic in the middle of an evening grocery run because I am inundated by living things. If everything disappeared, I would be at peace. But I know things can't disappear."

"Is there really nothing outside work that helps you?" She had no judgement as she had assured him before. Her sort of reliability really did comfort him.

"I had someone at work that bothered me constantly about hanging out, and it was kind of frustrating to be taken outside my predetermined schedule, though I was never really disappointed when I did. Time passed as well as it did at work." The thought crossed his mind that Caide may never talk to him again.

"I might understand having someone like that," Iramir said, her voice softer. "I have never had a chance to take advantage of such an opportunity."

"Never? Do you ever want to?"

Iramir said nothing else as she stretched her arms over the counter, letting the beetle waddle down the forearm stretch.

"We are both terrible conversationalists, it seems," attempted Venner.

"I have tried reading up on how to socialize," mumbled Iramir.

Venner chuckled and said, "Most stop at the first fifteen pages of one of those books." She sighed and nodded.

The sound of weights sliding across the room drew Venner's attention to the blackstone idol, which rolled past the hole and then began rolling up the wall. Gravity had no intention of bringing the bear back down as the blackstone continued skyward, rolling over the curtain nails as it ascended. On touching the blackstone, nails popped out from the wall and melded into the stone. A corner of the shower curtain draped over, letting in more rain to stain the furniture inside. Iramir walked over and gathered the bear into her hands. She shrugged with the faint expression of imploring some forgiveness for a misbehaving pet.

She attempted to retrieve some of the nails whose heads still showed. As iron scraped out of the crevices, the blackstone idol shuddered in her fingers. She wrested out the first nail. The iron had been bitten down into the shape of an evergreen tree. Gone were the swaths of forests and the links of mountain spines. Whole facets of the blackstone were swept flat and empty. The nails were substitutes, not mere dessert. She replaced the evergreen nail.

"Having trouble?" Venner asked. There was tepid worry on Iramir's brow. She placed the blackstone idol in Venner's hands.

"Would you kindly coax the bear out?" Iramir asked.

"How? It would come out on its own, would it not? The idol has changed. None of its markers still exist for a hint," said Venner. Iramir urged him despite his protests, and he felt pressured to try. Performing a quick inspection of the blackstone idol, he noted the odd scuff and chipped edge. If he managed the right orientation, he could redo that solution from earlier.

The inside was empty. Had he got it wrong? The bear that had eaten the unfigure should have been inside. The blackstone idol should have either unraveled to full size and crushed him under its bulk, or he should have found the bear neatly packed in an impossible space.

"Is it as easy as you make it seem? I did not think you would be so effective," she said, taking the empty blackstone idol back for closer viewing.

"It is almost rote most of the time, the abstractions of patterns and numbers," he said. The sight of the solved blackstone inspired that insipid compulsion. The brief reverie of relative normality had been broken. Thoughts of consequence, of murder, of obsession spilled into his mind yet again. "Where is the bear?" he asked, waiting for Iramir's explanation to distract him.

"Try telling me, Eram." Iramir used the empty idol as paperweight for Weill's bills. The corner of Venner's mouth twitched from the urge to pick at his teeth. The image of a dog skull swelled in remembrance. His insane veracity persuaded him the bear could not swim. Nothing could swim in his ocean. A man couldn't drown a bear in an ocean that only existed in dreams. It was an association gone awry, yet the more the thought lingered, the more he was unable to muster any alternate answer to offer Iramir.

"It is a bit late to print missing pet posters," she said without any ire of his mishandling or his sudden reticence. "Stay here. It will be safe enough despite how it appears. I will make the necessary calls for any compensation you require. A vehicle, I suppose, would be first on the list."

"Why are you doing this? You've already explained to me how I am a statistic to be measured. A lost cause by the byline. I'm beginning to think particular attention is not something I should be happy for."

"You need to go back to sleep," she said far too quickly for his liking. Those scant few words irked him. She meant only to keep him safe, possibly, but in the span of seven words, his hatred of his own dreams overflowed. The act of solving anything stemmed the madness. An empty idol only whetted his senseless appetite, stoking that desire for the missing paper man, for the resolution of his life in jeopardy, for a moon.

"I'm going. There are people I want," said Venner. Iramir broke with clear disappointment. She settled back in her seat by the countertop and helped the beetle that had gotten stuck in the bottleneck of her drink.

"I said the city abhors aberrations. There is a sense of regularity that should not be disturbed. Follow me and the city may end up considering you a troublemaker. Stay and keep it easy for my future interference. I will have you back at home then. There is simply too much to be dealt with at the moment. Weill is my guardian, my hound of the Library. She will have her way. You will not come."

"You will have your way," corrected Venner, denying her attempts to let him down gently. Iramir leaned on the table with a quiet glare. Moonlight washed over them, banking off impossible angles. He despised the moon's reflection upon a dreaming ocean. This reflection drove his habit for desire. He had been left so miserable and wanting by his failures to capture it; he would tolerate much more of it if it meant he could solve the problems within his grasp. "I want to know them, deeply, those that dare disturb my ocean."

A glass lance braced itself against his neck. There was no contact between glass and flesh, but the lance seared, nonetheless. It was Weill, still damp, still suspicious, having left her bedroom of upturned floorboards with her own weapon in hand.

"Explain," growled Weill. Her lance did not waver. The moonlight was a single spotlight upon him. The rest of the apartment had been cast into darkness. A neon air lingered in the light, ready at a moment's notice, building and binding from the girl and igniting from her guardian. Threads of gold weaved impossible words like that of oil around the apartment.

Venner stuttered, "I—I mean, I still hate this. I have to hate this, but, but . . ." he struggled. "If I set foot home, if I close my eyes and sleep, I will witness my inaction forever. My dreams have an agonizing continuity I can't change." He hunched over the countertop, having given up the linguistic auditing for benign subjects. "They haunt me, these things I can't drown. They displace my ocean with their horrid shapes. They escape me, and I so desperately want to fill these shapes in with brine. I must have them. I must. Despite you."

Weill turned her lance closer, but Iramir waved Weill away. The hound obeyed with bared teeth. "I must," Venner said again.

"Weill, we leave now. I tire of this waiting, and so does Mr. Eram Venner." Iramir sat back up and raised the collar of her coat. The apartment flooded with moonlight, and the edges of all things were highlighted in incandesce. Diligently measured was Iramir's cadence for this neon hymn. This was her illusive, oceanic reflection made real—he had no better word for it than that. The mercurial behavior of light beyond the explanation of proper physics felt so close to the senselessness of oiled words and paper existence.

"You," huffed Weill, trying to manage her tongue. "Lady Iramir, this is a mistake. He can't come . . ." Weill seemed ignorant of the sweep of golden threads that tugged at her edges and rounded away the corners of the apartment like it was sanding down space. Only Venner seemed to notice. Goodbye walls, floor, and hole.

Iramir readjusted her ribbon tie, umbrella in hand, before closing the door to the apartment. They all stood in the open hallway where the apartment door should have been half-embedded into the wall, but nothing remained. The unit did not exist.

Weill kicked the floor, folding her lance away and tucking the still massive weapon under her arm. She approached Iramir, standing between her and Venner. "You shouldn't be using your magic so liberally," said Weill, who was a poor whisperer. "We've got people on call for stuff like removing an apartment. You've already had to defend yourself alone." Weill's shoulders slumped. "I'm gonna be rude, but your life is short enough as it is. You know, no marathon, no walking even. Take it easy."

"I am able and therefore I act," rebuffed the hound's master.

"What did you do, Iramir?" asked Venner in shock.

"Must have been a trick of the light," said Iramir, calling the elevator. The noise of strummed cables and counterweights rumbled behind the metal doors. "My intentions are not his absolution, Weill, but my intentions are absolute." The light display above the doors marked the elevator's upcoming progress.

Weill tucked her cap low over her brow. She checked the time on her watch and smoothed down the masking tape of the cobalt crystal chunk barely stuffed in the jacket pocket. Venner ran his hand along the wall, feeling for the door that had once been. The wallpaper was mottled and dust lined. Reality disagreed with him, but he was convinced, like all of his insane maxims, of the neon air and gilded threads that were so tangible.

Weill nodded. "I'm your loyal hound, Lady Iramir."

The elevator doors slid open, and soon they were in a beat sedan glistening under the rain. The cobalt crystal sat in the center cup holders, nestled amongst napkins. Golden threads peeked out from between the cracks and swayed in the breeze of the heated ventilation like rippling wires of shorn electronics. Weill seemed not to appreciate a well-solved puzzle. These etchings arced over and through the crystal never to be completed.

The radio crackled and sounded an emergency alert. Their phones joined the collective noise with disaster texts. Weill threw her phone in annoyance on top the dashboard. A flood warning had been issued, promising that there would be enough rain to flood the underground train tunnels and make much of downtown impassable for standard clearance vehicles. Emergency response would be limited during the downpour. From the backseat, Venner watched Iramir check a map of affected areas on her phone.

"We're still away from the lower areas. If we stay west, we should be fine," said Venner from over her shoulder.

"I would think the city would welcome the rain, especially given the secrecy of its operators," said Iramir. "Does it rain often?"

"A constant reminder throughout the year, but this torrential pace is the tail of a season. The city is quiet because of it. I think it's lovely in the dead of night, standing under the rain where neon reflects off everything like city stars, where there is no one else to bother you."

Weill grumbled, "I hate the rain." She slid her hand from the shifter over to the cobalt, digging her fingers into the cracks. Inner fire flared inside the warped reflections of the crystal facets, shorting the gilded threads. Whatever stench the hound was following, Weill was steadfast.

Venner found himself impatient. There was a puzzle to be solved. The accountant, the paper man, the card. The way the world shifted as if turned by a mystic hand, from a stairway departure to an apartment erasure, only turned his gaze outward. The city was so loose in its wiles. Were all things like this? Out in the broad city, swollen with gilded magic, what was kept in its center? What beat as its heart that he could find and drown? Moonlight glittered off the rain, slicing along the edges of the speeding car.

Iramir fixed her collar, letting the ends of her tie slip between her fingers. Though she was outwardly serene, her hands betrayed her. "Was there really nothing else that could be collected from the car crash? No further clues as to what he is?" she asked Weill. A possible answer to his definition forced Venner to attention, but the city puzzle gnawed his mind.

Weill shifted in her seat and leaned her head on her arm that was braced against the door. She began tapping on the steering wheel. "No. He's caught up with some thieving necromancer. City doesn't seem to care about him. Fat load of good that does. You mind telling us then?" Weill nodded to him. "If you had shut up, it might've been better for you."

"Fortune tellers and soothsayers gain insight out of scissors, mirrors, teeth, and so on," said Iramir. "Eram simply understands without a need for any tools. All prophets are company sponsored in this day and age. Eram is a lost man of no association."

"Is that what made him a target?"

"It is appealing. Although, it's questionable whether anyone today could produce something so able." None of this was helping him.

"We can," mumbled Weill.

"Like a project hidden in the cobweb annals of my library," said Iramir. She was studying Venner's reactions again in the reflections of the rear-view mirror. She gave up the pretense and addressed him directly. The flicker of her grey eye captured him. This conversation was not hosted for his sake but for her continued data collection.

"But it does not matter if nature cannot oblige," Iramir continued. "Man-made creation would suffice, but failed projects get shut down. The researchers move on or die. Fit checks on satellites, correct? Is it a heavily success-oriented industry? My failures sting rather harshly, even when some of them are inherited. Yet I suppose that is why it is ever more important that I succeed. Generations of failure had to end eventually.

"I find oceans rather frightening sometimes. A few thousand people drown and become mere statistics. If I open one of my books in this library of mine, would I find you? I would hope not. If so, I would rather in a book that was loaned to me instead of my own."

Venner did not understand. An obtuse joke, perhaps? It did not seem like it. He needed to stop staring at her. A cloying anxiety disturbed more of his balance the longer he did. Iramir then turned away. Whether or not she had found what she wanted, Venner didn't know. Yet even in his release, his upturned sense of balance failed to settle. Seeking refuge in the storming city views, he saw white light skimming off the peaks of asphalt waves. The moon always just out of reach behind cloud cover and balance drowned in the ocean.

*Devour the moon.*

Venner crushed the card in his palm and ran a hand through his hair. He should not have looked out the window. He should not have looked up. He had forced his wonder and received the panic-inducing consequences as he should have expected. Shapes tumbled into nameless-ness. Neon dotted the landscape between the seams of a city lined with auric luster. There was neon where the brickwork shifted and turned, where the sting of magic rippled underneath wallpaper and echoed across drywall. The heart of a city ran like clockwork underneath him. Each movement of the gears disturbed the waters. Waves collided and mixed through the constant motions of a concrete heart built to last in the hands of a forgotten order. The city was alive, its inner mechanisms felt undeniably clear, almost as if he could see as this water itself.

Salt water had yet to breach the city bowels, which were kept cleaned and oiled by diligent paper hands. These same paper hands crumbled and sank beneath the waves that lapped the bulwarks. Water rippled to the rumbling of a thousand legs ticking in the depths of the city like a clock-work millipede. He suffered paper pareidolia wherever he looked. With trembling fingers, he unfolded the card. Seven drawn eyes stared back at him. He saw himself, the car, Iramir and Weill, the city outside and no more a city than it always was. But something saw madness. Impossible mental imagery intersected reason with a razor's edge.

Venner smoothed out the card's corners and kept it in the safety of his pocket. *I am the infinite ocean.* Oceans didn't have eyes, so why did he? Where were the rest of the seven? He traced the shape of himself. Five fingers, palm, wrist, forearm. Two eyes. He felt outside of his body. His sense of self leaked through these imagined holes. His perception poured onto the streets and rushed down the gutters.

Lost, liquid eyes saw to the skies. Asphalt rivers, even an ocean, had no choice but to look up. A cascade of shattering glass fell like rain. Moon-light danced amongst its favored medium, creating a mirrored maze of city blocks. Emergency responses were limited for the poor paper men that hated water. The millipede loved its paper playthings.

# FIFTEEN

VENNER WOKE TO THE SMELL OF SMOKE. IT WAS WEILL WITH A cigarette in hand.

"You alright?" she asked roughly. Weill had parked the car outside an entrance to an underground rail line. Iramir twirled her orange umbrella by the entrance.

"Yes, yes," muttered Venner, failing to get to grips with the sudden weight of a body and the exhaustion of speech. Weill shrugged and stalked off, calling to Iramir. Venner stepped out from the backseat. He had nothing but his hand to shield himself from the rain. The asphalt was solid. Beneath him would be the power and telephone lines or the sewers. Sand, aggregate rocks, tar. Concrete and rebar. There would be no reason for concrete hearts. Or eyes. This hidden space, these extra organs, lived only in his imagination, but now that he had thought of them, they existed, and their existence annoyed him. However, these concepts couldn't escape the ocean forever.

Rain pattered off Iramir's umbrella as she stretched to cover him. She huddled close. It was not a large umbrella. The nylon still brushed the top of his head.

"May I?" Venner offered to hold it.

"You could stand to lose a few inches," Iramir whispered before refusing. Weill took a final puff of her cigarette before flicking the snuffed end into a wet trash can.

Dusty construction tape was wrapped around the stone bollard chains, holding the turnstiles still. This was Lacrum station, closed for construction but never worked on. Even on a good day, this line was rarely used. Whatever traffic it handled was taken by the newer downtown line that had been built a few years prior. The city council had planned to connect the discontinued rail across the river instead, but proposals fell through. The council then made their promises to continue the project, but the public tacitly understood the line would never reopen.

"Why are we here?" asked Venner. "This is a dead station. It will be flooded too in this torrent."

"A good enough place to hide. Weill has followed her intuition, that is all," explained Iramir.

Chain-link fencing prevented access to the station, except where urban explorers had cut through. The cut links were bent and rusted, flouting the occasional scrap of fabric. A trail of graffiti art led down the station. Weill simply took the chain link in hand and widened the hole. Venner did not even need to bend down.

The only light was from Iramir's flashlight. No, perhaps Weill's, judging from the initials on the rim. Evidence of roughshod sleeping lined the walls. Graffiti wrangled for space, rising to the very roof. Discarded paint cans floated in the river that made its home over the rails. Air stilled and cooled. The storm had difficulty penetrating the thick concrete and left the station desolate and quiet.

Venner stood up to the blue painted line that reminded passengers not to approach the platform edge during their waiting. The river almost reached the lip of the platform. He peered down the tunnels. There was only darkness. No light for the maintenance workers, if there were any in there.

There were once barricades blocking the tunnels, but that plastic was now buried under silt. At the pace the river was moving and its sheer depth, it would be quite easy to drown in the undertow. The flashlight briefly outlined Venner on the tunnel wall. Iramir joined him on the blue line, tapping the end of her folded umbrella on the tile.

"Weill, go on ahead," said Iramir. Weill bounced the cobalt in her hand and approached the iron maintenance gate that allowed access to the sidewalk through the tunnels. She sheared open the gate with her bare hands before quickly disappearing into the dark. Golden sparks trailed from her hands as if the cobalt was alight, vanishing last.

"Are we not following?" Venner asked. Iramir unscrewed and removed the head of the flashlight and shined light from the bright, naked bulb down into the river. That white luster danced within the grasp of muddy rainwater, suffusing the underground station. Rippling reflections washed over the walls and ceiling, tracing the flow of swaying water. She flashed the sliver of metal she had held during the apartment brawl before recapping the now dead flashlight. Light, ignorant, continued to play in the water despite no source at all.

"This a conscious effort. Dedicated preparations before the application of intent," said Iramir. "Scene, apartment. When you threw that glass, how did you do it? Pull moonlight from thin air?" An active demonstration of mysticism invited Venner to work out the means. Either drawn from an LED or a bulb, there seemed only so much light to manipulate. A moon would be endless by comparison.

The light over the river stayed at Iramir's behest through a network of golden thread, stemming from her sliver of metal. A neon hymn was what he had associated with these impossible moments. These threads expressed an indescribable nuance, as if he were gazing at matters far beyond mere physicality, matters which demanded solemn regard. Oceanic veracity was escaping his dreams, but he didn't care. He took the time to trace every turn and straight of the threads, evaluating where the pattern kept diligent and where it wavered. It was more so an elaborate diagram that had been thoughtfully commented on by the occasional, entwining desire—fragments of frequencies strumming down the wire from a heartbeat or a voice, changing reality to her whim.

Divine circuitry was what armed mighty Jove with her lightning. Yet so fragile this power as golden thread warped in the water like all string did, drowning even. All things devoured in his dreams tasted just like this.

"Only you can control moonlight," said Venner. "Lightning spears and all. Perhaps you had an inkling to—"

"I am never disobeyed," said Iramir. She lifted a javelin from the liquid surface with a nudge of her hand. "My magic is not wild." The javelin floated above the water, a long, graceful spiral of light. Water dripped from its point, each drop escaping with gold in its belly.

"I did not do whatever you think I did," said Venner. He could not comprehend what she wanted. He got scared, that was all. He threw something at something he was scared of.

The javelin spun in the cool air. It was a fine creation, but as his gaze traced the shape where the light dipped and weighed, he realized that the javelin was hardly as gleaming as the first one he had witnessed impale the dog head. Even when plunged into black oil and red bone, that first shining blade of a moonlit night was effervescent. Moonlight followed in the wake of a moon and forged ahead, lighting forward, despite whatever intent a moon may have.

"If moonlight could want, would it want to protect you?" asked Venner. She remained still, her only movement was the slow tapping on the flashlight.

"You ask as if you do not know the answer," said Iramir.

*Last of her legacy, scorned.* That was what he'd called her when they'd had their difficult conversation. He wrung his hands. It was cruel of him to air what must have been sensitive matters, to affirm that she was unwanted. "I'm sorry about what I said earlier," he whispered.

"It is fine," said Iramir, "You repeated a statement of fact. I am not meant to be outside, to be here or any place like here. I am not meant to be. You heard Weill explain I am fragile? Like a particularly vicious autoimmune disorder, magic has the tendency to destroy its user for the crime of simply existing." She flicked her flashlight back on. The river light vanished instantly, focused once more through the lens. She urged him to follow the damp tracks of Weill, showing the way with her light.

Venner considered Iramir's words. The application of intent, of desire. It was an odd sensation to have put this phenomenon into words. To want something, to have reality listen, and then to oblige. He furrowed his brow. He remembered the words in a pool of black oil. *I want to live.* It had been unmistakable. If they lived—the patient paper man, the bear in the box, the unfigures prowling—he wondered if he could pluck their heartstrings and hear those words echoed back to him. He wondered if he could cause the gears and pulleys that comprised their very shapes to rust and tumble down.

This curated system, made with love, was one he could destroy. An ocean waited for them. If they wanted, then they existed, and therefore they had to be drowned. Blood seeped over his taste buds where he had bit his tongue. His blood tasted salty.

Underneath the moon, an anxious ocean waited. Venner followed Iramir down the tunnel. A coiling of gilded thread unraveled from this magic, or perhaps it was magic itself, the fabric of reality to be played with. It coiled around the sliver of metal she kept palmed in her hand. It seemed to coil around everything supernatural. It was a tentative contract between a bloom of pure potential, a person, and a thoughtful vessel lying in wait. From magic supplied, a tool bridged the gap to reality. Bear house, unfigure machinery, solid light from a sliver of metal in a hand. These means gave life to what normally could not live. But perhaps he should avoid such conjecture.

*Eyes forward.* What surrounded him was the glimmer leftover from a broken cobalt vine, the cold and lean intents of a moon, and the rumble of wilder things that may have known his insides. They were here to find his killer. He was here to confront what vexed him and then die again. The ocean devoured such sobriety.

Gilded threads swept against him as he followed Iramir. He felt convinced these threads were something only he, with his ocean eyes, had noticed. Threads reacted to his touch. They pushed back. He needed an incision within her shape for the ocean to seep through, like a crack in the city's foundation accessing clockwork, to pour the ocean in like white noise in the space behind 3 a.m. Any displacement within his waters must fill with brine. He coiled gold around his fingers and cut the thread on his teeth. So, the last moon had to fall into the ocean.

Iramir dropped to her knees, clutching her stomach in pain. The flashlight clattered into the river where the light was swallowed by the water. Venner curled up against the wall. Nausea gripped him. Acid rose up in his esophagus. Something bit back in his mind, a gravity ripping forward from 3 a.m. His vision burned and the senses of his limbs multiplied. Thoughts crumbled into salt. He staggered blindly in the darkness, almost tumbling over the sidewalk edge, and vomited. Gilded thread tied around his neck, cutting into his skin. It tied around his lower jaw and pulled. A dozen threads pulled the ocean as a moon played puppetry. The lethargy of dreams did not apply to waking reality.

The river was so loud. His hands grew suddenly warm. Someone leaned against his body. "Enough," Iramir spoke. A gravity well commanded his ocean outside his control. He scrambled at his jaw, ripping the threads by the handful. He had to. He had to. He had to. He had never been so close to devouring the moon, to bridging impossibility and making that dream true. Small hands gripped him by his shirt. The crescent moon summoned his waters and made his tides. There was nothing to misinterpret. Methodical and exact, Iramir's intent was paramount, irresistible—stop. She held him from falling into the river. "Go back to sleep," she whispered.

Weill rushed down the cracked concrete subway. Fire leapt in full ferocity, whipping and scoring the concrete upon the footfalls of the hound. She stood by them now. Her fury was hotly illuminated by the lance she wielded. The lance's molten core snapped savagely in its glass casing. The hound sniffed the air for any intruders.

"What the hell happened?" asked Weill. Her lance was aimed squarely at Venner. The heat was unbearable. Weill helped Iramir up and held her close. Iramir began to push away, but the worried look on Weill's face changed her mind, allowing Weill to hold her a moment longer. Venner tightened in frustration on the ground. He swallowed the bile. The salt only worsened the burning.

"Eram Venner will be taken to the Library," ordered Iramir calmly, wiping the blood that leaked from her nose on her sleeve. Weill was incredulous. The tip of the lance dropped to the ground. Iramir fixed her hair, pulling her bangs behind her ear. The eye her hair had hidden was carved from white porcelain, unpainted and pure. Where flesh could not provide, she was solid pale stone, hewn from magic. A doll. Gold spilled from the cracks in her porcelain eye and face. She touched her forehead and brushed loose chips of porcelain away. She dusted off her hands and the sound they made was like ceramic sliding against ceramic.

Iramir asked Weill for an empty vial. Weill could only produce a full vial of amber color tincture from her pocket. Iramir uncorked the tincture and poured the rest of it into the river. Venner was dumbfounded, unable to compute his mental break. He blankly watched Iramir kneel before him, lift his hand, and slice through his skin using her sliver of metal. She collected his blood and held her thumb over his wound until it scabbed.

"The sheer amount of protocol broken to let you exist, ocean," said Iramir.

Venner clutched his chest. His mind raced. He was desperate for action, but there was nothing to do. A sharp pang arrived in his throat, and he vomited over the edge again. Whatever response he might have mustered was expelled. Had he ever lost control like this before? Had he ever been in control at all? His life had always been dictated by insipid ideas. He was human, not some damned ocean. It was different with words, but what had spilled into reality—into waking, concrete reality—terrified him.

*Distraction, save me.* Down the river bend, lit from Weill's fire, there was the faint glow of a flashlight under the river muck. It would take far too much effort to retrieve. Bits of trash and detritus flowed and mingled in the muck. The remains of paper men swept by. Their parchment bodies were ripped in long, tangled strands. He heard the ticking of a thousand legs. The clockwork millipede had found him. Venner stood back up, taking a step away from where they had come.

"The matter of a murderer shall be left unsettled," said Iramir. "We are returning now." The paper remnants floated by, and jealousy gritted his teeth. He had wanted to solve these strange things. To be denied the opportunity to drown them was a blow to his fragile ego. The thrashing of things in his ocean only created more holes he could not fill.

Weill stuck out her tongue. "I had just found the ol' hidden door too." Iramir noticed his wandering attention tracing something in the darkness. Weill stopped him with her lance. "Running away?"

"We are not alone," said Venner grimly. Weill ran the end of her lance along the sidewalk, igniting a short trail. She would see to that.

"It seems so convenient for you that something comes your way to break the tension," said Iramir. "Why should I believe you?" Leaking water tapped on the pipes above them.

Venner huffed. "Iramir." He pointed to the river. "Can you not see them? The paper men in the water? They've been murdered, and it's coming." Iramir kicked a pebble into the river. There were no bodies to find, just paper. "It lives in the bowels of this city, a parasite feasting on the city's attendants." A crude feeling stirred inside him. It was as if the order of nature had betrayed him. "I—I need to explain this. They, they were . . ." Venner exhaled sharply. "They were mine."

Tapping pipes multiplied into the discord of rain. The brickwork shifted back into place. The city had transformed again, shifting its cellular pieces to and fro. The clockwork millipede tapped along the walls with a thousand legs, climbing, spiraling amongst the cancer of too many places in one moment.

Venner stumbled over roaming balconies. Concrete jutted like the crags of a mountain. Clockwork sprung under obscene pressure. Gears seized within doors. Storefronts hung upside down above him. Street signs bent and intersection signals blinked red again. Rain fell at odd angles. The city undulated as the millipede rebuilt its nest. Gold bled from the city, fusing together the final corners. He had been removed from Iramir and Weill as if the millipede had taken his slice of space for its own enjoyment.

The clockwork millipede wore sheets of paper men which flapped in the air. It hid amongst the corpses under the city's very nose, and the city obeyed the feigned voices of its many servants. They manned the streets, turned the gears, drove the buildings. The millipede scrambled around him, ducking about the concrete noise. Its empty eye sockets bubbled in silent delight. Emaciated human arms lined a ravenous, open gullet like teeth, beckoning him to oblige it.

Venner scrambled as it gave chase. The sheets of men tore on open rebar. He was blocked by endless dead ends. The flickering red lights painted roving shadows of the millipede. It was monstrously large and there was little he could do to protect himself. He could not conjure light or fire. He had nothing to say about his own death other than to hope for a savior. His back thumped against a brick wall, slick with rain. The sheets of men should be awash in his ocean.

The clockwork millipede leered over Venner. "I didn't expect you to be taken along," it said with a voice like a static whine. "I wanted you alone in that apartment for the easy collection. The Library should've stopped caring about you, caring too much instead about revenge than bedside manner. They should've given you their empty platitudes and no more. Now, I have a Library problem. That's very annoying." The millipede slithered closer. Arms caressed him by the cheek. "But the Library is invested in you. That's very intriguing. Stay and let me find out why."

Was it not just a few minutes ago that Venner thought himself infinite and unstoppable? Did he not decide to name those intervening shapes of paper men "wondrous distractions"? The clockwork millipede was no exception. In the span of all his abyssal depths, the millipede was no larger than a legfull thing. A wry smile crossed his face.

"I wonder if you understand," said Venner. His perception failed to steady on solid ground. His head hurt from too many eyes in improper places. "Things like you are a nuisance. You think you have such freedom to trespass at will, but you are all merely shapes. If I can solve you, break you down to the very last vertex, you will cease to exist, and I will be pure again."

He picked at the concrete around him, tugging the gilded thread used to stitch the nest together. If gold bribed impossibility to obey, then without it there would be rebellion. He strummed the heartstrings of a city alive, listening to the echoes. He found the heaviest rhythm, the string most taut. Perhaps a city was too large to swallow, but a little millipede's nest? Surely he could. "I think I might be fine with seconds," said Venner. "You must stay. I am furious." He cut the threads on his teeth.

The nest collapsed. In a faraway dream, murmuring in the back of his mind, salt water consumed glitter and gold. Magic commenced restructuring. The clockwork millipede slipped from its perch as the concrete ruptured. Foundations fell and swallowed chasing buildings. His smile began to hurt, pure glee drunk on the refuse of 3 a.m.

"You only become more valuable than what my thief has described," said the millipede. "I must have you." With arms for teeth, it weaved a runic circle, commanding magic in a copied voice, and a black expanse opened in a falling brick wall. Water leaked out, and the millipede scrambled through.

Venner was alarmed at the sight of this. The idea that the millipede would try to escape him was so foreign, then he remembered he had legs. He stumbled on his first step, trying to catch up. The sensation of physicality was a strange thing, as his body felt much too confined for the shape of himself. Rubble struck him on the shoulder. He gasped in pain, struggling to explain the existence of his own body. The shapes fell away, nameless and heavy.

The city slowly roused with the echoes of too many people of the distant surface. The millipede's nest had been punctured, its disguise done away. Like clockwork, the city righted the damage done by the parasite. The city was aware, and it dropped Venner anywhere he fit nearby. He stood upon damp linoleum; it smelled of corpses and mint. He found himself in a morgue, observing the embalmed bodies on operating tables and the stolen limbs suspended in acid, too damaged for use. He squeezed his arms and shoulders, rubbing where it hurt, remembering what shape he was.

On a nearby table lived notes of revivification. A half-built unfigure lay limp, hanging from a meat hook and connected to a series of pumps and tubes. There was an open fridge of empty blood bags raising the electric bill. Empty packaging was thrown in an overfilled hazard container. Cold alembics sat covered in dust. Reagents wasted away in open cardboard with no useable bodies to fill. The import documents collected in a pile. He read the shipping header on one of them: the accountant.

Oh. The memories came back quietly, filling in the gaps he preferred empty. "My name is Eram Venner," he whispered. Human. He had a job to answer to in the morning and bills to pay. He brushed a hand through his hair, surprised that his head was actually there. He shook his novel head, leaned against a table, and waited for the sensation of being on a swaying ship to fade away. He heard the grinding of a brick wall opening behind him.

# SIXTEEN

IRAMIR WALKED WITH WEILL IN STARK VIEW OF THE NECRO-mancer's sanctum. A true necromancer. How quaint. Rarely were people so personal with their creations these days.

The buzz of fluorescents was the only accompaniment to their footsteps. A few overhead lights would be enough in the case of noncompliance—certainly much better than the meager light from a cellphone. She released her hold on the tarnished metal and left it floating in midair behind her. What edge it once held had been rubbed down over the years.

The hidden door she and Weill had entered through still crackled from the fire. Heat had shattered stone and melted all manner of lock. This was a pocket world, an artificial insertion of space into reality. If sufficiently agitated, these pockets tended to implode, crushing everything within. Agitation came in many forms. For example: fire.

Supply boxes were filled with medical instruments and savage charms. People in the modern age preferred fast food—quick things for a single purpose—but there was a certain allure to good craftsmanship even if the world could no longer sustain such admirations. Too much effort was spent for things to die too quickly.

Eram was somewhere in this sectioned world. The night was still young enough, and the little location spell she'd told him had yet to wear off. She wondered how moonlight could have spotted him this deep underground—it implied that there was another exit to this pocket plane that led to the surface. No matter, she had Weill.

Iramir rubbed her neck, feeling where soft flesh transitioned to porcelain. She was patchwork, of some forty percent real meat and sorcerous automata for the rest. She rubbed her false eye and felt the noises of scraping ceramic. A crack trailed from her temple down her cheek. Porcelain dust coated her fingertips. The spell that kept her passable in public had failed. She stretched her hands and wrists. Joints were still movable, interior organs still warm, and a soul still attached.

The activation of a tool like her metal focus or Weill's lance was akin to a tugging, electric sensation across the spirit. It was that same unmistakable sensation she felt with Eram upon his touch. The resonance between tool and user formed the basis for magic. Overflowing resonance burned the spirit to cinders.

Eram was something contained in a human shape that could attune with that immaterial wellspring and grant another endless power. Yet unlike him, everyone else was fragile, incendiary even, at those terrifying amplitudes. Nothing could contain his gifted endlessness forever. Flesh and bone and twelve-volt batteries were quite enough. Any excess destroyed. She should be careful. Their connection was momentary, but the danger might linger.

That flicker of living circuits overloaded by magic, of thaumic autoimmune disorders on command, had not damaged her irreparably. Though it had certainly been strong enough to dissolve her partially. A lingering anxiety warned that she should not have shown Eram her magic so clearly. She picked up a tooled, brass heart from a nearby worktable just to have something that could kept idle hands from widening her cracks.

Weill paced the perimeter of the room. Her lance rested at her side, extinguished and dark. The hound instinctively kept to the shadows. Someone stepped down the stairs that led from the sanctum. He drew a pistol, finger resting on the trigger, and aimed squarely at Iramir. Weill seemed to recognize the gunman, but she stood silent and waited for her master's command. Ah, this was the necromancer then.

"How charming. Good evening to you as well," said Iramir, rolling the heart in her hands. She did not raise her voice. "A necromancer outside of an association. Now is that not lonely? The world can be quite frightening when you're alone. It is a shame about your dear minions.

You are in short supply by the looks of these stark shelves and partial cadavers." She put the heart back on the worktable. "You were so generous tonight hunting a man on the streets, stealing from Harken, and even making an attempt on my life. I must reciprocate."

Her metal focus shivered in the air where it floated. Light melted into quicksilver, forming an ornate white halo, thrice layered and pointed, centered about her. The necromancer would know her as most knew her, the Sovereign Moon. "Surrender," she commanded.

He shot. And shot again. The gunshots echoed around the empty space. Bullets tumbled through hard light, deflected through the spears that caught them midflight. The spears, never as good as moonlight and never as safe, shattered. Pain was rising again in her abdomen. Heat collected between the interfaces of flesh and porcelain. She rubbed her ear to dissuade the ringing.

Unfortunate. A threat like her typically inspired a lovely, quiet surrender. This had been a long enough night already. Solid outlines of her spears formed at the ready, and her halo distorted. Liquid light dripped up to the ceiling, unable to keep form. Magic bit back at her command, the small disobedience characteristic of more severe consequences in the future.

Iramir sighed, "Pity."

The hound emerged from hiding and struck her lance against the ground. The glass sparked but did not ignite. Weill gnashed her teeth. Iramir took note and another spear was thrown before the sound of another gunshot. Shattering glass filled the next beat and remnants of a light fixture showered over Iramir, a panicked misfire. The fluorescents shorted, darkening the rest of the room in quick succession. Her spear never made it to the necromancer. Iramir simply brushed the loose glass from her shoulders. The only light emitted from her halo, faintly illuminating the silver coin the necromancer held just before the gun barrel.

The necromancer spoke, "Brimstone begotten and aurora fed, be charged with mortal judgement, you have been sentenced. Fetch and be free." One more gunshot, bright in the darkness. The bullet impacted the silver and sliced through, dragging behind in its wake a torrent of blood. A beast of cloven hooves and ribbed horns burst from the coin, lit by auroras that showered the beast in cold majesty. Its weight broke the floor and shook the pocket space. The necromancer rushed back up the stairs, nursing his hand where he'd held the coin.

The beast threw tables, discarded corpses, and literal chunks of pocket reality. Cloven limbs scraped along the floor. A body heaved, ready to charge. Open holes in reality collapsed upon themselves as stress cracks traveled across the room. Iramir pulled out her phone. As damaged as she was now, it was unsafe to use the light made from the sorcery of other creatures. Weill, taking point, stood fast between Iramir and the cloven beast.

"Let me, Claire!" urged the hound. Weill took her lighter and bit down on the tin as hard as she could. There was much too little room to avoid a charging beast. Hooves shattered the floor with every thundering step. Weill raised her arm as a shield. The beast collided head first against her. Its horns cracked on impact. Weill was unyielding.

The cloven beast wrestled with the guardian before being forced away by a rough shoulder check. Weill dragged the tip of the lance against the ground, sparking a circle of flame. At last, her weapon ignited. Fire engulfed her arm and then jumped to all things flammable around the laboratory. Fire roared and crackled and smoked. A winged lion was etched upon the lighter, glittering in the orange glare between Weill's teeth. Her lance was the fang of the Library.

"Avoid the stairs," said Iramir, chastising Weill's uncontrolled inferno. Weill seemed so uncomfortable wielding her weapon these days. Iramir's halo reformed back into her metallic focus within the blink of a camera flash. The phone's LED light steadied. She would need cover anyways if Weill continued to have trouble.

The beast threw another chunk of floor space towards Weill and attempted again to gore her upon horns from under the shadow of a flying worktable. Weill parried the debris but failed to find a good angle for her lance against the oncoming enemy. The beast bit onto the weapon, cracking glass and tearing it from her hand. It swept Weill up onto its horns. She braced her arms inside of its maw, grunting from the sheer effort of prying bestial teeth apart. The jaws opened just enough for Weill to touch the exposed molten core of the lance. The crack of a lance exploding rang farther than the shredding of scorched hoof and horn and the confines of a pocket space.

# SEVENTEEN

THE CLOVEN BEAST WOULD ONLY FARE SO LONG AGAINST THE
Library. The accountant fumbled with his keys and locked the door
from inside the cleanroom. Harken had to have known the Library was
involved, but they neglected to tell him. This oversight meant that he
had become Harken's willing lamb of slaughter by incurring the Library's
wrath. Now, it did not quite mean he had been betrayed. Fervent pacing could not quell the sense of his world collapsing. It was going to be
okay. Harken would take care of him. Nervous laughter could not dry
the sweat dripping down his temples.

The accountant excavated his briefcase from a worktable littered with
creature blueprints and business magazines and searched it for another
pack of smokes. He found one, and unwound the seal on the plastic
sleeve, but he couldn't find his lighter. He tapped his foot, mentally
tracing where he had been and patting his empty pocket. He had been
caught after his theft of Harken property by the millipede, cornered into
a dead-end street by the city's shifting civil planning.

The millipede introduced itself as Vandheer, an agent of Harken and
the city, and demanded compensation for their stolen property and broken laws. Monetary sums did not count as adequate compliance. The
accountant, in a desperate bid to avoid paying with his life, dressed his
abnormal client as someone worth investigating.

He explained the impossible consumption of a parking lot creature,
the inexplicable extraction of it from its locked housing, lying through
clenched teeth about the sheer worth Venner had. It was not a complete

lie. There was a genuine anxiety associated with that man, almost dangerous even. Aberration always attracted Harken's attention, and such information may save the accountant.

However, Vandheer had only agreed to have the accountant collect the client. If Venner was any bit of the destructive force described, Vandheer would very much like Harken to inspect him themselves. Only then would they grant the accountant leniency.

What else could the accountant do to stop the Library? He may have bought himself time with Harken, but the Library had no such deferment. The resources Harken had given him were already exhausted. He could try a demon summoning with a circle drawn in blood. There was nothing wrong with being traditional. If it were only fifty years ago, he could bind a soul with nothing but the desire to do so. He kept pulling out a single cigarette from the pack and then sliding it back in.

It was not blood on the floor before him, just marker over the damp, linoleum tile. The accountant oversaw a crude ritual requested by Vandheer at the very last moment, before he had known the Library would arrive to take vengeance. He had not expected the millipede to deliver him the client, and his only task was to create an imprint of Mr. Venner. Every facet of Venner's physical make to be written down for perusal. Vandheer would do whatever they wished with it and in return, grant the accountant deliverance from the Library. An amendment in his favor, but that future was slipping away by the second.

The lights of dancing glyphs formed and dissolved over the ritual circle, merging and separating complex abstractions. The hastily drawn circle coiled around the open bottles of oil and flux. Venner lay within, unconscious from whatever the millipede had done. The client's chest had been pried apart, and his splayed ribs were held open by hooks. A sacrificial obelisk etched by invisible hands was suspended over him.

The accountant did not have the time to properly prepare another coin. However, while this ritual was not necessarily crafted for summoning, there was no reason it could not pull double duty. He just needed to be a bit inventive. Taking a marker in hand, he bent down and made several scrawling adjustments in glyphic words, being careful not to overwrite the ritual's function and equally careful not to step on Venner. On the back of his hand, the accountant scrawled a final inscription of his own name . . . . Now he simply needed to perform the magic.

Things were different now than they'd been fifty years ago. As he stood there today, nothing answered his soulful cry. The accountant quickly proofed his changes again as he paced the circle's perimeter, adding any missing hash or stroke. It was textbook correct, if muddling. Yet again, the world did not turn over in accordance to ordained prayer. Magic no longer functioned as intended. Something had changed, either in him or in the world. Constructs broke down from lack of maintenance no longer possible. Solely ethereal things did not decay but simply died. File the accountant in the former. He felt of missing limbs and stolen senses, of an emptiness that was literally suffocating.

This body was temporary, its successor had to be named, but death would not be cheated for much longer. He feared the emptiness outside of a name. He feared taking the leap into another body and finding no way to get back in. He had to choose between a death of thaumic entropy or flaming retribution. Or there was the pistol that weighed heavily in his pocket. There was nothing wrong with being a bit traditional.

The accountant could attempt to divert what powered the ritual for the demon summoning, but any disruption may stop it, and there was new doubt if he could restart it. He accidentally bit the marker as if it was a cigarette before replacing it in hand with the cyan carton. Where was his lighter? The sudden tapping of a thousand legs racing around the room startled him.

"The hound will hardly be deterred," said the millipede, nestling itself above as it pulled the rest of its body through a closing hole in the bricks. It arranged its teeth-arms in a crooked smile.

"Shut up, Vandheer. Manipulate the city. Get them away!"

The millipede laughed like hail striking gravestones. "Not anymore with this little millipede. Our strange man seems to have ruined the whole secrecy of it all. The city is staring. Can't do anything about that."

The accountant tightened. "Don't you speak on behalf of the city?" he asked. The millipede laughed again. The arms of its mouth all separately brought a finger to the rim of its lips.

"Give me what I want and I'll save you, if that's what you mean," said Vandheer.

The accountant balked, clutching his hands together behind his neck. He paced and whimpered and checked the time on his wristwatch. Seconds slipped into minutes. As long as the hound was not here in the cleanroom, he still had time. The accountant pored over an open notebook on the table. He had checked his calculations over and over. There was just enough fuel to complete the imprint.

One adult male would take about three minutes. The suspended obelisk kept on inscribing. The accountant kept counting time, but it was taking too long, especially to scan a person. It did not take that much effort to search up the composition of a human body in a textbook or on the internet. An imprint was more often used to map magic resonance, of how magic flowed and responded inside someone or something. He had nowhere near enough measurable resources for that. Entire institutions were set up to do just that and all manner of impossible things.

All Vandheer wanted was composition. Eram Venner was a man. Anyone could see that, but the tracing left on the obelisk, the map of personhood, did not look human. The accountant ran a finger under his collar. He kept pacing, watching his fuel reserves dip below the twenty, the ten. He tore the carton in his anxiety, spilling cigarettes onto the floor.

The etched obelisk was only partially complete. With limited resources should come corresponding goals—there was no need to compound disappointment. Yet, he found himself wrung with the same regret he proclaimed himself better than. He should have gone straight home tonight. He should have avoided the violence because he had only one body left and nothing to his name. He should not have bothered but for that one moment in his life, he had thought he had some sort of control. Now, he stared at his failure.

The sudden clap of a thunderous explosion rocked the cleanroom. There would be no deliverance. His anger snapped at the millipede and crushed the cigarettes underfoot. He shook his fists, shouting until his throat stung. The deal was rigged. He pointed at the closed door as the heat of judgement slowly engulfed the room. He threatened to expose the millipede and lord the Library over Vandheer.

The millipede investigated the half-finished product. Its hands felt every crevice of the obelisk and swallowed the wet crystal. The millipede ignored the accountant's words. The accountant put his hands together. He pleaded. The hound neared.

The accountant rushed through his pockets. No more coins to bribe death, but he found the revolver. Hardly had he begun aiming towards his own head when the millipede stole his finger, his hand, his forearm with its own mouthful of limbs tearing and snapping flesh like clay. The accountant stared at his missing limb, neatly torn and dripping. Pain then caught up with his vision. He screamed. The millipede picked the gun apart, dropping the components on the floor.

The millipede inspected Venner, hanging his body from its skittering mouthful as its human arms perused flesh and bone and teeth. Arms clattered about like a spider as it weaved the heart and spinal column to where they belonged, keeping Venner's consciousness alive just a little longer. The accountant swore and scrambled over to the table. He swept off the clutter and leftovers of this cursed ritual. He kicked open the drawers and grabbed a first aid kit.

The millipede cocked its head to one side, nudging the lifeless doll of a client. It finished stitching Venner's open chest back together with a cadaver's signature. The millipede listened closely to the chest and then clapped in apparent success. The accountant stuffed the end of his stump with cloth, hastily dousing the wound with stinging tincture. The millipede rumbled to the accountant, "You've failed to fulfill your terms of the deal. My business with you is almost over." It climbed back inside the city clockwork through the dark tears of the pocket realm opened by the fires.

"Be damned!" the accountant spat into the void. He threw the rest of the kit onto the floor and grabbed a book from underfoot. Fury found a new target: the body of Eram Venner, slowly stirring to life. The accountant screamed in anguish. If only he had more power, if only he did not waste his resources, if only he had not bothered. The accountant strangled Venner using a knee and the spine of the book to keep pressure on the windpipe. Venner gasped for breath. The accountant so desperately wanted to be more. He wanted the power to get revenge on Vandheer.

"Do you know what I can do to make it worse for you, Venner?"

seethed the accountant through clenched teeth. He coated his fingers in the blood of his cut limb and sketched the beginnings of a spell on Venner's forehead. "I'll rip your soul from you as slowly, as painfully as you'll ever experience."

Magic burned. The accountant's hand seized mid-stroke of a rune. Tendons contracted and skin bubbled. He lost his breath as his chest shuddered. Nausea leaked from him and an upset sense of balance forced him off Venner. He struggled to right himself in a coughing fit. His mind tumbled over itself from any change in height. The room slurred in after-images. He coughed again and stared at his ejected teeth. The accountant cupped his bleeding mouth.

His body burned. A single rune had undone him. The limit had been breached. This was magic turned traitor. Thermal runaway of the body skipped over the speed limit. Death commenced as melted meat spilled from the opening of his cut limb and strength turned to slurry. The accountant spat out bits of inner organs and curled up on the ground. He slammed the floor with his fist again and again. Strips of skin were left behind. *Please, make the pain stop.*

Everything burned. The final bulwark of the cleanroom caved in. He clutched his face to keep his eyes in. The hound advanced through the incoming blaze. The pocket realm scorched all around them. The hound stepped back in horror, holding back her Sovereign Moon.

"Please help me." The accountant struggled. The vibrations in his throat snapped the vocal chords. Magic ate through the connections of sinew and bone. It electrified the nerves into endless misery. He swayed upon the ocean from dizziness. The deafening crash of waves from him swelling with blood. He was drowning from breaths displaced with red water.

The Sovereign Moon approached, seemingly immune to his suffering like it was just business for her. She glanced over to Venner, writhing and scratching at the millipede's handiwork. She waved to her hound. "Collect Eram," she said. The hound hesitated. "Now."

The hound gathered the muttering man in her arms. The accountant reached out with a fingerless hand. From the firelight, the Moon summoned her divine weapon. The spear poised itself over him. Sparkling fire was encapsulated within hard light form. The spear dropped into piercing darkness.

# EIGHTEEN

THERE WAS STILL THE MATTER OF A COLLAPSING POCKET world. Weill was uncomfortable with Venner leaning on her shoulder. She did not want to irritate the already ruined stitching of her jacket. The delirious man muttered nonsense of oceans and drowning things and held on to her blindly. Weill stared at the melted remains of their necromancer. Too many body parts and facial features were still recognizable in their agony, a fate she was sure was Venner's doing somehow. A fate she did not want to share. As often as she had witnessed this sort of death, it never got any easier. Rather, every death made her feel closer and closer to her own.

The shadows of a lone spear, Iramir's mercy, chased the flickering of the room-consuming inferno. Iramir attempted to stem her nosebleed with the back of her hand and seemed intent on doing nothing more but waiting. Blood seeped between her fingers and dripped down her chin.

"Claire," started Weill. A sharp glance from Iramir shushed the hound. Whatever was to be done, Weill understood their return to the Library had to come first. The pocket world creaked, unable to handle its own weight. Weill loosened the chains that held the travel anchor off her back while making sure she still had a good grip on Venner.

This was a do-it-yourself emergency portal. The anchor was a collection of odds and ends not fully burned to ashes from the sanctum. Iramir had quickly duct taped half-decayed antlers carved with Nordic incantations to a photographer's tripod. There was no time for proper attunement to a destination elsewhere.

"Are you sure this'll be alright? We're aiming blind here," said Weill. The room was compacting as the pocket world imploded. "We might end up someplace we don't want to be if we don't take the time to count coordinates."

"It will be fine," said Iramir with an ease that Weill could not understand. Iramir picked through a ravaged first aid kit. "Besides, we are aiming for the infinite ocean. A landless mark quite difficult to miss." She wiped the blood off her false skin with a clean cloth and some rubbing alcohol.

Weill took a shard of flint taped to the tripod and struck the idols. The sight of flames mixed and congregated into a curtain of light. Weill stepped aside to let Iramir settle their destination. Iramir refused, abandoning the tripod. Surrounding landscape faded away like a burning photograph into absolute darkness. Iramir took Venner by the hand, wiped the blood off his forehead, and whispered to him, "Obey me, ocean."

The dark dropped away, revealing a set of massive lapis doors. They were the doors home, with nary a consideration for proper sorcerous procedure. Weill's grasp tightened on the pointless idols and tore the tape. The Lion's Gate of Babylon opened wide and awaited the return of their Sovereign Moon.

The Lion's Gate deposited them into Iramir's office without their idol compass. Weill remained astonished at the swift change of scenery. It couldn't have been this easy. She looked all around the office for any sign that they'd actually landed in some terrible place in disguise. Iramir closed the doors behind them, and on this side, the lapis doors seemed no more absurd than standard office modesty.

Venner groaned. Weill stiffened and, eager to avoid touching him any longer, hoisted him onto a desk. In her effort, she knocked over several stacks of documents and paper binders. The office was another nest of Iramir's cluttered decorum. Weill scratched the back of her neck, not quite as eager to restack papers.

Iramir waited at the latches and then opened the doors again. She peered out into the empty hallways. They were right back within the Library of Babylon, out of the fire and into the cold. Iramir was about to leave, but Weill stopped her.

"Claire, what the hell? What if we got lost? You can't just—" Weill grew crestfallen. Their dangerous escape would not have been necessary if she could control her own magic. Iramir knew better. Iramir would always be better. To question this fact served only to remind Weill she would never be better. It was a long, downhill slip and slide, and she was racing. "Are we really leaving him alone again? He's . . ."

Weill checked behind her at the sound of Venner moving on the desk. He was rubbing his head, examining his new surroundings. He laid his head back against the hardtop. Bloodstained loose documents creased from his thrashing. "He's troublesome," said Weill.

"There are a few places as secure as my office within the Library but nowhere else as private," said Iramir, scraping the fresh cracks across her porcelain hands. Weill huffed a sharp "stop," and Iramir ignored Weill with a wave. "Listen, Weill, I have no intentions to announce him to Grimleer, and I accept the risk."

Weill knitted her brow and bit back her tongue. She didn't like being rebuffed, but there was little to be done about that. Iramir always refused to speak about herself and her damage. It was just business all the time. Heavy silence and a slight shift of the eyes were the only warnings before Iramir exercised her authority, which she did often and without hesitation.

Iramir led Weill outside the office. "Eram is unable to act without another party," she said. "My office should be more than enough to handle him. In the meantime, finish your reports. You know what to say. Return as soon as you can and keep watch, out of Grimleer's sight, please."

"That's it?" asked Weill. Buying time, she flicked the punctured lighter open and closed. Lighter fluid had leaked and made the casing slick to the touch.

"Still worried? You are not going to end up—"

"I am," said Weill. "It's inevitable for everyone." Iramir closed the doors with a heavy metallic rattle. Moonlight sparked at Iramir's touch as she drew symbols down the latches.

"Then visit the thaumaturgists down in the labs if you are so concerned. Moonlight should be good enough to watch him then." Iramir tested the spell by opening and closing the doors.

"I didn't mean for you to do everything," mumbled Weill. She took her turn trying to open the door. Yeah, they were locked. The undercurrent of sorcery pricked her fingers and lurked around her grasp. Weill attempted to brute force the doors, and at the point she could feel the latches yield, her grip slipped from the blood on her hands. Faint cuts lined her fingers, a warning. To open these doors without Iramir's permission spelled casualty, or maiming at minimum. Weill wiped down the latches with her sleeve. Iramir's authority was bolstered by the fact that she wouldn't hesitate to hurt others.

Iramir wrote something else on the door. "You get the one," she said. "If you need another, it is because something has gone wrong and you will break down the doors anyway. Fair?" Weill nodded, keeping her hands well away from the latches. "It will be alright. I will make sure that you, along with all the others, will find the support you need. The Library will prosper. Before you leave, Weill, help Eram get comfortable, please. Calm, I mean. If you have immediate need of me, I will be with Samuel."

"Alright."

"And I am sorry about the apartment," added Iramir, apathetic as ever. "Are there any immediate requests for recompense?"

Weill soured. "Yeah, whatever. I'm in good hands. You always have these mishaps fixed up. Don't think me ungrateful now."

"Always. For the good of the Library and its persons."

Heading down the stairs that led from her office, Iramir paused on the fifth step. Weill closed the lighter with a final thunk. There was little else up here except the office and the gardens. The Moon kept herself far from the bustle of the lower levels. Iramir combed her hair over her cracked face and settled the great coat properly over her shoulders to hide some of the blood. The first footfall upon the sixth step summoned the lions from hiding. Their ears perked up at the sight of their Sovereign Moon and waited for her to pass by. They flanked her, escorting her wherever she needed to be.

Weill waited until Iramir was out of view before heading down herself. There were no lions to greet her from behind monuments and alcoves. The Library was more hospital-like these days, coldly clinical but compassionate. The clean-cut and high storied atriums were white and spotless. The ornaments of an aging renaissance had been moved into storage. Bronze castings of dead visionaries or collections of star-seeking tools, she used to read their brief histories on the plain-cut placards mounted next to them.

She was especially fond of the placard descriptions of taxidermied creatures. Stuffed specimens once roamed the halls. A lesser Ander's lundwurm had been posed hunting a red tailed deer in front of the first occult wing on the ground floor. As a cousin of the major draconis, it lacked the ability to breathe fire, but compensated its hunting prowess with a corrosive venom. The lundwurm had been declared extinct over a decade ago.

Instead, the Library harbored glimpses of polished machinery, ancient monoliths, and the people who attended them with spiraled notebooks in hand. She caught glimpses of golden lions standing guard at each archive wing, with a claw raised and flexed in quiet intimidation, glimpses of the sorcerous river that rippled above her, harboring tiny satellites and carelessly lost pens and glasses.

Weill made a return trek with a fresh hospital gown and a roll of clean bandages lifted from medical storage. If someone did find Venner, he wouldn't look too far out of place, just lost. She left ashen handprints on the white fabric. Whatever. Weill entered the office to find Venner trying to strike a match for the many candles that lounged in Iramir's possession.

"Those are safety matches," said Weill. "They'll only light with the box. We're in a library." An invading hallway study was damn better than the fire hazard that was the office. Candles were stowed too closely to dry books and their wax catches overfilled.

"There is no light anywhere else," said Venner. Weill shrugged. Only the laboratories were outfitted with modern electrical systems. The rest of the Library was slow going. Weill pointed to a box filled with wire spools and bulb housings hidden behind stacks of papers.

"Iramir planned to do it herself. She just doesn't have the time, like all the time. No time for other people either. She hates everyone, wants to keep away like they don't matter. I'm just a bar of morale to keep full. Try the desk."

Venner explored her suggestion, diving between documents and opening drawers. Weill adjusted the brim of her cap, carefully watching Venner in his motions. He seemed alright enough. She inspected the bandage roll, not particularly keen on helping him patch up either. His wounds hardly seemed too severe, and he was active and up.

"Does it hurt, your chest?" asked Weill. Venner laughed with a distinct unease.

"I, uh, I feel good, actually. Fairly pleased, like a full meal, like I had just solved something amazing." He wiped his thumb across the points of his lower teeth. Good enough for her. Weill tossed the roll onto the table as it clattered against the books.

Her thoughts turned to herself. She was still capable. She was the hound of the Library. Her lance, its fang. The title made Weill feel important. She wasn't going to roll over for nothing. She was distinguished. She was different, above the senselessness of decay. She was more than a rotting body in a trash bag. *Dream bigger. Be heroic.* These words were stolen from a passing billboard verbatim.

Venner stacked journals taped shut on top of the desk and continued to search the drawers. He found a silver box filled with a guardian spirit and bounced it in his hand. Weill watched. She had held highest honors in her class, which had granted her the appointment. Tonight was an utter mockery of that title. She flexed her hand. More often than not these days, she felt she was clawing at nothing. She missed those moments in childhood where she conjured fire from believing instead of from some tool like a lighter or lance. Hound of the Library, the least impressive by far. The paragon protector, and she could barely do her own magic.

"Do you want to be more?" asked Venner suddenly. A smile crept over him that Weill could not stand. There was something wrong with him, and she wasn't staying to find out what it was. Weill rolled her shoulders and bared her teeth before throwing the gown at him.

"Put this on," growled Weill. He winced at her tone and obeyed. "Someone'll be back shortly." Weill exited the office and made sure the doors were still locked with Iramir's spell. She coughed. Her bile tasted of lighter fluid and salt. If there was ever an all-cure, Weill decided then and there, she would not hesitate to spend her life for that scant hope. Anything to be useful for the good of the Library, to play the part of some grand savior, or at least, a part of that part. Heroes can't end up in trash bags.

# NINETEEN

WHETHER GILDED THREAD CHASED MAGIC OR MAGIC FOL-
lowed thread was a distinction Venner didn't care to contemplate. The
coexistence between the two was enough to be immediately enticing.

Weill walked out of the office, and sparks of neon vibrated along
magic's fragile patterning in her wake. An overlay of gilded webbing
shimmered across the surface of the doors. Having witnessed a living
city, he understood that these walls too might carry sorcery, impenetrable until not. Was it the final rot of his sanity that caused things to lose
names and become shapes brimming with gold to be devoured?

He had not found Weill's supposed matchbox, and the outside provided him only dim solace. The windows had frosted over, the world
beyond protected by an impenetrable blur. The Library could be anywhere. In the quiet, however, he knew at least it was not the city. His
vision was adjusting to the dark anyway.

His attention fell upon the box of lighting equipment, and then he
scanned the ceiling to find the leads that should trail from a transformer
or the like. Hot and neutral wires were used to complete the circuit. They
needed to be routed from the transformer through a switch to the fixture. The ground wire typically attached to bare metal plate as protection
from overvoltage. He had to shut off electricity at the fuse box first.

Venner blinked in a state of strange confusion. His mundane thoughts
sat oddly in his head as if they were never meant to fit. He scratched at
his wounds, an itch less painful and stranger, as if felt from far away. The
workings of a roaming hand, the slight stretch of his skin against sutures,

the sensations of exhausted eyes sliding in their sockets took nervous priority over sheared flesh, and all felt sickening. The giddy happenstance of a good distraction was fading quickly and demanded to be refreshed.

He was tempted by a nearby silver puzzle box, but for the moment felt too nauseated to move. Familiar reports stood rank and file on the shelves, the Library their research facility source. The pages were stamped in blue ink with a winged lion beneath a full moon and the words, *Property of the Third Gate of Babylon, Library Complete.*

He finally reached for the puzzle box, which opened under his touch, the gear teeth gently riding his thumb. After solving hundreds of these curious things, he had gotten quite proficient at their signs and patterns. He pulled gilded thread, stark against the darkness, between his fingertips. He watched luster dry and dull until the threads snapped into dust. They were not puzzles, but the homes of inexplicable lives. The bear had come out on its own and done its rough diligence. Yet they were always empty.

Venner traced the flat walls inside this house. He closed the shutter, keeping pressure with his thumb because it would open on its own with nothing inside. Or, more precisely, he had broken the seal, and he could not spin the magic to put it back together. He let go, opening the shutter, and the accountant stared back, a pile of melted disgrace.

He shoved the box back in the drawer and slammed it closed. He shook the water off his hand and bit his knuckles. Empty shapes that displaced water invaded his ocean. They pitted his wondrous uniformity. They mocked his divine work. These bodies of frustration could only be unraveled by the tugging and cutting of gilded heartstrings. Unravel the unwary inhabitant of a silver house and fill the empty space with brine.

Then what protected people from an ocean's hunger and frantic hands? What protected the accountant from his boiling insides and the hopes and dreams of a broken body? That one moment did not feel any different from countless, nameless creatures he had taken apart in the name of idle entertainment. His enjoyment was rote. By every puzzle increment, he grew more bored.

Desire let him in within the confines of other people. He followed the golden trail of their desires crumb by crumb to their very shapes. Give people what they wanted and they were exposed, cut open on his teeth, and then they drowned as water poured in. *Devour their names. Celebrate the nothingness. Sow cancer within the grammar of sorcery. Magic turned autoimmune disorder.*

He needed only to solve desires, like how a puzzle box demanded interaction. Strumming heartstrings of magic demanded the echo of its own needs. If he matched just the right frequency, the ocean was poured into these shapes of people, erasing their insipid existence. He could not explain exactly how, but there was an otherworldly perception that tapped perfectly in time.

Weill of fire and burning paw prints had scored the dreaming shoreline, invading just like legfull things. He had felt the desire to be more, to be greater than the mortal, failing shape that housed her. He had missed with his first guess, accountant solution not quite applicable. No spark of connection, no travel way for endless water to pour into. Weill's shape refused him. No two layouts of people alike. He wondered if she had noticed, and then he clutched his aching head. He wanted more outsider voices to silence, more beating hearts to rupture. He could not stop smiling.

Were there more people like the accountant, dressed to the nines of sorcery so taunting? He ran his thumb over his lower teeth again. The abstract jaw lived in his ocean, made from the broken bodies of moons. He laughed, his body shaking from exhaustion, and wiped over his stitched wound to clean up wet remnants, then dug his fingers into the gashes. He was chasing the whine of the living, breathing thing beneath his sutures.

Fulfillment of his compulsion gifted him ecstasy. The matter had been cleaved, and all things would be fed into the ocean. A thousand writhing people would make a good number. A Library staffed with people that Weill had to meet and Iramir had to attend to. A Library staffed full of those to be stripped of their identities. He wrung his wrists. They had eyes. Eyes multiplied amongst the facets of a broken flashlight lens. It did not matter if they were made from paper or flesh. They had to be unmade. By every puzzle increment, he was ever mesmerized.

He tried to open the doors. Locked, even from the inside. Magic weaved across the latches denied him. Digested puzzle box shapes bled together into a massless mess and satiated nothing. Everything he ate left him with a deeper hunger. There was an accountant-shaped obsession in him.

He rested his head against the door. Giddiness started at the back of the head. He could devour a whole library beneath his ocean. There was satisfaction in having things fall into place, of stonework buildings collapsing into the water and people drowning in whirlpools. This was the pleasure of absolute silence after a behemoth storm and the surface of an ocean quelled and clean. He would take scissors to the lines of magic that commanded reality and open wide for feasting.

He grabbed threads and wound them within his grasp, snapping them easily, one by one. He leaned his head back and swallowed a length of gold. It tasted like a moon.

# TWENTY

"ARE YOU CERTAIN, CLAIRE?" ASKED SAMUEL HELLION, appointed advisor to the Sovereign Moon. He flipped through the pages of a much-redacted work, salvaged by Claire herself. Samuel rubbed his forehead. It worried him enough that Claire had returned hurt, but to also be reminded of one of the Library's worst shames was even worse. He waved his hands and said, "Unimaginable. I mean it. A successful engine that's real, living, working?"

"Coming home from work," said Claire. Samuel scoffed.

"And where does it come from? A sanctuary or some heavenly haven? That's much easier to swallow than an evening commute."

Claire softly laughed, but the corners of her mouth still dropped. "He functions, Samuel. I do not know how or from where, but I assure you, he is capable. The Library will be saved if we are only a bit creative about it."

"I want a second opinion," said Samuel. Claire ignored him as she always did when she thought she knew better. The Library was now a misleading moniker. The days of free spirit and charity were shut behind lapis doors. There would be no one else to confer with outside these walls, and no one inside allowed to peer into her office.

An everlasting night watched over them under the apple tree of Claire's private garden, cultivated on the upper towers of the Library. The moon, alone, sat upon its throne of the evening sky. All the stars had been harpooned into the ocean by fishermen of distant epochs. Nets cast into the hidden sea pulled onto their decks an iron bounty of fallen meteors. This metal stone made the Library. Their narwhal bone hooks still hung flagship in the main lobby.

Nothing climbed higher than the full moon. No phases hid away the majesty. Impossibly near, this celestial god dominated the heavens. Its lower edges barely brushed the horizon. The sheer gravitas affected by sorcerous ingenuity lifted the Library—an immense castle cobbled together with changing sensibilities—into the sky. Towers grew from misplaced cliffs. Wings were built under dishonest gravity. In the vaults, the Library hoarded all that the moon pleased, and once upon a time, the vaults were open for the advancement of man.

The ocean, infinite and empty, stirred far beneath them, lapping at the heels of the floating Library. There were no more stars to harvest, nothing vibrant to be found. It nurtured only death. The apple tree used to bear fruit in Claire's formative years, back when she went without a name but existed as a spirit in a glass bottle looking out to sea. He remembered holding the jar in his arms as he showed her around the Library. He'd been smitten with that dream, with pressing his fingertips against the glass and having a spirit gravitate closer and nudge back. He remembered promising to bring her fresh apples to try.

Now, the tree bore only salt, which solidified on the branches from the ocean spray. The ocean had not used to reach so high. Now it eroded the Library's foundation. Claire stretched back in her seat before attending to the new reports and risk assessments that the Library produced in its meantime, thankfully penned on more fruitful matters than dead engines. She swirled her coffee, letting the sugar dissolve away. Samuel poured himself another cup, careful not to spill again on the lattice table. The medals on his lapel glinted in the moonlight. The Swiss flag was sewn above them as a personal distinction.

Salvation was a depressing topic. Magic was failing everyone, regardless of circumstance. The intrinsic spark waned within the lifeblood. A color fell through the rainbow. Thaumic possessions like third eyes and sixth senses were cut to two and five. Only forms insulated from magic seemed immune. Something was wrong with the world. The Library, long ago, chose itself to shoulder the divine duty of righting such wrongs.

Whitepapers named this solution the world engine, though the cynic called it a virus. It was designed to be a universal tool, the perfect obelisk, to not only uplift the personal spirit but to source magic indefinitely and indiscriminately. An unstoppable force to power all manner of impossibility in a world where the natural laws refused to shelter their poor. Believe and make abject existence submit. The worth of all life will defeat deathly finality.

However, such indiscriminate ease was likened to potent virality, and therefore, difficult to contain. Had an engine existed, it may have been capable of connecting with users without explicit permission. Even mere contact could expose users. To source such power without proper failsafe or anticipation could easily be fatal. A tool as such may be impossible to tame once out of control.

The world engine project was canceled decades ago due to unviable results and rampant costs. No engine was able to transform intent into result. All test units were then destroyed. They were too dangerous for storage. The best security was to not exist.

Then enough nerve moved Samuel's tongue. "Claire, it's not that I doubt you, but an absurd miracle like this demands Grimleer's attention. An engine's merely an assumption. I'll speak to Grimleer on your behalf if you wish." Claire had scanned through a brief report revision proposing an adjusted treatment schedule for failed bodily transfigurations and, evidently satisfied, signed her name as final approver just below the header.

"It might only be a false positive," suggested Samuel. "The project was a failure. The transplanted specimens died during their first attunement. The single one that survived had its insides melt and its head cracked open on try two. And yet, an engine is just alive out there? Free, even?"

"Well, I can see that fact bothers you greatly," Claire said. "May I ask that we do not engage in one of those conversations tonight? Let us keep firmly on the subject now." Samuel sipped his coffee. The fact that an engine had more freedom than Claire very much frustrated him. Her porcelain skin passed very well in the moonlight. By morning, however, it was quite easy to catch her artificial tendencies, and that would only garner unwanted attention. She would never be allowed outside that long anyway.

"Could it be just coincidence that an alchemist got lucky?" asked Samuel. "We can't claim it as ours. There are too many hoops to jump through just to leave the Library without triggering an alarm, much less with such precious information."

"We know people like this," Claire said, capping her pen. "We know worse things have happened without triggering an alarm, and neither do I claim we are the only institute capable of nurturing abominations."

"So one of our ex-employees got lucky then? The only thing we have hemorrhaging faster than our researchers is our dignity. We're on the lips of children as bogeymen." It was time to change the subject. Letting the conversation lull, Samuel took a moment to listen to the ocean and watch the garden flow in the sea breeze. "We need a proper test to find out what makes this engine different. If it is indeed the ocean, then we might be able to salvage a bit of our previous work. Better than starting from nothing. We have better technology this time."

"The engine has a particular ability to capture the perception," said Claire. She reached up to pluck a shard of salt that burdened the lower branches. "I was not physically transported anywhere, but I fell from the sky into the ocean. Like caught in a dream, Samuel, for the moment such idea made sense." Claire inspected the white crystal, letting porcelain fingers rub away salt a layer at a time. He hated the cracks of her face that ran beneath her collar. "The engine knows how to start a cascade."

Samuel chewed the inside of his cheek. Mordrem's cascade, a fatal phenomenon where magic decayed in a way that destroyed its user. Causes included overwork, excessive exhaustion, or even simply existing. There was something incompatible between the immaterial and the real. Not that Claire should be suffering from such an agonizing fate. The Library had an entire department meant to research cascade and its effects, but cascade realistically could only be managed. Its solved cases could never be repeated, as if reality was quick in plugging its loopholes.

Claire frowned. "I am not that fragile," she said. "Do not look at me like that."

Samuel did not apologize. She guided him away from holding her cheek. She allowed him only one moment. Porcelain never felt as warm as flesh. He tugged at her collar where blood dried into rust. Samuel straightened, let go, and grabbed his cup to take another sip but did not. He opened his mouth to speak. Claire stood up.

"I am an Iramir. I am the Sovereign Moon. The throne has been mine alone for years. The ocean is beneath me, and the ocean will obey me. I am not a child, Samuel."

Samuel closed the project files. She grew up with too little fear of a world beset with danger. Dangers were labeled so because they tested bravado and slayed those who failed. He pined for the softer conversations of minor quibbles and gentle inconveniences. She had asked for a cat two or three years ago. The request was denied because such an animal was deemed purposeless, Grimleer's words. Samuel said the cat would be miserable in the Library with too many rules.

There were lions, though they were Grimleer's tools. They functioned as keepers of the Library and its things. It was not the same. She was furious in her quiet way when she had found out Samuel had adopted a cat instead. Beans, a grey and white tabby, lived under the television set, chewing the wires. He made sure every kitty milestone was documented, as many interactions recorded, and he saved photos up to a thousand-fold just to share with her. He shared the country postcards, the videos of travelers from far and wide, of folk dances and midnight bonfires sparkling in town squares. She only left the Library—only another glass jar—to settle the unsavory valor of dry politics. Her caging was his failing.

"The world engine project was the Library's most damning disgrace. The fall of virtue," said Samuel. "Those children are not wrong when they look under their beds for us. Those people are not wrong when they open the door with a weapon in hand. People were counted by their weight in raw material. A damned consciousness rationalized taking people that no one would miss. A lie, Claire. There's no one that can be described like that. You shouldn't be reading through these shames. It, he," said Samuel in disbelief, "cannot exist. I'd like a new leaf."

"We do not have skeletons in our closet. They are taken, they are catalogued, and they are arranged on their backs to make our foundation," said Claire. "Our intention, my intention, is to save my Library, to save those who walk my halls, to save our dying world. I will stop this blight and usher us into a new age of prosperity. An endless sun to make irrelevant the stillborn souls." A close enough paraphrase of Grimleer's words again.

Samuel bit back, "And some of ours who have walked these halls with lower morals stole that same technology for a god delusion. There was too much sacrifice for a dream, and their scraps were too real to forget. We killed. We were very good at killing, slobbering over what if."

"We move forward. Saintly hands or otherwise," said Claire. "We are living in a dying era. Something is wrong in the center of our reality. A ravenous maw pursues the living, collapsing entire civilizations. We feel it prick the back of our necks, the bones of our soothsayers, and the glass eyes of mystics. The world is tainted and negligent. Existence demands turnover, restructuring, and everyone is scared. I simply want stability. Risks are risks, Samuel."

The Library in the absence of her mother needed leadership, or at least some physical representation that legacy had not abandoned them. Grimleer built upon the remains of the engine project to fill that void. Claire was the only good to ever come of that dark venture. Through her threats and domination, the Library was given nearly everything it ever wanted. Blood instead of trust. Long-term investments, she had told him, were too optimistic for her in a world that may perish the next morning.

She was not responsible for this. Do not follow the beast into darkness. It should not be hers to tame, as it was born from the optimism of a naïve generation passed. "Claire, I'm going to talk with Grimleer about the engine. This is our responsibility. Your mother would not have wanted this for you."

"It is because she died that I may exist," snapped Iramir. The garden, the ocean, the Library disappeared into black, and he sat underneath the spotlight of a moon for one scathing moment. He shut up. "In a forgiving world, my mother would have begot a real child. Any of the six of them. I am a contingency, a doll made to sate guilt and rally the flags. Remember that you should not have named me. Your sentimentality is interfering with work. I will do what the world no longer can. Alone, if I have to."

Conversations with her always raised the same thorns. She reminded him of his work and then reminded him how temporary she was. Turning the thumbscrew, she would reiterate her purpose to scour the world for the Library's aching solution. She would suffer if she must.

She did not continue. Samuel supposed it was because she had more immediate concerns. The most painful turn was the reminder she was no different from scrap after completing her duty. Grimleer's Library had no room for items of spent, singular purpose. She was devout to her death, just as planned. There was too much of Grimleer in her. Often it seemed as if all the time Samuel had spent with her simply escaped into the ocean. As Grimleer would say, noble purpose demanded self-sacrifice and diligence above all else.

"You are more than a doll," said Samuel through clenched teeth. "I've watched you grow up. You're alive. I didn't—I didn't mean to imply you were lesser because you're stuck here."

Claire rubbed the bridge of her nose in irritation. "Samuel, enough." He stood up. The chair scraped over the pavers. He cleaned up the cups of coffee. The rattle of cups signaled his haste.

"I should've brought the hot chocolate," he muttered. "It's cold up here, and the ocean's a menace. Something much sweeter would be better. I'd much rather be in my office. You remember where everything is? Claire?"

Claire checked the time on her phone, beheld her ocean, and then crossed her arms. "Yes," she said with a drop of her shoulders. "Lowest two drawers, second cabinet from the right of the door." Her gaze did not waver from the dark waters.

He kept blankets and cheap, instant hot chocolate kits complete with mugs and a hand crank lantern in that drawer. He would heat milk for his hot chocolate instead of water because he had standards. He used to pitch a misplaced tent in the middle of his office when career politics were out of mind. Turn off the lights and let the eternal night sneak in. Set a lantern on a tower of books and tell her stories when she nestled in his lap. He missed those younger days.

Shadow puppet creatures and folklore maxims, Aesop, Homer, him. In between the lessons and legends, he would wax lyrical about the working world outside. The rivers and mountains, the deserts and beaches, and the people that occupied them. Not just their mythos, but them.

To wake, work, love, and hate. To live. Really, Samuel knew he was just gossiping about his neighbors, but there was more to be had than her coursework in mathematics and alchemy.

"I'll take you camping one day," said Samuel, leaning against the table. "I want you to witness a world free from contracts or research, just the lovely expanse. There will be real stars. It'll be once, just once. It won't be a bother to business at all."

"I do not need real stars," whispered Claire. "I just need"—she sighed and shook her head—"I just need you, Samuel. You want the stars seen from Andermatt where you will take me home one day, I know. But I prefer the flashlight stars here." Samuel used to plaster butcher paper and tin foil over the windows and walls of his office. He made do even if a flashlight could not really replicate the stellar majesties. That was so long ago. All those toys and supplies hidden because Grimleer had warned him about becoming too attached.

"You need real stars," said Samuel. He kept framed one of Claire's revision spells, a page cut from her tutoring assignments. The shaking lines, the novice inefficiencies, but a star was a star even it was simply glass and fire. "I still keep your star hanging right in front of me." Claire hid her growing embarrassment under her hand. Samuel laughed.

"You have promised to take me outside for as long I have been alive," said Claire, finally shifting her attention away from the ocean. "It always makes you miserable when you talk about it."

"I mean it. If that engine is truly capable, then you'll be free," said Samuel. Claire made a strange expression. Samuel lit with sudden relief. "You'll be free," he repeated. "If we cannot use the engine as is, we'll dissect it. We'll make it properly ours, and all our problems will be solved. No more floundering for false promises or chasing dead-end ideas. You won't have to shoulder the failures of the Library."

"Eram needs to be taken home. I am to take care of everything of the Library's make, and he matters too."

"It doesn't matter. It's just an engine." He gestured for her to follow him back into the halls of the Library. Claire ignored him, walking away towards the center of the gardens. Grass crushed underfoot. Tall lilacs swayed and trailed her outstretched hands.

She drew a summoning circle in the air with moonlit ink, detailing the specifics with swift fingers. The stone shuddered underneath them. The apple tree rustled from the rumbling. Heavy chains rose from the dirt, dripping petals and leaves across the tumbling links. Spiraling from hidden aqueducts, water flowed droplet by droplet up from the garden. Suspended in the air by a ring of chains was a rippling blue sphere of swirling water and light entwined by her magic. It grew, towering over the silhouette of a small girl. The garden was bathed in this azure light under the starless skies.

"The world falters on occasion. What exists suffers. Yet wherever the living are failed, I must provide. I want to do what I can to quell the frightening tomorrow," Claire said. "An engine would save the Library, I understand."

The repository was the beating heart of the Library, an energy source that kept the facility floating and was used to fuel research. Its water had been derived from the ocean by methods that were no longer possible. Knowledge was fed into it, and it breathed insight. She approached her inheritance. Her halo draped from behind her, stemming from the metal shard. Samuel grimaced at the reminder.

A mage needed a focus to attune magic. It could be something inanimate such as a staff or wand, something living such as a familiar, or it could be the breathing self. Magic relied on the reflections memories made. Magic lived within the imprint of oneself, wandering and affecting the world. That shard was made from the blade that had killed her mother. The matter of a death was hushed quickly and quietly. It was simply an accident.

Liquid tendrils coiled around her outstretched hand. She called for the world engine, for the names of its romantics and the hands of its architects. The subtle acquisition of redacted documents from the archives was a trivial matter for Claire's authority. Access to the repository was surveilled entirely. Samuel sighed at her swift hypocrisy, having just chided him on wanting to inform Grimleer. It was ideal nonetheless. It meant she was deferring to them.

The repository reported to Grimleer, as Grand Magister and the repository's primary keeper, those that accessed its knowledge and on what—not even Claire could hide her usage. Grimleer preferred the written word and from the waters, he typically produced a stack of documents to peruse in his downtime. Claire preferred the intimate. She beheld the dreams of the Library with a feeling of intuition over confidential matters.

Samuel wondered how invasive that would have felt, whether the repository was kind enough to make room. He would not know. No ordinary mage could attune with it. The Library's mortal blow would fall upon the day there would be no one left to access these archives. Knowledge that once sat in the palms of their hands would be lost between their grasp forever.

Not all things were fed into the repository. There were always those bits of tribal knowledge, of informal conversations lost to the wayside. Samuel spied her slight frown. Good. No one wanted their failures or crimes immortalized. To ultimately announce to the world that atrocities had been committed for nothing. Certainly Grimleer knew how to circumvent Claire. The matter of an engine should be kept firmly out of Claire's hands and only between him, Grimleer, and a few of the old guard. She needed only to reap the reward.

Claire rubbed the bridge of her nose again and produced a vial from her pocket. The dark liquid it contained gleamed in the light. "I will talk to Grimleer myself," she said.

Samuel was surprised. "Claire, you should get some rest. I'll call the doctors for your repairs."

"You will return to your duties," ordered Claire. "We will have our engine. Rest assured."

# TWENTY-ONE



**THE LIBRARY WAS AS CALM AS THEIR PATIENT, PANTHERA** guards intended. An artificial lion made its round to the highest point of the Library available. It paced along the sixth step down from the Sovereign Moon's office. Soft footpads brushed along the marble steps. The lion slid its front paws forward and let a roll of stretching muscles sweep down its back and curl the tip of its tail. It yawned wide and shook itself with a huff.

Movement of the door latches alerted the lion, who turned its head and perked its ears. It sat down awaiting the journey of Iramir, its Sovereign Moon. The lion liked this moon the most. Iramir did not have the scent of people. She was pure like all creations of the Library, sweet to the senses and gentle to the touch.

It was, quite curiously, a man instead. He peered suspiciously from her office for a moment, and then walked out. Physical moonlight cracked around him along the outline of the doors. Sentries made from her austere light failed to activate. These shattered white shapes splashed across the walls and ceiling. The edges of these shapes started to round and drip luster onto the landing, painting it in a gleaming brilliance but leaving behind a darkness where magic spoiled.

The man brushed chips of hard light off his shoulder, caught sight of the lion, and then raised a finger to his lips. The lion leaned down and growled. It attempted to climb higher, but its paw flattened against an invisible wall. Outstretched claws skidded and sparked across the barrier. It did not know how the man had gotten there. Only a few people were able to climb above six. It stretched its jaws again, tongue sliding across its fangs.

From behind the wall, the man stopped on the fifth step and said something the lion couldn't hear. The man tapped at the invisible wall, disturbing the air into scintillating colors. The lion glowered at him. The man scratched at the surface of the barrier, but it had no effect. He investigated where the barrier would have intersected the walls, and the air warped to leave a trace everywhere he touched. Liquid moonlight escaped the office landing, traveling down step by step until it all collected before the barrier, becoming the visible boundary.

They met eyes again, and the lion repeated its guttural warning. It did not like being denied by a facet of the Library. It wanted in. The man kneeled down, placing a hand against the barrier as if he wanted the lion to copy him. The barrier denied it yet again. There was a good inch of empty space between them. The lion lay low and tense, ready to attack.

The man reached through the barrier and held the lion by its snout. The lion snapped its jaws and sank its teeth into his flesh. The man startled and observed his trapped, bleeding hand. The man's flesh tasted of salt and the ichor of alchemy. The lion let go immediately and stared at him. Growls simmered into inquisitive chirps. It sniffed his touch. It sniffed him. The man still smelled faintly human, perhaps leftover from his last user, but more importantly, he smelled of the very familiar ocean. The lion whined, ears pinned back. It hung its head in the man's wet grasp. It had made a mistake.

At heart, he was theirs, the Library's. The lions performed as shepherds for their dear flock of idols, instruments, and totems—all that was begotten or appropriated under the Library's banner. Vicious keepers, these shepherds of faint mercy, beating with the staff of a fanged maw all those that dared mistreat the ilk of the Library.

The lion plopped onto its side, keeping its gaze on the man. What a novel idea, an obelisk shaped like a man. He could walk himself, function for himself. The man slipped his salt fingers between the lion's teeth and pried its jaws gently open. The lion let the obelisk man follow the ridges of its canines and molars.

The collapse of a magic barrier peeled cinnabar petals from its own destruction. The lion batted at the falling petals, too wily in their movements. Mercury dripped from the barrier's growing lesions and mixed with the thin paint of melted moonlight that lit the steps. The man plucked a mineral petal from midair and tickled the lion on the nose with it. The lion sniffed and chuffed. It wrapped its paws around his arm and licked his skin. It enjoyed the salt.

Someone had been careless in putting the obelisk man away. Such carelessness needed to be reprimanded. He brushed through its mane and wrapped around its muzzle again. The man agitated his wound, and it tightened in pain. The smell of a human grew stronger. The lion whined for more attention. It had never had its back scratched before.

The man grew restless. "I want to leave. I should not be here," he said.

The lion pondered the request. All items of the Library were meant to stay within the Library, but it had never before encountered something that had asked to leave. The lion very much wanted to make the obelisk man happy, but he had to be safe most of all, even if that did make him a little unhappy. So the lion refused. It rolled onto its back, inviting the man to play again, to smile like he had when playing with its teeth. Moonlight clung to its fur in shining beads.

The man covered his eyes. "It is everywhere." He peeked through his fingers at the lion. "How can you all stand it?" The lion pressed its muzzle into his stomach and breathed hotly. The lion did not like the smell of a human growing more potent. The obelisk had to be returned to storage. The lion softly bit his undamaged hand and started to guide him down the steps. The man resisted the lion, but the lion pulled just enough to make him take a step. It kept doing that, patiently taking one step down the stairs to a faraway storage.

The lion felt the flex of the man's muscles between its teeth. He had dared to pull back against the sharpened grip. The lion let go, keeping its jaw wide to avoid harming him again. The man, failing to expect the sudden lack of resistance, slipped on the steps. The lion leapt into him and shouldered him from a long tumble. The obelisk was warm like they always were once running and going. The lion wanted to bask in this niceness.

"Please, there has to be a way out of here. Everything is wrong, even you are shaped too peculiar for your species." The lion whimpered. It wanted to save the obelisk and for it to feel safe. "Will you?" the obelisk asked, leaning into the lion's embrace. His fingers toyed within its fur. "Will you want me to go home?"

More of the barrier corrupted into darkness. More steps were dressed in blinding light. The lion licked his bloodied hand in apologies again. He flinched back. Iramir would know what to do, so it stretched its jaws and clicked its teeth together. Magic hummed within panthera bones. It approached the wall and scratched across the sideboards. The boards bent and broke into the shape of a hidden doorway. Frost and fog waved in and stirred in the breath of the lion. It could not see the destination, but it could smell the ocean.

The lion felt the weight of spiritual connection and the heat of magic filling its pores. It had not intended to use the obelisk man like a tool. Its own bones should have been enough. Yet the man had full access to its desires without permission. Strange, but not too terrible a problem. It did not want anything other than to help the obelisk.

Paws pattered about in the inch's worth of water that lined this extra space and spilled out into the Library proper, mixing with moonlit paint. The obelisk man entered the extra space. His grasp warped the outer edges of the hole. The lion groaned and lay down. Its heavy breathing disturbed the water. It felt tired. *It wanted the obelisk safe at home within the Library.* It nuzzled him. His touch hurt. It was scared he would be lost. Iramir would protect him.

# TWENTY-TWO

WARMTH AND THE SMELL OF SWEET INCENSE LINGERED IN THE office of Marcus Grimleer, Grand Magister and head of the Library's many sophist theurgic apparatuses. The bespectacled man stood before a fireplace, stoking the flames with a soot stained poker. He grabbed a half-cut log from a wood chest and stood it amongst the ashes. The wood began to crack and char. A lion lounged in front of the fire. Its tail swished along the floor. A researcher with notebook in hand reported to Grimleer.

"We're holding steady for now, much thanks to your expertise, Lord Magister. We are currently able to resonate twenty-eight of the thirty-five nodes. Though, our efficiency for fifth form attunement is . . . ," the researcher paused and folded a corner of a page, "diminishing. In the, well, rare likelihood we cannot achieve fifth form, as time passes, we may need to start sacrificing our extraneous activities to make do with diminishing resources and the shrinking energy cap. We need to set a limit that cannot be breached for the health of the Library or we'll fall into the ocean."

"And what do you propose? Every venture the Library undertakes is always with purpose. The collapse of our laws of sophistry demands innovation, desperation." Grimleer tugged at his beard, cleanly shaped and oiled. "Or sacrifice. Our solution may come from the oddest of places. Our life lines and our time are a resource, not an end goal. I understand that the levitation cipher has stopped responding to realignment procedures. Yes, yes, terrifying. But to cannibalize our own endeavors to impede the coming of midnight but a few minutes." Grimleer scoffed, digging the end of the poker into the mortar of the fireplace. His rings rubbed against the metal. "We must continue full steam no matter how dire our existence becomes. The world demands that we be adamant."

The researcher deflated. "We don't even have a year if we continue this pace, magister. All our efforts will be in vain. We need more time."

"The Library will not fall," said Grimleer. "I am the guardian of this wonder, and I have held this stead against plague and rapture. Reality will always find me difficult."

The researcher nodded and bade the magister good luck and a good day. "Magister," the researcher said at the door, "I believe we should merchant our work. We cannot save this place. Outside, we could lay profits several hundred, even thousand, fold. Our technology is worth more than legacy."

"Before I accuse you of treason, I will assume your talk is from a fear of failure," warned Grimleer. "Our halls are sacred, begotten from forces that the world can no longer fathom. Our work belongs to the betterment of man, not sold to scoundrels and corrupted fiends. The Library is not a secret club of failures hoarding treasure to be richest in an apocalypse. The Library is a divine trust. What we do here is because of the strength of existence to persist, because of the sea below us, and of the moon above. In return, we should aspire to be more than the common man." A shadow flickered beneath Grimleer's glasses as he adjusted with a finger to the bridge. "Leave."

The lion flanked the researcher, baring teeth and malicious eyes. The researcher left without another word, closing the door behind him. The lion returned to Grimleer, rousing to his touch as he bent down and brushed its fur. The Library's heart, a perpetual source of magic also used to power its own research, was failing, so the Library would slowly lose form and crumble. Its end was coming sooner than he had anticipated.

The lion laid its chin on his knee and Grimleer said his command: "There will be no more disturbances to the structural undercurrent of the Library, as its heart must not be stressed more than necessary." The lion whined to dissuade its master. "And thus, my lions must walk the halls properly and will be forbidden from folding Library space for travel until further notice."

There would be more gaps in surveillance as a result of slower patrols. So be it. The halls were his domain, bequeathed to him by the very legacy that blessed the Library. He had to keep his responsibilities well. That was the mark of a good man. The lion murmured that Claire was coming. Surprise, surprise.

The magister led the lion off his lap and brushed some stray fur off his leg. He walked over to his desk, tracing the corner with his hand. He cleared away some of his clutter, sorting reports and picking up the empty plates of silverware and crumbs. There was nowhere to place them other than the mess hall. Not that he had time for it. He reached over towards the side table and found more plates at his place of intention. That would not do, but it had to.

He then attended to his notes and the problem of waning sorcerous prospects. If base thaumaturgy would not do, then perhaps a return to more traditional alchemy might make for a finer solution. Perhaps simple was best.

Equivalent exchange, a reliable enough property. Desired results came about through offerings of equal value. The definition of equal value was at once strict but nebulous. Material transmutation was a science. The transmutation of reality itself, to pull and react to things that could not possibly be measured, was an art no one truly understood. That subset idea was the equivalent of throwing away a visualized future on pure hope. Such gambling was shameful.

There was no suitable replacement for a failing heart of the Library's need. The means were extinct. When reality conspired against itself, there was nothing to prevent reality simply saying no to the pleas of its constituents. Grimleer straightened his desk lamp. He took off his glasses and wiped the lenses with a faded cloth.

The Library would not suffer a dark age. No other magister before him had failed in their duties, and he would not be the first. He turned to the photos nestled amongst decorated achievements. They hid behind busts of old age scholars, and there were a few askew. He took to correcting them. He leveled the spines of his textbooks and journals to make more room.

Ah, he had looked so young then. He tried various angles of a photo of his team standing in front the operating theatre. The photo had been taken after their first successful recreation and rehabilitation of failed thaumic sources within terminal patients. No longer were these victims plagued by failing magic, by inaptitude for control, or by the mutilating decay of cascade. A new lease on life. His team's best success rate was one in three as processes improved, then the world faltered, and the dying had no recourse despite Grimleer's best efforts. His grey hairs and wrinkles were born from an age of worry.

Another framed photo captured them standing before the animated heart of a lunar familiar. Karina Iramir, the Sovereign Moon of his time and Claire's mother in a loose sense, stood front and center. The familiar had been meant to last a century, protecting the Library and controlling the ocean. An experiment conducted to master the elements of their own demesne. The familiar had gone missing, swallowed by the ocean, most likely.

The ocean was the Library's richest source of magic and its elements, perfect for providing the means of creation, but it was terribly hostile. It had claimed countless of his researcher's lives. One of the ocean's constants was that all who encounter the fateful Oceanus would be destroyed. Too difficult to replenish, the ocean's distillations then became too valuable to waste. These monuments forever taunted Grimleer about what could be if he simply did away with safety—if he flashed divinity in exchange for blood.

It unnerved him that despite the Library having existed solely in this domain, they had little understanding of the ocean it drew from. The ocean resisted all attempts of probing and inquiry and the sight of these modern-day magical regressions reminded him of just that. Waves could endlessly erode foundation. The ocean was ultimately confined in its own realm, but that was only an assumption. None of their research could ever verify it.

Where did the waterfalls lead to at the edges of the ocean if it did not fall back down as rain? There was little that could prevent the ocean from endlessly eroding reality. The inanimate were failing en masse, and the living were hardly any different. The quality of current magicians left something to be desired. He wondered if he was immune to the wasting of talent and body because he was born before these dying times or if it would simply take him longer. These morbid thoughts told of faraway things. The now had to be managed.

He folded the cloth and scrubbed dust from another photo frame. They had been on the cusp of their finest achievement: a world engine. Impossibility be damned. The power of gods in the hands of progress. The elimination of stratification amongst any and all people. The phenomenon of wasting magic was seen as part of the natural ebb and flow of time. However, predicted resurgences had failed to topple the sorcerous drought these past few centuries. The world had suffered a net loss, a fact easily measured. People of minor persuasions had heralded it as the end of days.

Yet even then, the Library worked miracles. They chained heaven by their fists. They were titans, but the world no longer supported titans. The earth was too fragile, and the air was too thin. The ocean no longer sustained. It had grown more insolent, threatening to devour his home should it fall ever lower.

His grip tightened on the frame. Karina's death was regrettable. It was an accident. At least her body had been reclaimed for good use, her organs saved and implanted into a doll. Grimleer pinched the bridge of his nose. He did not have the heart to do anything else but lay the photo down out of sight.

Familiar faces lived only in photographs. Most of his peers from his heyday had already departed, or simply died. Morale faltered across the Library. The sight of a hanged man in a third-floor office broke many more. A mass exodus of employees ensued in this bleakness. The Library's secrets were in jeopardy from more dishonest defectors.

Their longstanding suppliers dropped out of contact, and these were the blights that Claire spent much of her time fixing. Her efforts were of slight beneficial effects. It was increasingly difficult and frustrating to work with substandard equipment and material. Though he should not be so callous. There was only so much someone like her could do. She was a failsafe and nothing more. It should have never gotten to this point. They should have never devolved to such barbarity. The Library had once been the pride of Babylon.

Grimleer had cooled significantly in his elder years. His provocation in his prime could force reality to heel. Results oriented, no matter the cost. The prize was possession, proof of his superiority, not use. He was cursed with impatience, then the negligence of properly attending to consequence. Grimleer despised his younger self's imprudence. Every delay, every setback, every catastrophe culminated in an intolerable storm of behavior that caused present-day Grimleer to recoil in frustration. They'd gone faster and faster, and before they knew it, several thousand lives were consumed to understand an ocean.

So many mistakes were willfully overlooked because the promise of a perfect solution was too tempting. Growing pains, they rationalized. The reality was that they had no solution, and it was far too late to save what could have been. Things fell apart. Karina's health deteriorated over the course of the project. She had not produced an heir. The stillbirths were attributed to cascade. Everything was put on hold to attend to her, everything but the engine. Over a decade after her death, they had finally realized, raised, and then named a little spirit in a glass jar.

Grimleer found the book that hid his poison flask of choice. The dark amber was bitter and softly sweet, aged older than most of his current staff. There was a forwardness to Claire that he found as equally aggravating as his younger self. Impatience would be the death of men. There was a truth in the natural that could only be observed in peace. Yet, her bluntness did sharpen her threats. Bluffs belonged on maps, not before her presence. Her independence at least, he found admirable. He capped the flask and replaced the book. Hiding was a vestigial action. All of his staff drank openly.

It was cruel to expect Claire to match with her mother. Claire was made to be different and understand the very limits of her capability and responsibility. She was to provide for his Library and no more. His Library would be saved by his own hand and labor. The outside world would suffer as it must. So was the consequence of a world so negligent of its living.

The lion jolted to the door. It straightened and raised its claw. Grimleer returned to his desk. Claire entered. Her porcelain was cracked. There was blood on her clothes. He adjusted his glasses. The moon was fragile. That was another problem. Fragile bodies were an insult to noble intentions. Her appointed hound was a disgrace.

Fragile bodies made it difficult to consider a replacement. Not an easy venture to salvage already failing organs, but still possible. Occasionally, Claire's damage was too severe to repair with passable results. The accruing debt of surgeries made restoration ever worse. The doll grew more brittle every opportunity he let lapse for a new spirit to utilize those organs. There was nothing of consciousness these organs could hold on to. She had to be shattered, and the consciousness thus released, then the material requisitioned for a fresh doll to be inhabited by someone else.

Yet despite good material practice, he did not want someone else. Her name had been chosen by committee, and it was his suggestion.

Claire was meant to be the physical manifestation of the Library's authority, something to carry the Iramir name and assert such influence against the outside world. The Library would lose much of its sway if knowledge leaked that the legacy had been effectively undone decades ago.

Claire defied intentions. The spirit in a porcelain body had learned how to tug him by the sleeve to ask questions about magic sophistry. The spirit would hide in his laboratory whenever Samuel was too overbearing. Samuel had introduced her to music before he lost interest, then it fell upon him to continue that endeavor because he could not deny the spirit, her, whenever she caught him practicing in his office. The piano was long gone. Yet unlike Samuel, Grimleer knew how to temper her with duty first.

"Lady Claire," bowed Grimleer. "First matter, I must thank you for your negotiations with Harken. The laboratories will hardly have a day of respite with our new line of resources. However, your return is later than anticipated." Grimleer held his tongue on her appearance. So long as she was not broken, he had no concerns. Her repair would be scheduled soon. He sat back in his chair, resting his hands together on his lap. He watched her perhaps unwittingly trace the cracks of her body. "To what should I attribute this meeting? Or are you simply looking for a glib one-on-one?"

"What would you require to restart work on the world engine?" asked Claire, straight to the point.

Grimleer raised his eyebrows and glanced to his recent shelves. "Is that what you have demanded from the repository? I might have been notified of a glimmer of that. Lately, Samuel has been requesting I restrict your access to certain literature. Is that not insane?"

Claire followed his attention towards those figments of yonder days. "Samuel is just apprehensive about my position," she said. "It is rather ridiculous, yes, to hide from past mistakes. What else would provide that opportunity for growth?"

"Exactly. I do not know why you bother with that man. He should be kept solely to Library security and day-to-day admin instead of encouraging his private visitations. But I should hardly worry about you. You have yet to fumble your responsibilities. The care is well appreciated." Faint relief crossed Iramir's face. A relief, certainly, from knowing she was not alone in admonishing Samuel.

"Well," continued Grimleer, "my answer is no different from the repository's. Have you elucidated something rather miraculous that you think should be bothered with? Until I have something that changes the project landscape, it will stay defunct and shelved. We cannot afford to chase what is genuinely impossible."

"I do have something," said Claire. She kept her gaze on him and produced a small, corked vial of what was clearly blood. "Run this. I want a full report of its make. The base should be ichor." He wrapped the vial in a handkerchief. The vial contained enough for a few samples if conservative. It seemed quaint enough as he carefully raised it against the light. No immediate signs of any oddity, but that was why all things were tested.

"Where did you get this?" he asked. "You are implying this ichor is worth restarting such a resounding failure." It would have been sensationalist coming from anyone but Claire. There was a degree of veracity he had come to expect from her and the matters she shared with him. She trusted him, and thus he trusted her.

"Outside," Claire answered. Grimleer rubbed the bridge of his nose again, lifting his glasses along his knuckle. He let go, exhaled slowly, and straightened his glasses with a finger to the bridge. "And let us try not to have people run off with this knowledge," she continued.

"Our deserters are turncoats," said Grimleer with a scowl. "Is that the implication? That this vial was taken from a reject that could only owe their success to the groundwork the Library has laid? The world should not profit from the fruit of our divine providence."

"Alert me to your findings," said Claire, and swiftly left him to his devices.

# TWENTY-THREE

GRIMLEER FLICKED ON THE LIGHTS OF HIS PERSONAL LABO-
ratory. He locked the door, and his approaching footsteps lit the floor for
a moment. The measurement machines around his workspace began to
hum softly with the sounds of sorcery. Their spiritual anchors weighed on
him, making their connections with his source of magic. An imaginary
feeling but pervasive nonetheless. His devices awaited command. Stones
and hieroglyphs rose into the air. A summoning circle slowly began to
form as the devices warmed up. He navigated to his workstation.

He snugged on a new pair of nitrile gloves, carefully routing his fingers to not catch on his smoothbore rings. The vial was uncorked. The
stained stopper set on a cloth. He metered out half the substance in a
glass flask, then recorked the rest the vial on a rack.

He searched the drawers and found a thin metal prong wrapped in
sterilized protection. After opening the packaging, he inspected the vio-
let crystal inlaid within the metal for any defects before stirring it in the
liquid long enough for good saturation. The ichor substance bound to
the crystal. He turned to his computer to start a new test. Scratching his
brow, he read through the sticky notes plastered down the side of the
monitor. He should not have been so reliant on them, having assured
Samuel he could figure out the nuances of this technology on his own.

The data logger program began measurement. He carefully lifted
the soaked metal and transferred it over to his nearby devices, laying it
within the holds. A composition check needed only a brief moment. He
supported the floating summoning circle just above his hand and felt
pressure pushing back. Geometry reacted against the rings through the

glove. All magic started with the first echo to begin resonance, a small force supplied to zero the devices.

The crystal cracked instantly. Grimleer snapped back as shards fell to the floor. The summoning circle melted into a viscous, physical thing dripping in dull color. Pain started at his fingertips and quickly seeped into his arm, finding its way down into his marrow. Flesh constricted almost to the point of rupture. He struggled to avoid calling his rings on reflex. Any additional input of sorcery would encourage this destructive cascade. A hazardous prospect when a good mage has the habit of standing at the ready in uncertain danger.

Grimleer forced his shoulders to relax and waited for the echoes of resonance to fade away. It was genuine agony, slow in rise and fall. It permeated his organs and left him short of breath. The heat of spent sorcery scored the back of his neck. A primitive fear took hold of him. It draped over his work and old memories.

Mordrem's cascade was easily fatal. There was little to stop this existential feedback once it became self-sustaining. The saving grace was to abort all contact with magic, to block all possible pathways cascade could use to feed, a slim grace as hopeless as advising someone not to startle in the face of a phobia.

He was fettered by the grazing touch of death. There was no resistance against the feedback, no sliding scale between zero and everything. He had never encountered a system so unstable. He slipped off his gloves and inspected his hands. The skin was red and bruised from the spasms of muscle. Nothing seemed melted. His rings were tight with his fingers swollen. He checked the time on the wall. Safe practice demanded no thaumic contact for at least a half hour after a cascade scare. He gathered the shattered crystal in a glove and tied shut the opening, then threw these remains into a contamination bin.

He limped over to the computer, leaning against the table for support, and waited for the results to finish compiling. How fortunate. Had he taken a hardier instrument, the transferred resonance would have killed him before he could even register the pain. He was saved only by the grace of weak, crude things. All his mental fortitude and magical defenses did nothing. This primitive hunger made easy prey of his essence.

The engine might be real. It might be powerful enough to bend the rules of nature. Ninety-six percent pure chimeric ichor. The rest was water and trace amounts of salt. Obscenely pure. Unbelieving, he rechecked the program settings, combing through the calibration entries for a missed sensitivity. He checked every revision note. It might have been a fluke. The vial awaited its next result. He had to try again. He had to be sure. He set down the vial. He had to be wise.

Samples taken from the ocean only reached as high as fifty-three percent. The filtering effort proved too much for general consumption, thus these samples were cautiously doled out. The vial that Claire had given him easily overshadowed their finest work. Whatever force could concoct such potency would be a danger to the Library. No, they had to be a minor danger. He doubted Claire would handle such circumstances so lightly. She always had the Library's best intention in mind. Security was Samuel's purview. Thaumaturgy was his.

This vial was proof that the ocean could be tamed by an immaculate machine and thus by the Library. It was proof the powers of infinity could be controlled by mortal existence. His heart shuddered in his chest, skipping beats and doling out harm to his other organs. This mute sensation defied understanding. It was a sinister acclimation like the world turning outside the bounds of reality. A nightmare fear crumbled the cement of his soul. He turned to the contamination bin, but did not lift the lid. He knelt down and listened to the heartbeat of something that had become too real too quickly.

# TWENTY-FOUR

**THE LION HAD CLAWED OPEN AN IMPOSSIBLE HALL FROM THE** interior office landing into outside egress. Venner navigated the hidden bounds of the Library until its darkness gave way into a brightly lit garden that beheld the night sky. An inch's worth of water spilled from the open hole of extra space, pooled around his feet, and swept between tall ferns and flora. The cool air stung his skin. An ocean rumbled in the distance. He rubbed his eyes to assuage the headache biting along the optic nerves.

The lion's desire had been simple to solve—find the moon. The emptiness within its crooked lion shape was reminiscent of walls and stairs, of architecture smoothly gliding into place like carefully designed mechanisms. Brine replicated those well-trodden circuits of panthera magic carved into its bones, and thus he knew its outline swimming in imaginary water, how it interfered with his thought space, how desperately he needed it out of sight and out of mind. What else could he do but pour the ocean into it to settle his unease? *Consume the lion displacement.* He had no precision, but he had wealth. Enough to fill all empty things before him. A lion became indistinguishable from the ocean, perfect uniformity like the joy of ticking checkboxes.

He was disappointed. He had obliged the lion's traveling intent but attempted to insert his own intention into the lion's mode of magic, a forced solution from the thin air of thought. It was an effort that he could only describe as meaning harder, but reality did not turn and buckle then like it did for golden threads. The destination was set upon the lion's last breath. Satisfying an accountant's final desire to be more was easy. Fill the human shape will all manner of brine because the craving heart accepted with haste. However such effort only consumed. Far more difficult was to dictate magic. Venner did not have the authority of moons and lions.

Venner glanced around the swaying gardens to get a bearing of where he had been dropped off. Light glittered off dew. He looked up. The moon stared back at him in its majesty, impossibly large and gleaming. The open sky was spotless except for the very object of his desires. His heart panged from his fixations. He traced the outline of his neck, his jaw, and forced himself to look away. His hands slipped from sweat, clawing against the shape of himself. He counted his ribs and so desperately wanted all these compulsive reminders to leave him alone.

He became frightened of the ocean filling his headspace and drowning the sense of self. It all felt wrong, exercising qualities impossible for a human. It made him wrong. But he had a purpose to fulfill, and this compulsion was overwhelming.

The lion's travel way loomed in darkened silence. It led him one way in and one way out, but he knew how to destroy. Enter back behind the scenes of the Library and break down false wall after false wall until he found his destination free from this anguish. The lion was sized as a complete thing, starting and ending as one composite castle with a panthera viewfinder. It would never have been able to send him away from its programmed domain. Yet there had to be a way out. Perhaps the same way that Iramir had whispered him in. He just needed someone to say the words. And he would grab those words out of thin air and eat them and eat the speaker too.

The outline of the hole continued to decay into peeling, cinnabar petals. Mineral scraps, adrift on a breeze, floated through the garden. Their lawless shadows hunted between the lilacs and the heavy chains. Their distorted reflections colored a suspended sphere of light and water that illuminated the entire garden in a harsh luminance. Petals traversed the winding branches of a solitary tree burdened by salt and settled upon the one that waited underneath.

It was Iramir, looking out to sea. The background imagery hurt the mind. His approach through the flora caught her attention.

"Eram," she said. Her genuine surprise immediately turned to pity. The word that was his name pierced the regression of a mind into primal instincts. The word reminded him of his body, his identity, his function in society. People do not eat moons. People want to wire lights in their offices because it was dark at night. People fit quite nicely in the ocean. The word reminded him how fragile a person was.

No amount of physical persuasion could force himself to look away from Iramir. The captivating moon he had hammered into his knowledge as an impossible dream. However, Iramir was different. She was within reach. She was fully defined. She was solvable. Iramir took him by the arm and splayed her hand with his just as before, as if it was only in this way that Iramir could express anything resembling intimacy. She was much smaller. Abstract jaws would be able to handle her with ease.

"I was just about to look for you," she said. "You left a mess of broken things in my office, and I see you have invited water into the walls of the Library as well. This will not be good news for my grand magister." Their grasp entwined. His skin pinched between the cracks of her porcelain as she squeezed. Her delicate fingers were on the verge of breaking where gilt thread unraveled from the damage. "You are so far from home, so far from the city." She picked the petal blossoms off the top of her head and let them re-catch the breeze.

"You must be drowned within the ocean," he said. The clock had reset to 3 a.m. with the imagined image of her resplendent spear rising from the water. Stirring amongst the breaking waves of the mind's eye, 3 a.m. spilled. The dream captured center stage how it would sound with her voice filling with water, how she would wrestle with the weight of brine, unable to break into open air, how her soul was to be laid to rest. How easy it should have all been. Yet his own name reminded him of the limits of the physical jaw, the limits of a self-identity that could in no way be construed as infinite.

Iramir refused to let go. She took the time to find one of the few spots on her neck made of true flesh and mouthed the count of her heartbeat. Then bracing the wrist of the hand that held him, she led him to the edge of the garden balcony. Water sprayed the air from a wave's collision against the stonework.

It was an ocean lit by a lonely moon. This black expanse roiled as far as the eye could see. His wordlessness hung from his gaping jaw. Counting ribs and limbs could not save him. The word that was a name fell of out his head. Each acoustic echo of galloping tissue inside him shed the shapes of skin and bone like ripples of a stone thrown into water—shapes that once were human. His thoughts refused to ground. Nothing processed. A link was broken between the visual organs of a number too high for mortal men. Eyes had been turned inward, staring at themselves. She whispered into his ear, "Who are you?" and he replied with the answer he had always hated.

"I am the infinite ocean."

"Of course you are," said Iramir. "You simply had to be. I cannot deny the recounts of my researchers, the truth of my repository, the misfortune that must exist solely for me to settle." She brushed away the flakes of porcelain that littered their grasp.

"This is a dream," he said, desperate to find the cadence of denial that promised to soothe.

"Yes, that would be nice," agreed Iramir. "A night that disappears, forgotten and lost, upon a morning's break. For my repository to have lied to me, for you to be a regular man and not an ocean, for you to forget you had ever met me. If I keep you, what wonders may my Library wring from your corpse? If I take you home, that is a chance lost. There is no guarantee my Library can fully replicate what you are, but I do not need your processes in entirety. Just enough, even if a little shakier, a little less refined. Simply functional. An ephemeral nature is acceptable because my Library needs only one wish. Yet I can march you straight to Grimleer, and you must obey me."

Venner could not look away from the ocean, and the ocean could not look away from him. He confronted his own disassociation, identified the physical arms and legs and mouth so lacking for his ambitions. If something had to be undone to relieve him from this misery, it would be—.

"Are you ready to be taken home?" Iramir asked. Going home was the next best thing.

"I have been looking for you for a very long time," said Venner. "From all my shattered moons, I have built a jaw just to devour you. My life has been spent in anticipation, but I don't understand how it has gotten so difficult, cleaning up my ocean. I'm so anxious. Prior intrusions drowned without thought, without any preparation. Why is there so much left still, piling up within my knowledge? The unconscious reflex has slipped away from me, and I'm struggling to fill that void. Iramir, why has everything gone wrong?"

Iramir did not seem to immediately understand. Her expression echoed a careful analysis of his words as she toyed with his fingers. She inspected the bite marks across his hand, having barely scabbed over. "What happened to the lion?" she asked. A rather exacting question, but Venner supposed, perhaps, that only lions roamed the Library. The Library was made of only lions, to be exact.

"Drowned," was his answer, and because Iramir seemed unsatisfied, "within the ocean. Because it had a wish, and I granted it. Because the heart murmurs for fulfilment, and if I offer exactly what is needed, I am granted the very intimate knowledge of their whole and how to destroy them."

"Everyone wants something. What is it about lions that attracts you?"

"This is consequence for stepping into the ocean. If things kept well enough alone, kept out, it wouldn't be a problem." Again, Iramir lingered for a moment in thought. Venner was ashamed to think he only rarely had such gentle company.

"Was your hunger born from shattered moons? A sudden, emergent consciousness to better execute your most primal ambition, awakened by the thrashing of an outside existence? There is a coincidental truth that thrown into the ocean are the corpses of several unborn children and bits of their mother. They were moons, Eram. My predecessors.

"I imagined myself being able to force you, but how quickly such will dissolves. I had been confronted with the reality of being free, and I think you very much matter. Would you have ever said such things if I never got involved? I fear that I have ruined you." Venner did not know how to reply. To see Iramir so unsure absolutely bothered him. As the final moon, she had to give him final reassurance, the stillness promised by completed checklists.

"If it were just me," she continued, "would I be able to make something that could move the world like you do? Would it work even if I were not a whole moon?"

"Yes," said Venner. "The ocean would do anything for you." She smiled.

"What wonderful confirmation. After my own heart, are you? So not only can I protect my Library, I can protect you as well. I do not want to involve you any further. That is my decision."

She directed him to her ceramic skin and continued, "I would expect, having eaten so much of my legacy, that you would want to complete the collection. I am made from your leftovers of a crude feasting. The last of my mother, the real full moon that you desire, lives on through me, wrapped in bandage and suture." Iramir leaned closer. "I am not real, just like a glass star. I think I will only be a disappointment to you. The artificial never quite compares to the authentic article. Dear engine, confront your programming. Help me make my decision of whether you are fit to leave the Library. You should have stayed in my office. It would have guaranteed your freedom.

"Eram, go back to sleep. You were made from my legacy, from the industrious efforts of my Library, however distant. To all the Library, its believers and consequences, I have promised their peace of mind. It will be okay. I will patch the holes and soothe the aching thorns."

His gaze, the ocean's gaze, was drawn to her brilliance. He had to complete the next step of the enigmatic solution and shave down the shape, stress the vertices and find the opening where the ocean could leak in. The crescent moon had to be reduced to nothing. The crescent moon commanded his tides and refused his hunger. Gravity burdened him with his name. He must submit to the contour of humanity and be cowed.

Iramir rubbed her neck. "Tell me something of your life," she said. "How you have been? I still want to understand you."

"Me? I must—"

"Any hobbies? What about your career?" The idea of faraway salvation kept within a glass corporate tower cut through his compulsion with exacting precision, riling up mortal consequences that demanded he react.

"I work as structural analyst for a firm in the city. Mostly for flight vehicles. I have to settle the preliminary analysis for the block C wing design. Ah, I forgot to send Caide the draft of the acceptance plan. It needs a second party approver. I need to get home. I—I need to get back to work." Venner shook his head. "Caide needs to be prepped on taking over my responsibilities. And maybe I'll make it up to him by bribing him with donuts again. And lunch. And a case of beer."

"There it is, what exists beyond your programming," said Iramir, seemingly comforted. She added as a small aside, "I would like to be bribed like that once." She laughed. "You are alive. You have to be. Are you not tired of foolish moons and a mountain of strange business so difficult to manage? It is time to go home."

"Why are you helping me leave?" Because humans could ask, could wonder. Because water was mute, deaf, and blind to the world around itself except for its own purpose, and he was not water. "You brought me here because I was an aberration. Nothing about that has changed."

"I have shared more words with you than I thought I would," she sighed. "Listening to you is like listening to my own fears brought to life. Is this what Samuel feels when he looks at me as I look to you, oh ocean of mine? Ah, but I am not nearly as altruistic as Samuel. You just need to be helped back home. I do not need to overturn the world to save you."

Iramir tugged at her lips. "I do not mean to imply you are low hanging fruit, Eram. I will find a functional replacement in your stead. And while I cannot help dream of what could be, I cannot take that same freedom from you. You are not a question of what could be. You have made it. You are fully within the arms of a world that will behold you, and because of me, it would be ruined. It is not absurd to so desperately wish for comfort, for everything to just be fine."

"Why not experience it yourself?" asked Venner. "I wouldn't think anything could stop you from leaving."

"My duty is here. I want to be here. It would be negligent for me to leave my station and my responsibilities. The world will not have me. I am built to service it and what it needs. An accessory to the realer, fuller things."

"Are you so sure of that? There's no need to be self-deprecating. I would guide you around the city, if you wanted."

Iramir laughed again. "I did not think I would be so easily smitten by being asked to join. I appreciate it, but I have no interest in avoiding my work or the people that rely on me. There is a momentum already attached to your existence and to mine. No effort is needed from me to stay my course. You will survive without me." Out of all the things spoken like foregone conclusions, it was this. So much trust was inlaid within those last five words that he could very much believe nothing was wrong with the world.

"It is time to go home." Checking her pulse again, she guided him away from the ocean view. He felt nothing through her ceramic. "The long way, however. I will take you to the transport dock and then outside. There is a minimum of concern I should have for my current condition."

Iramir directed him back through the impossible hall of crumbling petals. The view of the gardens disappeared as moonlit gold stitched together his inflicted spatial wound. They were left without light. The rumble of an ocean became the sounds of their footsteps treading water. She navigated the pitch-black space with confident ease and never let go as she counted out loud the lengths of featureless walls. Once satisfied, the lunar lion mimic clawed at the paneling and opened their way out.

The translation of space had dropped them in a storage warehouse. They were surrounded by fibrous specimens wrapped in film and housed in glass containers, crates made from exotic wood branded with foreign lettering, and polished metal canisters plastic wrapped for safety. Cargo, shipment, and stock. The blue stamps of a winged lion assured him he was still within the Library. The floor was imprinted with an ornate summoning circle overlaid upon many others unlike it on every inch of open space.

Iramir smoothed down the wall they had exited. There was no lingering void, her magic exact and easy to follow. She checked her phone messages. Irritation crossed her features. "I had forgotten Samuel issued a lockdown once you were discovered missing," she said. Her tight-lipped nonchalance returned at the mention of Samuel. "You do not need to be anxious, Eram. If all the transport anchors are indeed nonfunctional, I can still just wish you home."

Iramir massaged her joints as if she was in pain. "Are you alright?" he asked.

"I am fine," Iramir mumbled. She let go of him, her hand with fewer fingers than when she'd started. Smooth ceramic had broken into rough patches. She shushed him, evidently noticing his apprehension. "I can be repaired." Venner was unconvinced, much less comforted. The magic that kept her spirit tied to porcelain was fraying thread by thread. He attempted to console her by the shoulder only for her to gently rebuff him. "You are almost free."

Her phone vibrated. She checked the name and rejected the call. "Quickly, please," she urged, pushing on Venner. Her phone vibrated again. She brought the phone to her ear. "Grimleer, what is it?" Iramir rubbed the bridge of her nose. "I cannot come to the lab right now. I need time for a short detour outside.... What sort of emergency?"

Iramir splayed her ruined hand on Venner's chest. She continued to speak over the phone. "You will be fine.... I will come by soon." She hung up and avoided Venner's gaze.

"Iramir," said Venner.

"Go home," she ordered with a serious and formal finality. In spite of his compulsion, Venner ignored the clamoring of abstract ocean eyes. Perhaps once away from the toil of water, he would relocate a sense of himself that demanded decency. He had been rescued from the ocean with such care, assured he could be beyond his obsessions.

"Not like this," was all he could muster. He knew he would not be able to resist a second command. He did not want to disappoint her. She had fed him her hopes and dreams, but the ocean did not know how to digest such soft ideals.

"It is for your own good. A bit of coarse medicine."

"I don't want to lose my name. I don't want to lose anything I hold in my hands or my own head. A wish undoes me. Context falls apart. Names and labels are stripped out of me and my surroundings. I am the ocean, and all that matters here and now becomes unspeakable words, hateful misfortunes, and dead things. It becomes much easier to swallow things when they have no meaning.

"And all I am left with is pieces when I am finally plucked out of the ocean. Just enough pieces to be fit together, to work out the course, and regret. Pieces of my relationships, my career, my life. I want to be free from this trap. I know your name, and I hope you can understand how much that means to me. How much all names mean to me."

"Then ignore me. You were given names to cherish, not to lose. Does it hurt to grant wishes? Then I am sorry too." Iramir started her retreat away from him. "I should not have put you through this anguish, and now I have to make you wait again. I need you to hide here, Eram, only for a little while. I just—I just need time. It will give me an opportunity to lift the lockdown for the more mundane way out. There should not be too many people here. Please, just wait." The crescent moon left no room for interaction, and the ocean obeyed.

# TWENTY-FIVE

ON HIS SEARCH FOR A QUIET CORNER, VENNER CROSSED PATHS
with an inspector marking off a clipboard of shipping transcripts and
checking import tags on various pieces of shipment.

"Who are you?" said the inspector, alarmed. "You aren't supposed to
be here." Venner refused to answer the question. The inspector checked
the floor, scuffed the sole of his shoe on the etched circles, and glanced at
a nearby steel beam embedded in the concrete floor that stretched up to
support the warehouse ceiling. Dark, esoteric markings with sharp, scat-
tering angles were carved all along its surfaces. "How did you get here?
Nothing can come or leave during a lockdown. You're not a stowaway?
Or"—the inspector soured at the patient smock—"a property, are you?"

Venner did not know what to say. The inspector sighed and pulled a
brass snuff box from his shirt pocket. His laboratory coat was stained at
the edges. His armband emblazoned with a lion was heavily wrinkled.
He took to fiddling with the brass box, opening the cover, taking a look
at the powder, and closing it back again. The inspector tried signing to
Venner with the snuff box in hand. It was a mumbling mix of an unprac-
ticed mute voice, shaking hands, and touching his chin in thought.

"I need to get home," Venner said. As much as Iramir assured him
she would be back, he did not want to see the moon again. Rather, he
wanted to get home with himself intact.

The inspector's face opened in surprise. "Oh. You still aren't supposed
to be here."

"I mean to be here."

"Look, I don't know where you're from," said the inspector, "but it's safer in the Library. More comfortable. It is. You have to realize the Library is one of the few places left that can help mend sorcery. Someone has moved heaven and earth to get you here. A lot of people would. I'll take you back to the medical wing. Come on. Let's find your doctor."

"I refuse." Venner stepped back towards the steel beam, hiding in its shadow. The inspector checked his watch. The glass was scratched, the case dull and leather tearing. His wedding ring glinted under the glaring light of the warehouse.

"How much longer do you have?" asked the inspector. The inspector slid his pen from the metal hinge of the clipboard and wrote something down on the sheets of inventory. "It's running out, right?" The inspector clicked the end of his pen and slid it back in the clasp. Venner stayed silent. Okay, the inspector mouthed, then, "There have been a few of you, I guess." The inspector pointed to the steel beam. "May I?"

"Who are you?" asked Venner. The inspector entered the etched circle that surrounded the steel beam. The invading presence activated this sigil in a soft glow. Venner supposed he was to be inside, stepping over the rings of hard light.

"Robin Hood," said the inspector with a scant smile over his shoulder. "Ah, I'm teasing. Don't take that too seriously." Not Robin Hood laughed and then spun his ring around his finger. "Don't look too worried. I can try to get you out of here. The lockdown might not be truly foolproof. Wherever you'll go, don't make too much noise. Thanks." He knocked the face of the beam with the back of his hand.

Not Robin Hood took a deep breath and knocked again. Nothing. He turned back around and motioned for Venner to wait a little, wiped the sweat off his hands with the corner of his coat, and tapped on the steel beam as he brought his wedding ring to his lips. A spark flared briefly as to obscure his features and shadow his shape. Venner supposed his ring must be the equivalent of Iramir's sliver of metal, a tool that amplified the intention, yet gold did not echo back. The inspector's shape was lacking.

Venner wrung his wrists. A lion's desire he saw through to fruition. A moon's gentle inquiry could have been easily answered. Not that Venner meant to demean Iramir's attempt to inspire a human confidence, but he would be home if he had solved the problem of silence within the inspector. Only the inspector had the right words to operate this steel beam. Staying here guaranteed his mindful self-destruction. It would only be a momentary swim to be free.

Not Robin Hood squeezed his ring. "I'm sorry," said the inspector. "I'm a bit exhausted already, even though the morning has just started. They usually have a tool, a key, for this, but it's all been confiscated. Cease and desist, the shipping, receiving. You're a little late, I'm sorry. I'm not Magister Grimleer, you know." Tarnished gold leaked from the wedding band and stained the hands of the inspector, unaware.

"What do you want?" asked Venner. The inspector startled at Venner's close approach and brought up his ringed hand as if to protect himself. Magic curled around the inspector's grasp. The ocean caught the tail of a lion named Not Robin Hood. Gilded threads, pulled from a ring, tangled in Venner's grasp. The ocean turned shape end over end, inspecting the inspector's nuances like the edges of a puzzle box. Unlike Iramir—for whom magic followed the tune of her will, fully entranced and docile—the inspector was a wall. He was impassible, mute, crumbling from the might of forces beyond him.

Not Robin Hood called and magic apathetically answered. The inspector had exhausted his inner talent. The ocean wondered how far it could reshape the inspector, as stretching thread distorted and altered all manner of person boundaries. The inspector pulled at his sleeve and apologized to Venner.

"I want, ah," the inspector started, "I want to be more, but I just don't have the talent for it. Is that the sort of answer you were looking for?" Venner was pleased. Not Robin Hood would hardly be defeated so easily. The inspector pulled a shipping receipt from nearby crates. It was flattened against the steel beam, and the inspector smoothed down the edges where adhesive rippled, letting it hang on its own. The inspector took his pen and started to sketch odd shapes and symbols.

"I've sunk too many hours here, working in these halls and seeing nothing else but suffering," said the inspector. "All this time and all this effort spent finding cures and helping people. I used to be in research, actually. And I had a good couple of years where I was feeling like I made a difference. Then everything broke. People died and nothing could be done. Then people became less like patients and more like means of experimentation for such cures. Products and resource.

"I ended up not being able to handle it, but I couldn't gather up the bravery to leave the Library. I still believe in the endeavor, and opportunities elsewhere for what I want to do are slim. I know a lot of people left because they felt it was pointless or that they had better financial prospects outside. I transferred from department to department until I ended up here, and I meet people like you." The inspector took a moment to appreciate his drawn abstraction on the receipt.

"I know outside might not be better, but it was where all the things I loved were." The inspector fidgeted with his wedding ring for a brief moment more. "Maybe I'm a bit of a defeatist, letting people leave because I don't think they should be spending the last of their time in this lonely place. But sometimes this is the closest to comfort we can actually offer." The inspector took something wrapped in a napkin from his pocket. The napkin unraveled. It was a crystal sliver, small and pale.

"Do you believe in me as a rogue in Sherwood Forest?" The inspector waved the crystal. "It's not a real obelisk, rather the scraps left over when you make one. Can't actually smuggle the real thing. You know, when the body fails, tools make up the difference. You can pretend to be Iramir or Grimleer when you can flick a switch and throw a lightning bolt. Or just start a fire. Even failed scraps like these are so rare outside nowadays. For so many of us even in this Library, we cast magic because someone else made us something to do so. Weapons, maker apparatuses, day-to-day living. Breathing for some of us."

The inspector pretended to nock an arrow with his pen. The obelisk scrap played the part of a bow. Not Robin Hood's slight smile turned crooked. "These scraps can make all the difference outside, instead of being hoarded and forgotten here. I guess I'll explain now so you don't get too hopeful. Maybe the lockdown is kind of absolute, not that I can subvert the Library."

The inspector wrapped the obelisk scrap in the receipt, hiding his work. Tools made all the difference for those quiet, stuttering voices asking reality to heed their intentions. They demanded weapons be born from moonlit artistry. They demanded steel take a man home. Unlike Iramir, so echoed in gold was Not Robin Hood's silence even with all his amplifiers.

Yet Venner heard and began to plan what could be done to solve the inspector's plight. There was a memory of a crescent moon that lived in his ocean, the mirror reflection, and if the ocean so desired, it could reflect this memory over the shape of a pretend bowman. He would redraw the lines and encourage the faltered shape to become more. Mismatched features and crossed connections, the ocean can transform flesh into more usable form. If everything was made like Iramir, would they not be happy when their rivers of gold flow so freely?

"I'll give it one last good try," said the inspector, clutching his wrapped obelisk tightly. The ocean smiled, tracing the final shape of Robin Hood with a lingering touch. To the inspector, it was just a pat on the shoulder as he knocked on the steel beam one more time.

# TWENTY-SIX



THE INSPECTOR STAGGERED AROUND IN THE THROES OF SUD-den terror. He clawed at the steel beam for support. The obelisk scrap boiled in the palm of his hand as the receipt covering decayed to ash. The skin of his palm softened and began to melt. His eyes widened in realization: this was a thermal reverberance, cascade. His inner source had had enough. The sending of a man outside, his single piece of straw. The obelisk shard fell from his hand. It tumbled, shaking strangely in its movements like the slosh of liquid in a half-empty bottle.

He choked and clutched his throat. The obelisk rolled and clattered, and the heart chased these movements in errant beats, each striving to be the last. He dropped to his knees as blood slowed and veins shriveled. Doom impending. He reached out and shoved the obelisk against his bare skin out of the insane desperation of the drowning to breathe. The crystal, once solid pale, was hollowed with a red liquid. Thicker than water, the liquid clung to the inner faces, bubbling in the corners.

A small malformed heart beat within the crystal, no bigger than the heart of a sparrow. The damp obelisk left stains as he slid the rock across his skin. He crept for some packing tape from nearby specimen jars and taped the obelisk around his forearm. No, somewhere safer. He unbuttoned his shirt and taped the obelisk over his heart, where it would have been. He had no words for what had just happened. All he understood was that this rock had transformed and somehow contained his life.

He stared at the steel beam supporting the ceiling of the warehouse. He was alone. The strange man that had touched him on the shoulder had been sent somewhere else. He had no destination in mind. The transportation spell had been completed with nary a conscious thought. Gravity was smothering. He had to find Grimleer. The Lord Magister must know what terror had just been released into the outside world.

He would be punished if Grimleer knew. He would be dead if Lady Iramir knew. He slumped into himself. He needed help, but he knew no one with the expertise to help him who would not report him. He tried to open his snuff box, but knocked it out of reach. The brass skated away under a palette.

The doors to Lady Iramir's gardens were plated bronze. It was within that arbor haven that the repository was housed. The repository would provide him answers without judgement. However, entrance was forbidden except by Grimleer's decree. Lady Iramir did not bother doling her own permissions.

The steel beam loomed. If it was at all possible to repeat that same thoughtless spell that had sent a monster away, he would not need permission. He could send himself anywhere as required. However, the Library had been built to prevent such flagrant spatial transgressions. The lions were the only exceptions. He would need something that violated the very sanctity of magic to defeat those fail-safes, a violation like his beating heart inside an obelisk shard.

He could not catch his breath. It was too foolish to try sending himself to the gardens. He climbed up the steel beam by its crevices, hugging it to keep his balance. The shard scraped against the steel where tape failed to protect the edges. Any movement sloshed the heart in its cage. Even his own heavy breathing unsettled him. He feared that with the smallest of sparks, the cascade would start again. He lived on borrowed time as a product of eldritch sophistry that must be inherently unstable. He needed help.

He felt the transportation circle activate as if he had always known how magic tapped to rhythm. The tower rings of hard light prepared for use. Coordinates were filled by the images in his head rather than through numbers. The world was racing through his hands, and to stop would rip his limbs apart. The throttle was jammed fully open. Reality catered. A single dark rumination could spell the end of him. A miscalculated direction would send him straight into brick. The steel beam unraveled into black, taking him so quickly that he could not refuse.

The bronze relief doors carved with the image of a whale leviathan stood solemn. Blind bronze eyes witnessed the transportation of a man into their sacred domain. Blind bronze eyes witnessed a man screaming.

He was in an emerald garden lit only by the repository upon its stage. The core of liquid knowledge was suffused with moonlight. He was here beyond the doors, beyond the need of blessings, beyond all reason. Suspended water rippled as he approached in utter disbelief. There was no room for his own reflection in this blinding light and no room for the consequences of trespass in his mind.

A sinking feeling stole the ground and all landmarks, leaving him stranded in water. He raised a hand to block out the sight of the repository. This disquiet resounded in his new age heart. He peeked between his fingers. The garden was dry and all there. A hallucination then. He could not stay like this. He was dying. Surely, he had to be dying. A home waited for him at the end of the day, as long as he didn't die. Secrets were not questioned if hidden well enough. No one would make him stay here forever. No one had to know what he had done.

He reached into the water, pleading with the repository for help. The repository heeded. The answer was torrential. Typeface leaked from his eyes and ears. Letters sprawled into wiry things waving serifs in adoration. Words climbed over blades of flora, dripping off petals.

Lady Iramir's voice was muffled through the brimming words that crowded his head. "How fascinating."

He struggled to rotate his eyes in their sockets. Letters stuck their points so painfully. She had found him. The light of her garden gathered around her. He stuttered but winced at his bitten tongue. Words failed to come, the endless fount of the repository suffocating. The scent of the ocean filled the air. She did not meet his eyes but focused on the bleeding shard taped to his chest.

"What did you do?" she asked.

He clutched his life tighter. He spat typeface onto the floor. She snapped her fingers. The repository collapsed into liquid light. Waves rushed through the flora and collected as a small lake. Her footsteps left widening rings that echoed her movements. The physical manifestations of sound lifted at her heels, forming droplets suspended in midair. Typeface appeared across the liquid surface. Massive letters slid over the lips and ledges of petals and ferns, compiling their most recent request.

*Lich. Phylactery from blood and stone. Spirit in a glass jar. A false moon begat from the ocean.* She paused before this phrase. Silhouetted beneath the inspector, letters merged and morphed, flickering like projector slides of a human recreated layer by layer. Typeface and diagram outlined where the human was cut, mended, replaced. A crude process did not bother to finely align torn organs and limbic systems. The human was barely functioning, animated purely by magic.

The inspector scraped words by the handful from his leaking head. Water flickered black and white to the tune of speeding letters. *Be drowned*, spoke the background. He tried to call for the anchor. Something else called back unlike the calibrated tool. He did not know this sorcery. His intentions felt weightless like mere thoughts made in idle daydreaming. Magic spun so finely out of his control. There was no point in reigning this wildness. He dropped all pretense of safety. He was beyond Lady Iramir as he let magic have its way. He kept his mouth shut. Consequence could not chase him.

☾

IRAMIR HEARD NOTHING OF A MAN RIPPED APART. A STAIN ON the liquid surface was made from meat, a stain that was smeared across the garden and rode over the balcony into the ocean. His corpse, piece by piece, peeled away from the stone with soft patters. She clasped her hands behind her back and bowed her head. *The moon disturbs the tides of the ocean*, said the typeface, immune to speeding tragedy. Thus the repository said its final piece.

She investigated the obelisk shard floating within sheared flesh and blood. A tiny heart ruptured in its crystal cage, damp to the touch. Whitepapers warned of uncontainable virality if the engine of brine could connect with people and their magic too easily. Simply existing within the gaze of an ocean would warrant retaliation. However, that risk was deemed acceptable. The test article was completely stationary, predictable. A terse abort plan recommended sealing the engine away until better technology offered an actual solution. It was unthinkable for an engine to be malevolent and actively seek its victims. It was terrifying. How could anyone anticipate that the act of contracting would be painful for the engine?

Consequence beckoned. The ocean had to be tamed, not merely calmed by insincere efforts. Samuel knew how to calm matters of the heart. If there was a voice that could cut water, it would be his. She had not the gift Samuel had. She was wrong to have left Eram alone. He had to be found. He had to be dealt with. He had to be saved. A matter such as this could not be treated so lightly. A heart had to tame the beast and guide the human from the wicked abyss. Not the machine that worked the ichor blood and porcelain frame, but the promethean in the first place. Out of pure care and patience, Samuel must be able to understand infinity. Despite the risk.

# TWENTY-SEVEN

**IT WAS FIRMLY MORNING. THE NIGHT STORM HAD BEEN SHELVED** into the eaves of mindfulness. The city beheld the next day swimming in coffee and easy breakfasts. Venner found himself in the front lobby of his apartment building. A mailman was filling the mailboxes. They met eyes only for the mailman to pull down his cap and continue on his duties.

There was no desire to peer into this person, Venner realized. Oh, he cherished this quiet. The world was steady. Home awaited with hot showers and email checkups. His thoughts were what he decided they would be, not stolen by absurd abstractions. He felt in control, so far away from impossible things. Entering the lobby elevator, he pressed for his floor as the doors slid shut. The elevator smelled faintly of bleach, rumbling as it climbed.

Apartment 325. His home. The door was locked, he just remembered. No keys, no wallet, no work badge. He had a broken phone. A screen smashed almost entirely unusable and the battery dead. He could head back down to the lobby and alert the manager. He traced the brass latch with his fingertips as he wondered if he could attempt the same mysticism that had freed him from Iramir's office. To his surprise, the latch easily turned, fully unlocked. The door swung open. He could have sworn he'd locked the door, but there were times, he knew, when his addled thoughts could lead him astray. He did not pull away gilt thread with his touch. Perhaps he had simply forgotten.

His apartment was as he'd left it, just enough for one person to stay sequestered from the outside. The blinds were kept closed and would stay that way. He was in no mood to see beyond his walls. He locked the door behind him and flicked the light switch. A moment's pause prompted him to relock the door twice more, listening to the mechanisms.

A stacked pyramid of puzzle boxes waited on his living room table. Hardly a bad omen when they were his in the first place. He spied the potted plant in the corner of the room. Disgust tightened his jaw. He lifted the plant by its pot and carefully moved it near the sink, then covered the drain with a plate before breaking stems and branches to fit the plant inside the basin. A turned faucet unleashed water, filling the sink. The levels rose, tipped over the ceramic brim, darkened the dirt, and then overflowed. He turned off the water when it began to spill onto the counter.

Retreating to his bedroom, he straightened the alarm clock on his nightstand, turned on the lamp, and plugged in the power cord to his phone despite its uselessness. He was late for work. Not that it would matter soon. He was most assuredly getting fired now. Yet after all these arcane nightmares, he pined for urban normality. The clock flashed 3 a.m. Perhaps it had lost power sometime during the night. A quick reset returned the clock in rightful order.

He undressed slowly so as not to irritate his wounds. His skin was inflamed around the stitches. There was pain medication in the bathroom cabinet. A car went by beneath his window in full disregard of noise laws. He tossed his clothes over the end of his bed and flipped the black card of Harken onto the nightstand. There was a whole procedure to go through. Report his wrecked car to the police, then insurance. Get a new license and other cards in the mail. Tidy up his resume for a new chapter in his life.

He turned on the shower and stood naked in front of the mirror. The showerhead hissed as steam enveloped the bathroom. To believe none of the night had been real would require him to swallow a mountain of denial. Yet here he was in his apartment, in nice, relative safety. He stared at his reflection, at the grisly wound across his chest. Do not look at it. It will spill out—organs, offal, him. The pain was not the problem. It was good work that put him back together. It was the unsettling sensation of faraway phantom limbs and optic disassociation that lingered beneath his punctured skin, coiling under his ribcage around his heart.

He tugged where stitching loosened and a decent length unraveled, free. He shuddered from the pain and chastised himself for his idiocy. He placed pressure over the broken scabs. It was not blood that leaked, but water, and it wasn't suture tied around his hand, but gilded thread. Refusing further comment, he washed his hands to drain the evidence away before stepping into the shower.

He would dress up and travel the underground. Midday arrival at the latest. He would check in with the secretary for a temporary pass, then tidy up loose ends at work. Check up on issue tickets, read team reports, and write up his own progress checks, reviewing the final corrections for the prototype models that would enter fabrication by the end of next week. Get called into the director's office. Get fired. Yes, a very fine plan. Very usual, very good. It would not take much to digest such normalcy in the safety of his own home. This was just part of the checklist, the occupational hazard that people dealt with.

The water that washed away sweat and dirt also irritated his cuts and bruises. The heat stung. He had abetted his own kidnapping, the very destruction of his own peace. He scrubbed the stubborn grime with more soap and inspected the various nicks that littered his body.

His world had been undone. No mere milieu, the world lived and breathed and pressed its body against his own perception. Most habits, the details of the habitable collective, flew under the limit of awareness. The movements of the eyelids, the pressure of the tongue, the cadence of breath, the sanctity of perceived normality. Attention had been drawn to these unconscious things, leaving him very uncomfortable over the whole gamut of unsettled feelings.

There was an outside to his plane of existence. An intersection of realities that dug into his mind and consumed his attention. An outside space so infinite and terrifying and full, he wished so desperately to close back in. Eventually, he had to forget, slip into unconscious habit, and life would continue as it had before. He just had to outwait this feeling of displacement. Water spiraled down the drain. He swallowed hard to keep the nausea down. The dripping upset the stomach. Please, not in the shower.

He dried off quickly and brushed his teeth until he could not stand the taste of salt anymore. He wet the razor and tugged at his cheek where he spread the foam. His coworkers would notice the cuts and bruises. How could they not? His eyes staring back in the mirror reminded him of the ocean. Weariness weighed on them. He raised the razor over his iris, barely nicking the eyelashes.

He could cut himself open and count how many eyes would spill out. People have two eyes, but there were unaccountable things in that outside space. The rest of his seven eyes had to float in the ocean because there was nowhere else Venner felt they could reside. He tapped the end of the razor against the side of the sink and continued to shave.

He finished preening himself in the mirror by the closet, tying, but also continually failing, a necktie. He held back a sigh and brushed a hand through his hair, now finally clean and slicked back. He preferred a white, collared shirt, pressed, and over that a sharp black suit. The futility of cleaning up so impeccably did flash occasionally in his mind, but it was a habit, and habits were comforting. It was time to go to work and then to never go back. At least, not there. Ah, he had not touched his resume in years. He tightened his necktie and squared his shoulders in the mirror. *Smile.*

He turned to look at the nightstand behind him. He reached over, took off the shade, and threw it onto the bed. He covered his eyes from the glare, but he had no intention to replace it. Squinting against the light, he grabbed the cufflinks and tiepin from the nightstand and turned away to secure them with his back to the glare of the naked lamp.

The tabs on one of his cufflinks were crooked. He walked over to his desk and rifled through drawers to find a pair of pliers. Small change clattered. Leftover papers from his planned tax return rested on their binder. He was supposed to have finished that last night. The image of a rotting skull reappeared in his mind.

While adjusting the knot of his necktie, he thought of the crude machinery that had powered the unfigure, the hanging skin and wasting bone. He made smaller adjustments. Attending to his cufflinks again, he straightened the tabs against the corner of his desk. He set the tiepin, smoothed the creases in his collar, and patted himself down the rest of the way. The accountant had been repaid with a melting body and a disfigured face.

Venner had *eaten* him. That was disingenuous. He hadn't eaten any-one. He was not an ocean. He scratched at his neck. He was just insane. There was a famed psychiatric hospital across the river. They had ads occasionally plastered over the boards in the subway, urging the public to keep their mental health in mind. He didn't want to be any later for work than he had to be.

He had a rail card stashed somewhere in this apartment. A card, he hoped, left with a charge or two. He opened the drawers again, finding no spare bills. An ATM was out of the question without a bank card, and the bank itself would give him at least an hour's worth of scrutiny, verifying his identity without plastic identification. The rail card stayed missing. It might have been used for balancing boxes then.

He stepped out into his living room to the stack of puzzle boxes that lived on his coffee table. The boxes that made up the foundation were coated in a heavy layer of dust. He'd used business cards and company advertisement placards to shore the odd corner and end. The yellowed plastic rail card sat nearer to the bottom. As a relic of older times, the card still bore a brief map from when there were only three main lines. He tried to gently slide it out but every movement shifted the stack precariously. They were empty anyway, these boxes of little use. What satisfaction he once gleaned from them could not compare to the excite-ment of people. He lifted the card and knocked them over. He then went to turn off the lights before leaving. There were still bills to pay. The bed-room, in fact, was dark. The light was out. The broken glass of the bulb twinkled on the ground.

He was halfway down the stairs of his complex before his mind caught up to him. His heart raced miles faster than his feet. He had left the door unlocked, but so what. All an intruder would find was his obses-sion. There was to be a fine separation of the normal and abnormal. He was supposed to be free from this terror. A broken bulb made not the hunting unfigure. That matter had been burned to ashes. He straight-ened his collar and smoothed down his hair. He absently examined the patterns in the brickwork as he walked down the stairs.

These were the kind of malignant thoughts that ran him to exhaus-tion. He was not okay. There were no skeletons in doors, millipedes in city nests, or moons to be devoured. This was to be the calm after a storm where he had cleaned up his wrecked identity, where he accounted his own memories and calculated if he was fit enough to enter back into society. Legfull things that had once lingered in his ocean lingered now underneath his stitches. The thought made his wounds itch.

The ocean used to stay contained in dreams, but it had escaped him and rampaged throughout his reality. He squeezed his eyeball between two fingers. The pressure was excruciating, and he felt proud for expecting such a sensation. He let go, blinking back the pain, and exited out of the stairwell to the lobby. The mailman was not there.

Venner walked briskly to the nearest underground station, cutting streets between idling taxis and roving things. There were people everywhere—workers, students, and travelers sharing the byways and enjoying their collective ignorance of one another. The cars, bikes, and distant sirens jackknifed an old city never made for such modern inefficiencies. The crackle of broken streetlights unable to turn off in broad day, the rustling of change in a tin cup, the rumbling of construction, the death of all silence. He hated everything.

He came to the turnstiles of the subway. A line of travelers stood at the manned booth, while none stood at the self-service terminal. The terminal monitor illuminated the dim underground with a faint green. The sounds of rushing metal raced up the stairs. His back tightened. It was only the trains. He glanced back up to the surface streets and to the people that walked up and down the steps. Backpacks, briefcases, a wedding ring, and a sliver of metal. Any one of them could spin gold.

The chatter of crowds was revolting, this living blight of so-called existence. He slipped his card into the awaiting insert. The machine scanned and repeated the remaining amount. There was the public bulletin board nearby that boasted the extended reach of upgraded rail lines. Brochures with more information were available for the taking. He watched someone peruse and take one.

There was nothing that differentiated those that spun gold from those that did not. He did not want to look inside the human boxes, but he needed to. He did not have enough eyelids for all of his eyes. People were the new puzzles. If only he could solve the enigma of their ribcages, their so-called desire, and devour their organs lined with gold. He pushed against the growing crick in his back. *Do not look.*

His account was empty. His account stayed empty. Someone tapped him on the shoulder. There was a line behind him, and he stepped away, making haste to the teller. He counted his change. Enough for a single trip with a bit of charity. There would be the problem getting back. Or not. After getting fired, he would have all the time in the world to wait at the bank. Or just walk. No one would hire him. That thought actually hurt. The sense of sanity that made him passable in society felt impossible to grasp.

The ocean had to be empty. The ocean had to be empty. The ocean had to. Be. "Sir, sir," the teller repeated. "Would you please come up to the counter? What do you need?" Venner was next in line. Yes, one ticket to Lorcaster-Shorn. No, no return charge, please. His mouth started on the wrong shape.

"I want to eat you." Coins spilled onto the counter. "I hate your voice, your heartbeat. There is just so much of you. I do not know what to do, but I have to start somewhere, right? Keep to the right waiting on the escalators, never talk in the presence of the captive subway audience. In fact, never bother anyone. Unobstructed, uninvited conversation invites the death of you. Societal courtesy keeps everyone out of trouble, but you all rebel. Mindful shapes need to be condemned," snarled Venner. "Please, I need my ocean empty, but existence outweighs my jaw. You cannot just open these borders that I have made and just leave me here to fester."

Venner was shaking. The teller stuttered some reply and stepped away from the transaction window. The noise of a crowd turned into unpleasant whispering. They stared at him. A few heads shook. *Be devoured. Oh please, just be devoured.*

These people things encroached with pure disregard. A shape dared come too close. He tried to keep it away. The shape guided him from the window. Paper was pressed into his hand. It was a train ticket, warm from the printer. He did not recognize the station name on it. The shapes made sharp edges that might have been pointing fingers, or maybe the sharp edges were their facial features. He did not care, having had enough of names and context. Frustrated hands tugged on the ends of the ticket.

Go to work. Drown in the distractions there. The ocean could not bother him in the midst of his paradise. The ticket was for the wrong destination. He did not care. He kept his head down and passed through the turnstiles as his ticket beeped against the reader.

The train pulled up to the station on howling brakes. The doors hissed open before the blue hatched lines. This outgoing crowd did not know him; they passed him right by. The ingoing crowd did. He took his seat at the end of the carriage. The other passengers kept away from the man that rocked in his seat, stared at the floor, scratched at his eye.

He could ruin them. His eye hurt from the pressure. He wanted so much to unplug the hole and release these black thoughts. The doors hissed closed. The announcement of the next station sounded overhead. Last night between abandoned stations of a long dead line, he learned that there lived a magic man amongst corpses and mint. The train shuddered as it began hauling its passengers. The magic man was an accountant. The people that stood leaned a bit as the train took a turn. Amongst the people here, huddled shoulder to shoulder, he wondered who else lived like the accountant. Who hid away the supernatural from prying eyes, who displayed little trinkets of nostalgia, who too longed for something more?

He hated how rattling travel reminded him of the rolling waves. More thoughts fell into that ocean at the sight of the accountant drowning. He flinched as he squeezed too hard. Instead, he rubbed his eyes with the heel of his hands. There was so much to clean up at work.

He pulled his hands away and saw the aftermath of a wreckage, long settled and cold. The carriage had been destroyed. Metal had warped around him. It smelled of gasoline. He had felt and heard nothing of the cacophony that made this. It was a sudden transposition within a moment of inattention that had displaced him into a likeness of his car crash. A discordant rhythm crept about the back of his head despite the silence surrounding him. He recognized the overbearing feeling, trapped in an oceanic dream, waiting for it to end. He climbed out into the cold night through steel gashes. Red emergency lights flashed on and off.

White sand billowed from his footsteps. The familiar ocean hung in the sky while he stayed on this inverted shoreline below.

Broken moons emerged from the water above him, collecting salt in their crevices. Their split bodies had been razed into teeth and reflected the red lights. The half skeleton of a dog head was abandoned mid-pounce, arcing right over the wreckage. Its legs were lost beneath the sand. A single one of its teeth was nearly the size of him. Venner sat down in the shade of the massive skull. He undid his necktie and unbuttoned his shirt, carefully treading back his earlier routine. He dug between his stitches, letting oil and water bleed.

"Did you know what would happen last night?" he asked to what was left of the accountant. "What would happen to you?" He spoke to the creeping thing in the pits of dog bone.

Venner was elbow-deep in his own body. His stitches all tore. "Do you know how to fix this? The shores, the ocean, the refuse I leave behind because I am not as diligent anymore? I hate having all my work upended. I used to wait, always, for the dream to end because there was nothing else to be done. Now there is too much, and I am just overwhelmed." Venner pulled the accountant's broken hand out from his chest. It was soft to the touch. "I want to forget how you tasted. How you writhed as your existence failed you."

Venner cradled the hand carefully to keep it from spilling. He reached up to feel the dog bone as he traveled underneath the spine. The rib cage rose higher, but as he left the confines of the skull, the open area shrunk, shaping back into that accounting office. Venner took his seat and laid the hand on freshly inked paper.

Red light navigated between the blinds. Fake plants were left unpotted, unable to thrive in the sand. The bookcases and display stands of once-cherished things were empty. Green glass tubes of occult purpose were filled with dying art and waxing nostalgia. There was nothing else alive here but Venner. Nothing else that thought or talked. Nothing else that was not made up. A hand did not a person make.

The accountant idea should have been stamped and sealed. Venner leaned back in his chair, gripping the armrests tightly. The hand deflated, leaking innards over the paper. Cleanup never felt so intensive or so personal before. Association refused to simply disappear, demanding that he repeat his experiences as part of a new clerical procedure. He did not sign off on this bothersome change. Breathing and blinking were automatic. Why was cleaning not? A function that had been completely reflexive until this body. Until he had eyes and a mouth and the whole terrible weight of a name.

Venner shifted to the edge of his seat and pulled gilt thread from the accountant's bloated fingers. He took a pen off the table, uncapped it, and drew around the hand the charnel beasts under leaves of mint. The context was forever mute. What was left of the accountant, dog bone made, steel wire anchored, and hand carried, stared back.

Venner wondered why he was here, acting through a body so useless for its intended function. When had he acquired this confined shape? He was the ocean. He did not need to bother with superfluous things like relation and introspection or engage with this strange ritual just to clean up.

The sky bound ocean fell in thundering terror and washed this world away.

# TWENTY-EIGHT



**IRAMIR WALKED UP THE STAIRS BACK TO HER OFFICE. THE LION** that escorted her kept nudging its head into her hand. They would hardly leave her out of their sight, and while she much preferred staying within the laboratories to continue work on a new engine, there was nowhere else for privacy. She just wanted a moment to herself, a break from the people and the stares of their expectations.

A new engine from the proof of concept, of impossible hearts within crystal cages, would be made to control the ocean. Effort would be revitalized and so would the bloodlust. People were broken down into the weights of their contributions, by the worth of their theories or the worth of their physical bodies and the materials they contained. They could not help but be expectant. The Library's salvation waited behind stark white walls and industrious machinery. It had never been closer.

The way Grimleer and his researchers trusted her and congratulated her made her little secret ever harder to hold. She was not known for half-measures. It was absurd that she could undermine her divine duty just to save one man. Yes, entirely ridiculous to hold Eram in such regard. She barely knew him, only his name and vague scraps of livelihood. Idle chatter just to pass the time, hardly poor conversation. She was quite used to others who were easily lost in their own reverie, where she only needed a passing reply to keep them going. It was a nice reprieve to feel included in such a way, pretending to explore any topic outside work.

These people urged themselves. They desired to be exceptional beyond the means of their current circumstances, a motive Iramir could not quite grasp. Their ambition and blind faith led them to believe, despite everything, that all would be well. She had often said that all would be well, or some close approximation of that, but by no means did she ever think she had made it. She was made to do as she was told, and she was committed to predestination still, just with a flagrant omission of the real engine.

What wonders the Library could do with an already functioning engine despite his name, despite everything that had brought him before her. A life measured by his own contributions and an ocean could be made to contribute infinity. She had brought him to the Library fully intent to break him down and find out what he was. It would have been unfortunate, Eram's death, but necessary.

This resolve had shattered once Samuel pressed her. To be free, to live outside. It did not feel right to stand before the world, having stolen another's place to behold it. All those moments attempting to be tender with Eram would turn into nothing. Eram was what could have been, like what Samuel had claimed, and to ensure Eram's continuation satisfied her. It had to satisfy her, this scant, fragile interaction with the outside.

She tugged on the lion's ears, feeling its soft velvety fur against her living skin but feeling nothing with her ceramic portions. Silver trails of mercury lined the steps up to her office. Scattered cinnabar petals lay quiet in their rest. There was someone waiting at the top, framed by the open doors of Eram's escape and the darkness that was her office. It was Weill.

"Why does it have to be Samuel?" demanded Weill as soon as Iramir crossed the sixth step up. Iramir remained serene against Weill's aggression. The hound towered over Iramir from the office landing. "I can find the engine a hell of a lot better than he can. We don't care about treaties anymore, right? So let me tear up some stupid city."

"I need tact," said Iramir. The lion stayed where the barrier once stood, sniffing at the broken boundary. A paw tested its new lands, patting the fifth step as if it should not exist. Iramir watched it whine softly and plead with a tilt of its head for permission to follow. The ensuing conversation would not be quiet. To keep any semblance of privacy would mean sending the lion away to prevent it from reporting to Grimleer.

Weill gritted her teeth. "The Library needs that engine. This broken world will change. My curse will get better because of him, right? So why am I not out there? Grimleer says our most valuable resource is time. So what about broken kneecaps and decapitated heads? It'll all be fixed in the end. Samuel's too slow for this stuff. He's too useless now. When was the last time he was out on duty?"

The lion narrowed its gaze and glared at Weill. Iramir realized the lion had caught her own irritation at the hound. She took a slow breath to correct the apparent displeasure in her face and posture. She very much believed in Samuel to correct her mistake for failing Eram, and it was frustrating to deal with Weill at the moment. Iramir did not want to be reminded how she was failing her Library as well. To risk being cajoled into reneging her promise to Eram. The lion growled. Iramir took the last few steps up to Weill and then past her into the shadows of her own office.

"I have full authority over you, Weill. You will stay in the Library. Return to your station and if I have need of you, I will request it." Iramir observed that even as Weill kept her hands in her pockets and kept her head down, the trembling of her body revealed Weill was keen on smashing something.

"I don't understand," admitted Weill. "And I know I don't need to understand, but this, this is so important. Grimleer says the new age is just around the corner. All that fear of, of dying, just goes away. It'll be better, it'll be alright, like you always say. Does that man mean more to you than the Library?"

Yes.

That was the split decision. She trusted the Library to handle itself well even with sub-optimal solutions. An alternative engine was feasible enough even if lives were lost along the way. Loss of life was business as usual now.

Even so, it felt uncomfortable denying the Library in such a way. It was not denial, just a shifting of what was allowed. Grimleer would be disappointed in her, as would Samuel, because another engine meant a missing moon. She had chosen the worst of all options, had she not? An ocean in tumult from her interference, a Library in discord throwing more bodies into an ocean without benefit, and Samuel to be denied what he had wished for all these years.

Samuel would fix her mistakes. Grimleer would fix her mistakes. Iramir had never felt so useless. She simply wanted to return to work. Impatience demanded all these problems be resolved, however poorly the current forecast was, and finally be over with. She was only valuable as a means to an engine. There was no freedom to be had for her, but she could assure Eram's. Eram had to survive her. She was not slave to misfortune. She could see to an ocean home, safe and sound and, by proxy, maybe Samuel would be content.

"He means enough to me to necessitate I send Samuel," was Iramir's muted response. Weill would only ruin the effort to keep an ocean dreaming. Eram would simply not survive a second return to the Library. It had to be selfishness, all this in repayment for an evening's company.

"Do you not trust me? It's because of last night, isn't it?" Weill lifted her fist from her pocket. The lion roared, leaping between them and forcing the hound back ungainly steps. Weill was shocked, having not realized the barrier was broken.

Too zealous, all her keepers. "Stop," she murmured to the lion, grabbing it by the scruff and pulling it away. Weill held nothing but a crumpled letter. The lion returned to Iramir's side, sweeping around her and licking her hand.

"I got a letter stating I was fit for duty," said Weill, "but that doesn't matter. If I had just done better, we wouldn't be in this situation." Weill nodded to the lion. "So it can go anywhere now, huh? I'm just being replaced?" Weill kicked the floor and crushed the letter under her foot. "I'm here to ask for permission. Grimleer is offering salvation. It's trial stuff, I'm sure you know, but I want to take the lab rat part. If I can do magic again, I can"—Weill breathed sharply—"I can give myself up. I'll be useful again. I'll do anything for the Library."

*Anything*, Iramir mouthed. "What does duty mean to you, Weill? There is no success rate to speak of."

"To make a difference. And anyway, if there's someplace that's going to help me, it's here. Whenever I go on assignment, I just hate how useless I am against whatever's wrong with me. And it's always been here that I've stayed powerful. I have a debt to the Library for what they've given me. What they let me hold on to past my prime."

"You want to be exceptional."

"Yeah, I don't want to be left behind. I want to be brave. I'm either gonna end up like that necromancer now or later. Or I won't. I usually beat the odds. I'm finding that engine. For the Library, sure, but also for myself. You're going to let me outside."

"I will not be ordered," snapped Iramir. Moonlit spears crowded the landing, scoring the air and edging painfully close to Weill. "Nothing will be decided for me. I am the Library's authority, and my word is the only command."

Porcelain certainly was not meant for easy assurances. Future companionship, well-kept relationships, and gentle introspection were not outlined in her stated purpose. What lofty goals for something that was not made for it. Iramir hated this razing incompatibility of what she wanted versus what the world demanded. And it had always been here that she had any authority to affect the world.

For the good of the Library, she would ignore all that walked its halls. So long as the Library succeeded, nothing else mattered. There was no need to engage with the outside world any further. It could handle itself without her interference. She did not want to be here, caught in these situations. She had never felt so frustrated and impatient. Please, she simply wanted word that Eram was fine, that the alternative engine was ready, that all her immediate problems had been settled for at least a moment. Relief taunted from distant horizons. She could not explain why this felt so much more suffocating than just business.

"You want to be useful?" asked Iramir. "Die for me. The new world awaits." Whatever it took to end this conversation. Whatever it took to escape this world that demanded the impossible from her, whatever it took to be left alone, to fast track her purpose and be done with everything. Weill left without another word.

The alternative engine would be made to grant a wish for a better world where the law of decay had been overturned. It would not be an instantaneous solution, most likely the foundation to shepherd the new world. To rewrite all of existence required the concept of infinity. Life would be erased and remade. A wish for happiness built brick by brick to Grimleer's specifications. Happiness in a job well done.

# TWENTY-NINE

**VENNER AWOKE AND FOUND THE CARRIAGE EMPTY AND WHOLE.** The train rumbled on the tracks, dipping and leaning. Its shattered wreckage was only a dream to be forgotten. Had the other passengers all gotten off? How many stations had he missed? Had he eaten them? He tugged on his shirt, feeling for the stitches. There was no aftertaste. Nothing queued for drowning. He had simply been left behind.

Foreign language announcements echoed in the empty space. Tunnel graffiti sped by: distorted names in bubble letters, distended caricatures rendered in two dimensions, and then a white face staring right through him, a face that had definitely looked three dimensional. Venner startled, stood up from his seat, and reached out for a tether to keep himself still. He looked down the train through the windows between the carriages. The train kept turning. The carriages responded one by one.

A figure in the shape of a man but made entirely of antlers except for its white, expressionless face and the hooves that grew out from the bottom of its antler legs opened one of the windows of a distant carriage with its pointed antler fingers and slipped in over the seat. It stared straight at Venner with its holes for eyes. Venner's foot slid out, ready to run. The antler man turned around on its cloven hooves and closed the window, even giving an extra shove on the pane to make sure it latched. It rubbed the seat cover where antler bit into the felt, and it brought its hands together near its chest. Its white face observed its surroundings, checking the overhead bins before bending down to search under the seats, row by row.

Venner wondered how this thing would displace his waters. He forced himself away, covering his mouth. The accountant was so beautiful while drowning. Complete and utter destruction, not the paltry dissolution of desire. The person was so unique and so alive compared to his shallow treats of boxes. The utter calm after such struggle was tantalizing when watched from all angles with so many eyes. His head hurt again, but he was filled with such glee. Would anyone miss the antler man if he plunged it into brine?

The antler man opened the door to his carriage. Its antlers rubbed and creaked as it moved. It had a stack of fliers in its antler hands. He did not know where it had found all that. It smelled of honey and freshly cut oak. It crept up to him and passed him what seemed to be a hand-drawn flier for penny cures and half dollar revolvers, though he could not read the language. On the back was the train schedule from a bulletin.

Painted horses sped by along the walls outside the train. They galloped and dived. Their forms broke apart into dots and splatters and reformed. Awkward imagery collected on the tip of his tongue and, as always, demanded to be explained. Say nothing and pretend to be sane. The pretending—the longest he had ever had others think him whole— had lasted no more than a year. He co-mingled with his coworkers. He put out the fires with them. He started a few of his own. There were certainly rumors circulating the office. His defense for keeping his station had been his workmanship. Now that this defense had faltered, he had nothing.

The antler man waited on him the entire while. Patting the stack of fliers in its lap, it had taken a seat across from him. It swayed slightly to its own unheard tune. Venner apologized and was rather thankful the antler man did not mime any judgement. Its expression did not change, but it did look to the floor for a moment. It shuffled the fliers and another set of arms—or antler tines, rather—slipped through the openings of its body. It held a ticket puncher and prodded Venner to reply. Through an opening of one its holes, he spied the light of a pocket watch dangling on a branch. It clicked the ticket puncher expectantly. The antler man was a conductor, it seemed. Venner fished for the ticket.

The conductor took his offering and turned the paper end to end. It seemed it could not read the language either. Venner leaned over and helped it orient the ticket correctly. Its pointed antler fingers were smooth and warm to the touch. He pointed out the box where it needed to punch. The ticket puncher made a hole in the shape of a horseshoe. The conductor raised the ticket to the light, inspecting its handiwork. The conductor then offered the flier again.

"Really, I am not interested," said Venner, taking back the ticket and giving the first flier back. The conductor showed Venner a small black and white photo, old and faded, with ragged edges that had been reinforced with tape. It pointed to the image of a riverbank surrounded by thick trees. There was a family dressed in period clothing. Their caravan was set up by the shore. A child rode atop one of the horses. There was nothing of an antler thing to be seen. Written in caption, the only word he recognized was the river Dneister.

Venner placed the location somewhere in Romania or Moldova. Though if this was the river, much of it had been modernized into cities, bridges, and country homes since this photo was taken. The conductor pantomimed a camera, bringing its hands together over its chest. It flipped to the back of the photo and referenced a monetary amount written in pencil. This was the reason for the fliers. There was a drawing of a boat scratched out for a drawing of an airplane. There was also a drawing of a spaceship attached to a horse in the corner. The conductor wanted to go home or somewhere equally as special.

It collected the rest of its items into itself and nodded at Venner before walking away. He wondered how much it would cost for the airfare, how many revolvers the conductor had to sell, how it was possible for an antler body to traverse in the public eye. It was evident that the conductor had been here for a very long time. It passed through another carriage, traveling to the front of the train.

The stack of fliers had been left on its previous seat. Venner took a page and picked at the edges. There was no gilded residue. It was just paint and paper. He laid the page back down and straightened the stack for the benefit of the conductor. For better benefit, he should return the fliers properly if the conductor was always searching for them. There were scratches in the seat plastic. They were made wider and deeper than with a pocketknife, as if made with claws in idleness.

The station map glued to the rim of the overhead bins was also scratched out in places, written over in marker in others, or plastered with paper amendments that unfolded down, revealing impossible dimensions. He took out his ticket with its preplanned destination to locate himself.

WHERE ARE YOU GOING, read the ticket in stark, black lettering. Whatever else had once been on that ticket had been erased. He checked the back. TURN AROUND. His thumb left a gilded imprint, and he ate his ticket.

# THIRTY

**THE CONDUCTOR MADE ITS WAY TO THE FRONT LOCOMOTIVE,** sliding the gate of its cabin closed behind it. The sound of its hoof falls transitioned from ringing metal to soft plush. It bent down and unrolled the corners of a stained rug that had bunched where the gate had rubbed over it. Steel gave way to wooden panels and a hay roof, yet the rocking on corroded rails reminded the conductor where it really was.

This caravan facsimile was cramped but homely. Ornate tapestries of owls and forests were draped along the wall. Orange glow bulbs hung on single wires from the ceiling. Handwritten letters were pinned across every empty space. Thin, off-white paisleys covered a splintered table burdened with subway brochures and newspaper clippings. Wet brushes clattered in their open bottles of paint.

There was a furnace in the corner. The fire was low and fading. The conductor opened the furnace and sifted through the trough of coals underneath it. There was not much left to sift through anymore, just scant shards and dust. The conductor took the trough by the sides and gave it a sharp tug to free it from the furnace drawer. The shards rattled and the dust displaced, but the trough remained unmoved. It checked the hidden drawer rails, feeling all the rust. The trough would not go anywhere.

It rubbed its antler fingers thoughtfully on the furnace before grabbing a subway brochure. It cupped the brochure and used it as a makeshift scoop for all the shards it could find and gathered all the dust it could until its very shaking disturbed its little mountain. It gently carried the scoop into the open fire, brochure and all. The fire crackled and sparked.

The conductor snapped a few of its own antlers and fed the fire for good measure. It rubbed the sharp edges of its fresh wounds, eroding them down to be as smooth as the rest of itself. It watched the fire claim its vestiges, scorching the surface and cracking open the marrow. It did not like the thought of being equated to a trough.

It stretched back, shifting its body so it did not rest on crooked antlers. It turned on the old television nestled amongst horseback figurines and mini succulents in painted pots. The screen flickered with static before warming back up, revealing where it last paused its movie. The word analog flashed in the corner. A cowboy frozen on screen was prepared to walk down an old, beaten path.

The conductor moved a pile of brochures away to get to its VCR. It lifted the doily from the controls and pressed play. The cowboy approached four men who eyed him warily. His boots crunched on the rough ground. The men asked him to leave, mocking him all the while. The cowboy's poncho rippled in the wind as he asked for an apology for his poor mule. The men laughed and the cowboy flipped his poncho over his shoulder.

The camera zoomed in and lingered for that iconic close-up on the cowboy. Smoke billowed from his mouth as his cigarette flared. He did not take too kindly to their laughter. The conductor leaned in, engrossed in the standoff. The scene quickly cut between the hero and villains with their shifting eyes and shaking hands. Their revolvers reflected in the sun.

The carriage gate opened outside its VCR world. It was the man again, carrying its fliers. The conductor perked up. It gestured to the man to come watch with it. The villains tried to act first, but scarcely had they brushed against their gunmetal. The cowboy was quicker on the draw. With ease, the cowboy dispatched all four of them. The tin can gunshots rang around the caravan, the only noise able to break through the rush of a train.

The conductor pulled away from the television and stopped the tape. The fliers were set on the floor by the leg of the table. The man looked around its home. He was dressed very nicely in his suit. The conductor had an idea. It searched through its chest of fabrics and brought out a red silk handkerchief. It offered the handkerchief to the man with a flier again. The man spoke. The conductor still did not understand. The man bit his thumb. He stepped forward and asked again. The room felt smaller and the man much too big.

The conductor stepped back and bumped against the furnace, spilling ash over its leg. It pulled a revolver from behind its makeshift mantelpiece. It cocked back the hammer and aimed squarely at the man. The man was not convinced. He came to the furnace. His hand traced the wall, over the cupboards, over the many westerns on video tape. He smiled and pointed on the flier where the conductor had indicated no bullets for sale to the pictogram of a crossed-out bullet.

The conductor lowered its weapon and placed it back on the mantle. The man gestured to the empty trough and the burning antler inside. He patted over his chest where his heart was, mimicking its own heartbeat uncomfortably well. The conductor sidled away. It did not understand, but felt doom in its core. The roar of the train sounded so foreign now.

The man offered a hand. The conductor shook its head. Its white face was impassioned still but the movement of its body seemed to upset the man, who looked to be growing impatient. He grabbed the gun, opened the empty chamber to one side, and then spun it, listening to the clicks. He ripped a strip of paper from a brochure. The paper was rolled up and slipped it in like a bullet. The paper bullet was centered as the next shot fired and he closed the chamber. He offered the gun to the conductor, handle first.

There was nowhere to escape, and the conductor supplied no resistance. The man showed the conductor how to hold the gun, with the barrel pointed against his chest. The roar of the train sounded like an ocean. The man had a tight grip on its wrist and said something again. The words had a familiar cadence. He was repeating something. This feeling of doom was suffocating. *Go away.*

The sharp point of the conductor's finger rubbed against the trigger. The conductor saw the bullet in the chamber, brass glittering from the fire. It dropped the gun in fright. The man let go. The conductor covered its head, scared the gun might misfire when it landed. The man caught the revolver. He raised an eyebrow to it as he opened the chamber and stood the bullet on the table, then he wiped the damp gun with the silk handkerchief and left it on the ground.

That was paper. The conductor watched him make the bullet and place it in. Yet it saw no magic performed, no transfiguration done. The conductor rubbed its wrist where the man had grabbed it. It glanced at the furnace. It had to ask him. The conductor crept up to the man, offering a scrap of antler. It pointed to the furnace but it looked to its video collection, to its fraying tapestries, and out the door of its false caravan. The train seized as the brakes engaged. The false caravan shuddered. The conductor, unaware of this sudden stop, was thrown around. The single bulbs cut out.

Without motion there was silence. The conductor shuffled in the dimness, surrounded by its shattered antlers. The fire still burned, though most of the fuel escaped through the open cover. Paint had been spilled and brochures scattered. The television and VCR stayed firmly in place, though the conductor needed to make inventory of its collection. There was no man. That was a minor issue. Its train had stopped. Had it hit something outside?

The antlers of its body spread apart to open a bigger cavity of storage. It reached inside the hole of its body. Its arm was swallowed up to the elbow but it did not penetrate to the other side. Tapping antler fingers counted interior items. Past the touch of a swinging pocket watch was cool metal. Its arm slowly retreated from storage and out came within its grasp was the long handle of a scratched grey pole. With a gentle clink, the dangling gaslit lantern was last revealed.

The conductor opened the valve on the propane bottle and took a match from the matchbox taped to the side. Dipping the matchstick inside the furnace, the phosphor lit, and then it dropped the matchstick inside the lantern, igniting the propane. The conductor fiddled with the knob and found a level it liked before leaving the false caravan. The gate closed behind it.

Tall ferns brushed past its antlers. There was no sky, simply a pitch-black backdrop. It stood within a clearing surrounded by strong oaks. There was no evidence of a tunnel or of the rest of its train. A small caravan squatted in the grass where the bucked locomotive should have been. The wooden window was open and the steam of a simmering soup escaped. Horse reins lay out in the open. A basket of freshly picked mushrooms and berries awaited use.

The conductor stooped down and sifted through the grass. It was too quiet here. There was only the noise that it produced—the crush of the ground underneath its hooves, the whipping of waving ferns from its motions. There were no insects or birds in youthful clamor. No horse filled the reins. No wind rustled through the arbor. There was nothing else.

The pole was stuck into the dirt. The lantern swung, squeaking on its hinge. The conductor stepped back into the caravan for a moment. It returned back to the dimness of a crashed train. It left the gate open. The lantern light streamed in. All the packets, all the fliers, all the baubles were carefully moved, along with the rest of its belongings, outside the train. It returned for the letters, unpinning them one by one. It sorted them by years, then months, then days. Then it kneeled down and blew out the fire in the furnace. A shiver ran up its antlers, and it stepped back into this strange vision.

# THIRTY-ONE

VENNER AND THE CONDUCTOR OCCUPIED THIS FALSE DREAM brought to life by the machinations of brine. All this desire for something that was barely even real.

He measured the conductor's shape from end to end as it swam in his ocean and the ocean found where the mind's eye lived. What a wondrous role model as always, the infinite water. The making of a bullet had given him the confidence to handle vague intentions. He could exercise some creativity adjusting the oceanic landscape to his benefit. The damp shale outcropping would be too lonesome a stage for many people.

He watched the conductor move its belongings from a distance. Its body had been carved down from an ocean's effort. The gilded threads that held its top layer together had turned sour. Its faint nostalgia of riverbank years produced intangible dreams that crumbled at the application of description. He had tried to make horses. They were not horses. Functional living things required too much detail. Snout, eyes, ears. Enough fur to fill four limbs and organs placed to equestrian compliance. These mistakes never broke the surface.

Venner dared not make anything more significant. He had only the single template of a moon, and the conductor did not want to improve itself. He could not pull another moon from the water without the willing flesh to mold.

A poor solving, this dream, lacking the required nuance the conductor demanded. By no means could Venner replicate the river photo completely. Landscape from the waves, it was simply too difficult to balance conscious compositing against devouring compulsion. Too many details to juggle without a few falling into the ocean; all the living things he could not help but omit. Ocean filled the trapped dead end of this antler puzzle box and not the conductor's proper shape. Perhaps it would have gone better if he was more attentive towards the conductor's soul, or if he had allowed enough time for it to explain itself, but he was not interested being generous toward shapes.

Vague, indirect desire was too tenuous to cheat. Instead of drowning the conductor, he considered whether it was possible that, during the solving, he could build into the unraveling abstraction the means for escape. His want to be free from this train heading nowhere, free from magical reminders, but he could not force the conductor to conform to his wishes. Indirect desire balanced the other side of the diligent lion spectrum too stubborn to move, but at either end, Venner could not affect magic in a way that benefitted him.

The encounter with Not Robin Hood was only successful because Not Robin Hood understood words. In between vague need and hyper focused intentions, his best bet was something conversational. Goodbye morning's normality, he had fallen right back into the arcane mire. Ah, well, practice made perfect. He was not completely condemned by literal interpretation now.

The conductor had made a wreath of spring flowers that perched on its lantern. The many letters rested on its lap where it sat down. The intangible tug of desire settled in acceptance. There was nothing more he could do.

Venner walked by for a final glance of the conductor. The conductor stared back. It gathered its letters close to itself as if it feared he would take them away. He shook his head and collected the single thread that led from the fire of the lantern and back through the caravan door. He was more curious about what lied at the end of this line.

The conductor seemed relieved and began to read again. It waved goodbye, and Venner reflexively waved back because his body was useful for that sort of thing. Though these interactive features did not properly compensate his uselessness at his intended function.

Venner still needed to clean up this troubled forest façade, but he bit his knuckles to help stem the abyssal pressure. This patience, somehow, felt like appropriate compensation for a wave of goodbye. He waited in the destroyed train, watching the conductor read through each letter within ocean dreams, watching the conductor decay in crackling ivory within waking reality. It passed finished letter after letter into the fire. Ash piled against the glass. The conductor read until there was no more and then blew out the fire. The ocean cleaned up all else.

# THIRTY-TWO

VENNER WALKED WARILY DOWN THE THIN METAL RAIL, CAREful not to slip. Water lapped the underside of his shoes. He stretched out his hand, letting the gold thread of a lantern slide through his fingers. The seized train engine had been left behind turns and straights he did not count. One step following the other, he walked by another missing piece of a carriage.

There had to be a way out, or another way at least for him to get more experience with these oceanic and magic things. The tunnel widened into a station expanse. This station was wedged inside a ring of railway exchanges. The ins and outs wound impossible tracks that spiraled up and across. A speeding train full of unwitting passengers curved around the ceiling.

Far up in the darkness were twinkling lights, and up out of sight beyond them trailed the thread. He tugged the thread, but it held fast. The stars chimed in their underground night. Getting to work should not be this difficult, but here he was, fishing for stars in the open air. He sighed and let go.

He hopped over the flooded rails onto the platform and looked back at the river. It had once been but a few inches high but had now risen to lap at the platform. The thread twisted and knotted in the currents.

"Hullo there," cried out a man who was rowing down the tracks. He tipped his bowler hat. "This is rather amazing, isn't it? I've never experienced flooding in my part of the tunnels before." His boat grazed the edges of the platform. "Dearie me." The man reached out and patted the painted concrete of the station. "Are you well?" asked the boatman.

Stunned, Venner made a few aggressive steps towards the boatman before stopping himself. Conversation instead of zeal, he quickly reminded himself. He cleared his throat and pointed up. "Are those your stars?" he asked. The boatman laughed.

"They are. They were once on loan, but it's been so long, I support the idea they're mine now." The boatman tried to lean over to board the station, but the boat kept floating away as he shifted his weight. The boatman paddled back until the wood graced the concrete again. The boatman scratched his forehead. The thread tangled in the paddle's movement. The stars above jingled whenever the boatman tugged.

The boatman checked his pocket watch, rubbing a thumb over the glass face to wipe away the water. He dragged a heavy crate coated in coal dust out from under his seat and motioned to Venner. "May I ask you to take this onto the platform? I shall not get them wet." Venner grabbed the crate from the boatman. "You may set it anywhere where there is no water," the boatman said. Venner set it where he stood.

The waterline for a moment spilled over the station's edge and soaked the concrete. Venner moved the box to a nearby bench of waiting instead. The boatman shook his pocket watch at Venner. "I had a schedule to keep, but this turn of circumstance makes such duty difficult. It makes it impossible to patrol certain bylines and overways. I've never had such a black mark on my file, and here I find myself quite ignoble about my first."

Venner made no comment. The boatman tucked his watch back in his vest pocket and slipped a leather-bound notebook from under his hat. He flipped to the next empty page, handily marked by a black binder clip, and made a few notes while glancing up and down at Venner. "Stranded by these rising tides, are ye?"

"I'm sorry for your tunnels and the flooding," said Venner. "I did this."

"Did you? That was quite rude of you," said the boatman, incredulous. He shifted the binder clip to a new page. "Then, man of water, may I ask that you lower the levels? I would like to have my nooks neat. You are quite compact for such a fearsome display of prowess. I have seen many people and the many things as their luggage. There's a certain gravitas that follows those powerful beings who consider the elements playthings. You, sir, seem like a madman."

Venner felt his face twitch. The boatman asked, "Do you mind returning my drowned trains? It would take ages to service them, but I suppose there is little you could do about that." Venner thought that he could, but he did not feel compelled to confront the boatman as he had the conductor. He felt quite grounded, properly anchored to an even-keeled existence. He had skimmed enough from the conductor to be satisfied for a while.

"Nothing leaves the ocean," said Venner. The boatman was certainly conversational, but he needed to wish Venner back into society, and right now, he seemed only in the mood for amusement.

"Do they not? Then is it the ocean that dares confound my work? There's business to be done. I have no time for ornery basins. When I mean to keep the bowels of the city clean, I do not mean like this. You are a cruel monkey's paw." The boatman tipped his hat again.

"Did your stars come from the Romanian steppes?" Venner asked. The boatman raised his brow, writing more on Venner's page. "What were they traded for? A pair of penny cures and a pistol?" Venner approached the concrete edge and leaned over the boatman. The boatman settled in his seat, lifting the paddle onto his lap.

"What property of stars could betray nationality, ocean?" asked the boatman. "These are hand-painted crafts, hardly the characters of constellations."

"Stars from antlers lonely, yearning for a home long displaced. The world cannot hold antlers together anymore, if you understand. To make a smile or make a frown, it takes monumental effort. Yet your trains are momentous beasts. So long as they run, so do your appointed conductors."

"I asked for gravitas," said the boatman. "So folds another finger of the paw. These stars were traded for a home. Yes. The best that I could do here and then. I would also like to comment that this is impossibly astute. How do you know of one of my conductors with such familiarity? I've never seen you before." The boatman tore out the page and slipped it beneath his hat.

"I gave the antler conductor what it wanted," said Venner. "The reflection of its dreams upon an ocean. A memory made real of a caravan home amongst the false forest. I would rather call it a poor performance though."

"And this water?"

"There was supposed to be a river but the shape of it slipped through my grasp. Unfortunate. Does it irk you that water seeps in between the cracks of the city foundation, where it seeps into the deeper bowels filled with clockwork and paper scraps?" Venner placed a finger over his lips. "Have you seen a clockwork millipede around here? Between two dead stations there was a little world full of mint leaves and corpses. Have you since then made your rounds and given a look? It was Lacrum towards the bay."

"A clockwork millipede, is that what you call it?" noted the boatman. Something was crossed out on one of the preceding pages.

"Are you uncaring for your conductors? You do not seem angry for what I have destroyed."

"Does one blame the storm for what it is wont to do?" The boatman tucked the notepad under his hat and his pencil up his sleeve.

"Am I a storm?"

"I don't know what else you can be. You are what I heard outside my own office. You have brought the impossible into my domain. I didn't know you could be a man. There was an error on the tracks and a storm surge came after me. Here I was believing that nature had turned over and the sanctity of my domain was now upon numbered days."

A sealed letter was pulled from the boatman's sleeve that was quickly read and just as quickly tucked back in. The boatman then paddled back out into the rail exchange and shouted, "Here I am believing that the storm can be reasoned with. Are you in the business with the likes of stars, o' sudden storm?"

"I am in the business of counting them," said Venner. "There are none, so it is quite an easy job. However, there is something so vexing. There is exactly one moon in the sky. That is one moon too many, you see."

"I've never heard of a storm so concerned with the sky above its body clouds," said the boatman. "Storms always like to look below. Who are you?" He changed the signals by jabbing the end of his paddle against the underwater levers. Venner stared at the boatman and laughed nervously. The speeding trains above them shifted destinations, spiraling between the stars.

"I am a good shape, am I not?" asked Venner. He traced the outline of his arm and his face.

"I suppose so. A head, two arms, two legs, and a torso to tie it all. Is that what you want?"

"I want—I want to leave," Venner said with relief. He patted himself down, somehow satisfied with the boatman's answer. "I need to get to work, the station at Lorcaster-Shorn."

The boatman brought his hands together. "I thought so. By no means are these tunnels homely, not even to a storm. Though you have caused quite a riot upon the city's surface streets. Not that I should worry." He took off his hat and picked at the rim. The leather notebook was nowhere to be found. "The city, she has faced worse even if her new attendants are less effective. Have you ever wondered why they're all allergic to the rain? I do.

"Many sordid lots come crawling in your wake when the enforcers do not chase them. Scoundrels, her new attendants. They may call themselves artful, but they're certainly indolent, ignoring you because you're a storm. If I had my way," grumbled the boatman. "I don't suppose you have a ticket? You're a passenger, correct?" Venner tensed. The boatman checked his pocket watch again and scanned the flooded passages around them. "Attendant visitations are instantaneous during drier circumstances. It has been minutes. Minutes! Their weather-born laziness must be curbed. Scoundrels."

"I," Venner started, but he did not want to reveal that he had eaten the gilded thing. "I had a ticket."

"Lost it? I can ferry you to the nearest nominal station, though you might have to remind me which ones are still on the map." The boatman paddled up to the station lip again.

"What would your way have been?" asked Venner. A train sheared through the flooded exchange. The cascade of waves rocked the boat.

"Diligence to their duty, that's all," said the boatman. "My due diligence is to this 'behind the scenes'. Recently, my responsibilities include homing the scores of displaced. For whoever asks and agrees to the conditions, I find places of privacy. The city has decreed to be welcoming to all as of late."

The boatman shrugged, evidently not fully on board with such a decree. He continued, "The city as built was never intended to be a haven, and there are no good places left to put them. The city prefers the honest living instead, burgeoning pure and innocent. So long as the people subsist and consider this city home, the city grows. People drunk like champagne, good for the concrete soul. Taxed a few heartbeats, but who's counting?

"But I say, however fortunate or unfortunate this statement may be, scores of the thaumic are dying. Less trouble, but also less to sustain. The future is uncertain for the city without these heartier meals. When we cross that bridge is when we cross. Every day, there is another train left cold which I must clean up. But you look to have a home, do you not, storm?"

The station began to drip from the ceiling. The boatman put his hat back on. Worry weighed on the boatman's brow. "You're amiable so far, storm, if still strange. I suppose today's a good day to learn how to negotiate with weather. May I ask that you stop whatever it is that you plan on doing? The health of the city is paramount to me."

"I am late for work," said Venner. "I need the distraction, and perhaps my divided attention will avoid turning upon the city. How much longer do I have to stay here?"

"Ah," said the boatman with a shake of his head. "Then may I ask for a reprieve of your request? I would like time. I must attend to this leak of yours. The residents of this background hostel may be familiar with the fluctuations of distaff beings, but the city must be kept functioning. I'm still an attendant myself. I clean the vermin. I repair the cracks. I transport unspeakable things through my passageways."

A terrible mass of raw metal and gnawed flesh fell from the overhead tunnels and into the water, almost capsizing the boatman. The momentary roar of trains sounded too alive and beastly up there. It was the corpse of the clockwork millipede. Its paper shroud had been ripped away. Its long body was crushed in oblong angles. The mass of oil and flesh leaked the smell of exhaust and freshly baked bread. Red brick dust seeped into the water.

The boatman cleared his throat. "I suppose you recognize this, your *millipede*, I believe you called it? I'm just a singular organism in this living city, working my best just to keep her alive. You've made quite the mess last night, but what a blaring whistle it was. We found this parasite due to your interference and dealt with it accordingly. If I were not so occupied with my tunnels and my brethren," the boatman threw up his hands. "There'll be vengeance to be taken on the rust you have caused. Mark my threat, storm."

"The holes were made by the millipede first," said Venner. The millipede had met its fate outside of his ocean, a fact Venner most despised. The millipede would forever remain unsolvable. Its shape, its memory imprint upon his brain matter, would be void of water and immortal. He glared at the boatman. "So the city is alive. The lines are a subsection of veins and arteries and through them are people as lifeblood. What of old lines? Where is this? I assure you there is nowhere you, or any bit of the city, can hide from water."

The boatman had slid another nearby lever closed. "I trim the fat," said the boatman, unfazed by Venner's outburst. "This is a dead station. It's not anywhere anymore. You will not find your way out of here. At the very least, a body like yours cannot travel between gears."

"That millipede was mine to drown. It graced me with a wondrous performance like the stars of crafted meridians. It showed me the rivers, the drowned rats, and where the piper would have come enticing children in tow. You are all Rattus children of gilded machinations. You ask for too much time when you are all in the act of spoiling. There must be repayment for the millipede transgression. Oh, world so large, I am infinite."

The boatman shifted in his seat. He rocked the boat to find a point of better balance and then stood up. He brought the paddle up with him, resting the end of it on the worm wreckage. "I do not imagine a fetid contraption such as this deserves an allusion to stellar majesties. Keep looking up, o' storm." The boatman dotted his forehead with the back of his hand, checking for sweat.

"All because we did not pay the piper," sighed the boatman. "The piper was a cheat. The contract stipulated only rats for slaughter, then the piper grew tired of rats. See the pits in the concrete and holes in the city fabric? Not by a Rattus tooth, but a beak. Many beaks and a racket of fraudulent, swarming feathers. We have our evidence, and we'll take the piper to the court of the city's make. Your assistance will be weighed in a future time. Mind you, this millipede is not yours."

Jealous ocean obsessions overwrote his personal authority. His human frailty was front and center under a spotlight. The boatman stood victorious over the poached shape. The ocean would not have let the millipede escape the first time. Who had put him in this bottle of flesh, capped by physical jaws? The boatman pulled another folded letter from his sleeve and read.

"Put down your hands, storm," said the boatman, turning his attention back to Venner. "Have some respect for yourself. It's a nice body for a storm." The stars jingled again as another train passed. "Oh, I've missed one." The boatman changed the tracks again, swinging the rusted iron with another heavy thud of his paddle. Then there was silence as the last tunnels closed with patching concrete. "The trains will not stop for you. You will neither have glimpses of them lest you be tempted to drown them too. You'll be kept here in quarantine until the city decides what must be done with you." The boatman waved the letter, indicating these commands had evidently been penned by the city.

The boatman rowed away into the roving brickwork, like his peers. The paper men and the boatman were the city's attendants, and for their gift of service, the city let them go anywhere. The desecrated millipede floated below. Whatever neon line Venner could follow had since wasted away. Something had to fill the worm's place, some close enough approximation so that by proxy the worm could be solved. The worm had been created, and by satisfaction of a devoured accountant did an ocean forget about the oil alphabet and the liquid voice. Find the worm's creator. Slay compulsion.

Venner wondered if this knowledge of a creator or who was the piper was shared amongst all the attendants. He wanted to return to his apartment and call that number written on the black card given to him by that paper man just to ask who. He had to solve himself into wellness with due diligence. Confine his dreams back into nonexistence and worry only about the consequences of deadlines and performance reviews.

But before he could do any of that, he needed to escape. He started to explore this dead station, its cracked tiles and paint wore thin. Stairs led nowhere. Band posters with their heads torn off plastered the walls. A dirty station mural was painted in gaudy colors and boorish font. The letters were too crowded and slack to make room for stallion beasts.

The rains intensified, leaking through cracks in the tunnel walls. A star splashed down. Its yellow paint bled out into the muddy water. What was the boatman made of if he could withstand the water opposite the paper men he called so lax? A pulp too premium for the high efficiency factory, perhaps. Another star was swallowed by the river.

This river flowed with trash and patchwork train, yet to hear every falling star adding to this mess aggravated him. To witness his river filling but be unable to be clean was excruciating. Whatever peace had carried him was stripped of a feather for every star. Wings flew too close to these handheld suns, and their heated wax dripped up.

A star knocked into a floating trash can. The resounding clang threw a small dark shape into the river as the makeshift raft overturned. It was a rat, paddling in the river currents. Venner bent down by the platform edge. The rat looked right at him with tiny beady eyes. It grasped desperately at the open air. Intent was intent, no matter man, lion, or rodent. He plucked the rat from the river and let it settle in his hands.

Certainly, he did not have the means to escape himself and work the magic that allowed the attendants to travel. He watched the rat rub its face with tiny paws and groom itself with a flickering pink tongue. It collected the tip of its tail into its paws and looked at him. Its nose twitched, and its ears changed from direction to direction. The rat made a small, high-pitched huff. The small breaths tickled his skin. It was bursting at the seams with vigor. Gold lined its existence, all existence, bled by the beating heart, created by the thoughtful mind. Think, exist, and then be damned. He bit his thumb. *Be gentle*, he chastised himself.

"It would be nice to be free from this dreary place, would it not?" asked Venner of the little rat. It tilted its head. Venner rubbed its cheeks and scratched behind its ears. Not that a rat could ever understand him. The rat held onto him with paws that patted and prodded him in curiosity. It climbed off his hands and onto the platform to run along the edge and watch the river flow. It circled him, standing up on its legs every so often to search.

The boatman had been thorough, diverting endless walls with nowhere to go. Venner scooped a wet star from the river into his hands. It was a painted glass bauble of winding features and tubes. Small candles lay waterlogged within its center. The rat investigated the bauble with the twitching of whiskers and the sliding of its furry body throughout the structure. Venner salvaged nearby star after star until he had a pile of them stacked beside him.

The rat climbed and explored his tower of stars. The concept of a rat lived solely within his mortal view. No extra eyes claimed their share. It was soothing to experience something that had no cognizance of supernatural things or had any sort of imposition upon reality. It amused him to see it play, to see it hop back down and attempt to drag his hand up the tower with it. The rat sat down upon its peak and looked up to the shower of falling painted stars.

It wanted to show him something that was not here. The sight of sparkling lights meant a busy station where people like Venner sometimes dropped food.

The Rattus shape emerged, or rather, Venner had realized its existence floundering in his ocean. Physical eyes could avoid seeing, but his other eyes had no eyelids and no hands to save them. The realization could not be undone. Infinity would never collapse so finely back in the body it was packaged in. To solve a Rattus shape was a simple matter.

The world righted itself in proper order. A train passed by, the river pushed out of mind. Venner staggered back from the blue line at the edge of the platform. The stack of glass stars collapsed from the tremors of heavy machinery and buried the remains of a rat. The train doors slid open, and the crowd stepped out. Living, groaning, wasteful things. After all his effort to wash a station clean of one, they made his nausea worse.

He would cut the threads of crowds and watch them drown. His wounds itched. There was infection in his station. Heat lingered on his brow. He would eat them and shrink his world back down to only him. What a beautiful idea. *Eat them and be small again.*

"You have done enough. Is this not what you wanted, storm? A chance to leave here. It would be useless to imprison you again," said the boatman at his side. "Your freedom had been negotiated by another attendant with the payment of one millipede contraption and the promise to keep you out of trouble, but you didn't give me the chance to unlock your prison door. No respect for the ceremony of it all." The boatman offered Venner a painted star plucked fresh from the concrete skies. The flickering light reflected the interior glass facets in vibrant color. "Whose business is this? Look up. Ignore the people."

"If you want to know why attendants are so fragile, it's because you are made of paper," said Venner. "You all are. You, in particular, are older than those quick-fire men made from a forest rationed." The boatman had been made of thicker and richer stock. A bygone product from a bygone age. Spy with inhuman eyes—.

Hands covered Venner's sight from behind, and the voice of that wondrous attendant, cleanly crimped and sweetly familiar, whispered into his ear, "Where is the man we had watched on those streets, who dreamed of tax exemptions and worker quandaries? Who took me by the coat and wanted connection? When did the ocean turn so ravenous?"

The paper man let go, but kept Venner from turning around. People jostled around them, but never made contact or notice. Venner heard the tearing of paper, the rustling of its folds, and saw the neat, little square offered to him.

"I think I've learned the rules by watching, even if a sample size of two is not quite sound," said the paper man. "I offer a part of me. I wish upon a shooting star for you to be home safe and sound, for you to be free from your terrors in a world so terrifying." Venner stared at the offering held by the quivering paper hand. Extra eyes might be blinded for a time, but paper was ultimately incompatible with water.

"What devilry is this?" decried the boatman to the paper man. "Don't shush me, you scoundrel. You are still disobeying our orders even if the storm can be tamed. He needs to be kept under finer watch. I have no trust you lot will be as diligent above ground." The boatman stamped his foot on the tile of the station platform and glanced at Venner with a thorough frown. "Do not send the storm down here again."

"The city doesn't need to know," said the paper man. "Out of sight, out of mind. Isn't everything alright, ocean?"

# THIRTY-THREE

**The machines of Grimleer's laboratory hummed gently** while Grimleer and Iramir checked the resonance on a new batch of false engines. Measurement sequences activated on a timed schedule, and a concurrently running post-processor on the computer analyzed for any frequency peaks. Eram's minor miracles of hearts inside crystal cages had been thoroughly examined, and at the moment, defied complete replication.

Iramir examined the results on the computer screen, keeping notes and hand calculations on a nearby journal. She tapped pen on page until it slipped out of her grasp and rolled across the worktable. Packing tape had been used to keep her hand together. The shattered ceramic was barely shaped into three fingers and a palm. Her heartbeat opened and closed these porcelain wounds ever so slightly.

She had refused repair, hiding the fact that her damage was progressing on its own despite how careful she'd been. Grimleer had always headed the effort, but her insistence on restarting research for a world engine changed his mind easily enough. She had assured both Grimleer and Samuel that she would not leave the Library again to settle any further worries.

The trials to reverse engineer the phylactery had shown promising if unstable results. Nothing obscured its function. It was anima at its purest, free from the perspective of a caster. An emergent order of magic as if reality simply decided for things to be and had always been. Missing were the mathematical foundations of any thaumic system from the last few millennia. By their nature, these were nigh unrepeatable except by luck and circumstance.

Grimleer had busied himself analyzing the various responses that his particular article emitted. He stopped bothering to cream and sugar his coffee after the third cup. They would need more recipients to implant these prototype obelisk designs. Hardly a day had passed and they had already lined up and thrown away a dozen lives.

Harken would not be receptive to any changes in contract, if the city would even tolerate her presence again. The act of grave robbing was impolite enough, and then to ask for the living, with expedited delivery, would not happen. There were other contacts, of course, where the stuck knives of favor could be pulled much to the relief of her third parties. If not quick enough, there was always the unwilling internal stock.

Too many human bodies failed, just like before when the project was still considered new. It was not enough to replicate the ley lines and circles. The rune words fashioned only lifelessness or a life too violent for its host. There was still much of the general framework to be deconstructed. Grimleer's fear was that there was not enough time to explore these possibilities, to be so close to greatness only to have the Library finally fall.

Iramir opened old reports and began annotating any frequency clusters and separating elements. Weill had been one of the first up and the few willing, not that this enthusiasm averted her death. A name, a life's worth of experience, and good luck sayings could not keep destruction forever at bay. Weill had become no different from the nameless once thrown into the sea.

*Anything for the Library*, Weill's words repeated in her mind. Other people had the right to their own decisions, this intrinsic property to real, living things, choosing with all the risks attached and dealing with the consequence as required. To go so far to gain nothing was a tragedy, objectively, but people chose tragedy regardless. All the more important that she makes the right decisions to help them avoid their miseries.

A dozen deaths could have been avoided if she had revealed a moon's hand in creating an engine. Weill could have been saved with fairer dice, but Samuel would despise the solution that Iramir throw herself into the ocean. Yet was it fair to the whole scheme of existence for her to place Samuel just a little higher than almost everyone else? The remains of her legacy made Eram. She was expected to give herself up to forge a temporary engine, however it had to happen. The world needed this, and to stand in the way of duty would be negligent. Had she no love for the world?

The real, living things needed comfort and assurance. Their scurrying could not be helped. They needed all the love they could get. She had to show concern, however muted and difficult it was. It would be much easier in the form of competence. The ocean would listen. Eram confirmed it. Progress demanded sacrifice and Grimleer needed a moon. Iramir hoped that Eram was well and that he was safely at home, free from the clawing desires of a legacy. It scared her, considering otherwise.

She massaged her loosening limbs. It was not painful, but it was uncomfortable. For the temporary good of Samuel, she kept quiet. For the ultimate good of the Library, she would have to tell Grimleer her revelation eventually. Grimleer still had his vigor, and Iramir only intended to make such a disclosure as an eleventh-hour grace. She sent a print request for her annotated reports and turned around to find Grimleer staring at her.

"What?" she asked. Grimleer shifted his glasses.

"I have seen more of you today than I have in a whole year," said Grimleer. Iramir made a noise in confusion.

"Well, I am quite interested in the success of this project," said Iramir, making her way to the printer located by Grimleer's desk. The machine clicked and whirred to life.

"I appreciate your presence and your initiative. Despite a wasting world, you have managed to keep the Library alive. You have grown to be so useful. I remember you so much smaller, running amok in the laboratories, being my littlest assistant. The lengths you would go to make your own light."

"Nostalgic, are we?" said Iramir. "You reprimand Samuel for the same sort of bothering."

"We are in the very midst of progress. A benign discussion would be forgivable, I would think. I heard Samuel was on assignment."

"I would think my grand magister would be above petty eavesdropping." She collected the warm pages and squared them against the desk.

"I was curious why your hound wanted to be part of the project and whether she had express permission. I have no interest in mission management, but on the subject of Samuel and nostalgia, we need to discuss his future in this institute. It would be good to return him to field duty. Do you still make your rounds in the medical wing?"

"I have had less time as of late. Political excursions do not rest as the Library demands more necessities. It has been a few years since I last wrote a prescription or provided any consultation. I think it was even before Weill was appointed."

Samuel had always called her rounds "playing doctor." It hurt to have her efforts diminished like this. He never seemed to trust her to fend for herself, insisting that she avoid all manner of Library work. She was too fragile and, by implication, useless. She preferred instead to follow in Grimleer's footsteps, trailing behind him when he used to head patient care. Eventually, Grimleer trusted her to provide aid when she was available. He never rejected her unprompted decision, even making sure to tell her she was appreciated then.

"Lost causes, most of them now. More dead than alive. This engine is our great equalizer. We will be beyond individual care. Bulk process is what we should strive for."

She began searching the drawers for a stapler or paperclip to bind the report. Pens, notepads, scrap metallics from old experiments, the music sheets for when Grimleer used to tutor her on how to play the piano and lesson plans detailed during testing lulls. This was his personal laboratory. Other than his office, he spent the most time here. It was different with Grimleer. He had always made it quite certain anything outside of her purpose was for mute amusement.

"It has been quite a while since our last lesson," murmured Grimleer. "I always meant to sort these things properly." Samuel wanted her to take up music, even after attempts to push her towards his favored violin had gone awry. It did him well, and he had hoped the same for her. She had taken a liking to the piano instead, an interest Grimleer actually encouraged. Music was one of those interests that Samuel threw to the wall to see what stuck and never asked about again.

Yet music became one of the few things she shared with Grimleer other than the research. It was difficult otherwise to have Grimleer be even the least bit satisfied with her. His present good mood was only a product of her agreement to give second wind to a world engine. But objectively, Grimleer would always have been the easiest to satisfy. So long as the Library continued, that was enough to fulfill the purposes of her creation.

What Samuel wanted was outside her documentation. All those small, tender moments culminated in Samuel's ever crushing pining for her freedom. Everything she did for the benefit of the Library always seemed to disappoint him.

She knew to love was important, that she should cherish the world, etcetera, etcetera. She'd never had the opportunity to exercise those virtues outside his tutelage, not without subterfuge. Now she had naïvely done so with something as dangerous as the ocean. She was not made for this heartfelt extoling. The pain of failing at something beyond her purpose hurt with a cruel sharpness. She should not have been left to experience such empathy.

And she should not have been so smitten with the world or with Eram. The talk of stars in a ruined apartment promised such wonder. If only she could accept his gentle nudging to stay outside and see the city skyline. She could witness where artificial stars lined the very horizons, live within the quiet moments where her legacy had been pushed out of mind. She wanted to be validated not as a means but as one of the realer things she admired. She wanted to make amends for terrible social habits and practice conversing out of self-improvement. Maybe she could even match Eram in spoken ambition, not the meager answers barely meant to move a single-sided dialogue along.

She must not want more. It would only lead to disappointment.

"Why did you bother?" asked Iramir. Grimleer would assure her proper place in the world and lay her doubts to rest. She examined the music sheets and all the notes Grimleer and she had made together, where he had helped her on more difficult sections, where he had even written notes of praise. "This is all so far in excess for just a means."

Grimleer rubbed the bridge of his nose. "You can be very frustrating, Claire. You always had the proper grasp of your purpose. I saw no reason other than malice to deny your interest. I am glad you did not end up sharing Samuel's sentiments and let interest interfere with divine duty. To dictate the future of man requires a strong hand but by no means a lonely one."

Iramir took the time to weigh Grimleer's words that perhaps he gave no second thought to. There was a strange relief that welled within her to know that Grimleer felt this way. It was amazing even, to have Grimleer never lord her enjoyment of certain outside things over her, or ever imply that she was lesser for what she was, that she was lesser than those real things. Enjoying outside things was not an exception, it was expected.

Grimleer squeezed back where her hand entwined within his. Oh, that was unintentional. She had not realized she was holding onto him. Grimleer only meant his best for the good of the Library. His sheer confidence put her at ease, the sheer love of validation. His absurd enthusiasm had hardly been beaten out of him by years of failure. He would stare down the face of fatalism and be victorious. She could not bear to disappoint him.

"Grimleer, I have a hypothesis on how the engine survives," said Iramir. "I believe the engine requires the sacrifice of a moon to function."

Grimleer stroked his beard. "Is it that indicative from those reports? Well, do you have something to test that?" Iramir flipped the sliver of metal in her hands and stepped into the open center of the lab. She declined the pre-drawn ritual circle of his workspace or any grandiose summon of her halo. The metal hovered in the air. With steadied breath, she imagined the ocean that lingered beneath the Library. It wanted her, waited for her, and always listened with rapt attention.

Metal crystallized into glass and filled with a liquid crimson. It was a quick transformation as if the ocean had waited forever for this appetizer moment. Iramir steadied herself against a chair. In the silence of their amazement, the telltale beatings of a living heart echoed through them. The glass engine quivered from the force of its newly begotten organ.

"Make a wish Grimleer. I suggest something inconsequential in case anything goes wrong," said Iramir. Grimleer recovered from his speechlessness and cleared his throat.

"I wish for another cup of coffee," said Grimleer. The false engine cracked and leaked ichor. Iramir gasped from the sudden surge of pain throughout her body. Ceramic cracked as she tightened against the chair involuntarily. The gasp, she hoped, would be misconstrued as surprise. The ichor darkened with the distinct smell of coffee. Barely a few ounces were squeezed from stone until the engine crumbled into dust, destroying her focus.

Iramir laughed softly. "Ah, that was a try. Not exactly edible, I apologize." The sight of Grimleer so astonished silenced her immediately. She was scared, imagining Samuel in his spot and starting another tirade about how fragile she was. Grimleer rushed to her side and held her close to him. Iramir froze. Please, she did not want to hear it from Grimleer too. He held her tightly, and despite herself, she leaned into his embrace. He was warm.

"A new world," said Grimleer, "free from the tyranny of decay. Existence will have its deserved tomorrow. Life will surpass its fated death. We can rewrite the world. This is so wonderful, Claire." Iramir shrunk in his arms. "You will herald the wondrous age. We must not waste time."

She waited and when she had gotten over feeling so small, said, "Of course I will. Of course there will be time." Any sacrifice as needed. Finally, salvation. She would be bright; she would be brave. This was the fearlessness Grimleer nurtured in her, for the world was fraught with difficulties. She hid the blood that leaked from her nose by pretending to be bashful under her stack of reports. Grimleer squeezed her shoulder and he offered to make another pot of coffee, leaving the laboratory without her reply.

It was a fundamental law, decay. The whole of reality had to be reset from the first insistence to remove such a rule, and the reinstatement of prior things were only assured by a tacit promise. There was too much detail to handle, merely impossible to remember and recreate perfectly. Set the world over again. Roll the new set of lives and experiences. By weight of existence, it evened out. The new world will be unknowable.

The old world effectively dead. Impossible parallels to be drawn, because who knew and who cared.

Iramir observed the remains of the false engine. She wished that Eram would be fine and that Samuel would understand. Her phone buzzed. It was Samuel calling at a bad time. Her heart went quiet and the silence plummeted in her chest. Samuel would never agree to this. Samuel must agree. The world needed to be turned over, to be kinder to its inhabitants. No more skeletons, Samuel. This was the opportunity to cleanse the Library of its bloodshed. She would be the last sacrifice and the Library would see to the new world.

# THIRTY-FOUR

"NOW LEAVING LORCASTER-SHORN. THIS IS THE YELLOW LINE to Epistal. Next stop, Truant," sounded the train announcements.

Eram had not been at work again. Caide sighed, tapping his fingers against his metal thermos. Eram could be very difficult at times when he actually had the presence for it. The database that Eram oversaw was entirely undecipherable, and the deadline to present the new block of wing designs was fast approaching. *Undecipherable*, a rather muted term. There was worse breakroom talk. Despite that, Caide did find himself respectful of Eram's work. Eram was competent when the state of mind allowed. The man thought a mile a minute, and his logs sprawled, tracking every foregone conclusion. He was an operator outside the bounds of convention.

The work was infallible. When it came. Eram's last check-in was a half-finished discussion on hyper-deformables and related amalgams. Caide planned to take these reports home for a more thorough reading. He might find the inspiration for some foothold in the comfort of his living room and the fourth marathon of police comedy.

If only he actually defended Eram at work. He started to grind his teeth. It didn't matter. Eram never acted like he was bothered by the rumors, and Caide wanted to keep good relations with other coworkers. Another stop forced him to squeeze against the interior wall of the train car, letting other people out, then in.

The last conversation they'd had was not pleasant. Caide had noticed Eram kept deliberately away. A sudden crossing of the maddening Rubicon and whatever tenuous thing they had, drowned. The new ordinary was keeping to themselves, alone.

"Just plain crazy," said those gathered round the water cooler, rarely considerate of the turned back. This exasperated sentiment was only deepened by others being forced to take over Eram's mishandled work. Yet none of them had any qualms about interacting with him under the thrash of deadlines. He was useful, then. It was the only time anyone might possibly want him around.

Caide thought of himself as better than that. All those little conversations without a project on the line had built a decent comradery between them, at least he thought so. Outside the mumbling discord of electric demons, Eram was quite nice to hang out with, though there was a certain coldness to him that Caide could never pierce. Eram never hesitated offering aid and always encouraged whatever new hobby Caide wanted to try. Eagerly confident to succeed, Eram chewed the scenery and obviously liked the sound of his own voice. The man loved to be right. All in good jest, however. Maybe.

Caide hoped Eram would have the confidence to confide in him one day. Eram probably did not see it the same way. He no doubt saw the conversation as a failure of his own character.

A pair of students with fraternity emblazoned sweatshirts took their spots across from the door and tucked their backpacks beneath the seat. A woman settled nearer the back, nestling her newly-purchased wares on her lap and her gym bag between her feet. Then entered a man dressed in a black suit, his skin pale but wound ridden. The scars were fresh. The smell of blood still lingered. He looked freshly mugged, robbed of gentle dreams as his dark eyes betrayed his nightmares. His body trembled as he found an empty seat, hands clutching at his head and clawing down his chest. Eram.

Caide navigated between people and placed his hand on the headrest next to Eram. Someone else paused mid-sitting. Caide shot the dirtiest glare he knew. He showed teeth and the seat was his.

"Eram," said Caide. The man startled in his seat. Fear first and then slowly, recognition.

"Caide," he said. Caide smiled in relief. Eram glanced around himself, unable to stop rocking his body. "Why are you here? You should be at work. I—I need to get to work," exclaimed Eram. Caide held him by the shoulder to keep him from standing.

"Eram," Caide urged. "Half day, remember? The end of two weeks. You know what day it is, right?" Eram swallowed hard and nodded feebly.

"I know. I know."

Such behavior could only be tolerated for so long, especially after this recent string of absences. Caide inspected his thermos, crisscrossing his nails down the burnished logo. He tugged on his necklace, twisting the chain around his silver charm of a seven headed spear. Oh the admonishment he would get from Eram if he got a single thing wrong about the work. How much clearer could it be, Eram would say. "Aloof" was a word that did not cover enough; frustration abounded with all the pages that Eram had torn away. Caide searched through his messenger bag.

Eram sat quietly in his seat, leaning on his arm. Caide handed over a binder. "I would like a second opinion. Or maybe just a clearing of the headspace. You think these flight margins are right for colder temps? I've added the preliminary CFD analysis. There are concerns if the heating elements fail. I'd like to know your number."

Eram agreed to this workplace consultation, turning the pages in review. "Work is the perfect medicine for dour nightmares," muttered Eram. "There are no demons between the lines of mathematics. Words do not have excess eyes. The moon stays firmly in a night sky that gives way to the rising sun. Land exists beyond the ocean." Yet past reports professionally articulated page after page after ten of straight nonsense. Caide did not want to comment. It was simply rude. Eram covered his mouth but failed to hide his scowl.

"Outsider thoughts slip in so often," Eram explained to Caide's surprise. "It is humiliating. I got assigned an editor, Caide, because I am a liability. Madness gets published and I cannot explain myself. Mental association folds into obscene shapes that are folded into nothingness." Eram ripped the pages out, crumpling these mental faults in hand. Caide stopped Eram from destroying his work any further. "I suppose I have been quite the topic for everyone else as of late. You must be so disappointed, if not repulsed."

"Hey, let's not be like this," said Caide, getting Eram to settle. "It's sometimes, I don't know, weird, I guess, but it's alright. It's alright." Caide squirmed in his seat. He wanted to comfort Eram, but there were no words to be had. He feared driving another divide between them, but was this not what he wanted? Maybe what Eram, preferred was simply commiseration instead of confrontation.

"I dream about work, honestly," said Eram. "Work is supposed to fix everything wrong with me. I forget about my faults. All the little successes spur a bit of confidence." Eram smoothed out the excised pages. Nonsense repeated endlessly. "This is the proof otherwise, that I am nothing more than my faults."

Caide tugged anxiously at his chain necklace, and it bit into the back of his neck. The thermos sat between his legs, ringing a little as he bounced his leg up and down. He stopped. "I don't want to pry, but is it alright if I take you home?" asked Caide. "I won't ask about anything. And thanks for covering me on the qualification planning for the aerocovers."

"That was a month ago," said Eram. "A bit belated, and anyway, I don't think I should be thanked for something I am expected to do as technical lead." Caide did not respond. He stared at his silver charm. The chain was broken in segments, metal links crushed. Caide then gave Eram another smile and a lift of the shoulders. Eram went back to his reading.

Caide massaged his fingers under the cover of his jacket. He tried to uncurl them from his necklace with his other hand. They were resistant. He leaned back in his seat and readjusted the ends of his jacket. He dug underneath the errant fingertips and clawed as best he could without clenching his jaw. At last, his efforts were fruitful, and he slid the broken necklace into his pocket. His hands hurt.

He unscrewed the cap of his thermos and took a sip of his coffee. The smell of maple spilled over. He really needed to cut back. The cap was crooked when he screwed it back on. The metal threads scraped against each other. He startled and quickly unscrewed. The metal was mangled. The rim of the opening deformed. He bit his lip and curled the edges back by hand.

"That is stainless steel, is it not?" said Eram, bemused. "I almost thought we broke something in test again."

Caide ducked his gaze. "Is it?" Eram looked uncomfortable smiling, as if he was so wary that such happiness would fall away from him at any moment. So Caide felt more uncomfortable too. The stainless steel would not accept the cap anymore. Caide balanced the cap on his knee and slowly flexed his hand and arm, inspecting his strength. He felt beneath his sleeve, checking to make sure the tape wrapped around his arm was holding and pinching his skin. Eram was distracted with work again and was now taking the time to jot notes in the margins. There would be no follow-up questions. Caide was thankful.

He wondered if the company would fill the technical director position or do away with it entirely. Eram would find another career opportunity with ease. Perhaps it would be better for him to find a more appreciative place. Somewhere more understanding.

There was a slow incline of the tracks. The underground tunnels cut into the light, and then they were above ground. Rain pattered across the glass windows and the metal body of the train as it crossed into the older districts. The two men turned to look out. Rain wiped the city streets and grey buildings in a glistening sheen. Caide swirled the coffee in his damaged tumbler. He had left his umbrella back at the office. Torment flickered across Eram's face.

"Is everything okay?" asked Caide. Eram replied with a soft chuckle.

"A headache, I guess," said Eram. The man rubbed his teeth. "You have a VPN on your phone? I need to check something."

"I'm not supposed to let you use my credentials." Caide turned in his seat to shield Eram from potential onlookers.

"This is my work," Eram snarled. "I am this project, and I will not have it undone by want of a nail." He pointed to the appended texts in his binder.

Speaking to his thermos, Caide said, "We're doing the best we can without you. Perhaps a little documentation wouldn't kill you." He dug his nails into the seat and picked away at the loose plastic there. He tried to calm himself. He would need to shave his nails at home. Eram breathed in sharply but bit his tongue.

"I am sorry," Eram said, continuing to detail his notes in the margins. "I will try to fill in as much as I can. How is the new house? I remember you closing on that a while back. You have extended your commute by twice as much. Is it worth it?"

"I'm slowly trying to find where I can cut streets. Maybe take the longer freeway because most of the traffic goes the other way in the morning. I haven't woken up early enough to try that yet. I mean, it's nice and quiet. I'm loving that. But, uh, the pipes burst in my kitchen last weekend. The steel all rusted up. Called up the plumbers and they told me all the pipework needs to be replaced in there. Quoted me the entire worth of my car. Say, do you want to help me replace pipes?"

"I am interested in tearing down your house if that is what you mean," said Eram.

Caide raised his eyebrows. "Or at least maybe help me fix up my drywall, and I'll have a professional fix up my pipes?" he said. Eram shrugged, then softly agreed.

There were certain allowances, Caide noticed, that Eram offered only to him. A certain patience was afforded. The way Eram would look up and ask if he needed more of something, or if he'd had a good weekend. Small talk was extravagant from a man who worked his weight in impassioned theory and ignored everyone else. Eram was good to him. On his more cynical days, Caide wondered if this goodness was born only from his silence about Eram's madness. Today in the breakroom had not been good.

"I need this. I need this job," said Eram in his scribbling. He paused for a moment, rolling the pen between his fingers. The nib rested against the paper, leaving behind a dark blob of ink.

"You have over a decade of experience," Caide said. "You could manage a ten, twenty percent raise, easy."

"Not the money, Caide. I need"—Eram breathed—"I need the distraction."

"A month of rest, I think, would do you better. Maybe therapy, but— but I don't want to push you. I mean." Caide gently stopped Eram by lifting his hand and prompting Eram to reread his work. The notes of competent, technical risk analysis tumbled into manic diatribe. Eram dropped the pen, and it rolled off the pages, clattering into an unseen crevice. Eram dropped his head into his hands.

"I'm right here when you feel ready," reassured Caide. Caide ran his query through his phone browser. The search for psychiatric help turned up various offices in the city and a couple institutions outside. There was a hotline even. He switched over to the city map for directions. They were very close to the ocean here as Caide scrolled across the coastline. He did not know how to swim. His mother used to tell him of the Fomorians who rose from the deep, blue sea. Their steps spread blight, and men feared their presence.

Caide blinked back this sudden nostalgia. His family had never lived near the coastline though. He loosened his tie. It was hot in the train. There was a cramp building in his abdomen. He did not want to, but he stood up, taking a standing spot and holding tightly onto the handrails. He looked around. There was enough room to pace.

He started to sidle about the middle of the train car. He bit his lip and squeezed his thigh with his hand, forcing himself to a slower gait. His muscles felt as if they were about to rip out of his skin, bulging against the athletic tape. The tiny spear bit into his palm where it jutted through the trouser pocket. He fished for the spear and opened the cuff of his sleeve. The seven silver points plunged into his flesh. His body shuddered, seized for a moment, then calmed. The cramp subsided.

Caide glanced over at Eram, who had been watching him the entire time. He did not like that look of pain. "I'll take you home," said Caide. "It'll be alright. Can you type in your address?" Eram bit his knuckles and covered his eyes with his other hand. Blood dripped onto the pages.

Caide stopped himself from touching Eram, wringing his hands instead. He did not trust himself enough to handle Eram right now. There was something off with muscle control. People were fragile and Caide had fallen out of practice over these years. He kneeled next to Eram, using the tumbler as a physical barrier between them.

"Eram, stop," urged Caide. Eram's red luster had faded, but his wound still leaked. A clear liquid, like water, pattered and mixed with spilled blood. Caide stared at this sudden shift. His hair stood on end as he picked up the scent. Magic.

The Fomorians had become children's tales. The beasts were taken to extinction by a plague from old worlds across whole oceans. Magic was thinning, the mystics claimed. The toil of the divine wheel had stopped. The ties that bound the ethereal were decaying. It was one thing to hear it from a phone call away of acquaintances disappearing, of childhood bridges having lost their toll keeper, but it was too sobering to see such wasting affliction in person. To know that it could just as well be him in that seat inspired weary acceptance.

Even on the commute home, Caide could not avoid reminders of his lineage. These sorts of abnormal encounters were rare unless actively sought within their community pockets, but in a city populous enough, they weren't impossible. The company branch employed several hundred.

He kept quiet, because who knew and who cared. If other context matters happened to come up in conversation, okay, cool, but typically they never had any bearing on anything. Nervous smiles and faint laughter, no one wanted to be reminded of how useless magic was or how scary the thaumic aneurism. The anxiety stopped conversion and dissuaded further interaction. It was just weird, an untouchable subject because nothing about it helped.

Accepting the end of an abnormal world would not make Eram go away. Not that Caide wanted Eram to go away, but Caide did not know how to act. He knew he had to do something, and yet he also did not want to be in this position. He wanted to slink away and let bad things happen elsewhere. Eram was here, right in front of him. With his shoulder, Caide nudged Eram. Eram did not respond as teeth gnawed on flesh and spilled more water from opened veins.

Caide swallowed his apprehension and slowly, painfully, took Eram's hands in his own. Fingers slid between the bleeding joints, and Caide hated how loose and soft other people felt. *Gentler, please.* The idea that he was only helping because Eram was cursed with magic was shoved deep into shame. Eram was a friend, a good friend. Caide directed Eram to look at him. Eram stared at his wounds in shock. "It'll be alright," said Caide. "Please, let me take you home."

# THIRTY-FIVE

A PALL FOLLOWED THEM FROM THE TRAIN THROUGH THE lobby and up to Eram's apartment. Caide suppressed the urge to shake his head after finding that Eram had not locked the door. Caide let Eram in first and slowly shut the door. It smelled of fresh ichor here like from the alchemists in the early morning, preparing for prescription tincture orders.

The puzzle boxes caught Caide's attention first. They were scattered about the living room, resting on the couches, the table, and floor. There were so many of them, and Caide was a bit intimidated. Eram, red-faced, was piling the guardians back on the table. "I am sorry about this," Eram said. "I will clean up."

Caide dropped his belongings on the kitchen counter and tightened the dripping tap that overfilled a potted plant sitting in the sink. He came by Eram, left the reports binder on the table as a reminder, and then bent down to help clean. Caide's nails scratched the matte metal of the puzzle box housing, leaving white scars. They were empty. He picked at the mineral build up in the interior corners. "You do not need to stay," sighed Eram.

Caide ignored him and lined some of the puzzle boxes on the edge of the table. He did not want to discuss the revelation on the train that now painted the years they had worked together darkly. It was rude to imply Eram's madness was a result of his nature as a thaumically aligned existence. It was callous to say Eram was made to suffer, because Eram did not ask for this. It was cruel to have just enough magic to understand how very little things could change and to suffer because of that lack of choice.

Caide snapped the tip of his nail off. He knew he should not pry, that he should keep his head down and close his eyes. He was outside the breakroom, miles from the water cooler. His imagined bravery was his ultimate damnation.

"These are the puzzles you've talked about, you know, sometimes?" Caide liked the nice, neutral memories. He hid his broken nail in a housing and laid the housing on its lids to keep it closed. One or two he could reason as toys awfully similar to guardian homes. A coincidence firmly grounded in the mundane from an artificer making a quick buck, not needing to perform the actual spells.

The metal puzzle box was heavy and smelled of burnt sorcery and the ocean. Guardians were no mere things. They were expensive. They were designed to protect things worth far more than they were. Fearsome guards for the rich and famous. These were most likely minor spirits then, yet to have so many made Caide balk. They could not just be housings either. Eram simply would not have been interested. He had never considered Eram appreciative of a journey. A man with as much intent as Eram demanded destination before the journey even started. "Where do you get all of these?" Caide asked.

"Places," said Eram. "Estate sales. Black market downtown. Online? I would like to think I have moved on." Caide swept under the table for more. "Though, they served their purpose. They filled the time between work. Good distractions until I became too good at them. Now I find myself wanting more."

He wanted more than this? It was absurd to see this many empty housings, because all those guardian spirits had to go somewhere. Caide hit his head on the underside of the table. Eram placed a hand on his shoulder and asked if he was okay. Caide nodded, rubbing the back of his head. To Caide's disappointment, some housings had rolled off in that impact. He counted the rest to be collected and was further discouraged.

Eram's obsession took the shape of empty vessels displayed atop the cabinets, rolling off the coffee table, and lounging on the kitchen countertops. His obsession was sitting on the couch emptying these vessels, going to sleep, going to work, and then starting all over again. Was this where Eram's spark of life had been extinguished? A stillness in the air convinced Caide that nothing could thrive here. It must be so suffocating. "Do you know what was in them?" he asked.

"Nothing. Well, they are always empty," said Eram with a strange smile. "They are to be solved and then you put something of yours inside."

Caide gave a better smile to lighten the mood. He scratched the back of his hand, pinching the skin whenever he was in mood for an escapade. Maybe it was a year back? Caide had shown Eram the list of about ten pubs about the city, a drink per place. Places of victory celebrations, awkward dates, awkward breakups. A lot of breakups. It was probably because of a breakup that Caide wanted distraction. They had managed eight, amazingly. Eram had kept the coasters, some of them found scattered underneath these housings. It warmed Caide to see them.

He had not expected Eram to say yes. Until then, their relationship had stayed mostly professional. It still mostly was, but exceptions came by more often. He must have been obviously inconsolable for Eram to have agreed. Eram would then learn about Caide's pets or his failing to pick up skiing last winter. He was closer to Eram than he had thought and that thought only made the inattentiveness more painful. Eram was defined solely by work, a singular hobby, and a madness for all to see. Above all else, Caide wanted to make sure Eram did not feel alone.

There was a noise in the bedroom like something had fallen. The door was ajar. "You've got a pet?" asked Caide, brightening at the thought of friendly discourse to share between them. "It's not a dog, right? Dogs make me kinda uncomfortable. Ever thought about getting cats? I've got more photos to share of my two girls, and my neighbor is looking for people to adopt her kittens." Caide began to scroll through his phone. There was a particularly good video of his cats playing with a new duck toy.

"Caide, you should get home," said Eram, who now rose to his feet. Eram did not look into his bedroom but slowly shut the door. "You do not need to be here." Something heavy banged into the door from the other side, almost knocking Eram over. He staggered away. Caide tensed, rubbing his arms, and stood up rather hunched.

"What's in there?" asked Caide.

"Leave." Eram clutched a housing tightly, bringing it up to shield his sight of Caide. Something was certainly wrong here. Whatever it was made Eram visibly uncomfortable. Caide refused to be put off so easily. He put away his phone and stretched his arms. He felt the spark of sorcery etch through his muscles. Caide confronted the door, bearing teeth, nicely cut and fanged.

The door opened and a creature with a human body but a radio for a head walked out, rubbing its shoulder. With a gloved hand, it inspected the dent it had made in the door. It was a gangly being, sharply dressed in a tuxedo and tails. It closed the door behind it with its coattails slipping through the crack. The radio shuddered on its head with a chasing whine of static. The needle was frantic in its search.

The standing radio reached up and extended its antenna. It carefully angled this way and that. The radio case was beat, the paint rubbed off from constant use. Track names and length were written on a fraying piece of white duct tape over the front hinge, keeping the door shut. The cassettes inside spun vinyl film behind the plastic windows.

The standing radio nestled a tattered black card between its play buttons. Caide realized what it was and finally relented. This intruder was a Harken enforcer. He let the enforcer investigate their cleanup progress. It reached out and toppled the small tower of empty housings. The rules of the city had been broken and so began the consequences. Caide kept his head down. He had no outstanding problems with the city, and there was no issue associated with being near an enforcer, as long as he didn't stand in its way.

Eram also refused to acknowledge this enforcer. He wrapped his arms around himself and stared pointedly at the floor. The standing radio stalked around the room. It ran its gloved hand along the TV, distorting the screen with a magnetic haze. It picked through the books on the shelves.

Had a black card caused Eram's injuries? Eram was biting his knuckles again, and Caide silently pleaded for him to stop. Caide thought about doing nothing. Fear this fearsome world. Keep quiet and let workplace gossip consume his fifteen-minute break without issue. Cross the ocean after graduation and forget about the wasting family land. Imagine the healthy homestead through the landline. There was no landline to shield him from Eram's suffering. So much nothing recounted, and now he could not stand doing nothing.

Caide loosened his tie. A black card would end him too. He was far from the breakroom, miles from the water cooler, deep within the over-grown forests. His forests. A ten-year-old boy climbed the white rocks and proclaimed himself protector of his mother's fields and all the crea-tures that nestled underneath the poppies. A little lamb in the shade of a puzzle box home hid from the city hawk. His skin burned.

He rolled up his sleeves, revealing the tight tape coverings lined with handwritten Gaelic. A human shape from thine own flesh, oh hound of Chulainn. But muted flesh indeed, he who could not defend his fellow with words in a breakroom. Was he only good for herding sheep and cattle? For hunting elk and foxes? A lazy fisher boy dreamed on the gentle riverbank, finally free from school, of days young and everlast-ing, of his domain so easily kept. Eram's social stigma was infectious. Caide feared breakroom words, but by claw and teeth, he feared no man nor fey.

The standing radio slid its radio/head off its neck, grabbed it by its handle, and tucked it under its arm. Smooth glass cut across its neck. The image of a pacing Caide reflected on this surface. It flicked a switch on its radio/head and the ever-present static finally stopped.

Eram gasped for air. He collapsed to the floor, knocking over a lamp. Caide was forced to take a knee. His lungs felt engorged, gripped by the lining to tear themselves apart. His organs turned, ready for rupture. His claws dragged across the floor as he forced himself forward.

"I do not need breath to act nor flesh to support me," heaved the wolf named Caide. Caide pounced across the room. Claws first, teeth second. The enforcer raised a hand to protect itself. Caide buried his claws between the enforcers ribs and lifted it off the ground. The slice of its neck clinked against the ceiling. Glass shattered under its clothes as Caide crushed its chest. The enforcer struggled to turn its knobs. The radio voice echoed in their minds.

<< Emergency signal, red alert, the planned circumstance did not account for such an extinct thing! Wolfman, you are three thousand

miles too far from home! >> Whatever setting the radio could find could not persuade the man of Ulster.

"I exist. That is enough to proclaim myself mighty," said Caide.

With a wolf's fury, he began dismantling the enforcer. Anachronistic radios tumbled from the beaten shape. Their overlaid voices and discordant static mingled and swore. Caide crushed this cursed machinery and spilled audio tape and oil. Radio weaponry, acoustic reformation, had no stay against a man of Ulster. The last voice was a small hand radio with a crank, hidden in Caide's grasp. It was the kind used for camping in a wild forest.

<< Are you listening, ocean? I fear the wolf! I want my heart to beat forever. >>

The hand radio twitched as bolts cascaded. Metal deformed and sheared itself apart in Caide's rough hand. Pieces dropped to the ground. << VANDHEER SAVE ME. >> The ravaged, headless body crawled blindly away from Caide.

Caide stood tall. His muscles settled from their acoustic reformation. He gave a low growl and attended to Eram, kneeling and lifting him against his chest. Disembodied arms climbed up a cabinet to a waylaid globe. The body recoiled as it pricked itself with the flag pins Eram used to mark where he had been. All its clumsiness was gone. With deft hands, it set upon this capture, unscrewing the globe from its frame. It set the world on its shoulders. It groped over mountain ridges to keep the world steady.

Mountain ridges scratched the glass. Magic tarnished as headless skin thinned. It attempted to screw the globe into its neck to tie itself together, but no connection could be made. Water leaked between the interfaces. With a jerk of its body, the world was thrown off, leaving a sizable dent on the floor. The headless creature found the table, cleared the way of empty houses, and sat down. It slumped, audibly cooling in front of them.

Eram was in Caide's arms, resting against his shoulder. Caide's muscles turned in their places again. He glared at the pile of deconstructed radios. They were silent. The smell of dying sorcery filled the air. The fur on Caide's back was standing on end. Something was still not right here.

This was magic that did not return to any cycle or that gave way to entropy, off to be somewhere else. This was dead magic. Its death left empty spaces in reality. Spaces so empty that they came alive, ready to devour everything that crossed into the void. There was no satiation. This negative void only grew deeper the more it was fed. A wolf heart worked harder, beating faster to replace what was being taken. This hunger was a match for a man of Ulster.

Caide covered his face. His teeth were far too large for his own mouth. His jaw hung wide. A human's skin flayed at the edges, barely held by tape. His human form had faltered, and he wanted very much for Eram not to look his way again.

Eram was not human. Caide saw not with his eyes, but with the scent of outsider things. Instinct painted over the eyes a figment of a simulated experience. A false place and time that Caide understood could not actually be where he was, firmly in Eram's apartment. Yet the sensation was so captivating.

The here and now, within the foggy glen of a nameless forest, floated a dark, crystalline object just as big as werewolf him and within arm's reach. Polished facets were shaved without pattern and specked with dew. Its bright halos enveloped and rotated about its body, light reflecting across its form. Water dripped from these divine tines, glittering like stars. And just staring at this silent, monolithic thing struck Caide as almost blasphemous, like finding the most vulnerable of things at the ends of the world.

Caide felt the weight of a sorcerous tool within himself, an extension of the verbatim word. He had not allowed this tool, this obelisk, to listen in or to act in his stead. Someone had forged his signature on this contract. In fact, a maligned and misaligned tool could undo him so easily, taking any request too far and running his body too hard into the ground. The resonance overpowered his fragile eardrums. Caide's body wasted and his blood boiled. He was lost in the salty fog.

With a sharpened claw, Caide etched spells of protection and disownment into the floor. The cessation of a contract. *Let me be unburdened.* The obelisk cared not. A forced forfeiture of choice cursed the wolf. The obelisk imparted its own will and resonated with a howling he did not know existed. Halos started to stutter in their rotations like something caught between immaterial gears. Caide started with a sudden fright. He felt hands upon his person. He felt he was being pried apart as water entered his lungs. There were no hands, no rupture of the werewolf body. Yet the intrinsic, vital stuff within him, his very name, was being displaced.

Caide continued writing from plank to plank, devouring empty space. He could afford leisure but could not afford to make mistakes. Magic was flippant. Magic was killing him, and his only out was to ask magic to save him. His roving claws bumped into Eram, who was trembling, holding tightly and burying his head into Caide.

Caide held Eram tighter. Caide within the here and now laid hands against the obelisk without conscious decision. The dichotomy startled him for a moment. Here and now was just him. Or not. He stared at the obelisk and wiped the polished surface, collecting beads of dew. Water climbed across his palms and down his arms. The crystal material was barely transparent and there was water inside it.

Endless water and a horizon line, like an ocean. Ah yes, Caide remembered Eram leaking the subject on occasion in between meetings and risk discussions, how he viewed the ocean through a crystal looking glass. Caide did not understand what this obelisk was entirely, but it was linked to Eram somehow.

*I am the infinite ocean*, what a strange phrase that was. One no more sensical than Eram's other ramblings, but one that he associated more strongly with him nevertheless. There was a sheer conviction that always convinced him. And Caide listened, even though he was not really good at replying back. The werewolf laid his head against the obelisk. He flicked an ear. "You'll listen to me too, Eram? I wonder how other people would see you then?" mumbled Caide. "If they had senses like mine."

Caide found a small crevice on the obelisk and hooked his fingers underneath. The warmth of flesh pushed back. "Because I know this isn't that real," whispered Caide. "I'm holding you."

They were not in a glen of a false forest, but the mental imagery was powerful as he had to constantly remind himself otherwise. Caide brushed the wood chips away. An obelisk was deaf, blind, and mute.

Eram was not and this spell crafting was certainly not working. Claws scratched the underside of halos because Caide wanted some way to ask for attention.

"I'm right here. Eram, stop," said Caide, taking Eram by the chin. A sudden pain enveloped his arm.

"I want this," said Eram, as if halos could hum.

"Want what?" Halos broke free from whatever stalled their gears and advanced another full rotation before catching again. The pain bloomed into fire. Caide prodded at his balding spots and the growing lesions that started them. Cascade. Magic forgave nothing. Not even a man of Ulster was immune.

Eram whispered his answer, "You."

Caide's ears perked up. "If I had a tail to wag in happiness," he huffed softly. Caide shifted closer to the obelisk and laid the whole of his upper body against the cold crystal. The back of his hand rubbed sharp edges gingerly out of the need to comfort Eram.

Magic had cursed both of them, having brought nothing good into their lives. His ears pinned back in thought. He reminded himself again that the forest was not real. He opened the cover of the binder on the table, but found no pen clasped to the rings. It had been lost on the train. He hovered over the radio remains warily and then picked up a shard of the hand radio dripping in oil. He scribed a small charm on his flesh, peeling back tape to make more room. Oil transferred into his blood. He pressed his palm against his charm and pulled away a sticky mixture of stretching tendrils. It smelled of honey.

"I want you safe and sound," he said, and gently pried Eram's mouth open. Caide measured by his knuckles not to open too far. Delicate touch was difficult and often deceiving. Those mistakes were only made once. It was unnerving to see polished crystal fold open so easily whenever the scene switched back. Caide offered the liquid to Eram, who choked on the taste. He then massaged Eram's throat, enticing him to swallow more, and watched his oiled blood spill into the interior ocean.

The contract collapsed and Eram was pulled out from the deep blue sea. Caide sighed. Perception now rightly grounded within the apartment. The burn of cascade did not stop, but the lack of pressure from an overeager obelisk gave the body of Ulster the advantage. *Out of the glen and into the fire,* Caide thought grimly. His body only had a slight advantage. Whatever rot had been induced inside of him was furious and forever. Like no more exercise because he was missing a lung or no more drinking because of kidneys, he only had one. Cascade was never put out once it began, it was just delayed by better practices. If he was careful, he might make it almost as long as he would have. He hated magic.

Caide was now part man and part lupine creature. His ancestry leaked through where his form was no longer bound. Scraps of athletic tape were scattered around. Caide cupped his hands together to hide his claws and spoke lightly, moving his jaw as little as possible, "You okay?"

"No." Eram rubbed his throat. "It feels like I swallowed knives." Caide moved his snout to avoid hitting Eram as Eram brushed through Caide's grey fur. "You are a lycanthrope."

"How clinical," said Caide. "Do you also call them the Grigori and the Blajini?" Eram grew red. Caide softly chuckled, but even as soft as a wolf could go, the thunder reverberated still. "I'm a descendent of the hound of Chulainn. You know, somewhere up there however long back. It's not actually that impressive. What about you? No spark? No blessing or demon's deal?" Caide leaned in. The fur of his neck brushed against Eram's cheek. Eram tightened up. Caide pulled back. "Sorry."

Eram looked so amazed. Caide offered a claw, letting Eram inspect the appendage. For once, Caide felt rather proud to show off. Eram noticed the sores. "I did this to you."

"Like the molting of a spider, I can shed my form and regrow a limb or two if needed. Hah, wolf spider, get it? Oh, I'm sorry. It might be slower though. I think I've got cascade biting at my heels forever now." Caide read Eram's puzzlement. "Death by resonance? Mordrem's cascade? Screw Mordrem, but I suppose it ain't his fault for giving it a name. Uh, um, resonance is, you know, like magic. Like seeing, feeling, one of those appendix organs in your body.

"Well, it's maybe more like a muscle injury, I guess. When you work out and think about how your ligaments move and tendons stretch and pull against your bone. And you think about just them pulling themselves apart. Like every time you push another rep or lap, a microscopic layer detaches, a rip grows bigger. Then it snaps clean through and your football career is over or something. Only people die. Exercising magic feels so dangerous because you can't help thinking 'is this it?' Most people don't feel good doing magic. Something grates in the back of the mind, like something's failing."

"Will you really be alright then?"

"I will be. Lycanthropes are hardy creatures." Caide flexed for a moment, but let go with a chuckle.

Eram's captivation at his form made Caide's ear flick. Eram was so small and, for once, did not have all the right answers. Eram kept fidgeting and asking and rubbing his wounds. It must have been nice to live so unburdened from the failings of magic. Well, it was just shifting the point of horror from childhood nightmares to end-of-life dementia. Neither was actually that good. He had known other people that lived that gaily. Magic was the cool double-thumb, not the guillotine. They did not have to see their family fall apart at the ligaments and neurons.

Obelisk man, that was quite new to Caide. An obelisk was a tool. Good but inflexible. But it was not out of the realm of possibility for a "smart" one. Everything's smart in modern business. Tools starting contracts on their own, that is the real spooky action. Something that should have been ironed out before production.

Caide's ears raised back up. Eram was not a tool, and Caide hugged him tighter. Smaller things always needed guidance. "Be mindful," warned Caide. "Have discretion because others need it. No one can really stop what you do. Because—because, now this is a quote here more or less from one of them sophists: What can one do when reality conspires against the existence of all things inside of it? Ask reality to be forgiving, I think."

Eram inspected the ruined floor. Oil dried into the wood and splayed like a spider's web, anchored from etched rune to etched rune. The morning dew might have broken these very strands.

Caide helped Eram up. "I gave you what you wanted," Caide said and licked his fangs. "But in a werewolf's tincture for hunger. It's meant for growing children to dull instinct, especially on the heels of the first kill." Caide stayed sitting on the floor. His scars from the athletic tape showed through where his fur was missing. "I'm fine. Don't worry. Hey, don't go near that thing." Eram had approached the slumped body of a once-standing radio.

"How do you handle it, living as you are?" asked Eram.

"Hmm? Just the butcher, Eram. It's just shopping. Groceries, toilet paper, another set of guitar picks, that peach protein powder, and enchanted athletic tape." Eram picked up the black card from the broken electronics. Caide growled. "People like Harken take terms like magician so seriously. The age of Cu Chulainn is a bygone era. I can't really cast magic. I've got a magic body, but that doesn't really count."

Caide gestured to the floorboards. "I shouldn't have been wasting my time. Should've gone straight for the blood. Because if I could spin a spell, I wouldn't need tape to hide myself." He started to clean up such tape. "I need a good tailor. Enchanters and artificers make good money, not gods. Tools help us pretend we are not powerless. It's flicking a switch to pretend to be a legend. It's a tall task to ask a lot of people to flick a switch, actually."

Caide thought for a moment. "What can I pretend to be with you? A miracle worker?" He showed his clawed hand with a broken nail. "I hate this. Stay human, Eram. Ignore the stupidity of magic things. You hardly know anything. Keep it that way. It won't go on for much longer."

"Have you ever thought to move somewhere more accommodating?" asked Eram. Caide turned his head in confusion. His ears made a slow circle in the air.

"It's not the place. It's reality that's the problem. Or so goes the whispers in the back alley. Anyway, my doctor is here. The last of the few that decide to help instead of just lament. People stay here because Harken makes it easier, if only slightly, to get what we need to house our ailments and homeless lives. I would like to return home, but I also don't. There's a rot in the old lands that my family has told me to avoid. I haven't heard from them in a very long time." Caide gathered some radio parts into his trash pile.

"Is there nothing to be done? It sounds as if the world is dying." Eram passed his collection of scrap to Caide.

Caide shrugged. "As many people have their tales of origin, they have their end times. They contradict, squabble, and unite as all myths are wont to do. They are all true and not. Yet all kinds look upon the horizons and find the coming storm. What's your favorite nightmare?" Eram did not answer. "I know a handful of stories of how the world will end. That's what I meant. It could be useful to know what to expect. One tale at least should be right.

"When I was a child, I was always told to bring a map into the folds of nature. Know where all the lakes were, the ponds and rivers, because of the maidens. Maidens stranded in the midst of sudden water made from their own tears." Caide raised his hands. "If that water had no name, that was no stranded fair lady. A banshee wailed for your death. I saw the face of a crone when I was a kid, might've kidnapped me if I hadn't taken that advice. I wonder if the banshees still exist back home or if they have traveled to more fertile ground. I have seen beautiful things too. I have seen the Tuatha ride across the oaken crests, brushing sunlight at autumn's first daybreak.

"I never got the chance to meet them, the ones up the glen from my grandfather's. They were on a first-name basis. Good for him. My parents were bit on one side, bit on the other. Father was alright with my outings in the woods. The fey dreamt dreams you could touch. Rivers filled with honey. Fields bloomed with flowers that could only be imagined. Mother would always remind me to never miss homework." Caide laughed but it was short. "They had never seen the Tuatha, actually. That sighting on the eve of autumn was my first and last.

"Perhaps like an atmosphere grown too thin, those faery creatures can no more exist than the massive prehistorics. The rot starts from the top down and comes to me. Unfortunately, it's the enchantments that are failing, not my beast. It takes an extra roll in the morning to wrap myself up. I just want to get on without trouble."

Caide finished rolling his remaining tape in a small spool. The Gaelic sagged and draped over themselves, peeling right off the plastic. There was a wet squishiness to the spool and lettering squeezed out between the layers. Caide shivered and stopped handling the tape. He dropped the roll into the trash pile.

Eram polished the glass neck of the radio body with his sleeve. Caide made an anxious noise as he watched Eram pull an auxiliary jack from under its collar. It was connected, somewhere. Eram went into the bedroom and came back with his phone, plugging the body in.

Caide raised his brow. "We had an entire work safety meeting about picking up and using unidentified electronics from the floor of our parking lot. You have no idea where that's been. It's common sense. You'd think people wouldn't need that sort of training."

"I want to hear about an ocean," interrupted Eram, laying the phone down on the neck. "If you have a story."

"Hmm. I had the tale of Eiocha growing up, where seafoam mated with the shores of barren land of what would become the Emerald Isles. But tales are fickle, and that is the same everywhere. I might have a good one."

# THIRTY-SIX

"BEFORE THE ADVENT OF TIME, THERE WAS ONLY THE PRI-mordial sea. The water was alive with two faces. The water that gave life, sweet to the touch of the ephemeral stars it begot. The water that devoured, a salt that strickened the blood. Until the waters in their mixing, came anima. Or perhaps the waters were always anima. Liquid magic. I think so. The sea was pure without anything but itself in the cosmos of its own creation.

"Out from the sea was born all things. The Moon was the eldest and thus knew all that came after. It made a throne upon the sea, looking upon itself, knowing itself, but there was nothing to rule over. Its siblings were noisy and brash and the little things they had made to serve them were just the same. The siblings made their places over land, for it was unlike the sea. The new gods knew themselves only through their reflections in the carved idols and casted icons of their people. It was the gift the little things graced their gods with, an image and name born from cherished hearts.

"This moon, what became of it?" The way Eram stood up straighter, the way he approached bright eyed for understanding pinned back Caide's ears in a phantom pet. He was a strange one, Eram. Caide felt better as his lupine features simmered down. He would have to be careful to not break what little guise he had left. Some scant lines of tape were left around his abdomen.

The city loved its sanctity and would not abide the sight of a were-wolf, but its rule ended at its borders. Home was not far from here. He should pack for a few days and escort Eram beyond the boundaries of petty magic. He could not stop thinking about the autumn day. He had lost the leaves shaped like wings once collected in a child's shirt.

"It was jealous, the Moon. The first Moon was before all things and could not stand to be akin its lesser siblings. So, in secret, it made its little things, things born from the ashes of fallen meteors and the wellspring that was the sea. The younger gods made do with the rain that fell from the heavens, but the Moon had the waters of heaven itself. Its people were told to never leave the ocean. They lived upon the sea and fished from it the rock that was their home. The moon was their giver and tasked them to record all that it knew.

"The centuries passed. The lunar people grew bored of their heavens for often nothing beheld them. Only rarely did fish live in the ocean. They came in fleeting schools until the salt of the sea turned and mired and did away with all things. There was no land to sport the kinds of things the Moon claimed roamed on mountains, fields, and desert. The sea was deep, dark, and endless. The endless empty.

"So, ah, I forget the name, the wisest of the tribe who wished the best for his people—he knew his people's plight. He told his greatest fishermen to travel to the land of younger gods. He asked the stars—the stars the Moon let grace its heavens—to lead his people safely and to help avoid all manner of storms. The stars watched over both heaven and earth and came to love the little things that gave them names and gifts. The constellations were born from the competitions between stars for the best name, but that's for another time.

"The Moon kept constant measures of its creations, making sure its garden was exactly how it was meant to be. Missing fishermen were too easy to audit, and the curious little things that came from under the wings of younger gods, perhaps even empathetic to their distant cousins, were struck by lightning on their first footfall into the sea. A very lonely cage that was the ocean and a throne.

"The wise chief knew the Moon was vain, and every night the chief would come with adulations and meager questions. The Moon answered all of them. How many grains of sand made the deserts? How did the stars orbit in the skies? How many, how odd, how strange. The Moon engorged itself on its infallibility. Until one day, he asked the Moon what size the ocean was and what its provenance prior the birth of knowing things had been. He asked if it was truly indisputable that the Moon was the only ruler of the sea and even if the Moon was the ocean's eldest creation.

"The Moon would not be humble to admit ignorance. It knew all there was to be known but not anything before it. Its sights lingered farther and farther out to the edges of the ocean for its infallible answer. The ocean was infinite, or at least very, very large said the stars, so this task would have been almost impossible. Accounting was forgotten, for the Moon could not waste its traveling progress coming back home every day. Attention was finite and under this distraction, heaven and earth became one.

"For centuries, the heavens and earth conversed. An errant star, wily and capricious, learned that if it led its lost sailors to shore, the sailors would shower the star with more and more gifts. The more treacherous the journey, the more relief the sailors had upon finding their destinations. So, this star led its charges farther and farther out to sea until they met the eyes of the Moon.

"The Moon now knew it had been tricked. It became enraged at learning its people's betrayal and how its people made do with the things of lesser gods and lesser places. Its pristine garden had spoiled. The Moon in its fury threw all the stars into the sea. It made so much ruckus and noise that the earth itself shook. It schemed to flood the little things of its siblings and all the little things of its own.

"War was wrought between a lesser world and the Moon that despised all things. The Moon became pockmarked from all its numerous battles, until at last the Moon relented. A wealth of knowledge was shared across cooperative hands. A new age was born.

"I don't claim that's the whole tale, spoken right from the elder, but that is how all spoken myths are. They are half-phrased wisps here or there that're about the same thing. One day, the salt riddled waters will devour all that is sweet in the ocean. The ending of togetherness is optimistic but the many wars were not. All that death fed into the bitter ocean half. All the screams of stars drowned together. All the hate of a

Moon that despised existence made the endless abyss. So corrupted the salt and poisoned the wellspring of anima.

"That ocean was the Moon's weapon. A terrifying force of destruction this great flood never to come. Everything that was ever built will be devoured by the flood. Forty days, forty nights, what not. The ocean never forgot and will find a way to escape the heavens that keep it contained, but all end-of-the-world myths are like that. Ragnarok, Armageddon, Seven Suns. I would prefer the final quiet sleep myself."

Caide cleared his throat and rubbed his reddening face. "I didn't think I'd get through most of it," he said. "I get self-conscious eventually. It all seems so silly." He stretched his arms, now more human on the whole. He asked Eram if had enjoyed the tale. Eram had.

Caide gathered the trash scraps into his torn shirt and headed into the kitchen. He threw the scraps into the waste bin and began digging through his bag. He found and put on a loose gym shirt. He wanted another swig of coffee, but his thermos was empty and stained with dried remnants.

"What do you think of the Library?" asked Eram.

"Rumor is that the Library kidnaps people for experiments," said Caide. "The human experimentation is truth. The kidnapping maybe a little less so. Not that they'll ever show up in this sort of city. They used to be the pioneers of innovation. Red Cross with a little bit of peace prize-ism. Nowadays, they pour salt in a wound they refuse to let settle."

Caide lifted the plate from underneath the submerged plant to let the water drain. The levels lowered with a groaning tumble. There was no convenient place to set the rescued plant but on the stovetop. He used a dishcloth to soak the excess water around its base, then washed his thermos out.

"They are not the only ones," continued Caide. "Desperate wraiths scrape the land for anything left of sustenance. To pick up whatever scrap of magic they can hoard. Doomsday preparation, if you understand it. Let them be kings of wastelands. Many cannot afford to look forward." Caide dried the cap with a paper towel.

"Are you going to be alright?" Caide asked. "I want you to be safe. I didn't realize you had this sort of problem. That you were someone

I could've talked to about these stupid things. If I had your answers of confidence, I would have liked a bit more time."

"I would have liked to as well," said Eram. "I apologize greatly for my absences, but I am sure you will do just fine." Eram's attempt to shake Caide's hand remained unreciprocated, fingers curling in dejection.

"If you ever want to talk more about myths or anything, I don't mind if you call me. Company is sorely lacking these days." The prospect of sharing stories again anywhere in the future seemed grim, and a wolfman's strength could not change that.

"Do you hate what you are?"

"That's rude, Eram, but I'm just not sure. My fur may bristle, and I may bare my fangs, but my spirit is voiceless. I failed all examinations despite the pleas of my parents. I can't see what lies at the ends of rainbows. I wouldn't know how to imagine it, being actually talented. Magic is a color I can't see, a noise pitched too odd, a sight that defies explanation." Caide nodded to the floor of his efforts again.

"Those runes mean nothing. They were rote exercises from my childhood, but I thought that maybe, you know, in times of crisis, the body rises beyond conventional circumstance. I could lift a burning car to save a child. I could actually," Caide sighed. "My form is my only reminder that I could've been a bit more. But I have other dreams, and my body's a hindrance."

Eram's touch was cold and painful on Caide's forearm. A creeping anxiety haunted the forming wolf body and made Caide very conscious of his breathing. He leaned against the counter to steady himself, grip cracking the granite top. Human flesh subsumed wolf features in patchwork agony. Cascade wasted the body, making it quite obvious turning back would be just as painful.

"I can fix you," said Eram. "I can snip the roots of your ancestry. Shapes are lithe and nimble. You may choose any template that roams the earth. Or farther. Allow me to solve your apprehensions." Eram spoke so smoothly, as if he were simply advising the next step of design improvement at work, a confidence born from years of experience.

Caide had no words. Once, a wolfman had wanted to be a hero of legend. As a child, he would perch atop the largest cross in the graveyard looking for fiends to slay. He glanced at the fallen radio. The idea of playing hero was embarrassing. It was far better to do nothing and be untroubled. He would be troubled anyway by things which could have gone better if he just acted.

"I imagine that you could if you so wanted it," said Caide. "You don't make false claims at work. Why start now? No. I want you safe. Family, friends, you. I didn't run away. I don't want to run away." He wrapped a heavy hand over Eram's touch. "What I want fixed isn't me. I just want everything to be okay somehow. I don't like feeling useless, avoiding problems because it'll just make everything more difficult. I imagine you're having a tough time at it all, and I admit that sometimes I wish I didn't have to deal with you at work. That you and your insanity aren't my problems because I have all of mine to handle."

Caide looked away in shame. "I still enjoy the company. Would you agree that we'll have the chance to meet up again? You and me as is? Not dead. Ah, that last part sounds too miserable." Caide let go, letting Eram step away and pick at his own teeth. Eram fidgeted with his collar and tie.

"I—I would have to want to keep your name then," said Eram, whimpering and pacing and seemingly lost. His gaze flickered about the entire apartment but avoided Caide entirely. "If I have to promise, I would have to stay like this even if I hate my jaw and my sensations, because you only know this me. When did everything become so mired in ocean dreams? The order of operations has changed. A top level ocean view drips through the human lens when there used to be only humanity. As if what I want must be filtered through what a human body can achieve. There is an awareness that I am something outside my proper shape. This awareness demands I eat your name."

Caide did not quite understand, but that simply meant he had to prod Eram to explain, as usual. "Do you need it then?" he asked. "My name? How do I help?" This was not the tuning out of strange off-topic matters whenever they babbled up at work. This was to know Eram beyond the workplace condition.

"You mentioned discretion," said Eram. "The ability to discern. That I could stop if I really wanted to, that I could listen. I want you. I cannot have you disappear, but I am not quite good enough to really say no to my own compulsion. All I do is find some alternative satisfaction. Either a puzzle or me, I suppose. I will wish for you. I am the same as you, a body, two arms, a head. An empty shape that displaces water in some far off dream. A shape I can grab and rip apart at the seams."

Caide held Eram by the shoulder. There was no crystal obelisk, just a man looking back at him in confusion. "It'll be alright," said Caide. There was no angle he could imagine that could piece Eram's deliberate obscurity.

"I do not think I can give you everything you want," said Eram, "but that does not mean I will not give a good effort. There will have to be compromises. Don't look at me like that. I know—I know what you want, but I have found myself, and I am scared. I can't promise you anything." Eram glanced away, prodding beneath Caide's grasp. "It hurts, a little."

Caide was disappointed in the answer and let go. Eram's unwavering confidence was nowhere to be found. Maybe it was a mistake trying to push sensitive topics again. Yet Eram had not been rebuffed! He just needed to take the time to settle down and explore the matter thoroughly. He had no immediate plans, so spending the weekend with Eram fit his schedule quite nicely. Sudden duress captured him.

"I'm sorry," Caide gasped. "We don't have the time for this. We need to leave the city. Harken doesn't bother past city lines. I'm sorry. This is a real problem. I end up thinking I have more time than I have. Harken will come again. I know people in the back alley. I can get you out, maybe if I cash a few favors. Harken doesn't like having things they hate escape them."

Caide's thoughts raced. "I miss my home. I miss the autumn days. I thought I would be happier when I left the country, but now I always think about what I could've saved. What I could've changed. I'm miserable just like everyone because of this plague over the ocean. It's not my problem, but now I know you, and I'll think of you. I'll help you. I want to help you whether or not you're up for it."

Caide cracked three canines from his mouth, slipping the teeth out from his gums. Blood spilled down his chin. He spat blood into the sink. "Preemptive measures," he mumbled. "My body isn't useless. It can be priceless to the right buyer. Might as well get it over with." Caide stood the teeth on the counter, then felt the open pits of his jaw. He felt the slow advance of flesh wrapping around his finger, but not the enamel of regained bite. They might not actually grow back, but three should be enough. Caide held the phone to his ear, attempting the first of his favors.

# THIRTY-SEVEN



**VENNER WAS LEFT FRUSTRATED AGAIN. CAIDE, AS A WORKING** man, as a humanoid, magical shape, was to be the closest thing to the accountant ideal. He checked just enough boxes to guarantee a wondrous meal. Sentimentality turned his oceanic gaze away. Or rather, turned his extra eyes against himself. The ocean had seen the man named Venner. The ocean had experienced the man stand in the way of work and cleansing salvation.

Work. To. Be. Done. Was this not gospel? This human apparatus that attached itself to infinity must be undone. It was not merely useless. It was inhibitive.

The momentary disassociation really hurt the head. Caide's wish to have things be better was too abstract to solve well, like the nebulous inklings of antlers. But that was not the problem. The ocean demanded fulfilment because Caide could not be tolerated writhing in the brain stem of perception. Caide had been noticed swimming in the bitter water. In that moment, Venner set himself as the alternate solution to his own compulsion. And the ocean took.

Caide busied himself with various calls, wandering between the entry hallway and kitchen. He started to inscribe another spell on the frame of the front door using one of his pulled teeth. A dead spell just like the empty exercises that scaled the floorboards. Venner excused himself. He found distraction inspecting the body of the standing radio slumped on the living room table.

Venner noisily cracked his jaw at the hinges. His hands were numb, and the sensation of movement felt wrong, as if he were being controlled by someone else, someone far away. His vision seemed far too confined. He rubbed his eyes. Oh, he was blind in one of them. Brine dripped off his fingers. It was a strange sensation, a fingernail scraping across the eye of a severed optic nerve. Brine bled from his nose as well. There was still too much of that insidious shape named Eram Venner that thrashed in the water.

His phone interrupted him. He stretched his jaw again. The screen lit in white and then made more noise. An incoming text. The message was mostly unreadable through the cracked screen and distorted colors. Venner could only read nonsense noise, built by tumbling letters and numbers. Another jumble of text demanded attention.

F-ND HIM, VANDHEER COMMANDS, amongst the fragments. VANDHEER DOES00NOT TOLERATE FAI—then followed by enough pieces of his address and his identity. The repeated commands on high stopped and were replaced by cries of help sent out. HELP-MEHELPMEHELPMEHELPMEHELPME000. It was like the last thoughts of a fading consciousness. The screen froze into a harsh array of colors. OCEANSPAREME. The messages repeated endlessly. The screen refused to shut off. His phone felt unnaturally warm.

The standing radio felt very similar to the clockwork millipede. An extraneous property that was too large to properly fit within their normal shapes, like a distant master controlling their puppets. This vague origin slipped through his grasp. Venner had to find the source. He had a name and renewed purpose to devour such name.

Work was gospel. The ocean's task, his task, was to clean up. He needed to be discreet, and he decided then and there that to sanctify his fragile human existence, he simply had to erase everything that upset the checklist. He did not need to go so far as to erase Caide's ancestry or a moon's true body. He just had to forget, or at least be distracted enough to not care.

Was that not the most amazing cheat? Puzzle boxes passed the time and if he needed something bigger now, then so be it. He would give them no chance for outcry, so he did not have to be burdened by things like names. He would eat and be happy, healthy, and sane.

If this was the alternative, this life or death of one monumental struggle after another, he was fine with his ostracism, minor by respective comparison. Caide had offered to keep quiet about all this magical nonsense. Iramir expressed the desire to never see him again. So, Venner whimpered, eat Vandheer and all the biggest obstacles for a clean checklist would have been dealt with.

Venner entered his bedroom and shut the door behind him. The black card flipped in his grasp. He could have kept a quiet life even amongst these empty vessels, but the strange other world intervened enough for him to never forget what 3 a.m. felt like. A world filled with cruelty that stole all his wondrous distractions and left him with nothing but his wandering eyes. He was furious.

What turned his waters into turmoil was the one that put teeth in his chest and fed him the meat of people: Vandheer. All his lost opportunities, his very peace, demanded compensation. He had to placate the ocean. There would be nothing, surely, that would stop him from this drowning. He had to. He had to. He had to.

Slowly, he worked the written number one frustrating digit at a time into the noise of his phone screen. The dial tone droned without response. The call dropped and the door opened.

Venner walked through and found himself in the same stairwell where he had met the paper man. The door that led back into his apartment was gone. It had been replaced with whitewashed walls. Out of sight, out of mind. He leaned over the railing and the stairs wound down, deep into the darkness. Looking up was the same digression of impossible space. The floor numbers were painted on the walls in ridiculous digits. A million one and three. A few floors down and the numbers climbed astronomically.

"I didn't expect you to call," said the paper man, waiting with his umbrella over his head on the landing below Venner. "I had hoped we would've gone past the matter of sordid oceans and dead things. That a Library or a werewolf would manage to keep you above water, so to speak." The paper man was missing an arm. There was no rooftop storm to break the silence around them. This space seemed fully excised from a city proper, a nostalgic facsimile most likely slotted somewhere within the city bowels. So was the playground of paper attendants. "You shouldn't be here," sighed the paper man.

"I called and you answered," said Venner. "I mean very much to be here. Who is Vandheer, and how do I find them?"

The paper man crinkled at Venner's question. He squared his shoulders. "I met you last night to see if you were an aberration. If you were just a normal person, I would have left you to the city or the Library. Your choice. What would happen to you was not Vandheer's concern. If you had a bit of a spark, you would have disappeared, taken to the foundry. I know how to forge reports so the city is none the wiser to parasites. I know how to lie, and the city would have never known about you."

"I told you what I was," said Venner. "No one could have stopped you."

"It was too difficult an operation. I barely escaped with my life against the might of a hound," lied the paper man, and then he started up the stairs. "I didn't think helping you get to work would go so wrong. It was just a ticket, a strip off the shoulder to be more exact. Neither did I expect that an enforcer would try to take you back to the foundry, but it's only a natural course of events. Vandheer knows how valuable you are, and he would want you whole and alive to preserve your value until he figures out how to extract it. Despite what it may seem, the corrupted enforcers are his gentler options."

The paper man stopped before Venner, his umbrella still obscuring his face. "You asked me to listen," said the paper man. "You asked for permission. It was so novel that I might as well. I listened to you and yes, the world is very terrifying. I am not as hardy as living things, yet I am tasked to observe them, to herd them, to pick and choose for slaughter. I am fit for no more than what I was made for. You listened to me so well, grabbing a miraculous, momentary sentiment out of my head.

The paper man leaned in, lifting the umbrella over Venner's head. "I wished to be free from my terrors." An origami crow was folded from the stump of a head neatly cut across halfway up the nose. The crow pranced but never left its paper stage. It flapped its wings, but its legs stayed attached. This was the source of the errant folds and the reason why the paper man was cut incorrectly. He had been made to harbor extra prying eyes.

"To be free from the dismal weather as a jest," continued the paper man, "but to be free from Vandheer as one of his stolen tools. Maybe even free from the city, if a little less so. I had a thought out of the blue sea that I had the clout to do what I wanted. I had no immediate master, no world and no parasite. I'm a garish sight, I know, but my head's open just for you. My fellow, the one that manages the trains and rode that boat, told me the storm was cruel. Maybe, but I know the man behind that storm can be quite gentle. Where is that man?"

"Answer my question. Where is Vandheer?" Venner scowled. "You must know as well as anyone else about what murmurs beneath this city. Fail me and I will strip every word from your headspace. I will reduce you back to the dreamless scraps you were made from. I have found my purpose, and I am much more capable this time. I am a working man, paper, and the world becomes my plaything if I have the mind for it."

Venner scratched his fingernails down the wall. Gold dust of a stairwell facsimile rotted at his touch. Upstairs digressions melted away. Concrete bubbled into water, and the sudden echoes of tumbling rapids barreled down towards them. The paper man bit his lip in dismay. Rain invaded the facsimile, and the rapids charged ever closer.

"Meet me in my entirety. No city will save you," said Venner.

Rain tapped on the umbrella and slid down the walls, leaking between the railings. "I really do believe you can demonstrate discretion," said the paper man, who lost his nerve and retreated a step, careful to not slip from the rushing water that pulled at the ankles. The paper man shrunk under his umbrella from the torrent. He bared his teeth and threw the umbrella down the steps. It clattered and was taken by the quickening river. The paper man grabbed Venner by the lapels. "Not believe, I know this. That one moment cannot be swallowed by an ocean. You think. You act. You choose. You are more than a mindless storm."

The paper man brought Venner's hand to his chest, roughened by chasing a storm. Venner felt the heartbeat that should not exist echoing in proclamation. Meat was incompatible with mulch. Rain left dark imprints upon the paper man's head, distorting its shape and ruining its function.

"You gave me this, not an ocean," said the paper man. "What can I do to help you? Do you think I am blind that I cannot see you struggle?

That I'm somehow incapable of concern as I check up on you because I worry?" Venner clenched his teeth, straining the raw joints of his jaw.

"And I will take it right back," said Venner. "You will be taken under like the rest of your brethren, shredded at the hands of vermin."

"Then take it back," said the paper man. "Devour it whole. I wouldn't know what to do as a real boy. You chose to listen to me and helped, even if at the time we thought it was only words of sympathy. No discussions on deals or contracts. Have you no faith in yourself? What made you forget to collect the debt I'd incurred for my heart? Explain to me how I was an exception. What is it that you want?"

"You. I wanted to find you and prove to you I was not just water." Then Venner added, much more quietly, "I enjoyed the company." The paper man defied the checklist. Weekday corporatism and weekend consumerism disallowed the existence of animated pages. Partial success for partial happiness. He had failed his oceanic principles over and over, but felt relief regardless. He felt relief listening to the paper man and was so impossibly content to be in the company of something meant to be erased. He was ashamed to want this, despite his endeavors otherwise.

The paper man waited for him all the while, keeping gentle hold of his hand and letting him go when he was ready. The rain abated. Water settled into a smooth surface above them. The paper man gazed up in astonishment at the ensuing body of water that encompassed the entire upstairs. The surface remained mostly horizontal, swaying in an invisible breeze. This stairwell sea extended down to just above Venner's head.

"Flesh is incompatible with an ocean," said Venner. "I want to know that I am just insane, that my actions have no consequences, that I do not actually eat people, that this is all just daylight delusions. I was happiest when I first emptied my ocean. Infinite from end to end, but nothing lingered. The abyss swallowed all that drowned. There was nothing to compare against the serenity of nonexistence. That was my world, polished to the most exacting angles possible. I wish I had never looked up.

"What was once uncommon occurrence has reared new life. I am haunted. The boundaries of my world have changed without my consent, and they will not close back in. I cannot ignore these intrusions.

Yet I cannot even interact with these new anomalies unless it is by their good graces I am allowed. It did not used to be like that. If they existed, they were gone until one day I became incapable. Until one day I found myself with a jaw. Everything that I once could shield my gaze from is now everywhere. And out of further insult, all my self-medicating, all my distractions to keep all my eyes from seeing, were taken from me.

"And you have the gall, the very gall to tell me everything will be okay, that I am better than this," snarled Venner. "I am told to enjoy life without being hung up on my frustrations, told that I can enjoy company without ever thinking about how much I despise everything, told that I must be better than whatever failure I am now! You cannot comprehend how distant I feel from that. I get it. I objectively get it and what steps I need to take to get there, but I am incapable. All a checklist does is mock me. It had worked, all my efforts to keep this under control. A nameless salve for my affliction that allowed me to make it so long in this world. And what works now is an abomination to existence.

"Would I have broken down despite otherworldly intrusion? My efforts are pointless, as I lose control no matter what I do. I should have died. There were so many chances. I want the quiet, the calm, the very stillness that belies the end. My world either needs to converge down to the proper shape of a man that had no dealings with an ocean or my world needs to be rid of everything. Choose for me, paper, or the one that has opened me has to put me back together. It must be."

"You know that won't happen," said the paper man in somber tones. Venner pressed the heel of his hand against his blind eye until it hurt.

"I am an ocean made a man. My worldview is skewed through the limitations of flesh. I have a worldview now. Is that not novel? The ocean speaks! The ocean went through university and has learned to design planes. This is the dreaming, not my grey ocean expanse but my life over the last few decades. An ocean believes itself to be alive and dares interact with an outside world." Venner struggled for breath. "I have my solution. I have found myself. The name is Eram Venner; my perception I will devour to finally soothe my beast. So ends all my interactions with everything. I do want to go home. I just do not know which one. Please, wish for me. Wish for that man you want to speak to or free me, if you have any semblance of mercy."

"Wish for you," repeated the paper man, hurt. "What do you want? For me to halve you? For me cut out everything you hate about yourself? I understand it's difficult, but I don't want to hurt you like that. I'd rather be here as needed. No, I won't choose for you. I shouldn't have asked where the man was. The better question would've been about you and your ocean and your desire to live. A strange existence in a strange world. There's nothing wrong with that. Experience all the things so unlike your perfect singularity. Your dissolution is not guaranteed because you have hope for yourself, don't you? Does your purpose truly damn you without recourse? Is there nothing outside duty that can comfort you? You have as much a right as anything else to live. All of you, even in infinity."

"A nonanswer," gnashed Venner.

"It's the only answer I want," said the paper man. Venner stared at the crow that hopped around the paper man's head and then plucked it from its trap. Its legs ripped apart. He unfolded the crow and the name Vandheer was written upon the page. The paper man patted his cut head in disbelief.

"Take me to Vandheer," said Venner. "One favor for another. I am asking for you to trust me. I can fix myself. I—I have to fix myself."

"Or else you'll eat yourself," said the paper man. "I hear you. You make it seem so easy, your situation and your absolute irreverence for the laws of magic. You have the best chance out of anything against Vandheer, I suppose. Fine then, I will because I want so desperately to trust you."

They started walking down, their footsteps echoing together. The paper man watched the waterline follow them down each floor. Venner skimmed his knuckles across the surface. The ripples chased his movements, widening in rings to bounce off the walls of the stairwell. Ripples and echoes coalesced and divided. The drowned florescent lights shimmered through the chaos, showering them in waxing twilight.

"The city is an ancient and generous entity, and she is powerful in terms of longevity," said the paper man. "Not all powerful. We're her attendants, her children in a way, created to provide her day-to-day necessities. There's a hearty momentum to this city that can be electric to opportunists. Vandheer was brought into the city under contract to help clean up our undesirables. Just a modest fee for his efforts, then he held eyes with her wealth.

"We did attempt to pay him fairly. He wanted more. Wilder ambitions sought to melt down the heart of the city and every body of magic along the way, fueling his dream of immortality. What better victim, so reliant on her crafted children so easily hijacked." Galloping flickers of light chased between the railings or alongside mortar lines of brick. Light slipped between their legs and slid down the stairs. "Then may I accompany you?" asked the paper man.

"No."

"Am I too much a sight for sore eyes?" asked the paper man. "I'm sorry. I'll find you again. I'll be better prepared next time, a lifeline in hand. I promise. Welcome to the foundry that toils beneath the city." The paper man opened the brick wall at no particular junction, making it quite evident that the paper man was grasping for more time with Venner. "Please, stay safe."

# THIRTY-EIGHT

**NOW WAS A GOOD TIME FOR SAMUEL TO UPDATE CLAIRE ON** his search for the engine, and perhaps she would have better news herself. The phone rang. The blinds were open for more light in a living room dressed in Gaelic script over the floorboards. Crows cut across the setting sun and orange horizons. Their shadows leapt through the glass barrier into the room. The line clicked.

"Hello, Samuel. How goes your search?" Claire asked. "Might I remind you that not a single wish may be commanded from the engine. It is simply for your safety."

"Late. Harken's been to his apartment first," said Samuel, kneeling in front of the dead enforcer. He squeezed the phone between his ear and shoulder as he dove through the machinery. Its ribs were splayed open neatly, its heart missing. He pulled out the audio jack from underneath the collar. It was cut and collected in a plastic bag as part of a growing collection of handovers to the researchers. "Do you think Harken will hand over anything about the engine nicely? Though by sending an enforcer, the consequences of a trade contract are the last things on their minds."

Samuel sifted through the remains of wet radio parts and empty housings. "How about a night around the city? No business allowed, Claire, purely entertainment. I've seen ads for an art museum and newly opened exhibits. We can find the nearest tourist trap to start building the list of regrets. Experience the bustle of so many people you just don't get in the Library. Places where they don't know your legacy or your name. You're lost in the sea of just living."

She sighed. "Downtown is always rife with flavor. The marina is currently set up for celebrations when I passed by. Ride the ferris wheel. Win a prize. Watch the performances. The city is beautiful at night."

"There will be no time for that," she said.

"Yes, but you've always heard me plan, and you've always listened."

"I do not like people."

"I know, but I want to give you the chance to be disappointed. Where else then? Any places you've dreamed of?"

"They will stay dreams, Samuel, because dreams are so wonderfully benign. An impermanence that cannot stay duty."

Samuel stacked radio pieces vaguely back together. "You won't even tell me what they are? I'll find the engine, Claire. I'll set you free." No reply. The lack of trust hurt. "How goes the research? Have you and Grimleer found a better solution?"

"No. Grimleer's engine will be made from me. There will be no discussion."

Samuel threw a housing against the drywall, cracking both. Time unwound so quickly out of control. He needed to find the engine now. He had taken great pains to find the apartment. Claire refused to offer any leads. The shards of red bone Weill had collected were his only physical evidence. Everything else had been lost to inferno and collapsing spaces. He had interrogated suppliers in back alleys for the name of a necromancer, and broken into an accounting office for the engine's address. The mere validation of the engine's identity turned immediately into a conversation about despair when she explained her upsetting intentions.

There was noise at the door. Samuel slipped his pistol out from its holster, firmly gripped it with both hands, and aimed at the person that had just entered. The haggard intruder raised both his hands, revealing scars that ran down the length of his arms.

"Identify yourself," ordered Samuel.

"Where is he?" the intruder said. "Where did you take Eram?"

"One moment, Lady Iramir," said Samuel. He grabbed the phone with one hand, keeping only one hand on the pistol. The intruder rushed towards him. Its human guise split into bristling fur and shining teeth. Samuel fired. The enclosed room only heightened the muzzle report and heavy thud of the lycan hitting the floor. The heat of sorcery warmed the pistol. The lycan writhed on the floor, a bullet in its gut. Its shattered flesh was chipped with frostbite. "A lycanthrope. You are far from the Emerald Isles."

Samuel would have preferred to have not shot at all, lowering the counter on his watch. Three now. There was only so many times he could use magic tools without harm. To Samuel's surprise, the lycan was slow in healing. The lycan, maybe a half breed, was missing a few fangs. Their teeth fetched a decent price on the market as parts of charms or potions. Desperate for money then? Samuel leered over the fallen wolf. "You are not worth whatever Harken paid for you."

"I'm not with the bastards," growled the lycan. "Where is he?" Samuel remained unconvinced. He stepped over the wolf and examined the door. Teeth were embedded in the wood, and there were inscriptions along the inside of the frame—items initially overlooked because the slumped headless body was more intriguing. There was a messenger bag on the kitchen counter. Samuel fished a wallet from the bag. He inspected the driver's license and then the company identification card, photographing both. It looked like the intruder before he'd transformed into a wolf. Samuel tucked his phone into his breast pocket and adjusted it to still pick up the conversation. The call was still running.

"You work at the same company as Mr. Venner, and you are kind enough to give a house call. I would like to know as well, Mr. Caide Braonain. Where is Eram Venner? You've been here before. These are your teeth, aren't they?" Samuel showed the lycan his own fangs. "You had a violent encounter with Harken. That is evident. The modern office doesn't provide the proper exercise that a creature like you may enjoy. Explain."

The lycanthrope became reticent. Samuel dropped the items back on the counter. He inspected the mechanisms of his gun before approaching the lycanthrope again. "Perhaps if I introduced myself, you might feel more comfortable. I am a Library agent sent against Harken."

"Why does the Library care?" asked Caide, getting up. Flakes of frozen skin scattered as muscles stretched, revealing a bright crimson welt in sluggish renewal. The lycan licked the holes in his gums, eyeing the gun aimed at his heart.

"Mr. Venner is a very desirable man," said Samuel. "The Library wants to make sure that no one else takes advantage of his unfortunate property. We want to rescue him."

"I don't believe the Library has turned a new leaf for charity."

Samuel chuckled. "This isn't a charity case. We understand that Venner won't cooperate. If we can't have him, then no one will."

"If you dare hurt him, I'll rip you to shreds."

"Mr. Venner doesn't have to die. He just needs to be out of Harken hands or the hands of anyone else that dares to intercede in our business."

"He was here. He really was," snarled the lycan. "Just some time alone in the next room. It was just one door between us, then I go get him and he's gone. The city took him. I was going to get him out of the city."

"Very noble. The Library has the same goals, Mr. Braonain, though we won't be satisfied with simply leaving the city. We want to remove all traces of his existence. Again, do not misunderstand me. All he needs is a new name. New identity. Witness protection is rote for us." Samuel handed over the phone. Claire was still on the line. "We will give you fair compensation for your aid and knowledge of the city. I hear the old emerald fields are rife with plague. We can offer our specialists if you so want."

"What happened to 'first do no harm'? You are no doctors. You are all murderers, wearing crosses like wolves pretending to be sheep."

Claire spoke over the speaker. "The death of an age requires sacrifice to prevent it. Our talent is our currency. There is treating the disaster and there is cure by any means necessary. The world does not offer a bloodless solution. Our mercy is to keep such blood out of your hands." The lycan stiffened at the sound of her authoritative voice.

"Listen to me, Caide," she continued. "I will see Eram home, safe and sound. He needs help and we are the only ones left that can help him. His home seems to have been violated by more surreptitious parties. Would you kindly wait for him? When he is finally with you, I trust you to keep him well, and I ask you to trust me. You would not want to drag this ordeal out longer than it has to be. Time is not his friend, and you are only one man. There is a distinct difference between extricating a man from the surface streets of a city and the very confines of Harken.

"I know no one will help you," she warned. Caide did not refute this. "An agreement, how delightful. We will deliver you Mr. Venner." Samuel stared at the phone in surprise. He knew better than to actively question her during negotiations, but that engine had to be returned to the Library. It could not leave their hands to be cared for by a wailing wolf.

Caide took the phone, cupping it near his lupine ears. "Then what are the terms? What do you want?" he asked. Samuel chewed the inside of his mouth. It was absurd that the lycan was being given so much of Claire's attention and absolutely infuriating that he was being offered genuine salvation.

"May I enjoy my life and practice my art, respected by all men and in all times. That is what I want." Caide fumbled with her words, confusion lining his lycan features. Samuel recognized it as part of the medical oath. Claire had loved to play doctor when she was younger. Providing aid was a better use of Library resources than slaughter. Thinking about what could have been only made Samuel hate the current circumstances ever more.

"Where does your family live, Caide?" she asked. "I would like confirmation." Caide snarled with a thunderous roll. His lupine shoulders tightened as he searched for something to hurt her with, finding Samuel. Even without canines, the wolf was fearsome. Samuel's trigger finger twitched. "I have not hurt them, and I will not," said Iramir. "I simply want to help."

"You can get whatever you want with your power and influence. Why bother with a nobody and his family? To bring up hope only to crush it? This is pointless. You have even admitted your doctors don't help."

"It is not pointless. It is to stand before desolation, before the impending doom, and to act anyway, up until the final second and then onwards. And if not the Library, then me in their stead. Always in their stead. There will be no question of the light at the end of the tunnel. I know everyone knows someone affected by it. Tell me what they need."

Claire did not have to offer help. This was nothing but the last-minute busywork, moments too small to seriously attend. Time must be better spent than offering care for a world indifferent to her condition.

"What makes you bastard master of a decrepit tunnel?" said Caide.

"Because I choose to be. I choose to man the station when the sirens call to evacuate. I choose to help the last one out. I will always choose to stay." Caide could not hide his sudden whimper. He fell into shame and covered his face.

Claire coaxed the wolf to voice his plea. Samuel listened while the lycan told of how his father lost the use of his body trying to save his mother. How that failed twice, and Caide could not stand performing hospice care anymore on things that once were his parents. How the winds of autumn now poisoned the forest of the old home. How roots, grown vicious and callous, leeches off a grandfather who had refused too many times to leave the ancestral grounds because who else would man the manor. How the memories were all taken first. How the turning of spring meant the discovery of the freshly dead because winter winds had turned foul and destroyed all magic of metamorphosis.

Caide was asked to wait, and then asked to verify the names. Samuel dropped the aim of his gun. The family of a werewolf would be managed for a time, but Claire would not be. Samuel was nowhere closer to finding the engine, his endeavor impossible. He must rid himself of this wolf matter as soon as Claire hung up.

Samuel checked the time and saw the water. He lifted his feet. Water flooded the scratched floor, leaking from the dissected enforcer. He inspected this rift in the chest cavity with the tip of his gun. Reality itself easily tore as he widened the hole into this extradimensional expanse of pitch darkness. Petals of cinnabar flaked from the enforcer body. Samuel glanced at the lycan, who worried but could not end his own house call.

A hand grabbed Samuel by the shoulder and dragged its wasting body through the opened enforcer. It was a red skeleton facsimile of a painted human doll. It grabbed him tightly, threatening to pull him into the void. "TAKEMYPLACE. RELIEVEME," shouted a broken skull. The body struggled pitifully as the living currents tore its lower half away, disconnecting at the spine. Samuel shoved the end of his gun against its neck but the hum in his bones, the traces of a moonlight spell, stayed his finger. The lycan readied for another fight but Samuel's shifting aim cowed him.

The setting sun lit the skeleton in harsh, burnished gold. It held onto his body with a grip that cracked its joints. Moonlight spells end at the strike of dawn. The sorcery burns away in daylight. He could not surmise who had made this spell or what it was for. Or was it only a bait for an agent like him? Yet this spell transcended its limits.

THEOCEANHASNOMERCY. At this noise, Samuel widened his eyes. Impossible magic but the engine specialized in just that. The sequel to a phylactery and a flattened lich had found him. The ocean was to be found across the void. He weighed the possibility of having another chance in more forgiving circumstances. STOPTHEOCEAN. SAVEME. He had no time. Samuel shouldered the red skeleton into the graveyard of oceans and was swept into the very currents of oblivion.

# THIRTY-NINE

WITHIN THE FOUNDRY, VENNER BEHELD A HIDDEN HOLLOW of the city's crooked reflection. The noise of toiling machines filled the stagnant air. The high wires of transmission towers crossed the hazy sky and dipped to touch each streetlight one by one. Glass towers were stripped of their glimmering façades and stuffed to the brim with meat and gold bulging between steel and rivet structures. This wasted metropolis had been reduced to a mere scrapyard filled with captured beasts and inexplicable curios trapped inside their tower cages. Not all captured were dead. They screamed, they shook their chains, they wished until their hearts burst.

Parts of a city, of buildings, bridges, and monuments were scattered on the highway paths. Painted lane dividers and carpool indicators were scuffed from something scraping along the roads. The route signs read of places Venner did not know. He had climbed out of a shattered vinyl record storefront that had been thrown aside like a forgotten dollhouse. The open door lingered in black as if inviting him back to the surface, to slip back into changing spatial sensibilities and find himself properly within societal humdrum and good providence. He could use more sleep, a hot meal to settle the hunger, a conversation to prove he was not alone.

To sleep would be to dream of oceans and bygone memories, to get lost in unconscious squall, to stoke the deep-seated hunger within abyssal depths. There was always room for more, the incalculable seafloor, because every puzzle increment had negative weight. Yet to converse with others, to witness the movements and hear the noise of ecstatic life, truly confounded him. Existence was rotten. A visual blight to be fixed after 3 a.m. Yet those named displacements within the ocean defied him in his most pristine, and he let them. Because he was fond of them.

He was obligated to prove the paper man correct, somehow.

He had to stare into his own abstract jaw of lunar lithic teeth, find Vandheer, and devour the name. He had to remove all reminders that interfered with the efforts to mindlessly distract himself, and be saved. His impatience drew him to the normality of structural analysis work and binges of late night shows. It meant that happiness was always just out of reach.

He walked along the streets under skies of unchanging grey and navigated the urban jungle. Attempting to stretch his muscles and relieve some tension only caused his body to bite back in pain. Surrounding him were cages filled with candles and preserved praying hands, cages of spined creatures that ducked his gaze and hid behind their motionless fellows, cages all so gilded that he could not bear to keep his attention focused. He climbed up a hillside of bones and scrap metal to the roof of a small building.

The ground shook and rattled amongst the building supports. Sharp cracks in the distance sounded the fall of a concrete tower that had had enough of its breathing charges. From the cascade of dust and rubble came the freed shapes of howling meat. They were not free for long. A massive tentacled machine emerged from the decrepit skyline. Swift limbs whipped these beasts into submission. A cycloptic eye sparked with bright blue electricity and struck with a heavenly fury at the heathens that soiled its domain.

The machine commenced collection, stuffing charred bodies into its embracing limbs. The crooked city creaked to life. Unmanned cranes dredged shipping crates from the spoiled earth. The machine deposited its gilded treasure into these crates and compressed meat in stilted progress for maximum space. Dark liquid leaked through the failing welded seams.

These cranes and machines built the laden crates into the foundations of the stripped towers. Steam gyres shot into the skies as the foundations sucked dry their meal. Gold funneled up the glass pipes, up the transmission towers, and through the cloud cover. Behind the haze of a forlorn sky, a bright fire burned brighter for every drop. The weight of these nameless creatures did not last long, and the haze dimmed.

More of the city fell through the clouds and crashed into this domain. So filed these depositions from attendants with crows inside heads. More machines scoured for wailing leftovers to feed the factory the means of its elixir of immortality. One of them carried stacks of mirrors. The faces within their silver prisons were frozen in anguish. The factory was an autonomous collection, plucking from the refuse mountains all fruits of anima to be devoured. Part of him delighted in this apparent cleanliness.

A sudden spotlight found him. Stripped towers hummed with the electricity of biding sadism. A distant machine began crawling toward him alarmingly fast. Venner tensed. It was a far drop down from the rooftop. He could barely stand, much less run. Yet he was hardly defenseless. Consciousness was prey, and if this machine had an ounce of thought to itself, an ocean would find the exact edge to cut open on abstract teeth. Even mere machines overflowed with life.

His phone vibrated in his pocket. Low battery. The red icon blinked in the corner and a red oil seeped from between the aluminum covers. A sudden message, TASK88CO&PLETE. Here in the home of its master, the standing radio answered. Venner kept the phone in his hands. "Oh, do you miss home?" he whispered to the radio's mobile soul.

The stalking machine made no noise as it approached. It leaned down close to the rooftop, close enough that Venner's breath condensed on its metallic surface. Its eye tumbled in its artificial orbit, switching between different drawn expressions on its pearl surface. Venner attempted to touch the machine. The machine stopped him with a rough tentacle coiled tightly around his arm. A grip of iron forced Venner to stop struggling to avoid agitating his fresh bruises.

The machine spoke with a voice of buzzing fluorescents, "Are you thief or are you treasure?"

"Neither," said Venner. The machine yanked him off the roof and held him suspended by his arm. Venner struggled to balance himself, reaching blindly for a handhold. The clink of the phone hitting iron convinced him to keep the device safe instead. Dangling was still painful, however.

The spinning eye settled on anger. "Your heart beats with vitality too natural. You are a human. Like all living things of such brimming serendipity, you will be destroyed. No one and no thing of the natural world will penetrate our heaven." Runic patterns materialized from the eye like threatening halos. Gilded paths of winding magic completed and transformed. Aggression written in every way as the machine readied lightning to strike him like the charred beasts.

Following its programming without hesitation, the machine had no other desire than his own destruction. There was nothing to debate. Tightening coils threatened to crush his arm as a wincing body only reminded him of his pathetic shape. He should have shaved farther than just his eyes. He should have ripped a hole inside himself to the very size of infinity. His grip tightened on the phone, squeezing out more oil from between the plates. The circuit heart trembled and the mobile soul whined.

Venner showed the phone to the machine and said to the mobile soul, "Death is a hair's breadth away. You cling to your shape so stubbornly. A phone, even a radio man, pales against the mighty machine. How fragile are your fiberglass bones, your silicon blood? Spy down the barrel and glimpse the molten lead. Atom by flesh by consciousness, you can be reborn. Surrender to me and embrace immortality."

The trembling radio heart captured in its aluminum box said, "*I do not want to die.*"

From the machine, lightning struck without mercy.

It was a silent strike as all lightning was. Thunder was a forgotten afterthought. Venner fell from the machine's grasp, and it crashed into the ground, skidding across the pavement, without support of its tentacles. It was a rough landing as he braced to keep the phone safe. The pearl eye had ruptured in its shattered orbit; lightning misfired. Protective charms had been devoured by salt water, and its own magic electrified its organs.

Venner curled up in vile disgust, groaning with his hand over his blind eye. Festering sensations revived and doubled their displacements. The partial erasure of his human body meant the feeling passed through into the ocean unimpeded and true. The acts of mortal satiation, of scratching the itch, of retching the building nausea, of hurting himself to ignore the very revulsion, no longer functioned. Shapes writhed within his ribcage. Existence was so much more sickening when felt in the literal ocean.

The mobile soul awaited him, praying along the phone line. The wish ticket had been created, yearning to be resolved. Work delivered him free. Venner dragged himself to his feet. What had been automatic unconscious effort had stalled. The ocean's momentum, his hunger that had always hurried him now felt too patient. It was as if reality waited for his middleman direction. The mindless disappearance of things inside their boxes, he felt was no longer possible. He had become too aware. With shaking hands, he pried apart the phone and revealed the quivering little heart.

He viewed the ticket from the safety of an imaginary office space and read the requirements washed in a sea of glimmering pixels and almost-wolves and lost heads. Powerful and immortal, spoken right through the microphone. He answered the mobile soul with a strange intuition riding the waves as always. He began to tie thread, mixing gold in a bizarre pattern, between a steel body of lightning and a once-standing radio. It was a solution inspired from what magic he had seen before or known through rote puzzle exercises. To feel this body move and work left him wondering how surprisingly dexterous the infinite whole of him was to pilot a numb and pathetic human.

*Enough.* The intersection of this human body within water was becoming increasingly bothersome. The fine line that delineated him from himself had failed, and association was mingling, or rather, the line that delineated him from the ocean. His hands bled from catching on sharpened glass and metal. He felt nothing through his bleeding brine. Compulsion was the perfect soporific.

There was no part of the mobile soul that could sustain its impossible ambition. Yet whatever a mobile soul lacked, the ocean provided. Infinite water poured infinite gold. He squared the soul against the template of that wondrous moon because he could not help but look up. Impossibility be damned.

Venner hung his thumb over the quivering heart that shook loose phone components with every beat. Then, Venner gently punctured the living thing. The heart popped and leaked like a cracked egg before birth. Pierce the shape and pour the ocean in.

Black feathers rained over him and the slumbering machine. Crows flew circles above. The gold extended farther than the shape of physical things. The name that rode a once-standing radio and a clockwork millipede had come to investigate an ocean's disturbance in its factory heaven.

# FORTY

SAMUEL STEPPED OUT OF THE HOLE MADE FROM AN ENFORC-er's body. In the blink of an eye, the scene of a wrecked apartment hard-cut into an open metropolis. Water splashed underfoot as the streets flooded and submerged all manner of trash and rubble. It seemed he had entered another part of the city, one destroyed and precariously piled. Derelict skyscrapers lined the horizons in looming threat. Ocean sophistry was certainly effective. The way back, imprinted on a leaning brick wall, was obscured in pitch. He could only hope it would lead him back to the apartment if he found no other way to leave this place.

The engine was nowhere to be found. The wailing construct was also missing except for its breadcrumb trail of viscera melting in stagnant water. Samuel followed, keeping his gun at the ready. Landscape became consumed by more industrial machinations. Factory schemes intertwined civil planning.

The trail stopped. The red creature hid within a broken metallic shell, the interior heavily scratched. Fingernails shorn stuck in the crevices. The shell had been peeled open as if something had escaped. It squirmed in its juices marred with mud and knocked against a leg that would have been part of it.

"I WANT TO LIVE," it said to the shell, and did not look at him. It cowered and covered its head. "IT BURNS!" it cried. "DO YOU HEAR ME?"

"What are you?" Samuel asked. It ignored him.

"I WANT MY LEGS. I WANT MY BODY BACK. I WANT TO

GO HOME." The desolate city remained apathetic. It turned to Samuel with a fright. "YOU HAVE RUINED THE ESCAPE. IT WAS SO HARD TO MOVE SPACE TO GO BACK HOME. THIS CITY IS ALL WRONG."

"You're my only lead as to the whereabouts of a very peculiar ocean. I'm quite certain you know whom I speak of. Where is it?" The red creature dragged its upper body as high as a single arm could manage up against the machine carapace.

"THE OCEAN WILL DEVOUR YOU," it said, and gathered its leg tightly and rocked itself for comfort.

"The engine must obey its user, and I refuse to be dealt with so easily," said Samuel. The leg dropped out of its grasp as it tilted its head in seeming realization.

"THE OCEAN WILL NOT LISTEN TO MINOR THINGS. THE OCEAN WILL LISTEN TO THINGS LIKE YOU." It reached for him. Samuel shot it. The ringing of a biting bullet was swallowed by the silence of a broken city. The red corpse slumped over and the frost-bitten wound in its chest grew larger and larger. He lowered the counter on his watch. Two.

The flesh around the bullet hole began to suck in. Bone bowed and cracked. A gurgle of deflating lungs upset him. He questioned the purpose of a pathetic creature like this. In what frame of mind did the ocean deem this acceptable? It was made only to suffer. He steeled his nerves. Duty demanded completion, not fawning over every poor thing he came across.

"SAVE ME." The rattle of a red corpse surprised him. Another red creature dragged itself through the widening hole of its original, reborn from death. The smell of thaumic rot, like bittersweet ash, filled the air. Reality clung to this new body like webbing, stretching and warping perception. "SAVE ME," it repeated. This replication was corrupted. Features doubled up upon themselves. Two thirds of two bodies combined together without mirroring. It had too many eyes and too many arms. Its legs bent backward and black feathers discharged from its orifices.

Samuel's vision shook. The red creature reached out again. Its body splintered from internal fire and out of these fresh cinder holes came more damaged replications. Samuel could not move. Each successive iteration suffered worse from corruption. The creature, creatures, climbed upon him. It/they grabbed at his coat. It/they cupped his face. It/they wailed. "SAVE ME." Its/their discordant voice filtered through too many mouths.

Samuel tasted blood from his biting habit. The Library's mission was once to save the unfortunate, regardless of who or what, and he was still its agent. He held the flat of the gun barrel against its neck and snapped his fingers on the metal. It rung, then resonated. Red bones started to boil. Sorcery ruptured from cascade. The advent of ashes sped up and burned with a revived ferocity, but replication would not let its death be kind. It/they could not hold on. It/they flailed on the ground. Samuel looked away, but he could still hear its/their wails. He waited for silence. It/they would not be silenced. Pattering hands grabbed at water, searching for him.

This was how the ocean chose to spend its talent, sowing visceral misery. The engine was too dangerous to let free. It had to return to the Library to take Claire's place. He was not prepared to see her die, but he had not the heart to be deaf against the creature, no matter the wasted time. It had no one else.

Just one more minute. Duty must wait just one more minute.

He broke off part of a femur bone from the dismembered leg left within the metal shell. More fragments were made that he bagged carefully. He approached the creature multitude having grown too massive to move. Heads grew into themselves, bodies inseparable. His splashing footsteps alerted the multitude, and it clamored for him. It tried. Limbs snapped under their own weight. Febrile hands tugged at his legs.

Samuel kneeled down. He splayed his hand against a red-handed miscreation, carefully aiding the creature to match him. Then he entwined his fingers around its own. Red fingers stuttered closed in reply. Samuel arranged the bone fragments in a pattern on the floor. The water traced their shapes in tiny waves. He pinched his gun between his legs. With his free hand, he released the magazine and unloaded one of the bullets. The bullet casing was unscrewed, and out poured the ichor as Samuel drew a small ritual circle into water. White luster disturbed water's mirror finish, clouding but lingering where he had drawn.

Samuel rolled the empty casing in his palm. This suffering was the result of the Library's legacy. They had created the engine and thus appropriated all horror that stemmed from it. Samuel held the red hand tighter, using his thumb to comfort as best he could. He had drawn a repeating spell to summon a little light. A good student was able to induce cascade in minor spells as a defense or utility. Crude creations were also easy to manipulate this way. Even if he could not cast magic himself, he had the tools enough to do so.

"Perform the spell," said Samuel. "It'll help. I'm right here, don't worry." The red hand twitched. He laid the hand flat over the circle and stroked the back of it. Summoned light escaped between the gaps of broken flesh. Cascade fed on repeat and finally overtook endless replication. Ash soiled the water with a growing dark stain, a marked grave in final silence.

Samuel checked his watch, debating whether he should decrease the counter. Better to be safe as he dropped it down to one. The gun could only ignite ichor a limited number of times. He could always elect to ignore his cascade attempts. The bullets were also sufficiently lethal without magic. Water splashed from footsteps that were not his.

Another man forded his approach. Dead crows were gathered in his grasp. Their wings were bent crooked and their heads ripped wide at the beak. The man was ragged and soaked to the bone. One blind eye leaked water. Bits of his skin sloughed. Rusted blood stained the ends of his cuffs and collar. Samuel stood up, keeping the gun hidden behind his back with clasped hands. The man looked past Samuel to the stain of a buried creature and brought the bundle of crows up for further inspection. Feathers drifted and settled on the water.

"You are not Vandheer," the man said. "The radio did not last as long as I hoped. I had planned to make a god out of crows and radios until their collective prayers forced Vandheer down from his heaven. He refuses to act but instead watches through vermin, despite how many eyes have had their wings clipped." The man pointed to the grey sky that occasionally flashed with a vicious green leer.

Samuel hardened and revealed his gun. "You're the engine."

"I am the infinite ocean," corrected the man.

"Yes, you are. You could've been used for such good, but the fatal flaws can't be forgiven. You're a failed prototype, a cruel thing at that."

"Are you going to shoot me?" asked the ocean.

"You will be brought back to the Library," said Samuel. "With you, Claire will bring forth the new world."

The ocean smiled wryly. "Now, I do not think I am anywhere large enough to devour a whole world. Though if you ask kindly, from the very heart, I might make an exception." The ocean's spoken serenity was infuriating. Right behind Samuel was its abject wickedness in full view. "And I am quite curious how Claire would achieve such a goal. In delight, even. She is a gentle thought on my waves, of finely tuned instructions and unerring confidence. *The* moonlight ideal, even when she is one moon and not even a whole one.

"I remember feasting on seven, wonderful concepts. They forged my teeth and salted my waters. Claire has eluded me thus far, and I have grown so fond of the singular view. Has she been unable to concoct another body?" The ocean traced over his chest with a ginger touch. "Has her confidence wavered by sending you?" Seven was a number too close for coincidence for Samuel. Six unborn children and their mother. The ocean came forward until the end of the gun could almost tap it on the chest.

"I eat moons," said the ocean, and he calmly nudged the floating bodies of the dead crows around them. Samuel realized it was the ocean that had planted that poisoned thought into Claire. If the repository had not told her everything, the ocean had. A solution was a solution no matter the cost to her. What chance did she have? He could have stopped her then, could have held on to her so tightly and never let go, but he had been so eager to leave and find the engine.

Claire should not have been responsible for the failings of the Library. The consequences of thousands slaughtered, the burdens of futures destroyed, the agony of unstoppable destruction were the Library's to reconcile. Those that had created such misery should slay their demons and lead ghosts to rest, and yet she was made to stand for those that refused the call. Such dire consequence could not be swept away, ignored until it knocked upon the door, and ignored again. He would stand and take the lashings lest those that did not deserve it take the place.

"We fed so many people into the ocean," said Samuel, "all for a wish that the world be saved. Magic is failing and it'll take everyone that it has cursed. My reality, my world, is dying. Everything the Library has ever worked for would be pointless. How are you alive when the efforts of the Library failed? Whoever made you, were they simply lucky? Did fortune pat them on the head and curse the world through your existence?

"Why does it have to be you? You live free from the Library and Claire is trapped within. What did we do wrong? She won't survive too long outside. She wasn't made for it, but you have no care for the sanctity of your life. You were given a stolen happiness."

The ocean fumbled with his smile. His attention wandered. With wet fingers, he picked at the remains of his damaged eye. A phantom pain mapped this wound onto Samuel and the cries for help from a red creature lingered too fresh on the mind. The ocean did not deserve mercy. Of Samuel's many wasteful expenditures of time, the ocean warranted none of it.

All those years living without a care were wasted over the span of a single night. Claire needed to be different from her predecessors. She was not made to suffer, but to be safe and sound in his arms again. He grabbed the ocean by the collar, shoving the tip of the gun under its chin. "Move." The hole in the wall was hardly far from here. Given the gravity of this shipment, it would not be hard to arrange quick transport back to the Library.

The ocean's brief disquiet sharpened into anger. He grabbed the barrel of the gun and magic burned Samuel's hand, forcing him to let go. "I can make as many dolls as your heart desires," the ocean said, "and your incessant self will finally be reduced to nothing."

He discarded the gun, and its molten metal cooled in the water. A grazing touch, the ocean tapping the back of Samuel's hand stole his breath. His body tightened, flesh turned inwards underneath softening skin. Heat clawed down his throat. This ruin should not be happening. He had no innate magic to foul, but he felt the symptoms as easily as reading off the definition of the word *cascade*.

"I cannot forget how the world feels swimming in my thoughts," the ocean continued. "What is ever more frustrating is that you all act so ignorant of your crimes, demanding my presence yet gnawing down my peace. Everything must be drowned. The spark of life is just the same as sorcery and will not be spared. I suppose I can take a world under. There is a corner by the name of Claire where your shape falters and I can pull you apart. You exist, that is enough for you to be condemned."

Samuel punched the ocean in the jaw. He staggered back. It was unfair that something so inhuman enjoyed living so easily. It was infuriating that such a gift would be used to raze a thousand more lives if left unchecked.

Samuel coughed and struggled to move tearing muscles. "Claire could be saved because of you," he said. "All your ill-gotten years are over. Do you have friends or family? Who would miss you?" Those questions only further angered him. "Don't answer. You have nothing!" Claire understood how important this engine was and how potent it could be. She would've never let him leave. She would've never let the situation spiral like this. Why?

Another punch. The ocean did not fight back, and Samuel pinned him to the ground, raising another fist to strike.

"Have you never felt pain before, ocean?" asked Samuel, the ocean in anguish. "How did you escape the Library?"

"Iramir let me free," he breathlessly replied. Samuel's fist hung in the air. The ocean looked so vulnerable, plugging his palms over his eyes. The way he shuddered and seemed so suddenly terrified.

"She would never."

"Iramir trusted me enough to send me home, to tell me I would be fine. It was simply a matter of settling into old habits again. It will not end up like that. It will never end up like that. I am not happy," whispered the ocean. "I do not want any of this. What I want is impossible: for everything to be quiet and forgotten. I—I do not like existing. It is diffi-cult and excruciating. I am scared constantly that I am doing something wrong. There is something so fundamentally missing, and all I do makes it worse. But I cannot help it. My purpose is supposed to fulfill me. Work is supposed to save me.

"How do I fix this?" asked the ocean. "The disassociation is painful. It feels like I am piloting a body from afar through controls too frus-trating to wield. My world was no larger than my career, my immediate weekend, my name. Someone has shown me how to find the terrible things everywhere I look, how it feels to be beyond mortal sensations, how much I was just pretending to be fine."

It was a living being that stared in torment at Samuel, not some ocean of a Library far, far away. A living being tallied by its hopes and dreams and terrors that had just espoused its own suffering, a creature that had asked for help, that had grown so frustrated for salvation. This engine did as it was designed to do, promised so long ago to do as told to be happy.

That was what Claire had meant. It could not have been the hound that was sent to hunt. Weill was too dogged. It had to be him who had Claire's confidence and a weakness of heart for cases like her. Perhaps it was her vengeance for the times he told her she was too young or too fragile. Or perhaps who else? If Claire did indeed grant freedom to the ocean, then Samuel was not meant to bring the engine back.

A living being, a man, to be seen once in passing then forgotten. Just another person that lives and dies without leaving so much as a footnote. Samuel dropped his arms.

No, it was an engine the ocean contained. It languished in mediocrity and would be nothing more than a waste. Returning the engine would make the last of Claire's efforts a waste. Samuel felt so ashamed of outliving Claire. He would not be able to handle ruining her last request.

Cascade burning through his veins exhausted him. He wanted more time to avoid his task of gathering all the things needed to dissect a doll. One morning was not enough time to make a fatal decision. He stared at the ocean writhing in unknown horror. The ocean hated its own body and its own existence. The ocean had a name. It was alive. It occupied a space in the world. It was no different from everything that dreamed. His conviction failed and the realization could not be unthought. A fear struck him that even if he returned the engine, Claire would still go through with the ritual. She had that authority, after all. She was stalwart where he was not.

The world conspired against its living. Samuel could move heaven and earth and Claire would never be dissuaded. She was loyal to her purpose. Of all the things the Library would leave behind, he preferred it not be the final dissolution of everything he knew. A new world with Grimleer as god. No room for him, for Claire, for all those promises never to be fulfilled. A wish upon a star would not change the unwavering end.

Samuel leaned onto the ground, off of the ocean, to steady his swimming perception. He stopped the ocean from ruining its flesh by keeping its scratching hands at bay. Samuel gently cupped the newly emptied orbit. The eye had been crushed into useless tissue. He felt the warmth of a human body bleed into his. He felt the ocean's heartbeat. He just wanted everything to be okay.

"You've made it so far into your life only to have it ripped away from you in a day," said Samuel. This engine was what the Library needed. It was always about what the Library needed. What Claire needed was never really a consideration. Those interactions were, at most, some entertainment to help pass the time or to gauge her response if any adjustment was needed. If he were not so attached to Claire, nursing a sentimentality too obstructive of his duty, he could have wrangled the engine for her already.

Another life to throw into the literal ocean, the engine's or Claire's, but this time it really might work. Salvation was nascent upon the horizon. He gritted his teeth. Grimleer, himself, and all the other project members had felt the same way countless times they had living people right before them to be executed. But just one more, always one more. The next death would do it.

Claire knew this would break him because he had rounded the living personally and sent them to their deaths. Because she knew he hated the talks of legacy and failure. Because even if the Library could drop the idea of engines and new worlds, Claire would always be imprisoned within it. There would always be a new glimmer of hope on the horizon that Claire must break herself to find. Her presence and capability were a marked success for Grimleer, a shame for him. He never could deny the needs of the Library over her, but he wasn't here for the Library. He was here because she believed he could save the ocean.

"I want you to listen to me, ocean. My name is Samuel Hellion," he said. "I work for the Library. I've seen Claire grow up. I've been with her through her entire life, but I've never been able to save her. I wish—" Samuel stopped himself because he felt the ocean flinch. Not a single wish should be demanded from the engine, that was what Claire had said. "Who are you?" he asked instead, taking deeper breaths to stem the feeling of drowning.

"The infinite ocean."

"Would you like to be called something else or is 'ocean' fine?"

"Eram Venner and I want to keep this name," said the ocean in quiet astonishment. It was a faint relief for Samuel to hear the ocean speak of its apparent identity. The weight of cascade lifted, and he breathed with cold clarity. Samuel sat up. Water lapped at his edges as he situated himself for better comfort.

"What would it take to help you? I know you asked, but I'm at a bit of a loss here. A little direction wouldn't hurt."

"I either want to be without my compulsion or to have all things solved and settled. I have worked it out to these two solutions. Will you wish for me, Hellion, how I am supposed to be?" asked Venner. "My life consists of rushing from one distraction to the next so I can ignore my problems. I know how people taste, and I cannot stop thinking about it." Venner looked as if he knew how Samuel tasted as well.

"What sort of distractions?"

"A career that helps me reframe human interaction, where people are momentarily immune to my disgust. I can listen and engage all the wonderful distractions a body like this can afford me. Or I can murder those little spirits no one misses. A casual weekend afternoon, really, just to wear down the teeth. Any sort of diversion where there is no room, no lull where I can step back and realize what the hell I am doing while playing with my horrors.

"It is just absurd," Venner sighed, "because when I do step back, I find it very horrific, the social aftertaste. An ocean should not contend with existence. Eyes kept to themselves, an ocean's to an ocean, a man's to a man. The ocean has forgotten how to method act. Gone is the suspension of disbelief that worked the human dream."

Samuel rubbed his softened flesh and forced himself to stand. He was at that age where he could not do anything without grunting all the time. He helped Venner up. He kept his palm pressed against Venner's open eye.

"Those pursuits sound so lacking," said Samuel. "There's more to life than just work. Slow down, take in the sights and sounds. The touch of a world cradling you by the hand. If you feel the need to ignore me, ignore that thought. Talk to me and I will listen. You would need a rather nuanced wish, I would think, to comfort you. Something that carefully considers the result of you, not something that demands your problems go away. Crude cuts hurt. Nebulous limitations only induce anxiety. It won't be right the first time, but that's why we'll go slow with multiple attempts. Little by little, we'll do good."

Samuel let go of Venner, and Venner raised his hands in a taciturn agreement to stop fidgeting. Samuel huffed and grabbed Venner by the hand again, squeezing tightly. "I do want to exchange favors, however, and I need you to say yes," said Samuel. "Claire expects me to be too late to save her, and I know she wants to finally fulfill what she was made to do. She's wrong. Will you do it for me, Venner? Will you convince her to stop and give up the insipid idea of sacrifice? She has a soft spot for you—maybe a kinship in creation. She'll listen to you." Samuel watched the crows fly above.

The crows had gathered in unnerving numbers since the ocean had stopped grazing. Samuel rubbed his chin, readying another question. He tapped his shoulder, mimicking the motions of holding notes on string. Crows were perched everywhere on the branches and power lines. A thousand beady eyes stared down at them. "If you had stayed unfound, perhaps I could've succeeded in goading her outside after what should've been business as usual. I make so many itineraries for places I've been, all useless efforts."

Samuel swallowed his salted bile. "It's time to return to the Library. Straight to Claire mind you, at least for consultation on your condition. I know well enough how to keep you safe. Grimleer may have his designs," said Samuel, rolling his shoulders, "but there has to be another way that does not involve such death, and I say this knowing the Library has already soaked the past hours in red. Listen to me, Venner. If you agree, I wish to return to the—"

A steel bolt crashed into the ground where Samuel had just stood as if it had been thrown from the high heavens. Samuel grasped his chest from his sudden exertion of reflex. The bolt was nearly a man's height and was stuck fast into the shattered concrete.

Samuel scanned the area for any enemies. His gun was melted scrap, so his effectiveness was limited. He had no idea how quickly Venner could fulfill wishes. It was too dangerous to stay out in the open. They needed to escape to safety somewhere. Samuel took off his watch and held it tight against his palm. He picked up a shard of bent metal and began scratching a crude spell into the watch back. He led Venner through the urban jungle to where he remembered the enforcer hole was etched in a leaning brick wall.

Crows trailed them. Some fell into the water. Their feathers were stripped from their bodies, mangled by obscene replication. Every path they took through the city refuse led only to dead ends. Samuel tensed and nursed the cuts made in his speed through sharpened rebar brambles. Venner chewed on his knuckles. Crows flocked on walls and confronted them.

What avian consciousness survived the engine's transfiguration joined the hawking voices of a discordant choir. Corvus bones and flesh-feathered pitch made a walking entity that waved and clapped. Slithering feathers revealed two arms, two legs, and a torso to tie it all together. A head was fashioned from churning eyes stitched upon avian bosoms. Beaks formed its crown and made teeth for its smile.

"Ocean, you just had to make it harder for me," said the crowned mass of crow bodies and their harsh whispers. "Have some patience. I had to make sure I could survive you. I heard your call, and I must stress I am a better deal than the half-dead lunatic agent. I can gift you that quiet, ocean. I can pluck those maddening thoughts from your head and leave you spotless. I'll take everything from you, and I promise that it will all be put to good use. My foundry is very thorough."

Blue electricity lit the flickering eyes of the metallic beasts climbing from behind skinned towers. Whipping tendrils enclosed Samuel. The watch burned his hand. "Who are you?" asked Samuel.

"My name is Vandheer," it said, "and this is all of me." The advent of crows screamed at him.

"Venner!" shouted Samuel. "Take us back to the Library. Now."

# FORTY-ONE



**HELLION SAID SOMETHING. VENNER WAS NOT QUITE LISTENING.**
Venner stared at the crow shape before him, forming, malforming. Nothing mattered but witnessing actualization. The false cityscape crowded the shine of a sculpted, avian man. Vandheer bled gold and black feathers, features made from reassembled city dredges that an ocean could easily hold in its grasp. Vandheer was a pretend little bauble, avoiding any scrutiny that would pry him apart and rust the seams of crudely wielded magic. Vandheer fantasized about transcending death. His consciousness was a city wide and an inch deep.

The ocean rioted behind the controls of a human just as furious. Venner beheld this wriggling thing. Legfull, pale, and built by the masses. There was nothing unique to shadowbox and sink his teeth into. This shape was a stitched amalgam of melted things, soured by the aftertaste of lightning and oil. It was a pre-solved puzzle to be swallowed like charred beasts, shattered mirrors, and crows.

Live forever, all its voices shouted, tuned to the single channel. All deviating thoughts were melted down again and again until properly reformed. All the little souls dwelled amongst the walls of a fake man like a house made for bears. All this magic had been condensed down into doomsday rations and locked away to be cashed out in a dead era. It was an investment to be a god amongst departed men.

Vandheer had to prove the paper man wrong. He had to put an ocean back together.

"You must be more," whispered Venner. Drowned birds snapped

their ribs and ruptured their headspace under his approaching feet. "You must be more than all this." People resist being swallowed in a single bound. They had their intricacies and regrets, a wavering need that doubled back and wandered. The first solution often failed because of that. "I can count you down to the first broken egg. I can find all your tiny shapes swimming in my ocean. I can solve you in one. What keeps you here? It is merely your quantity?

"Where is that feeling past my grasp of a presence beyond the means of mortal bodies? There is no trick with you. No subterfuge to pick apart. I advance the steps, turn you end over end, and find nothing but chains of smaller things desperate to be more. Your heaven is silent because every voice is melted down into your foundry. Your machines are hollow nomenclature. You are a parasite that cannot survive on its own.

"No matter how much magic you pour inside of that head of yours, you will still be no more than a legfull thing. No part of you will echo back like that accountant you stuffed into me. You only want one thing. You are incapable of being misunderstood."

Crows plunged with devoured wings into pavement. "You are like the stars in the sky," Venner said. "If I lay on my back under the quiet night and reached as far as my limbs would take me, I could pluck these stars from their heavens. They taught me how to look up. They fit within my grasp like a handful of white beetles, scared and struggling to be free. I picked constellations clean. Yet where is your gravitas? Why are you so small for what you have taken from me?"

This amalgam god stuck inside a city copy, this human extrapolated from the creations of others, this incoherent noise excavated from the refuse of memory—the ocean despised it. Vandheer was made from melted scrap poured over top again and again, growing the ever few inches for however long the name Vandheer lingered on its lips.

The amalgam god had been gouged with crystal salt emerging from its failing body. The ocean torrent that had begun filling shapes slowed to a few droplets and then stopped leaking entirely. Wasting organs of an amalgam god remained dry and whole. Venner stared in shock at the steel bolt that ran through him, dividing his ribs.

The thing that had impaled him walked around him into view.

Venner clutched the steel and dropped to his knees. The thing was an exact copy of the amalgam god. Another Vandheer to be cheated by. Vandheer grabbed Venner by the jaw and drove the steel deeper, scraping along bone. Nerves wracked in agony.

"Your dreams are powerful, my headspace caught in your delusions," said Vandheer. "You weren't joking. I died in this head of mine, but I have many heads, and I don't fear you. I've seen how you work. How you snatch the perception and make it your plaything. I'm not big, but I'm the horde everlasting. You can only eat one at a time, right?" The sorcery of Vandheer extended far past his shape, traveling through city destruction and skinned towers. The factory sky kept Vandheer alive, forever feeding him the magic to be reborn.

"The ocean may be omnipotent, but the vessel is not," said Vandheer. "How little of a man would I need to control the ocean? I'll squeeze your infinity dry. Your crystal imprint was a phenomenal gift, leaving me ever wanting. I want immortality. I want to be perfect. Endless. You."

Cold, empty steel. There was nothing to be devoured in a nail that could undo Venner's impalement. He was in excruciating pain, and by proxy, the water too knew his suffering. More gods were born from feathered prayers. Steel glittered in their hands, ready to be pinned. It hurt as the next nail broke through his shoulder. The many was made from one. A conglomerate of minor things should be trivial. What was the point of him with a body so limited in scope? Why was he made to be so useless? All the goodness of his past interactions could not stem his absolute hate.

Venner heard Hellion, not his voice but the displacement within his waves. Lighthouse upon the black sea, the golden wealth of a man broke through a storm with ease. The difference was stark. Hellion was complicated. To fully solve Hellion's shape was to give everything into a desire and for Hellion to pour all of himself out to sea. To be so swept up in folly and rash decisions. To regret. To be scared. To have the shape defy the ocean. Hellion's gold bribe was accepted, and the ocean forced reality to oblige by sheer depth of infinity.

*Destroy.* Thus the contract between tool and man was mutual for once. The existence of blue lightning eyes and soulless amalgams could no longer be abided by the concept of gravity. Enemies were crushed into infinitesimal points. The immediate ideas of crows and machines fell into the ocean. Hellion fell onto the ground into the water with a sound of wet meat opening inside a bag of bones. Venner struggled to breathe. The white noise of a failing body overtook his senses.

*I don't want to die.* The ocean did not think this. The foreign thought was Hellion's. The contract terms had changed and appeared now as the new, willful departure from the disappointment an ocean had for its own body and for Vandheer. It would forget pain, once at work again.

However, it would need to be more discerning. It had failed to build a horse or a body free from blight. It had made monsters of men. They were solved enough. The desire to live was too loose with details and too easy to fall into a bare minimum effort. The bare minimum left all the ocean's victims broken, reduced to nothing but a whim. After all, that was what they had all wanted, a whim despite everything. Their forgotten senses were the ocean's reward.

Hellion was not made from a mold. What was Hellion's shape as it crumbled apart in the ocean's hands and Hellion's spirit whimpered? The ocean could not substitute anything. It needed the template, the human recipe, the original Samuel with whole hands, whole body, and whole heart. Memories of a passing hour would not do.

The ocean looked upon himself. He was human enough, was he not? He counted the limbs and measured the features. Where did ocean end and human begin? No more divide, too many thoughts and features melded.

He was not the magician at the helm. He was not the designer of a grand assembly. He was the engine itself. But of course, he had a mouth, a voice, and a body to interact with the world, to prod the wisher in ways the mindless ocean never could. He had thought and reason. "Hellion, are you listening? I need help."

# FORTY-TWO



**SAMUEL CONFRONTED THE DARK INFINITE OCEAN. HIS FEET** slid over the wet sand that covered his shale ground. Mud scuffed his soles, and the rasps followed his slow progress to the edge. Samuel was unwilling to lift his feet for fear of slipping into the deep waters. He scanned the ground carefully, noting ever crack, every hitch, every bit of the pitted rock he stood upon. He did not know how he had gotten here, but he was sure that Venner had managed some sort of impossibility.

The roar of the rushing water shook his chest. Waves were split by the efforts of a single outcropping and what had barely allowed him this scant sliver of ground. The splashing nipped at his feet. Every wave that managed to drag itself across the rock shocked him into stillness.

Something shaped like a human shared his space in the distance, standing upon the ocean. Something shaped like a human broke at the eye and out stepped something less than human.

"I know what you are," said Samuel. The rock ground crumbled away, and he found purchase upon the corpses of people. Their faces had been carved through, leaving nothing but holes in their heads. Water no longer, the sea of corpses shuffled under his weight. The Library made this. They had numbered all these lives. The soul was powerful, and the many was a tool. From the seed of a few hundred thousand people grew a tempered ocean. Samuel approached the inhuman engine. The halo of their finest thought experiment was magnificent.

Corpses grabbed him by the ankles. They reached up to his waist and shoulders. The empty people crowded over him. Samuel swallowed hard. He had ignored their pleas as he dreamed of vacations and happy futures. He moved the prodding hands away from his face but paused to embrace those that clutched his shoulders.

Samuel held the faceless things tightly. "It is an endemic feeling, that nothing outside the walls of the Library means anything," he said to the engine. "Things exist. They can be replaced. There is nothing innately valuable. Everything is quantifiable. What makes anything unique is so astronomically insignificant in the face of existence. Copy enough monkeys, let them procreate long enough, and there we go, our random set of experiences. Uniqueness is not special. Entropy is guaranteed.

"There is something so comforting about believing you're in good hands, about believing someone out there will make sure everything is well, believing you're not alone. Grimleer wants to build a new world, a perfect one where things do matter, whatever that means to him. I disagree with him in a way. Everything has always mattered, but I understand him. It would be purely negligent not to if you had the power, but this world is already here. You already exist. That's the difficult part. Because there could have been a better you, do you matter less? I don't know, but I might as well believe that reality tends towards the betterment of things.

"I want—I might want to see Claire again," said Samuel. "When she was only so tall, when she still followed me around, when she would annoy everyone by hiding everywhere in the Library, and then we would all have to find her. When," he sighed, "we did not quite understand the world was ending. Tell her that she deserves better. She deserves a world that wanted her rather than needed her. Tell all these people I'm sorry." He shook his head and knelt before the roving faceless. "I am sorry."

Samuel stood up before the brilliant winding engine, his hands still entwined within the grasps of the faceless. "I prefer the man," he said. "You are Eram Venner, not some cubic monolith."

The engine seized for a crackling moment. "I know that," said Venner, who now stood in place of the rippling shape. Venner shifted his weight on the uneven surface of people and investigated himself, straightening his tie and cuffs. He manipulated his halo into a flat surface like they were real, physical things, so he could rest upon the floating tines. He laid his head in his arms and covered his eyes. "No one wants to see the ocean or what you think I am as a machine."

"We had talks," said Samuel, "about the ethics of the project. One matter that never received enough attention was what we would do if the project actually succeeded, and what came about was conscious. Conscious thought implies learning and living. That there was nothing that separated you from us. Such concepts aren't new. They're well-tread amongst golems and homunculi.

"Yet an obelisk capable of dynamic intervention is a powerful tool. It is a dangerous tool with no comparison. You were reduced to one sentence. We would lobotomize you and make you no more than an engine. Sixty percent engine efficiency? Even twenty could still move the world. You might have been happier like that. Sentimentality gets in the way of progress. Our family, friends, and lives held higher precedence than the likes of you. It's different now. Progress became so unappealing."

"It seems a fair enough discussion," said Venner, "but it is an irrelevant one now. Once I have rebuilt you, you will take me back to the Library."

"To be with her, yes. There might be a way."

Samuel reassured himself that Venner was negotiable. He gestured for Venner's hand, and Venner obliged for a firm handshake. As physical a contract as ever. Mere pageantry since he was already within the ocean's impossibility, but it cemented the magnitude of what Samuel faced. He had to buoy the ocean before time was up.

"Wish," said Venner, "and be done with it," implying that Samuel should let go when he was ready.

Samuel listened to the voice that could not be, felt the heat of a body that should not exist, witnessed the bruises, the blood, the missing ocular organ. The engine was made like her, so fragile to the touch. Was it really for Samuel's safety that Claire had given him that instruction to never wish? He still felt whole at the moment after his singular call for destruction. Was there something so malignant within a wish that it could harm an ocean?

"What happens when I wish?" asked Samuel.

"You are wasting time," said Venner.

"I understand, but what happens?"

Venner spent some time for thought. "It starts with a framework, like a distant modeling program, I guess."

"I meant for you."

"For me to lose my name. That is literally how it is. A moment swallowed by an ocean, everything I behold picked and perused, and not all of it given back." Tools did not need names, but they had named Claire anyway. "It is easy enough to divert the preference of brine away from what I would like to keep."

"How easy?"

"Me, as human, as alive a stand-in as anything else. Bit by bit, I am devoured. Then all else continues as nominal." Ocean personified or person true, however the scales balanced, none of this contract was in Venner's favor. "You are very close to death, Hellion. Wish."

Ah, so he was at death's door, listening in on the other side, or here after all, amongst the arms of the faceless dead. It cannot be that easy to cheat death. Reemergence ruined the body of a red-handed creation. But more damning about it all, for the ocean to revive his body without cascade must mean the erasure of the Venner identity. For a wisher to survive the ocean and not be stripped by grazing brine, something must take its place. That something was Venner.

Samuel shifted their handshake, careful not to lose touch, and splayed his hand with Venner's. Hardly perfect, but good enough. There was a moment's recognition from Venner. "I would hold Claire's hand to comfort her. Size hers against mine, toy with the fingers, massage the palm. Because I think to feel touch is important. It's very connective." Venner closed his hand and entwined their fingers together. "And then to hold ourselves together," continued Samuel, a bit surprised to see Venner act first. "To know we are not alone. Celebrate us and our possibilities."

"I have been through this before with Iramir," said Venner.

"Have you?" asked Samuel, genuinely stunned.

"I see where it comes from, her care, or would you rather the word *love*? Though you know she would hate referring to this effort that way. It is just business."

Samuel collected himself with a sigh. "You really do know her quite well. I worry so much about Claire. I worry that I only bother her and all my efforts mean nothing."

"I remember offering her the opportunity to visit the city observatory to the see the stars," said Venner.

"What did she say?"

"Yes. She wanted to see the world, if she ever found a way to escape her work. Which I suppose was through me, though I am not that much satisfied by it either."

"I'm sorry," said Samuel. "You, you really matter that much to her, and I don't know whether to say I'm actually happy. She never seemed interested in the outside, and then she chooses you to start."

Samuel sighed again. "That's it, Venner. You're the validation that what I taught her is not lost. What lofty hopes she had for an ocean, for you. How could I compare as I thought you nothing more than a tool? I feel much lighter, certainly. Claire will be fine on her own. Her wiles will keep her afloat in your ocean. You aren't a beast of burden. I can't make you die for her sake. But—but if you ever find yourself in a situation where you could convince her, please, just a few words. That's what I ask for, person to person."

"Give me permission to revive you," said Venner with a scowl. "Say it. Save yourself. I have your image. I finally have your image, and I was wrong. Do not waste this time. I have made mistakes, but mistakes I can rewind. I can fix you, and then you could save her."

"Yes, you could," said Samuel, "but who else will be here? Who else can point you away from the ocean? I am here because Claire trusts me. Maybe not enough to tell me. And she told me how dangerous it was to be here, in this dream, but I did not listen. It's unfortunate how it has turned out, but it's not too terrible. It's just dangerous, my line of work, but sometimes very necessary." Samuel took a shaking breath. "A bit fast though. Claire goes so far because of what we have taught her. That the world cannot handle itself, that it needs some higher authority, that it needs to be loved. It is what makes it easy for her to follow through with this disaster. Show her she is wrong. You are that proof."

"You will be unsalvageable," said Venner. "Once you let go of your contract with me, that will be it. How do you expect me to save Claire? How am I supposed to handle your vague need?"

"I will be dead," said Samuel. "And if we go through this remaking of mine, you will be unmade yourself. Am I not right? I have no commands for you, just requests that can be ignored. You'll be beyond the Library's problems and our mismanagement. You said you were an ocean gazing through the human glass. How is it, the world outside?"

"I hate it," Venner said. "What was supposed to fix me cannot. I do not understand what you want from me. I do not understand why the world refuses me after I give it everything it wants." Samuel nodded and sat down upon the surface of crawling, faceless people. He cradled a restless one against his chest.

"What do you want then, Venner?"

"I want to be left with nothing because I cannot handle more than that."

"The world is scary, but lonely most of all," said Samuel. "Do you really want to be lonely?"

Venner froze.

"I would've liked to kiss Claire on the forehead," Samuel sighed. "All those years and I never managed the bravery. It just seemed odd. I wanted to show her what it was like to have someone love you that way." The least Samuel could do was to bolster that wondrous hope of Claire's and have it be known that no one was alone.

"Be given your name back, Venner. I'll do so as often as I can, and if I do it, then others will also. You too have someone that is looking desperately for you. Complain to them, decry everything in their presence. Confront your troubles and let yourself be known by the world at large. Take all of me, use me as however you must, and find them. Do not drown. Find them and you'll be fine."

Venner gnashed his teeth. "You cannot say that. You cannot keep saying that as if it means something."

"Then I'm sorry again, but I wish for you to live."

# FORTY-THREE

SAMUEL WAS GONE AND THE SHALE HAD BEEN WIPED CLEAN. There was no more desire to sustain an extradimensional perspective. Venner was back underground in the abandoned station where the train tracks were once hindered by rivers of rain. Well, the rivers had returned. Perhaps his oceanic exit had leaked a little. It was the emptiest place he could think of that was not his ocean.

Venner had finally done it. He had manipulated the means of a wish for physical escape despite the wisher having no intent to send him elsewhere at all. Neither an inflexible lion nor a meandering antler conductor, Hellion had offered enough thoughtful leeway for an ocean to do as it wanted. He celebrated the belated success.

Yet an ocean was hardly content. Venner felt much worse, burdened by so many other problems. The ocean was confounded. How was it supposed to find a wolf on its own? Or save a moon from her own destructions? And Hellion's delirious wish to have Venner live was as frustrating to handle as Caide's benign sentiment. Hellion had chosen incorrectly, like the paper man had. At least with Hellion erased, he would have a moment of reprieve from his compulsions. He could pretend all was well.

He moved a leg to walk and explore his surroundings. The sensations of flesh broke him. He had a body. He could not understand why he had a body. Did he need a body to carry his awareness? But why did he need an awareness at all? A vivid hate festered in his blind eye. He made a noise. Were they words? His ears could not determine their task.

He clutched himself, commotions cracking in his head. He could not understand why Hellion did not taste as good. He could not understand why a second time did not make his ocean as pure. Hellion must have been deficient somehow, or the accountant was some rare breed.

He felt around and found the steel bolts embedded within the body. The feeling of these bolts sliding out of him mingled into the white noise of nervous muscle spasms. It did not hurt, the nerves long since eaten. Corvus steel clattered onto the ground. He plugged the holes of his body, becoming slick with water, with blood replaced. What means kept this body standing other than the sheer force of infinity? A pure disregard for the lifespan, the ocean cradling its last heard wish.

Vandheer had failed the grand purpose of achieving peace. A part of Venner knew it was impossible to reclaim his previous sense of existence, but he had blind hope, nonetheless. Yet no comfort could be found within the confusing trajectories and half-hearted consolations of an outside world. He was part of that same assault upon his own senses. One eye gone, the other lined up to be drowned. A world could be left as it was so long as he had no capacity to interface with it. A part of him applauded the pure viability of plan B. Full success for full happiness. *Eat me.* He bit his finger by the knuckle. He bit harder.

"Do you need to be helped again, storm?" asked the boatman, hoisting himself off his boat onto the station platform. The boatman seemed quite pleased with himself. The journal was tipped from under his hat and was readied on the next blank page. He took a closer look at Venner and was surprised. "Oh, your good shape." The boatman rubbed his eye uncomfortably.

Venner shook his head. "Please shut up," said Venner. "I would much rather be alone right now." He did not want company, much less someone that knew him and took the chance to bother him as if they could expect something outside destruction and madness. The boatman checked the time on his pocket watch. A letter was pulled from his sleeve, pristine and red stamped. The boatman threw the letter into the river. Water tore it apart.

"You weren't supposed to come back," said the boatman. "The storm has subsided above ground, though something still leaks down here."

The boatman spied his boat floating away from the platform and shook his fist at his disobedient craft. Venner inspected his bodily wounds, wondering where the best place to start the cleansing was. "Are you okay, storm?" asked the boatman, calming himself down. "Do you need any first aid?"

"I'm fine. This is only a temporary problem." Venner wanted to close the viewfinder and go back to sleep, to cease his wanderings and slip into nothingness. His thoughts lingered on Caide, who may very well have been searching for him in the city streets. His thoughts were swept along the currents to a faraway place of a lonely moon preparing herself for the final plunge. He forced himself back into the current reality. He would only be met with disappointment outside. An ocean cannot be fond of its horrors. To be fond enough to chase them was unthinkable.

The station was as cold and decrepit as he had left it, with wild caricatures and names graffitied across cracked walls. There were no painted stars to dot the darkness above.

"Are you still in the business of looking up?" asked the boatman, also trying to find any glimmer of light.

"I'm in the business of looking through," said Venner. Even free from steel and graced by oceanic divinity, the body faltered. It shook and slipped and barely held itself together. The sound of his voice and the gurgles of a body functioning sickened him. He felt the stretch of wounds and the ache of melting flesh, the choking sensation creep up his brain stem whenever he took too long between breaths. The automatic habits that had driven the human vehicle had abandoned their posts and the ocean found manual operation so exhausting.

"I am the ocean looking through the human keyhole. That keyhole was my only known view. Peripheral vision was devoured by the mind's generous blind spots. Then I understood the keyhole, the locked door, and me, neglected and suffering, stuck on the other side of what was my content life."

The boatman was on his hands and knees at the very edge of the platform. With an arm outstretched, the boatman attempted to grab the paddle that leaned from the prow of his boat. His fingers only brushed the wood. "Would you want to be let in?" asked the boatman, glancing over his shoulder. "I wouldn't know if you would fit in my station, storm. The human is compact, but you're clearly unhappy. I'll try to find a place if you need it."

Venner said, "I want to forget I ever saw the door and that I ever knew a world so vast and terrifying. I wished I never looked up to know the stars and moon. My distractions are all spent. Minor things lost their standing against the living giants and their wealth of drama. Then the living giants paled against the massive influx that is life in general. The heartstrings of existence pluck throughout all time and space, and I was given eyes to see this damned blight. I was given thought to meander and understand my futility. I would just rather not."

Venner struggled to remain standing as he held his leaking head. The boatman lost his balance and splashed into the water. Despite himself, Venner went over to help. The spluttering boatman grabbed his hand, and he helped him back onto the platform. The boatman jumped to his soaked feet but kept a firm hand on Venner. The boatman even took the time to help right Venner, letting him lean on a wet shoulder if needed.

Venner scooped the hat from the river and offered it back to the boatman. The boatman nodded in thanks, turned aside, and flicked as much water as he could from the fabric. Not that this did much as the boatman sat the tired article on his head. The leather-bound journal, however, was lost out of sight.

"Is that how it is?" asked the boatman, who was in constant motion of wiping dripping water from his forehead. The boat was farther off now and impossible to retrieve without a swim.

"What do you want?" asked Venner. The boatman placed hands on his hips and surveyed the river.

"Ah yes, you grant wishes," said the boatman. "But I have not the shooting star to do it. I would think a real star would give me a better result. Counterfeit ones only turn my wishes rotten. What I'm saying is, if I had a real star, I might wish to clean my tunnels from all this water." The boatman, with expectation on the brow, turned to Venner.

Venner calculated that the boatman's request would most likely kill him and finally snip the threads that tied geography to humanity. He would refuse the examination of the boatman's shape and focus only on his own name. The ocean will be appeased with sacrificial substitution, then he would disappear like all things did when opened underwater. Venner brought a finger to his lips.

The boatman crossed his arms. "I've had enough of that attendant," he said. "Don't remind me of him."

A speeding train rushed passed the station, stealing the boatman's attention. There was no more water to impede. The wind disturbed loose newspapers and hidden trash around the station.

Venner's heart shuddered. He spat red blood into the palm of his hand and shook it off out of sight of the boatman. Sitting down on a nearby bench, he rolled up his sleeves and inspected the open sores where his skin melted and burned. Oh, right. He had to fix Caide, but where would he start searching for the wolfman? He was in no condition to even try. It was much easier to give up. So Venner lay down on the bench, feeling the cold of the sheet metal radiate throughout his body. He covered his eyes from the light of the station.

"What do you want?" whispered the boatman. "I will wish for you. Whatever care you need, I will grant you." Startled, Venner sat up on his elbow. The boatman held a painted star that was water damaged and unlit. "You did not take it the first time you were here. Lucky me."

"Are you sure?" asked Venner. "It is not the star I seek as price."

The boatman wiped his brow again. "I'm not," he said with slight annoyance, "but I trust the word of my fellow who trusts you very much and has pleaded so much with me. Oh no, I'm not angry at you. My fellow offered his arm to wish you well. If I must offer my body, then so be it. There will be another me. It'll be that the lost will find a place in this city. You have cleaned up the water without asking for payment, so what do you wish for, storm? I'm good for a hot meal myself after this drink in the river. I suppose you might be as well. Or not. I think I would be greatly upset, in fact, taking orders from other people for so long."

The boatman waited with him, waited as an ocean fumbled with its need for happiness. The ocean enjoyed the company. It was an impossible experience to be had, which made it ever captivating. The ocean had never realized what it was missing until confronted by the consequences of its name. The ocean did not want to be alone. Right now, under the dim cyan of buzzing lights and the slow, disordered dripping of a boat-man, Venner desired only to be able to move a mouth, to touch and fidget with hands, to assert himself true. But he was so tired of everything.

He could not wish to fulfill Hellion's requests. Too many variables needed to be made up. Too much effort was required of the body. The ocean was supposed to avoid instigating its own vague desires. To be less alone was also an inconvenient request. Making the boatman stay here did not count as companionship nor was foisting his burdens onto the boatman. Yet work was reliable and predictable. It always was the right answer if Venner was ever conflicted. He wanted it even if it was tempo-rary until his body surrendered. Even if it was not right.

"I wish to go to work," said Venner softly. "That is insane, is it not? I just don't like being alone, and I have never been around so many peo-ple I knew, if only a little, than at work. I'm obsessed with it as the only choice possible because to be free and content outside of work doesn't make sense. My distractions led me by the hand for all my life and to be without them scares me."

The boatman did not laugh. "There's nothing wrong with that. Even the little comforts are important. That bothersome attendant, he would know what to do, wouldn't he? I wish upon a star—"

## FORTY-FOUR

**THE ELEVATOR DOORS OPENED WITH A SOFT DING. VENNER** was greeted by replica office cubicles and shadow prop people. He was in a likeness of his workplace rousing in the early morning. Rain pattered the windows. Through them, he viewed the indistinct blurs of streetlights yet to darken and aircraft beacons on neighboring office towers. Inspecting himself, he was quite whole. The pecking of a crow had not chased him into this dream, but he was still missing an eye. Ocean wounds were permanent, it seemed.

It was a transfiguration of Venner's own dreaming, his shale upon the ocean. Though a bit cheated, he admitted, because it was the boatman that had wished for him and that had listened to him and abided. It did not hurt to live another day at the office. He was getting used to manipulating the landscape. Practiced lucidity produced finer command. Things came to be as if the world was constantly listening to his thoughts.

He looked around for a certain werewolf man, but he wasn't there. It made sense. If he had been there, it would mean the rest of him had been finalized into nonexistence. The coworkers here were nameless people with holes in their heads, mimicking life. Venner adjusted the grip on his briefcase. He navigated through the cubicles and peered over the half-walls at people working and having conversations. Not that Hellion should have been there either.

He should really clean up the rest of Hellion's traces, a once-around for anything that lingered like an accountant's hand. His workplace had set up informal meeting areas by the windows. A better environment to encourage the sudden idea, according to HR. He passed by faceless colleagues next to marker boards and offered a few suggestions on process improvements. They nodded and thanked him.

Their whiteboard notes of manufacturing planning changed hands into a trip itinerary. The city was the subject, and next to the list was a marker drawing of a sky brimming with stars over a mountain range. Written below this landscape in fading color was Andermatt with Claire. Venner tapped the whiteboard eraser against the back of his hand.

Not that he fully understood Hellion or his devotion, but he understood enough about stars. The pining, the regret, a love with no context but a love nonetheless. These were the dreams they'd poured all of themselves into, or at least an important part of themselves. The last of Hellion would live here if he did nothing. It would live beneath the ocean until he could no longer tolerate its existence or until he simply forgot.

In this moment, Venner was glad of the irreverent change order that forced him to confront his habits. Here he stood, of sound mind and body, confronted by the last of Hellion, and instead of erasing the message, he left the eraser where it was. It was a decision that felt no different than any other, but the breakdown of his automatic consciousness allowed him this very moment. One moment against the rules of his consuming obsession, even if his answer was to save this trace for another time. To clean the last bits of things in a place that did not exist was by no means gospel.

Venner started to count the faceless people that lingered in the office. Water pounded against the glass of his office floor with a low thunder. The skyline became submerged within his ocean. City lights shimmered and threw chasing shadows over steel and glass and office space. Faceless people lingered in their clothes, clattering on keyboards, pretending to be diligent and well. They leaned against water coolers and plants. They gestured with empty cups and scooted between cubicles on rolling chairs.

The more he watched them scurry and handle themselves, the less they seemed to impersonate his memories and the more they seemed truly alive, playing their parts like actors, and trying their best to guess at the nuances of office standards. A few observed their reflections in the glass, accounting themselves just as he would. He was a pretender just like them, an ocean engaged with dollhouse living.

He could try working like they did and finally conduct that wondrous distraction. He propped himself at a meeting table and faced away from the window. He laid the briefcase on the tabletop, opened the clasps, and took out his laptop. He turned on the power and typed in his credentials. His projects were in the midst of cleanup for his eventual departure. He minimized the problem emails and ignored the reminders of his lively ruin. He deleted past messages from Caide so wayward eyes would not be reminded in errant places.

He sorted through his finite element analyses and checked results against his hand calculated sheets. He made a few tweaks to his model, reviewing the layup schedule across the stabilizer and adjusted the drop off area around a few splices. A good hour passed before his effort died and he found himself simply staring at his work. He scratched idly at the backlit keys. Faceless bodies hit the carpeted floor like rain. Golden threads decayed around him. Foreign identities collapsed, and their shapes failed against oceanic need.

His computer screen went dark from his lack of activity. He stared at his reflection in the monitor, at the hole leaking brine where his eye should have been. Under the rain, under the city skies, under the desires and wishes of everything, he broke. Ignorance was bliss, but he didn't know how to recapture it. Infinity saw and attempted every shape of solution, only to make things worse. Devouring faceless spirits provided him no satisfaction. Work was rote. The effort was exhausting when filtered through too many middlemen limbs and conscious thoughts.

In the reflection of his computer screen, he watched himself wrap his hands around his neck. He was capsized in the dream that slowed the human sensation and halted the nervous mind. He slumped over onto his desk, then leaned back into his seat. He tried to relax, but his shoulders remained tight. His eyes refused to close.

In the reflection of his computer screen, the ocean wondered if it could excise itself from this person, whether it could let go of the reins and let the man named Eram Venner enjoy his life. Could the ocean return to being blind and mute and dumb? Oceans had no need of organs.

It would be a lot to miss, and there was so much to settle still. The ocean worried about leaving its work so abruptly and causing stress for its coworkers. It worried about the means of its future and even a search for a new, less consequential hobby. It liked being able to walk down the pier or catch a movie and dinner downtown. It liked spending time with Caide when madness never became a sticking point and gossip or TV show commentary ran amok. It liked spending time with Iramir, even with their brevity of interactions. There were stars to be seen, a city to show her and meander through, more conversations to be had about just how pointless work was.

Iramir had believed in the ocean, and it wanted very much to return that belief. It was an understanding, a company that left the ocean wanting. There was nothing wrong with the idea of Eram. The ocean just could not handle it. It would not last long in the proper waking world outside.

He turned around and faced the ocean that stared at him all the while, wrapped amongst dark towers. Or he could return to the dreams of yesteryear, however long ago that might have been during the age of legends and myths, where all he could ever worry about was the rare thing that landed in his body.

The ocean had no eyes or thoughts to process the happenstance. Events came and passed with no recollection. Where did his own voice come from? Why were events now becoming so important they must be remembered and solved by the act of unwrapping nostalgia? Memories were funny like that. Neurons stripped one by one like letters thrown into a fire. Every relived experience shaved the human-self down into nothing.

This office dream would not end with the playful stage exit beneath the waves. This would be it. He had found the shape of himself and his solution. The evening neon lights of a sunken city flickered to life, building by building. The city was stirring. A desire interfered from a source of crimped familiarity. Compulsion worked the abstract jaw. He knew that shape cut wrong by the edges and stuffed with oceanic wonder. The crow had been excised but the hole still remained.

Venner covered his hollow orbit with his hand. He wondered what the scene was like in waking reality. He imagined the forlorn scene of a paper man huddled from the bustling city streets, deep underground where stations no longer existed, where the railway river flowed salted with his blood. A paper man taking watch over an impudent ocean, maybe with a sigh or a spoken solace.

However the scene was set, he heard the paper man's plea offering the weight of a crafted body as a token to cross into what was supposed to be a solitary dream. Venner could deny the paper man. The ocean no longer groveled at every wish. Yet Venner had been asked to listen so gently, and he found the gesture genuinely soothing. Imagine pulling the paper man under water. A notepad was procured from his briefcase. He closed the lid of the laptop and set the notepad on the scratched aluminum.

Words appeared on the paper, as if scrawled by an invisible hand. "I've brought someone just as I promised I would. Thank you for accepting." The wet ink displaced itself like heartbeats. "I am not ready to put the matter of helping you to rest, not entirely. I still want to respect your decision, but . . . never mind. Call upon me if you need. I'll try not to listen in too much." The paper man wrote no more.

"Hey, Eram," said Caide from the other side of the table. Caide looked astonished to see him, and then equally astonished by where they were. Wherever Caide had come from, it certainly was not an office full of faceless corpses surrounded by ocean panorama. Caide's attention lingered on the corpses. "Is this what makes you happy?"

"I am not sure," said Venner. "They were eaten a lifetime ago. Ah, I should have cleaned up before you came in. My apologies, I really was in the process of sweeping house." As soon as the words left his mouth, the corpses were undreamt, erased from existence. Caide rubbed the back of his neck, visibly uncomfortable. "Think of it as laying them to rest. Nothing upsetting like that will happened again, I assure you.

"Ready for our one-on-one?" asked Venner with a sly smile. He drew his hand from his wound for a moment and gestured for Caide to sit down. Caide startled at the sight of his face, and grabbed his hand to keep him from covering it again. The damage clearly worried him. Either the wolfman's strength had waned or Venner's extremities had lost all feeling. Venner had no concern for the latter.

"What happened?" asked Caide. The wolfman's Gaelic scars had hardly healed.

"It is fine, really," said Venner. "The body is merely a suggestion anyways. But about you, are you feeling well? I suppose while I have the cognizance, I would very much like to fix what I have done to you. Then I will send you back home. It will take more than one pass to clean myself out and you are just the ticket."

"Don't you dare," growled Caide, his werewolf features rippling out against his human outline. "I don't care what you are. I want you, Eram, or—or the ocean. Does it matter? Iramir told me it's all the same, that you just needed someone to be there for you. Listening to her explain how to settle your upturned life, how to help negotiate with Harken, and how to find you in any possible way made me feel so lacking towards you. I didn't know you liked stars. Even someone from Harken offered to help."

Venner was surprised. "Are you that worried about me?" asked Venner, beside himself. He was just as uncomfortable here as he'd been with the boatman. The idea that the outside world would show concern for his safety had never crossed his mind. Not just show it, but conspire to reach him. The windows cracked from the abyssal pressure. Water seeped into the office space. The very fact that these things could chase him into his solemn privacy deeply unsettled him, and he had obliged them so easily as well.

"Of course I'm worried about you. Can we just leave this weird place?" Caide glanced around them, obviously expecting another someone. It was just the two of them in this replica office. The paper man declined to comment at Caide's insistence. "Would you want to leave here?" asked Caide softly.

"It depends on what you want," said Venner. "I am the engine that affects reality by throwing around the weight of infinity. I was made to solve your sorrowful matters. I was made to listen. It is quite amazing to be able to negotiate with destruction, with infinity. Desires get solved. My users disappear, perhaps satisfied, but really out of impatience on my end. I suppose if I were solved, if I were given the last piece of my puzzle—maybe a moon, or just nothingness—I would do anything and everything.

"I want to destroy, if that is what you are really asking. I am inseparable from that. My only solace from this obsession was when I did not know the very implications."

Caide rubbed his skin and showed teeth in his anguish. Bristled fur struggled to soften as he checked around the office, seemingly searching for any inspiration to spur his next words or actions. "Not that I want that fight in your apartment again," he said, "but I knew what to do then. What good is a body like mine if I can do nothing here? I want you to be okay, whatever that means for you. I can imagine how relieved you would feel finally retired, without being forced to be with anyone anymore, but I don't want you gone."

"It has been nice," said Venner. Caide did not hide his disappointment.

Caide took out his phone, and he searched his recent calls. He rubbed the back of his neck and held the phone tightly to his ear. "Please," whispered Caide. The wolfman's expression stayed dark. "I was told this was a dream, but it is much more lucid than I am comfortable with." Caide opened his jaw and tapped the tips of his claws to his last canine tooth. The wolfman still had strength enough to make it seem as if this tooth were never attached at all. He licked his wound and rubbed the back of his hand against the side of his mouth. The tooth lay on the meeting table, warm and quiet.

"I want to make a call," said Caide. The influx of blood in his mouth slurred the words, and he swallowed another mouthful. "And even though I don't get signal in a dream, that's not a problem for you, is it? I don't want to ask too much from you or ruin whatever makes you happy.

"But please. I've spent all my life leaning about creatures and their eccentricities. There are too many tales that warn children not to be rude or disruptive to others—mostly out of fear, because those unwitting children tend to die. Fear the world at large, all the monsters lurking under the bed and the closets. But we're not rote bedtime stories. Things aren't easily solved in a single good moral or a checklist. We're alive, alive enough to deal with our now and aftermath. I want to help you because I really like hanging out with you. I mean, just give me a sec.

"To be accommodating, to understand that the world is shared and not some binary competition where you've either made it or you haven't.

And you're forced to ignore everyone else getting there. Things exist with needs, with the intent to live. It's hard and no one wants anyone to see. No one cares, apparently. Everyone was made incorrectly for the world at large, I think. They're just better liars. It's okay to be scared. Those that understand will be with you.

"Now I'm not advocating free-for-all hugs here, because there are still genuinely threatening things out there, but you aren't those things. You're my drinking buddy, and I just want to go home with you. All these years of what could have been. I want that time back. I wouldn't have been so irreverent. But the next best time is now, right?"

"Yeah," said Venner. He tried to pick up the bloodied tooth but dropped it a few times before Caide helped him to cup it gently. The tooth awaited the ocean. It was filled with a vulnerable trust that made it so different from mere edges and vertices. It was a tooth, Caide's tooth. It had ridges and blood and the distress of use. Context was glued as stoutly as if it were impossible to have viewed it, to have viewed Caide, any other way. It seemed so absurd to know anything so abstractly as an empty shape.

What did the ocean want but more? It was so novel for a wolf to prowl its shoreline and wait within the foam of breaking waves to play and yap. The ocean could survive a few painful points for the good of its novel interactions. The phone started ringing. Caide's expression lit up, and he put the caller on speaker.

"Yes, Caide? Close timing you have," said Iramir, clear as day.

"Convince Eram that's everything going to be okay. Maybe he'll listen to you."

Venner stared at the phone. He did not anticipate coming to terms with Hellion's final love for Iramir at all. He did not anticipate Caide imploring Iramir to save him like how Hellion imagined it for her. The ocean was awestruck at reality's impudence.

"Eram? Are you listening?" she asked. The whiteboard message still remained in his memory, waiting for affirmation. There were matters of the heart to be managed, and the ocean very much wanted matters to be settled. He should tell her about Hellion and not have her wonder. Really, he was just delaying discussing the whiteboard at all. The number of vulnerable items and names he wanted to keep dry was growing uncomfortably out of hand.

"Hellion is dead, Iramir," he said. "I don't know if this is better than never hearing back, but I am sorry." Caide startled and spoke a swift apology as well, with the odd mention of a forgotten phone. The line was silent, and then Iramir sighed.

"That was the risk," she said in her soft-spoken apathy. "Thank you for telling me."

"Hellion could have been saved if he wanted to be," said Venner. "He wanted to save you instead."

"I apologize for forcing you into that uncomfortable position," she said. "I am sure Samuel has commented in passing about how disappointing I am or how terrible my circumstances. It is none of your concern, Eram. I am here to comfort you and send you on your way."

"He said that he trusts you, that he would understand. He loves you."

She paused. "That does hurt a little," she said. "He never managed to say anything like that to me. He always looked at me with such fear for my life. But I will settle my affairs out of your prying eyes. I am here to talk about you, Eram. You were meant to be more. Either you were created to live or you have escaped your design, but you have made your place. I was told the world is lovely beyond the castle walls. What do you see, ocean?"

"That I am not alone," said Venner, clutching the tooth. "I think I rather enjoy the outside. There is much more than what nothingness can provide. The world is no mere figment to be experienced. It acts. It takes you by the hand and leads. That companionship is irreplaceable." Caide smiled. "Come outside, Iramir. I managed to get here because you let me go, because you believe in the living spirit."

"Outside," said Iramir, as if she were gently cradling the word. "Oh engine, dear, stay free."

"Iramir, do not hang up! To be beyond your programming, to be beyond the means of a moon," shouted Venner. "Where is the girl I met in the rain? The one who said everything was going to be fine? What can I do to make that true for you? What nightmares must be drowned to free you from your destructive purpose? You delivered me from my compulsion, then. You saved me."

"Samuel saved you. I did as I was told." Her voice wavered.

"You did what you wanted," corrected Venner. "You told me how much I reminded you of yourself. I am what made it. I am what must survive. Do you not think you should be here as well? I want to return that trust you placed in me, the belief that things will be alright. I ask you to trust me. Escape your legacy. Escape with me. Know that I am listening. Claire, tell me what you want, and we will get there."

"I want to help, and my most maximized impact is the dissolution…" She paused. "Cases like Caide. Low efficiency items like personalized care. A useless endeavor by the numbers game because one person means nothing against the masses. Yet to work with numbers for so long, to even have a name attached, carries such special considerations. I have already told you about the stars, but I am not satisfied with just stars. I want to see the world. I—I am envious of you, Eram, so please understand I cannot have you ruin yourself."

"Why couldn't you come with us. Iramir?" asked Caide. But Iramir had hung up. The wolfman wrung his hands, clearly agitated. Venner was dissatisfied. There was a lack of force in a phone call that only face-to-face conversations provided. He didn't want to leave the matter like this. Iramir would of course pull authority if she had to, but he had the cognition to deny wishes and divert his compulsion. In a way, Iramir was not absolute. If it came to that sort of confrontation, then so be it. Venner settled his crooked tie and brushed back his hair.

The world interceded. The world demanded. The world worried about him and invited him into its problems. His thumb felt over the ridges of his lower teeth. He heard the intents of Caide and Iramir. He felt the changing sensibilities he could have grasped by the tail and begun the cleansing. He had paid attention and context never dropped away. Perhaps it was only a temporary liberation. Perhaps the world had finally solved him. Even if it was temporary, he was very happy to pretend for now.

The details of teeth and jaws and dead bodies were lost within the abyssal vast. He did not need to wait for words or to find the right rhythmic wish by chance. He had to speak. He was just as much displacement as anything else, and he would make room for Iramir just as she needed, just as she had given him.

"Is Iramir going to be okay?" asked Caide. "I don't feel good about that."

Venner looked down at his notebook and said, "Are you able to take me to the Library?"

Caide tilted his head in confusion while ink appeared on its pages. "You have to know everything about a place before I can take you there," Venner quietly read aloud as the words appeared. "I know only the city and its confines, and even then I do not know everything. I still do a fair bit of walking."

"Take us home," interrupted Caide, evidently realizing that the notebook was his missing Harken man. "Get us out right now." Caide turned to Venner. "You're not really leaving for something dangerous again? He'll take us back to the city. It'll all be normal. We'll go back to working, to our small talk, to just normal things. Do you actually want this?"

"I want to clean up my messes. I want to show the world that I am more than a mere ocean," said Venner. He took the time to measure his hand against Caide's and closed Caide's hand over the bloody tooth. The ocean nudged the faltered wolf shape swimming in its waters. Cascade gnawed down its vertexes, forever threatening to poke a hole and let water in. Caide could not be perfectly remade. The ocean should have paid more attention the first time the wolf fell into it. Displacement memory did not exalt Caide as it did Iramir. Another regret.

However, werewolves were vigorous creatures. He would take the existing lines of a werewolf's regeneration and redouble this code to offer the body better advantage, but only barely. A safe enough modification if not taken too far. He had to avoid the mistakes of a mobile soul only made once. Caide inspected his healing wounds with astonishment. Venner was quiet and only let go once assured that Caide stayed very singular.

"I have not actually fixed the problem," said Venner. "A bit of werewolf cheating for now. It is not enough for me to guess at the best way to solve cascade. I would like actual research to back my efforts. A later day, if you're interested. Maybe with Iramir." Venner nodded and added in slight aside, "Were you thinking of running away with me?" Caide looked betrayed by Venner's prying.

"I guess—I guess so. I guessed that what you would've wanted was avoiding all this stupidity." Caide opened his hand and inspected the tooth. "You looked so miserable. I can't deal with losing people I know. And I assume, since you want to go to the Library, that this is for Iramir? I can't let you go, not for Iramir. She's—" Caide palmed his phone and rubbed the back plate gingerly. "She's helped my family, I suppose, and then helped me find you. Is there really something of serendipity here?"

"I want to see the isles," said Venner. "I know I am trying your patience, but I ask you to trust me. I will come back home. Let us have that autumn day. Will you answer me this, Caide? What kind of ocean do think I am?"

"That was a meaningless tale," said Caide. "Where has all the care come from to displace all that hate, all that death and vitriol?" Venner leaned in and whispered into Caide's ear that same answer in the heart of an impossible forest. Caide tensed with Venner so close and could only muster a cracked clearing of the throat.

"It was not the violence I was impressed with," said Venner. "You, along with the world at large, have taught me to listen, so just wait for me."

"You've left my flock, and I wasn't prepared for this," said Caide, carefully settling his last canine within his pocket. "I've had worse tooth fairies. IOU, huh."

Venner took the notebook in hand and dictated to paper, "I am the infinite ocean. Wherever you point yourself, paper, you cannot miss. I assure you that you are not the first one to perform this trick."

"I think it's just because of you that alright things seem so weird," mumbled Caide with a lift of his shoulders. "I've talked with living books before, but why do you have to do it like that?" Caide's concern was purposefully addressed with a coy smile.

"Let me deal with Vandheer again," said Venner, more tempered to paper. The corners of the page folded over in apparent anxiety. "Are you not tired of chasing and worrying about me? I think the city would appreciate a little cleanup."

"Such confidence is quite aggravating," wrote paper. "This desire is not at the top of my list right now, ocean. Even if you somehow rout Vandheer, that does not make me capable of transporting you. Leave with the werewolf back to your apartment. The mess was no problem for a cleaner as me. All's right with the world. Whatever hope you believe lies across the factory horizon does not exist. I am not your lovestruck puppy. Perhaps we may attend to your desire to return to the Library if you will drop the Vandheer matter. The city will take care of the piper."

"I am there," said Venner in full confidence and then gestured to himself, "and I will come to collect thereafter, to take her outside and see the stars. Iramir does not need to be watched and fretted over to act. Just assurance."

Paper drew an arrow pointing to Caide. "Tell me werewolf, how do you deal with this man?"

Venner motioned to himself again and said, "Offer some advice to our Harken man on how to expect me."

Caide rolled his eyes.

"When he has the confidence, you have to offer irrefutable proof it will not work," said Caide. "If you think he's a bit stuffy now, wait until you see him talking about structures."

"I know you are concerned about me," said Venner, "but I want to do more than simply defer your terrors. Please allow me to settle the business that so unwinds you. That ticket you gave me still needs to be repaid, especially for the trip back. Or perhaps consider this the price for your heart, so will you oblige mine? I have my own tricks, paper, to ensure success." Venner considered paper the quickest travel, the thaumic connections already well made. If he could excise the Corvus anxieties, then to wish for home with all the heart became all the easier.

Ink trailed in stuttering phrases, crossing out lines and restarting constantly. That Venner was being ridiculous, that the wolfman needed to leash Venner better, that paper could not in good faith save an ocean.

"I have listened to you," another sentence finished. "And thus I know you. That sort of suffering cannot be undone, can it? To worry, to miss, to wonder about you. To look forward, how strange that is to me, because no attendant needs that sort of forecasted existence. I was built to be replaceable, but I find myself quite the opposite with an ocean. You need someone to watch over you still." A moment of pause until, as the final *t* was crossed, Venner quietly read it aloud: "I accept."

Paper folded into a hand and grabbed onto Venner's awaiting handshake. Venner tore away the living page and let it climb up his arm. Fingers for legs, a palm for a body, ragged tears for pincers, and the ocean enjoyed the company. Words rippled across the paper appendage. "I'll have to stretch myself sparingly."

Caide stared at the window where cracks grew in warping echoes. "This is going to be a scary way out, isn't it?" he said. It amused Venner to hear an outside view of oceanic stage exits.

"I am sorry. Never really sat down and thought it any other way," said Venner. "A bit of restructuring is in order, I suppose."

The glass exploded and water rushed in. In quick work, the ocean took care to lay the wolf home exactly as whole as it had been. Then led by paper's light, the ocean followed the piper's gilded tune to the crow's nest filled with dead children.

# FORTY-FIVE

**THE MOON, CRADLED BY THE MONOLITHS OF THE LIBRARY,** sat high above Iramir's garden. Moonlight bathed her with a soft blue hue as she stood out in the open, overlooking the ocean. Spraying water from crashing waves collected between her cracks and scattered moonlight across the empty night. Almost like stars, this glimmering map of entropic constellations. If stars shattered like glass in the darkness, then an ocean could slay impossibility and bring real stars into this lonely domain. This lunar shine rode the wind-swept ferns and chased the lilac petals that escaped out into the open ocean.

Iramir counted the seconds to help steady her breathing, her broken hand splayed over her chest, but she beheld no warmth. Tears slipped across her stony features. She needed time to settle Samuel's affairs and provide financial compensation to his widow. She disliked that this meager compensation and perhaps a funeral were the only comforts she could provide. Samuel was certainly worth more than this, but she did not know how to express it.

He was dead. It was too late. All semblance of posthumous business needed to stand aside for the ever-mounting need of the now. She did not have the time. Yet tomorrow could be different. Eram was proof of the heart, of the world responding well to the stimuli that she believed impossible of conducting herself. Caide would be the first of many consultations, the forging of her own path regardless of the climb for perfect efficiency. This was fantasy.

It did not have to go so far, this pretending for hopeful futures. It would have been easier if she had managed the bravery to say no to Samuel and firmly put to bed the idea of her own salvation. Samuel would have simply tried harder. She did want, so much, to make him happy. Why else would she have taken her time with an ocean? To take Eram by the hand and lead him home, but then just dawdle a tad because she liked the company. A rarity, the lulls in business, which allowed the imagined paradigms of an outside world to flourish. If only momentary dogmatism had not brought Eram here in the first place, but at least that mistake had been rectified despite great pains.

Eram just a needed small pat on the head. His foundation in the outside world had already been set. Barely a step out of line for him to be okay again. Samuel must have seen it the same way for her. Just a step outside and she would be there with him. Her fate was not insurmountable. There was nothing that could stop her if she ceased saying no. This regret hurt. Her gaze dropped to her phone and caught the reflection of Grimleer in his approach. She put it away and wiped the tears.

"I said it would only be a moment," whispered Iramir. Grimleer nudged the broken chains of the repository out of the way with his foot. The repository framework, the very means of a Library, had been used as basis for his engine, and now it awaited its final piece.

"You still left rather hurriedly," said Grimleer, now realizing he had unwittingly brought his notebook all the way from the laboratory. He nestled the notebook beneath his arm and tapped along its spine. He took in the ocean and then glanced up to the object of her namesake. "Have you any concerns for the ritual?" he asked. "I think we have done well with the previous trials. Risks accessed and sorted. We have been quite thorough in the mitigations, so I have nothing but confidence for our success."

A soft-spoken tenacity aloft amongst unfaltering belief in his own abilities and unfaltering trust in her had led her so easily to this point. His smile, his ease—it would never have crossed his mind that she did not share his convictions. It was simply easier to follow along. Validation spurred her.

The future of the Library and her legacy were contingent on her. A new world would invalidate all current existence. All those things that Samuel ever promised would not matter. He shared his love of the world with her so earnestly. It was not her place to wonder what could have been, but Samuel had nurtured that dissenting yearning well. It was strange, not to regret a mistake in workmanship, but to regret what had never existed in the first place. To grant the Library and Grimleer the power to reduce this world into a primordial state would be despicable. She had ordered Eram to be free in a world that would soon disallow that chance.

She wanted both Grimleer and Samuel to be happy, to at last be satisfied with the cost of her creation. She wanted to be more than the reminder of grim fatalism. Iramir took Grimleer by the hand. Failing magic robbed ceramic of touch receptors and now flesh.

She had to be satisfied with the knowledge that Eram was better off now. That for the briefest moment, he would be free from the weight of his shackles. Please, Samuel, she really did want the world to be better. Iramir buried herself in Grimleer's chest. She tugged at his shirt and felt the tears welling up again. Grimleer returned the embrace. The notebook spilled to the ground. Loose paper inserts scattered amongst the flora and collected the dew of brine and ichor.

Iramir then pushed away from her weakness and tucked her hair behind her ear. Chipped porcelain fell from her as she collected the notes of her planned dissolution. Water blurred her drawn outlines. Die for the single wish to remake the world. There was little that could stop infinity if properly motivated.

"There is something wrong. You are making that quite evident," said Grimleer. He rubbed his thumb over the stain her tears left behind. He crouched down to help gather the rest of the pages. Sea spray fell as rain.

"Samuel is dead," said Iramir.

Grimleer was speechless. He sat down in the grass, tugged on his beard, and started cleaning his glasses with his sleeve. He hung his glasses from his collar and offered a hand to Iramir. "It will be alright. As much as I had difficulties with the man, we both wanted a better world. There would be no better celebration of him than to make that come true."

"I killed him," said Iramir. "I sent him to find the engine even when it did not matter. If only I had confidence in myself, the solution is here."

Few staff had still been laboring within the Library. They had quickly rounded volunteers for oceanic sacrifice. Many were not volunteers. She had killed them by turning the blind eye. Their names drowned. Their fears and aspirations were forgotten. Only empty shapes of what could have been were left behind. They didn't deserve what had happened to them. Iramir could not apply the apathy she felt about her own life to others. It was ridiculous to apply such self-criticism to these lives. How unlike Samuel she was, poisoned by the ire of the Library.

Some had escaped by ability or luck. Those living dissidents were allowed because their lack of contribution would be rectified in the new world. Crimes against the legacy would be erased. If she wavered from her purpose, these killings would have been conducted for no reason other than sheer malice. The bodies were meant to prep an ocean, and she was the keystone. She had to command the ocean, to bring glory back to the Library. She had to be brave so their deaths would not be wasted, but what could be said for their own wishes? Of those that wanted all this madness to stop or those that had cursed her because she was meant for their hatred. She deposited her stack of wet pages and notebook back to Grimleer.

She felt so useless. She needed time to compensate their families. Was she only good for business and accounting human resource? She wanted time instead to genuinely help the world. Cases so rare like a lycanthrope's family where she could exercise the medical knowledge meant to save. She wanted to devise treatment tinctures and prescribe self-care rituals. Her ambitions seemed so meager and wasteful against Grimleer's. She was not made to play doctor. She was made to preserve this era full of established life. The more discerning survivors would settle the policies and direction of the new, emptier world.

Or, she could destroy the institution too devoted to internal cause, too negligent of a world that could and wanted to change. She could manage one fragile lycan case at a time to the best of her abilities. Bespoke care stemmed from the loving heart, a proof to herself that she could exist outside her planned delineation.

The knowledge of an engine could not be undone. No other means of salvation would satisfy the Library. Even if she failed to create a new engine now, perishing in the attempt, Grimleer would continue the work. Perhaps there would be another doll. There was irrefutable proof enough bloodshed could work miracles of magic. Within the Library, death was only novelty, paradise was always just around the corner, nothing outside the institution mattered. An endless cycle of insulated, cruel toiling. *Stop.*

"Come outside," the ocean had said over the phone, and she had almost said yes. She was vaguely proud of him, hearing him so certain and seemingly freed from his nightmares.

"The engine," said Grimleer. He gathered the stack and squared it against his leg. "It is good to be diligent. You could not have anticipated our quick success. We were fortunate because of our persistence, but we do not need the scraps of our turncoat peers." Iramir did not reply, and Grimleer scowled at her.

"The world is failing," he continued. "Too much has been left fallow. The foundation shudders beneath our feet. To build atop this dying world will be irresponsible to future generations. It will be painful, yes, but it is necessary. The world will be rebuilt into its stronger image where no one will ever fear the next tomorrow. Where no one will question whether time is unceasing or matter is omniscient. Reality will not die because I will erase such concepts from the annals of existence. The Library will properly contain reality. Be proud, Claire, you have realized your purpose."

Everything Samuel loved and hated will have never existed. He would never know this new world. Nothing would be known of it. The reaffirmation of her purpose no longer comforted her, but she knew better than to stay silent again. Grimleer knew her habits too well, but she did not know what to say. She had never defied him the way she occasionally had with Samuel.

Grimleer began idly notating within an open stretch of space in his notebook. "You can be recreated, Claire. I still have your schematics. I made you the first time, and I can do so again. Improvements will be made in regards to your fragility."

"I worry about what will be left behind of the outside world."

"There will be nothing left behind. Nothing I think is salvageable."

Iramir looked away from him. "This world fears its tomorrow because its days are in jeopardy," she said. "We are the background discussion, the final crossroads before calamity, and the world barely knows how quickly it must count down its final minute. We are destruction, not an ocean."

Grimleer started to his feet and pointed the notebook at her. "Claire, are your concerns beginning to interfere with our marvelous creation?"

Iramir held herself. "I cannot make either of you happy. I thought so lightly of your validation, Grimleer. How easy it must be. My error. I want this world. There are investments of mine I want to see bloom." She bit her lip. Had she really not a better phrase for explanation? Burned bridges and soured relationships were simply products of her impermanence. To ascribe something belonging to the quality of Samuel and his like to herself seemed far too selfish. She was making the wrong decision.

Erasure and recreation was the most complete solution. Not all leaks could be plugged and the fall of the dam of existence would ruin all previous effort. Then it must be folly, arrogance of the highest transgression, to stand before the break of tragedy and declare that the world would be okay. Because the world was not a dam, it was all that it entailed with and within it. Because the world must have the means to overturn reality and keep itself whole. Impossibility had been proven mortal.

"You have been poisoned by worldly desires," said Grimleer. "Samuel should never have been left alone with you. A family man without a family. Of course he would latch onto you. You will submit. This is not up for debate. I will make the Library drink the infinite ocean. It is our salvation." Grimleer rubbed the rings on his fingers, igniting with his touch brief flames licking around his hand.

Grimleer grabbed her by the chin, and she beheld her namesake. The moon always seemed so formidable, so far in excess of her fragile body. As damaged as she was, she was in no position to stop Grimleer. Sorcery refused her command without the attunement of her focus. More rain fell from ocean swells.

There was a framed spell hidden within the Library, a star likeness of glass and fire. She wished upon the shooting star because that was what Samuel told her was done outside. Grimleer softened as Iramir did not retaliate or run. "Claire," he pressed. "You must understand. I know you do. The new world is the right decision. I understand it can be terrifying right before the final push." He let go and held her gently in apology. "It will be okay."

Iramir took a shaking breath. Everything was supposed to be okay if she did as she was told, if she did not dream of anything more than what she was made for. This assurance had been broken long ago. She had ended up loving her caregivers, enjoying their company so far in excess of her design. She had worked tirelessly to grant them their happiness and she had never felt emptier. Her happiness was not here.

"It is terrifying, the unknown," she said. She tugged on his sleeve and Grimleer relented like he always had when she was younger. Grimleer picked her up in his arms. She loved this, listening to his heartbeat as he cradled her. The dark ocean glimmered under the touch of blinding light. The ocean listened. The ocean waited for her. The ocean spoke of stars because it shared a connection with her. Outside, what a delirious dream. The ocean believed in her anyway. How amazing the world must be to transform infinity, to want her in her uselessness and not her assigned merit.

"I loved all the time I spent with you and Samuel, but I am sorry." She made her silent wish to the moonlight that the ocean had assured her long ago was listening, moonlight that would protect her. She bit back the blood of her consumed organs. "But I will not allow this world to be erased, not from the works of my Library."

She felt the thaumic touch of a spear in formation within unseen heavens. The Library was already doomed to fall into the ocean without support from the repository, but she wanted to lay it to rest herself. *It stops now.* "There will always be a million worlds and infinite lives," she continued, "but this world and the few I know that inhabit it, the few I want more for, this world is mine to keep for another tomorrow. Please understand, Grimleer, because I do not quite understand it myself. Ah, is devotion not intoxicating? I have never had it not coupled with duty."

The full moon was lit in brilliant majesty tonight, and the sudden darkness of its disappearance haunted the very ocean end to end.

# FORTY-SIX

City towers invaded Vandheer's foundry like malig-nant growths and assured Venner he was once again where he ought to be. Upside down skyscrapers descended from a mirrored city skyline. If he reached up, he could tap against their lightning rods. Red blinking aviation lights forewarned the danger of capsizing midair. Steel towers of linguistic measures echoed their songs on the radio. Their electric lines choked the miscreation of emergent city cancer and dived through the clouds to feed the skinned towers below.

Gilded thread stitched together lost city streets. Shattered asphalt floated without regard to sensibility. Crude rebar, bolts, and welds made physical the bare minimum of a factory to conspire. Red light climbed through the antenna briars and HVAC monoliths. They scoured the scattered shadows and chased the ocean adrift in his dreaming. Deep under the streets of clamorous motors hid the heart of the city. Vandheer would excavate until he struck gold.

He would enchant the village darlings with the thaumic tune and lead them to the foundry. Every attendant spy would leak more secrets to the ears of an overeager crow. He would build its heaven from the stolen refuse collected by turncoat paper hands. He would source the flesh of a city's concrete body and the blood of her undesirables paving the dead end streets, then drown her children in the ravenous water. The crow grew full in blissful feasting.

Blue lightning sparked in the distance, building electric charge that pricked the air. Machines continued to feed the factory sweating in the discourse of dismantling. Gargoyles, petrified with their teeth in leer, rode meat hooks on the line. The heads of blind, sharp-horned beasts had been scooped empty and left decaying in buckets right after. Shuttling conveyors dropped magic refuse into the foundry's molten metal. Gears stalled as they slipped on shattered teeth. Magic sizzled from the heat. Exotic insides were seared to the bone and out bubbled thick slag. Here in the center of this heaven was Vandheer's sea of ichor and existential swill, an infinite ocean by the diligence of a crow. Venner enjoyed the flattery.

A paper hand tapped across Venner's shoulders and down his arm, looking for attention. "I'm still not sure what you plan to do," wrote paper, the words appearing over the palm and the back of its fingers. Venner stroked paper knuckles. Fingers tapped uncertainly, folding the fabric of Venner's suit. It seemed to fear that any misstep would have it fall out of Venner's grasp. "You mentioned you would eat him. I'm quite sure you would've tried that already. What makes this different?"

Venner held a finger to his lips. A paper hand kneeled and quivered in a silent breeze. "I vote no confidence," wrote paper.

"Vandheer bested me in my mindfulness, so I would rather ignore the Corvus man and see what must be done to dismantle his factory," said Venner, rubbing the wounds made from steel. His body was still damaged, and he missed the ease found in a replica office. It was difficult enough to slowly wander. He was glad Caide did not see him like this. "I am relying on you, paper."

The paper hand rested against the crook of his elbow and waved a white finger in the air. "I'd much rather fix you first. I will not be second-rate to a wolfman, but there will not be much left of me for your own use. In a worsening situation, my wish will be used to save you instead of killing Vandheer. No negotiation."

There was only so much the paper man had left to give. As much as the paper mind devised and threw suggestions to the wind about how to handle the piper crow, eagerness could not cover how ill-thought they were. Paper suggested erasing Vandheer, but it offered none of the mechanics of how, no plan for A to B.

The paper man did not have the fury to outmatch the factory. Even then, paper remained too distracted about Venner's own safety, that they had come unprepared, that this tribulation was pointless and that they were too foolish to escape. He gambled on the strength of paper's own oceanic empathy. If the ocean must react to the final capsize of the attendant body, Venner wanted to hear the true cry of the paper soul. This finest material of intent, with a little creativity on his part, must solve the Vandheer impossibility. A proper problem to showcase his lessons learned.

This was simply the cleanup of minor things, a practice that he had persistently exercised even as a human construct. Whatever Vandheer was, it could not be perfectly immune. Venner picked at the nearby growths of city cancer. He pulled thread from concrete dust. He had performed this trick before to undo a nest. He stretched magic taut by the fulcrum of his teeth. However, it seemed the city could not handle Vandheer and his factory like it could a millipede or two. It would have done so by now.

The bespoke drowning of singular shapes failed in effectiveness. Venner had no practice in expediency. Drowning was excruciating after all, and immensely personal. The foundry kept Vandheer immortal, endlessly replicable. An ocean's solution was to corrupt the foundry somehow. It was a singular point of origin. The crow had to be of one mind, deep under melted depths, tugging the heartstrings of its puppets. The crow had only one voice and one identity, but too many false solutions and false entrances to entrap the ocean and stab it again. Repeat exposure to Vandheer had to elucidate new solutions.

Venner approached the edges of the foundry sea. The sheer heat of molten essence stung his skin and consumed the sweat of his brow. All he needed was to find where to pour the ocean in. A steel nail clattered and rolled across the metal floor before coming to a stop by Venner's foot. Black feathers swept around Venner in his pacing.

One crow, two crows had fallen into the ocean's quiet murmuring. Vandheer, the various Vandheers, were solved trifles. They were too easy and self-contained to illuminate any easement into the foundry seen from outside the man's eye view. Venner folded the paper hand and ignored its written warning of ambush too difficult to express with any actual warning. The paper man was tucked away from prying crow eyes.

Another Vandheer formed from a rise of black feathers. All magic was patterning of composite commands, unseen and unheard. There was nothing immediate that tied the foundry to a crow's rebirth other than the nebulous feeling of something always out of grasp. There would be no closer physical contact than to be consumed by the sea. He simply needed some assurance that the ocean consciousness would survive it.

Venner was confronted by the many Corvus men with talon smiles and black-beaked crowns, stillborn feathers and meat singed from the molten heat. An ocean could eat magic from the speeding womb but Vandheer still functioned with his malformations. As soon as the ocean would ease its pressure, Vandheer would function pristine and new.

Spindly claws of six fingers and mouths for palms gestured to the main Vandheer that took command. "It's kind of you to drop by again," said Vandheer in the lilt of chirp and crow. "My roaming eyes were searching in such fever only for you to invalidate all my hard work." The black mass of bodies advanced towards Venner. They all had hearts beating fresh on their sleeves, but it ultimately was a futile endeavor for an ocean to keep pursuing. "Why are you back? It seems you are less equipped than last time, and you are falling apart at the sinew. There'll be no one else that will save you."

"I wanted your foundry," said Venner. "This second look on the lot of you should be more than enough. I will warn you again, it is a terrifying feeling to be overwritten by infinity. The mind sees no out. Compulsion steals reason with utter ease. As small as you are, close your eyes and do not struggle."

Claws flexed in anger. A flicker of blue light cut through the whine of red aviation warnings. A machine escaped from the confines of the antenna briars and stalked amongst its masters. Its eye bled lightning and spinning expressions. A tentacle wrapped around Venner's neck and lifted him over the boiling ichor. Venner shifted uncomfortably, barely holding up his own weight on the slick steel to prevent choking. Be fed into the foundry and confront the absolute prospect of Vandheer, across all of him everywhere and every instance. Brine would line its belly with gold until there was nothing left.

Paper would wish for him, Venner knew.

"Dispose of him," said Vandheer. "With you, ocean, I will outlast the ages. I alone will have everything under my name."

Paper wriggled in Venner's pocket. He reached in to comfort the leg-full thing, but the snap reaction of the lightning machine plunged him into the sea. Within the ravenous foundry, he was dissolved flesh and bone. Blind nerves rumbling up his spine gauged his own annihilation, until nerves became mute, afloat in endlessness.

☾

PAPER RESISTED ITS END. IT CLUTCHED ITS OWN SHAPE SO tightly against the maligned forces that demanded sacrifice. The foundry howled through its throat of biting metallics. The wraiths of forgotten things haunted the resistant paper thought. They promised peace if paper would let go and join the choir. They promised the end of all troubles if paper would let go and be lost in the crowd. They promised that paper would be no different from its brethren, together forever, hand in hand against the end of the world. To join the collective that was Vandheer. They promised immortality. They promised nothing the paper man wanted and the ocean listened well as a paper denied the death of a man.

# FORTY-SEVEN

THE FOUNDRY SEIZED FOR A MOMENT. CITY VENUES OF DYS-lexic words spilled from the Vandheer's concrete heaven clone. Street signs climbed, crashing into the false sky with a sudden tremor. A few of the Corvus men ruptured into free ichor and rotting magic. An acceptable loss. Black feathers dropped away into pallid skin. Vandheer inspected his newfound body; his limbs and torso and heart all seemed to be real. He had assumed the stolen identity of a modern god.

Revenge against the crow was shaped in human form and cut roughly at the edges. Anger was drawn in a fanged scowl. A folded, paper man stepped out of the sea in the reference shape that all things of the factory were hammered to: Vandheer. This errant body accused Vandheer.

The ocean must have stashed a vapid desire in its pocket. It did not matter. Nothing could hope to stop Vandheer. The ocean was his to tame. What could fear achieve but to balk at his majesty? He supped from the font of endlessness. He had enough fuel to outlast the very concept of epochs. Cost was no object. No spell was too large or complex. All bothers could simply be wished away.

The surrounding air and city lights converged into liquid neon and crowned the halos around Vandheer. The inner ring draped across his shoulders. The foundry glowed with moonlight. The factory groaned from the pressure. Pipes leaked. Gears melted. The system could not bear the resurgence of a new existence. Lightning machines stopped their work as the factory crumbled into its own crucible.

Vandheer commanded. The other Vandheers were destroyed unto his sea in mindless suicide. This splendor belonged only to himself. He did not need to hide behind things that pretended to be him. He granted his own salvation. He was realized. He was unique. He was alive!

The paper copy disobeyed. The paper copy remained. The paper copy approached. The fledgling god of white halos and black wings looked on with amusement at the shambling beast who shed bits of its body with every step. The paper hand kept its head from lolling too far. The new god snapped his fingers and blue lightning sparked from his touch. A god smites and so the paper copy was burned to cinders.

The clockwork millipede with a thousand arms for teeth had found its tail and so began to swallow. Vandheer had no more need for a factory. His sea self-sustained, the world his very paradise. Eager to continue testing his new ease, he commanded the city, not bothering to disguise his voice as her attendants. The city obeyed readily. Concrete turned and asphalt fell. The cracks of a destroyed world repaired themselves with swift expertise.

Vandheer beheld the thriving city under evening light pollution. Wind howled around him as he stood upon the highest tower that overlooked the entire skyline from its very center. The rooftop conditioners hummed. The aircraft warning lights bled bright red. The neon shimmer of a living city glowed below him, shadowing the people in their busywork and amusement. Civilization trailed from the ocean waterfront through the metropolitan discourse and climbed up the mountain spines.

The winds hunted. He shivered from the cold. He fell to his knees, and he did not understand why. The paper man stood behind him and forced him to lean over the rooftop edge. The shape of a forge refugee fit too well, stepping into the Vandheer namesake and taking control with puppet strings. Vandheer turned around but there was no image to vindicate this paranoia. There was no one else here. He would feel the disruption of any that dared to confront him. Fear began to creep in, constricting his veins and pooling in his throat.

He stood back up and stepped away from the rooftop edge. His body obeyed with no hint of rebellion. There was no one else here, he repeated. The underground factory had collapsed into itself. All things died behind civic walls, crushed into an infinitesimal point called his sea. This point was housed within himself, and thus he could not be taken from his factory. Paranoia had no place with all his power. Fear not, he was simply overwhelmed from his success.

His halo turned another half step in replication, another coil to echo the voice of sorcery. He could rip this city asunder. He could fold the city into himself and be ever more. It started to rain. Droplets splashed off his halo and slid down the tines. This was a fine perch from which to witness calamity.

He raised his arms wide and felt the folds of the world in his palms. Magic sung across the countenance of a fledgling god. He felt so free. There was so much power aching to be unleashed. A single thought upset the balance of intentions and blue lightning shorted across his body. His thoughts stumbled, racing and overawed by the possibilities. Magic crackled, reacting almost as if it tried to precede himself. Giddiness pricked the back of his neck and made his heart beat fast.

His reach felt endless. He was endless. The cost of negligent metropolitan destruction would be astronomical, but his factory afforded him everything. Let him start with the city borders and take everything that made her. Deplete her dimensions until she was gone. The feeling of infinity compelled him on, faster and faster. He would dive within the very atoms of magic and force it to heed. Perfectly deny the advent of thaumic entropy, reverse its decay, and be rebuilt into perpetual motion. Sorcery embraced his hands and chased his movements. A thoughtless mind surrendered to intoxication.

A circle of light encompassed the city from mountain ridge to seaport, lounging over every geological feature. The circle ignited. This shining abstraction raised into the sky and took the buildings with them. The earth screamed. Inverted mountains were made from the collapsing refuse of civilization. He threw all of himself into his powers, wrung all possible work from the ocean thought experiment.

*Are you satisfied?* Asked the infinite ocean with a silent voice. From behind a blink of Vandheer's eyes, a dark smear was left in his vision. This smear did not leave him, no matter where he looked. Inverted mountains crashed into each other. Magic worked without delay. Vandheer rubbed his eyes, damp. The smear became more defined. It was not human, of course not. Yet to be confronted without the ocean's human guise was another nightmare entirely.

Words spilled from the chalk lines that drew its seven eyes, one of them blind. The outline of an enigmatic engine rotating in inexplicable convolution scored the skies. This engine heart of an ocean could not be unseen despite Vandheer's protest as it took more and more of his vision. Words sprawled on inverted mountains and draped across tenant buildings. Font rose from the water.

*You are made from your own sweat*, it read. Letters climbed up the high-rise perch and folded over the edge, circling and hunting him. *How sweet. How beautiful. How divine. You are perfect. You are living and breathing. You have emerged from the singularity of existential boredom as something introspective and not instinctual. Exalt your revenge against the city that thought you insignificant. I was wrong. I want you.*

"I am immortal," said Vandheer. "I have erased the concept of death from the tapestry of my being. You cannot harm me." The ocean leaked between the mass of halos that adorned this exquisite piece of existence. Vandheer threw up salt water. His halo completed another ring that burdened the body. The compression of a city demanded more from him. Reality obliged this effortless task and pulled ever more from the poisoned, internal factory. Every advance in thaumic mathematics invited the ocean in between the cracks of Vandheer's name. The ocean was a virus. It was hostile. It was uncontrollable. It was in him, and he was hostage.

Words shifted across the concrete like pop art on display. *I will make you more. Endlessly absolute. The true paradigm of a species*, read dripping graffiti.

There was nothing for Vandheer to struggle against. He clawed at his halo tines, unable to stop the ritual he had started. He could not fathom the concept of his own sorcery corrupting. The ocean ate those unthought names. Magic became perpetual beyond the means of a fragile body. Entropy, formerly denied by the internal factory, was freed into externality and started with haste the irreversible destruction of a name. The weight of his halo hurt. Every new layer grew blacker and more crooked.

Cascade burned. Vandheer was not a city prepared for the wrath of the sea. The levees breached. No storm break would save him. Unraveling halos impaled and opened Vandheer's chest. His ribs cracked down the sternum and spread wide. Tines sliced skin and nailed limbs motionless. He writhed as the paper man unfolded out of him, wracking the muscles, redefining tissue. From himself, the paper man made his torso complete with arms and an empty head.

Vandheer stared at the paper man. "You, you're just an attendant. This . . . the ocean listens to you? You're meant to be scrap, destroyed from a bit of rain. I am to be beyond things like you. I am to be the only thing. How can you be more than me?"

The paper man was a pale facsimile, but everything made from Vandheer was Vandheer true. The paper man said, "I wish to be mortal. I must die."

BEMORTAL. BEMORTAL. BEMORTAL. BEMORTAL. BEMORTAL. BEMORTAL. BEMOR—. The words repeated across the starless skies.

"I am forever—I am nothing—I am a god!" proclaimed the conflicting twin voices of a fledgling god.

BEDENIED.

The words were written endlessly upon Vandheer's shape, chasing the very limits of effort from the factory sea. The ocean was infinite and whatever his factory would be was but a shadow of this demon. Vandheer was emptied out by a mad paper torso shoving its body into its creator and casting these organs out and away.

It was not rain. It was the weight of the ocean breaking through. Thunder was the ceiling cracking. Lightning were the strands of sorcery snapping at the junction. Here came the storm. The sea climbed upon the distant shores and navigated the asphalt streets. The sea rose to topple the mountain peaks and towers sunk beneath the waves. Cascade set alight the false sea of oil.

Vandheer had never left his wasting planes. This was the illusion constructed by the ocean in this head of his. Yet there was no escaping the ocean dream and teeth. The ocean had poisoned the sea and every new man to take the prior's failing place was infected too. Vandheer died in every head of his.

BEDEVOURED.

# FORTY-EIGHT

VANDHEER'S FRACTURED FACTORY FELL INTO THE INFINITE ocean by foundry, by machines, by fuel. Stripped towers dislodged from their stations into the violent water. Stolen city ruins became the inverted tower of calamity's make and dipped far enough down to scratch the water's surface. Its cancerous base hid deep within a starless, evening sky. The sea of immortality overflowed heaven and navigated the ruins in discordant trample, feeding the ocean.

The paper man lay on the shale, half-made. The open wound created from its missing lower body leaked feathers and typeface. The rain of breaking waves corroded on contact. The paper man split in layers, and a paper outline was left behind. The breathing ocean shape sat up and sized himself proper. The strands of spent sorcery, dark and viscous, tugged and stretched around the ocean's carved crystal spine. The ocean's heart beat in his exposed ribcage. His polished bones were slow in their healing as legs developed and finer human features detailed underneath the shadow of rain.

The ocean stood up, paper outline folding beneath his feet. The ocean patted down his suit and straightened his tie. He ran his thumb over his lower teeth as he inventoried the stock of his body, his limbs and their positions, their reactions in his pacing. A body sore in its freshness, the dissociation between his perceptions as nauseating as ever.

Mortal eyes trailed along water that stared back with its own set of eyes, perhaps wished into existence by a desire from long ago. He had found himself once again, and if he focused on the shaking feeling at the edges of his thoughts, he could see himself from outside the human view and feel the delicate controls used to pilot his body. He was mostly whole, his wounds repaired and himself clean cut. He had six eyes left, hopefully no fewer.

The ocean despised its own flesh still, but the possibilities that a body and a name afforded outstripped that discomfort and revulsion. The ocean wanted more time to witness the outside world. The world had grown so large and unknown, and an age had passed since Venner took to sailing. To travel and understand were the whims of once-zealous brine, as it found the human quite a sturdy vessel.

What had always been out of reach, the moon within its celestial heaven, mortal eyes found missing. The night was empty, broken only by the massive pillar of light driven deep into the ocean. This spear of Damocles, of material moonlight the ocean had come to know so well, had fallen. The child sailor never needed to stand on tiptoe. The ocean never needed to riot with ever-rising waves or fall as rain. The moon had stepped down and offered the whole of herself, denying the future of her Library. There will be no turnover. The means of a new engine would be broken down and destroyed. He would wipe clean all traces of the living within the ocean.

Orbiting this spear were the Library's shattered foundations, these vague lion shapes dripping in shattered cinnabar. Wreckage traveled in slow malaise, shifting under her light and casting shadows like petals across the pillar. Orbit paths would decay and be inescapable from brine.

The moon had been the only source of light in his ocean. Its solitude only emphasized its brilliance. The pillar lighthouse dragged his shadow long behind him, and there was a distinct darkness that now enveloped his namesake. No longer did he have his stellar prize overhead. No longer could he see from infinite end to infinite end. At last, the collection was complete and this thorn was excised as promised.

"You're such a sight like this," said the paper man. Venner was not alone. The paper man was now nothing more than a formed mold of him, a two-dimensional thing that disappeared for a moment as it tried to turn and prop itself on its elbows. The shorn body slowly took on water as it dragged itself along the wet sand. "Do they keep time in a place like this? An endless night, it would always be 2 or 3 a.m. here. Just an odd enough time to help nurture more surreptitious things in their laboratories." The paper man lifted its shoulders. "I didn't think you would take to my suggestion so well. You look good. Though, I wished for only two eyes, ocean."

Venner rubbed his only eye. The request from the paper man's beating heart contained only vague memories of stairwell matters. The ocean had to fill the missing rest, and the ocean knew itself well. By the ocean's own admission, the shape of the body named Eram was appreciated and carefully remembered down to the very last vertex. He had been solved and had put himself back to together again.

"I do have two eyes," said Venner. "Well, there is room for two eyes. I am what you requested. Yet how could you see the rest of them? I would have never figured that translation of madness. Maybe."

"Because I was lost for a distant moment in a lethargic dream," said the paper man. "I saw you through the human shape, like peeling layers of cut pages away. I saw this ocean like a black canvas with all your painted eyes, all vast and alone. The werewolf argued with me about your number of eyes by the way. The dog can't count. I found myself enthralled by this ocean. The moment lingered. You lingered. You waited for me to find my words. You listened."

A crick between Venner's shoulders and at the back of his skull reminded him there were displacements to be cleaned up, of a paper man, of a Library, of a moon, but he had discretion and the shapes had names. The world would never relent. Its existence was inimical with his own. If he thought too long, looked too closely at the bits and pieces of memory adrift in the water, compulsion would prod extra eyes into action. Yet to be swept along currents like the dreams of paper—to work reality for a shape that so entranced perception—was a liberating distraction from ocean fatalism.

"You were too greedy," said Venner. "You pushed the idea of my reconstruction with such force of will that there is barely anything of you left to take back to the city." Venner wanted this moment framed and kept forever. He was surrounded by the infinite ocean, by silence and peace everlasting, and he didn't have a single thought that demanded sustenance. He could enjoy the company, the real contentment. His childhood dreams had been achieved, finally. All he had left were scraps here or there, but he was in no hurry. The most significant checkboxes had been checked, and his obsession had been left to flounder without the reminder of failure.

"You're the one that obliged," said the paper man, "and I daresay I've ended up more than just a hand. The deal's gone the wrong way for you, ocean. I feel lucky that you're so generous. You suspended your sensibilities of balance just for me." The paper man tried to laugh but only crinkled. "What of your new trick with the wolfman? Do you think you truly reverse cascade with a little more knowledge? It would be miraculous if you had wholesale application. There is a lot of ocean around."

"Perhaps this is something a moon may have a better idea of how to exploit," said Venner. "Personal salvation and then maybe more. What do you want next?"

The paper man dragged its body to the edge of the shale and dipped its paper arms in the water. Fibers swelled and splayed wide into the waves, as if in embrace. What a comforting, revolting feeling.

"You first," said the paper man.

"I want to see Iramir well," said Venner. "She told me that I had made it. She should feel included."

"She's not here to wish for that."

"I will wish for myself, and I will do it myself. I want to show her she is not alone."

The paper man raised his wrist as if pretending to check the time. "Do not worry about me. My business is done, and I've done what I wanted," he said. "The city will be a little more at ease for a while, and I a little more restful."

"I can still take you back to the city," said Venner. "I think I can get back on my own. There are still things yet to be digested from a factory. A soul somewhere yearning to be elsewhere."

"You won't be able to forget about me," said the paper man. "I'll become the object of your terrors. Just because your needs are not human does not make your needs any lesser. I see the dark before me. Paper is meant to be replaced. Print another good attendant to man the streets and clean the offal. The city waits for you. I am its guarantee. Harken will call again, and we'll be more receptive this time. Climb up and find yourself in your other home." The paper man gestured toward the dilapidated spire. It would be quite the labor to hike, and as equal a labor to not idly swallow the concrete mountain from beneath unsure feet.

Venner was alone again. The shale had been wiped clean by the waves. He adjusted his damp clothes and swept back wet hair. He bit on one of his knuckles and waited for the reviled aftertaste. He waited for the train that would crash into him, the realization that the meal filled nothing and left him wanting more. Any sort of fulfillment must beget only deeper hunger and a lingering dissatisfaction. He felt a maddening joy at the idea that the outside world was just as contemptable as promised.

It was frightening because he felt such peace must be fragile. Any tribulation would shatter his calm in an instant. He had waited so long for this, the culmination of a dream's satisfaction, but he felt just as impatient, just as restless as before, floundering underneath puzzle boxes and thoughtless absurdity. He wanted to save Iramir, he wanted to go back to Caide and spend that time to settle everything. He wanted to travel, to *live*, that was the word he'd heard thrown so haphazardly around the past few days. The world had wished him to live several more times than he'd ever expected. *Live*, what a delirious word.

What worked the jaw now was not hunger, but a need to talk and interact, a compulsion nurtured by paper affection, wolves, and moons. He would cherish the moments that lived in quiet stairwells under cyan fluorescent tubes, in destroyed apartments under the spell of a spoken myth, in the garden where the moon watched over the ocean and took him by the hand and comforted him. Life given willingly was really another breed, sorted so neatly and filled to the brim with assurance.

Something clattered onto the ground by his feet. It was a glass star, waterlogged but glimmering from the moonlight. It must have fallen from the spire, or perhaps it was a trace left behind by a hopeful boatman, another addition to the cleanup of traces. It was another addition to the vulnerable collection instead, saved from the malice of brine. Venner traced the seams of its creation, not that it was any wonder what it contained. It was empty and he spied the blinding tower through its partially painted, fractal lenses.

Venner held his breath and jumped into the ocean. He barely made a splash. The cold wracked his flesh and bones. Shock stole his air and let water into his lungs. Glass points punctured skin as his grip on the star tightened in his panic. The stupor of dreams could hardly compare to the real element. Emergency alert, he was going to drown. He sank down the water column and pressure mounted. Moonlight rippled through the surface and stirred to his frantic motions. Brainstem reflexes forced him to take breaths, one mouthful of water after another until it did not matter.

Venner was suspended in a dream come true, surrounded by emptiness and thundering quiet. He never drowned in his ocean. Why start now? Emergency sensations lay numb. A slow exhale stirred the water and released the last of his air in rising bubbles. He held his arms out towards the moonlit beacon and embraced his waters. And he waited, wondering if this was at all appropriate, but he wanted to try nonetheless, to call a moon outside once more.

"I have listened," Venner said to the fallen moon, "and I am listening still. Rub the lamp with hands of sweet hope. The djinn has been released. Little spirit in your porcelain bottle, what do you wish?" The blurred, moonlight pillar flickered and went off. Pitch black enveloped the ocean. No more intrusions could be discerned, and his world collapsed to a single point of perception.

He strained for the touch of a world pushing back and struggled to see the break in the darkness. There were no more reminders that delineated his perceptions between man and ocean. He was the ocean through and through, and he took himself, all of himself, in his arms. From here on, he would move forward by weight of a name.

The moon had refused him, a fading, fluttering heartbeat evading his efforts. Venner rolled the star between his hands and then released it to the currents. "I have a star if you can see. Made out of glass and carefully painted. This star was traded for a home. It was traded for favors, but always with the intent of making things better, however slightly.

"The stars await," he said. "Whatever your decision will be, will be. Defy me even, but I want to hear from you, Iramir. Decide for yourself your very future." Venner splayed his unseen hand and felt points stab in response. The star had found its way back. Gold threads wrapped around his fingers and tickled his skin as they fluttered long into the dark.

"I want this. I want to understand you," said Venner. "If you agree to it, I assure you I will only be the first. It is nice outside. Maybe we will start with a walk."

A fire lit inside the glass star and illuminated his human shape in a faint, dancing glow. This light could barely pierce the darkness surrounding him. Venner cupped the star close to his chest. He felt her heartbeat against his. He leaned back and cradled the star.

"Let us go outside," said Venner. "I am getting tired of my ocean views. There is nothing here. Is that alright with you, Iramir, that I will take you too? You have as much a right as anything else to live."

"I want to make amends," flickered white typeface huddling inside the fragile star. "Whatever that entails, I want to start to find my place in the world. If you . . . if you think I am worth the effort."

"Yes. Wish granted," said the ocean. "All I ask for in return is that you keep me updated on whatever you plan to do. I am curious about the future, about how much you have planned. We will work through trouble as it comes. I hope this is not the end of our correspondence." With ease, the ocean rebuilt Iramir to her template of flesh and porcelain worn from repeated use, an artificial creation brimming with newfound freedom. The ocean was proud of her.

Using the building antennas as handholds, Venner climbed out of the water and up the first few steps of the city spire, then lifted Iramir from the water. She was warm to the touch like the fire of a star, freed from all pretense of a namesake. All things moonlike had been swallowed by the deep. She stared at him in astonishment with her newfound features, and he made certain to smile back. Venner led her through the concrete tower slopes and beheld the darkness broken only by the blinking signs of civilization.

"Everything will disappear in your ocean?" asked Iramir. She was shaking and held him tightly, as if frightened that the magnitude of her new life would slip away from her at any moment. She tried to spot something out in the ocean, but signal lights only provided so much to be seen, and it was all just water.

"Depends," said Venner as he helped Iramir up a particularly steep wall. "Most things will be devoured, but there are always things left behind after the first pass. I find myself with a start of a collection a bit more wholesome. Is there something from your Library you want to find?"

"Bits of research, if you can find something that theoretical to be still intact. It would make charity cases like a wolfman a somewhat easier endeavor. Other than that, I will be working from scratch." Iramir tugged on her lips. "So I have chosen the unknown. My ordained fate has been subverted, and I find myself without direction. Should there not be some purpose I must fulfill? Is this alright? For me to be brought back like this? It should not be. I have done and allowed terrible things."

"Who will be offended? You said it yourself. You want to make amends, having not given up your legacy but wanting a new direction. The same mercy you granted me, I will return. You have made an ocean more content than it thought it could be, and I hope you will find that same contentment somewhere out there. You have chosen the world. You are no stranger to a challenge." He shrugged his shoulders. "Well, see to it, and by no means will you be alone." Venner directed her gaze from the burial of the Library to look up. Distant streetlights of golden glow shimmered like stars in the sky of a devoured moon.

# ACKNOWLEDGMENTS

I'D LIKE TO GIVE A HEARTY THANK YOU TO JOEL BAHR. YOUR ongoing support and guidance has been greatly appreciated. I suppose you know I am not a particularly motivated person, but your enthusiasm has certainly cultivated and blessed new wings where I could not. It's because of you that this exists outside of my hands. It would've never been otherwise. So, good luck and godspeed.

To the readers who gave this strange story an idle chance, whether or not you ever get to this page, thank you as well. I do hope you had fun somewhere along the lines.

# ABOUT THE AUTHOR

**BORN AND RAISED IN SOUTHERN CALIFORNIA WHERE THE** concept of seasons is just mere legend, I am an aerospace engineer with a particular hobby that invites pen to page and makes an ocean infinite. Building rocket parts and seeing them fly impresses the idea that impossibility can be tamed. Not that all impossibility can, but the matter isn't truly impervious. Due diligence and a dream can make wonders and now the hobby has come into something a bit more permanent. Beyond the stars, beneath the deep blue sea, within the roiling consciousness of a good beer with friends on a lazy Saturday evening overlooking the backyard and just looking abroad, is wonder. Of this wonder I write about and enjoy exploring to the strangest of ends, having some fun along the way.